I0823656

Praise for *A Stage Set for Villains*

"Dark fantasy at its most intoxicating. Shannon Spann delivers a world where gods crave applause, mortals bleed for love, and every truth feels like a curse. I was completely enthralled."

– #1 *NYT* bestselling author Jennifer L. Armentrout

"*A Stage Set for Villains* is a love story drenched in beauty, blood, and betrayal—a performance so mesmerizing you forget where the fiction ends. I couldn't put it down."

– J. Elle, *NYT* bestselling author of the House of Marionne series

"Absolutely thrilling. Be ready to be hooked from the first page to the shocking end."

– *NYT* bestselling author Elise Kova

"As enthralling as it is unique, *A Stage Set for Villains* will have you spellbound!"

– #1 *NYT* bestselling author Mai Corland

"Part novel, part script, *A Stage Set For Villains* is a fascinatingly unique world like nothing you've ever read before, where mirrors are to be feared, life-eating curses abound, and vicious humans-turned-gods called Players perform on a voracious playhouse stage, that will have you riveted from the first casting call!"

– *USA Today* bestselling author Amalie Howard

A STAGE SET FOR VILLAINS

SHANNON J. SPANN

Entangled Publishing, LLC
644 Shrewsbury Commons Ave., STE 181
Shrewsbury, PA 17361
rights@entangledpublishing.com

Mayhem Books is an imprint of Entangled Publishing, LLC.
Visit our website at www.entangledpublishing.com.

Edited by Liz Pelletier and Jen Bouvier
Original cover illustration and design by Elizabeth Turner Stokes
Edge design by Elizabeth Turner Stokes
Edge image by Bourbon-88/Shutterstock
Endpapers design by Elizabeth Turner Stokes
Endpaper image by OlgaBegak/Shutterstock
Original mask art by Sheila Avellino
Interior map design by Elizabeth Turner Stokes
Interior design by Britt Marczak

HC ISBN 978-1-64937-951-1
Ebook ISBN 978-1-64937-952-8

Manufactured in the United States of America
First Edition February 2026

10 9 8 7 6 5 4 3 2 1

For Grandma
Who always believed in me, but had to go home before this book made its way to shelves. I'm sure you've already requested it at heaven's library. I miss you.

And for Star
Hey, look! Look, buddy! I did it!!

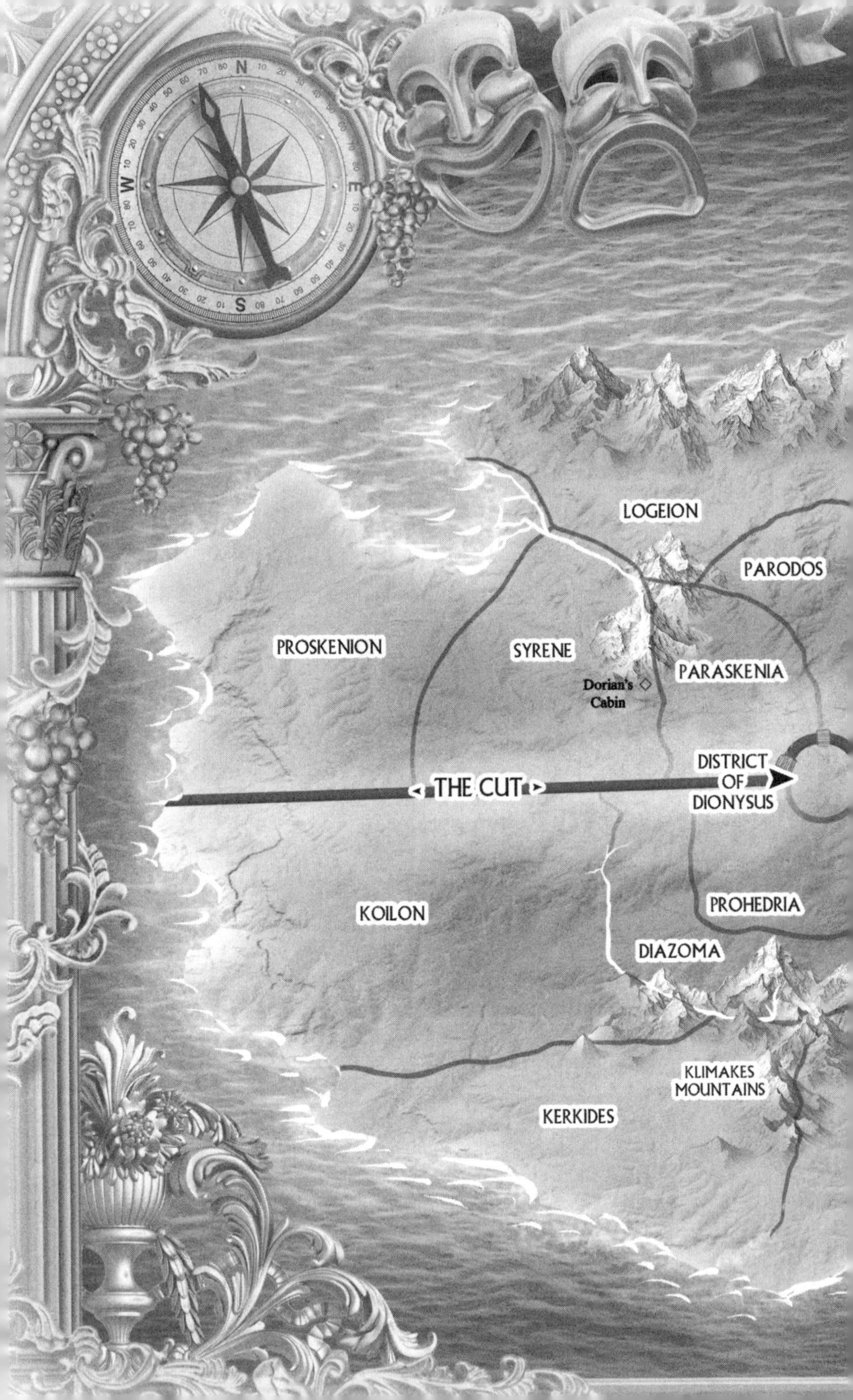

N
E
S
W
LOGEION
PARODOS
PROSKENION
SYRENE
PARASKENIA
Dorian's Cabin
THE CUT
DISTRICT OF DIONYSUS
PROHEDRIA
KOILON
DIAZOMA
KLIMAKES MOUNTAINS
KERKIDES

THEATRON
Eleutheraen well
MOUNT ELEUTHERAE
CHARONIA
THE MASKIRA SEA
ORKESTRA
Orkestrian Academy
Riven's Home
THE CUT
CAVEA
EDOLIA
KLIMAKES

A Stage Set for Villains is an atmospheric dark fantasy set in the brilliant and brutal world of Theatron. The story features elements that might not be suitable for all readers, including death, blood, violence, illness, torture, imprisonment, starvation, loss of autonomy, murder, burning, and graphic language. Suicide and poison are discussed in backstory. Readers who may be sensitive to these elements, please take note, and prepare to enter the Playhouse...

OVERTURE

For as long as I can remember, we have feared the Players. I know of only three ways to survive an encounter with one.

"Never look a Player in the eye," I recite as we shuffle a few steps forward in line. My older brother's hand clutches my gloved fingers a little too tight, and I wonder if he's nervous, too. Last night, I was so excited that I couldn't sleep. But the longer we wait, the more I wonder if being marked will hurt.

"That's right," Galen says. "Remember, that *doesn't* mean ignoring them, Riv."

I nod eagerly. If you're going to bruise a Player's ego, you might as well throw yourself off a cliff while you're at it. It would be less painful.

"What's the second rule?" Galen quizzes as another newly marked boy, somewhere between my eight years of age and my brother's twelve, passes us on his way out of the enormous courthouse ahead.

There's a bandage pressed just below the boy's throat like a necklace, gold bleeding through the layers. He's crying.

"Just ten minutes," Aunt Cassia told us before we left this morning. *"Ten minutes of discomfort for a lifetime of protection against the Players. Against the lure of the Playhouse."*

I touch the tips of my fingers to the dip between my collarbones, trying to imagine the mark that will go there soon.

"The Three Compliments Rule," I finally answer, mentally reading the memory cards I made in class last week. "Pay a Player three compliments and you might satisfy their ego long enough to get away."

"Good!" My brother offers an encouraging smile while I throw another searching look over my shoulder, trying to spot where we left our mother at the gates in the distance. "And the third way to escape a Player?"

I press my lips together, my thoughts stalling back to that crying boy. The bandage. My heart begins to pound in my chest. How badly *will* it hurt?

Galen squeezes my hand, and I realize I haven't answered his question. "Oh, um—give them a gift?" I guess, my memory cards momentarily fleeing my mind.

He shakes his head while a voice somewhere ahead shouts out, "Keep it moving!"

They call us next, and we're ushered into a bare, circular atrium, interrupted by a single stone hallway. My brother herds me up to a half-moon granite desk beside a gurgling fountain, our steps echoing.

"Fill these out," instructs a sour-faced woman from behind the desk, extending several pages of parchment to Galen. I snatch the forms indignantly, and the woman startles.

"I can read. I'm *eight*," I announce, plucking a pen from the jar on the desk while Galen apologizes for my brash behavior.

"Eight, is she? Tall for her age, I think." I feel the woman's gaze linger on my pen as I spell out my name: *Riven Hesper*. She inhales sharply.

I peer up to deal the woman a venomous look. It's easy to tell when people are mentally comparing me to my father; they always stare like I've risen from the dirt of his grave. My father's face is nearly as infamous as the Players who murdered him.

I go back to ignoring her and concentrate on filling out today's date.

Until my pen freezes at the sound of a scream.

It all happens at once. The desk woman jumps to her feet as the shriek ricochets off the vaulted ceilings, followed by a second scream—this one, in the shape of the word *help*. Then another scream, and another. At the frantic pounding of feet, my attention startles toward the cavernous hall. Somewhere, a man's voice yells out a warning that makes my blood run cold.

Player.

The word scorches my mind, fear wiping it blank of everything I have been taught. Instinctively, my eyes search for the closest grown-up, but the woman behind the desk has dropped to the ground, covering her eyes.

Before I can move, a tall, angelic figure flutters into the atrium, layers of purple rippling behind her. The Player whips around, a curtain of dark curls toppling over her shoulder. As if she senses an audience.

Her eyes glimmer like live embers, and I think she must be the most dreadful and beautiful thing I have ever seen. Catching my eye, the Player smiles—it's a wrong smile, though. It stretches wider and wider until each side reaches the blood rubies that dangle from her earlobes.

Aunt Cassia warned me of their unnatural faces—exaggerated so patrons in even the worst seats of the Playhouse can still make out a Player's expressions. Up close, it's as breathtaking as it is grotesque. She looks like a god.

But we don't have gods anymore.

We only have Players.

Sentries uniformed in black and silver fill the room, encircling the woman and barking orders at one another as she extends her palms out. Broken, golden shackles dangle at her wrists.

There's blood on her hands.

Suddenly, my brother's panicked face fills my vision, his hands clamping around my shoulders. "You look at me, okay? Look *only* at me, Riven," he whispers, frantic.

How could I have already forgotten the first rule?

I nod rapidly and focus hard on my brother's gaze—wide and round and scared. Except something is wrong with his eyes. They're too still—glassy, like a doll's.

"Galen?" I ask. Why isn't he blinking? "Galen!" I try again, alarmed at the sound of my own voice.

Because my voice is *all* I can hear.

The shouts echo into nothing, the world shuddering to a stop. I look from Galen's frozen stare to the fountain behind him, where the water is stuck in midair like it's hardened into ice. Around me, the sentries are locked in place, a museum of lifeless statues. Galen's hands press on my shoulders, cold and heavy as marble.

I blink a few times, baffled.

The whole world is still.

In the silence, a hand peels over my brother's collar. I shiver, watching as it hooks around his shoulder one long, elegant finger at a time—each adorned with a ring. Several nails are stained red.

Then the Player's face appears, hovering just over Galen's shoulder.

I glance back at Galen, obeying his instructions *not* to look. But the Player's skin glows so bright, it feels impossible to keep my eyes away.

"Oh, dear heart. You look so scared." I shudder at the sound of her voice. It's slow, the timbre light and airy, like silk. It fills the room, sinks into the walls. "At least look at me, won't you?"

Never look a Player in the eye, I chant mentally. My breaths are coming too quick, my vision beginning to swim.

In the corner of my eye, her smile falls at my silence and her hand lifts off Galen's shoulder, glides to his face. To my horror, the Player sets the sharpened edge of her ring against his cheek. Then drags it across his skin, slicing open the soft area below his eye.

Still, Galen doesn't move. Doesn't react.

And suddenly, I forget everything I should—and should *not*—do in this situation.

"Stop it!" I shout, locking eyes on the Player. Fear gathers in my throat, and I spit it back out as fury. "Or *else*," I add, hoping she doesn't notice the way my knees are trembling.

The Player tilts her head at me, curious. "Why, what lovely golden eyes you have."

A compliment? Wait—three! I'm supposed to pay her three compl—

"They're *brown*," I hiss at her. Like my father's were. *"Liar."*

She throws her head back and laughs. The sound ricochets off the stone, ringing in my ears. "What a *beautiful* temper," the Player muses. "*Lying* is a part of living. The truth is too often vile, wouldn't you say?"

I'm not sure, really. Most people I know *can't* lie. Pulling in a breath, I cast a nervous glance around the room. "Why aren't they moving?"

"Well, I've suspended our reality, you see," she whispers, like it's a shared secret between us. "Do you know what that means?"

I press my lips into a frown, frustrated. I *don't* know.

"It means this conversation doesn't happen," she says, gathering her robes as she settles on her knees before me. Her figure still towers over me at this height. I straighten my shoulders and stretch my neck a little higher, searching for confidence.

"They're going to take you away," I warn in a way I think sounds threatening.

"Oh, I know!" the Player says, excited. "You see, they've promised to burn me at the stake. And I cannot resist a spectacle." She smiles softly. "What is your name?"

Before I can speak, her gilded eyes fall to the pages in my hands—documents that declare I'm to be marked. Safe. Protected from Players. At the top of them, my name.

"Riven!" She howls another laugh that shakes my boots. "What could divide you so fiercely to merit such a name?"

I don't answer, keeping one eye just to her right, to the blood now trickling down Galen's neck. I wonder if he can feel it. The Player pulls the pages from my hands, the startling warmth of her touch loosening my grip like melting ice. She raises them between our faces, then, in one beautiful, violent motion, tears them to shreds. They fall around us like new snow, landing gently in the quiet.

"You aren't getting marked, Riven," the Player murmurs, and it's then that I notice how white and pointed her teeth look up close. "*You* are coming with me."

I don't even hear myself scream. The will, the *desire* to follow her overwhelms my every thought as the Player reaches for my hand and summons me forward. I watch her golden eyes.

Compelled, my hand reaches for hers. I'm not marked yet. I can't help it.

Maybe *this* is how it feels to watch a Playhouse performance. Galen says Players pluck the heartstrings of thousands in the audience every night like delicate threads on a quilt, wiping away and rearranging their spectators' thoughts, ideas, and beliefs with little more than a pretty word.

Players can make you believe anything.

But there is at least one thought she has no hold on: *She's going to kill me.* She's going to force me to follow her, an eternal audience, until my legs give out. Until I die from exhaustion or starvation.

An audience, wholly and solely devoted. This is what all Players crave.

As my mind blurs, I grip the edge of my brother's coat, cling to it, certain I'll be gone forever if I let go. My arm stretches and stretches as the Player drags me away, the gap between Galen and me widening.

Then I see it—a glint of gold in Galen's pocket. Father's knife. Galen carries it everywhere.

The third rule for surviving a Player flashes through my mind: *A Player can only be slain with Eleutheraen gold.* I squeeze my eyes tight and reach for the handle. My fingers scrape at the wood—

"Riven," the Player chimes sweetly. It sounds a little forced now.

I stretch my fingers, clawing at the knife.

"Riven, darling, there's no reason to make this difficult—"

It all seems to happen in a blink. One second my fingers are wrapping around the knife's hilt and the next, I'm bringing the blade down as hard as I can.

The Player's words shatter into the most terrible scream I have ever heard. She falls onto her knees, wailing and clutching her hand. A puddle of gold gathers beneath it, dripping onto the stone floor like drops of sun. *Player blood.* Brimming with power, with *Craft.*

She looks at me with eyes full of hellfire, rising from the ground with a lethal sort of calm. I scramble away, bracing myself, waiting for her to rip my eyes from their sockets. To break my legs and drag me to the Playhouse—

But a gold chain loops around the Player's throat, and a man holding it wrenches her backward. He screams something I barely register, his face white with terror. Almost instantly, a dozen more sentries are upon the Player.

All around me, everything starts to move again, free from her charm. *I* am free from her charm. That desire to follow the Player unclenches from my heart, lifts off my shoulders like a bird.

It occurs to me it was never real to begin with.

But before I can realize what's happened, before I can so much as *think* to move, the Player wrenches free and is on me again, gripping my coat collar and holding me too close, like she's about to bite my neck.

She whispers into my ear, and I freeze.

And then it's over. Guards rip her away.

Weight crushes around my arms as Galen whirls me to face him. Relief fills me to see him moving again, *breathing* again. He's blinking, too—wincing as he dabs a hand over the open cut on his cheek, bewildered.

Behind him, the Player thrashes, stretching those long fingers toward me. *"Riven!"* she screams, her anger shifting into hysteria. *"Riven!"*

"How does she know your name?" Galen asks, panicked. The Player's screams ring out all the way down the hall, my name echoing off the stone. Did no one else notice the world go still?

Galen's gaze drops to the knife in my hand, slick with golden blood. The Player's blood. Before I can release the knife, droplets of it drip down the handle and sink into my skin, warm—*too* warm, like I'm holding my hands over an open flame. I cry out and drop the blade.

But inside, my chest feels like it cracks open. Something sharp and hungry rushes in to fill the space.

"Riven, what did you do?" my brother asks, and I think the answer is that I have made a very dangerous enemy. I do not say this out loud to Galen.

And I most *certainly* don't tell him what the Player whispered in my ear.

PROLOGUE

The mortals made a treaty, to keep the Players South
And when the treaty ended, a wall to keep them out
And if the wall should crumble, then marks will keep us safe
And if our marks should fail us, gods have mercy on our fate

ACT I

Act I: Scene I

TEN YEARS LATER

If I had a coin for every time I was warned about the Playhouse, I'd have enough to buy a front row seat.

One for last week, when the papers warned of its rumored grand return and the looming end of the treaty.

And then about a hundred more for this morning, when news broke the Playhouse had posted a bulletin announcing their next tour stop—the District of Dionysus—and all hell subsequently broke loose.

To make things worse, the bulletin listed no date. No arrival, no performances scheduled, nothing. Like the tense speculation of their return—and the fear it drives into the air—is just another glorious part of the show. I'll bet they do it on purpose.

I push myself to tread faster, my eyes focused on the afternoon sun dipping lower on the horizon as I weave through a sea of faded coats and skirts blurring into gray streets, the word *"Players"* swarming in the air. They've been closing in for weeks, their theatre sinking and vanishing beneath the earth, only to impossibly rise up somewhere else.

I tuck my chin and urge my legs to *move*.

You will cooperate, I command my limbs, most of which have already gone numb and cold. *You will work today and not—*

As if to argue with the thought, the wind smacks me with a gust that soaks through both of my coats and unfurls a paralyzing chill down my bones. I buckle and swear under my breath.

"Cursed, I heard—" someone utters to their companion in passing, eyes flickering in my direction. I bristle at the word, straightening. *Cursed.*

The Player's promise from ten years ago hovers at the edges of my memory, sending a shiver down my spine.

Glass smacks the sidewalk in front of me, shattering, and I shriek, shielding my face.

"Sorry—gods, so sorry!" calls a woman through a window two stories up, who just nearly murdered me with a slab of falling glass. What a way to go *that* would have been. "Can't be too careful."

She isn't the only one. The path ahead is littered with broken mirrors catching the light like specks of gold. The Playhouse is moving closer every day, and people are *still* harboring them? Gods help us.

Mirrors are practically an invitation for a Player to come inside. Or worse, to snatch someone through their reflection. I wait a beat, just in case anyone else feels like chucking more glass out their window, before moving again, taking care to sidestep a large chunk.

I avert my eyes from the shards; I haven't seen my own reflection in years.

From the way people stare, I gather this is a good thing.

Glass crunches under my boots all the way to the Cut—a deep trench of dark water on either side of a wall rising out of it. Both look a little ominous today.

The Cut divides Theatron in half, separating us in the North from the Player worshippers of the South. In the center between them is the only shared territory, the District, which sits low and flat like the bottom of a bowl. It's a wildly unhappy marriage, and probably the only place you can find a temple dedicated to the Players just two streets away from an apothecary that sells the Eleutheraen gold that kills them.

"Did you miss me, Jak?" I call mockingly to the usual guard from the footbridge as I approach the closest gateway.

Jak's face pinches at my greeting. "Riven. Still alive, I see." He doesn't sound pleased by this, nor amused by the little bow I offer in response.

"When do you think it'll be?" I ask.

He huffs a humorless laugh, but there's a strained edge to it. "I've heard guesses ranging from three days to three months, based on their patterns. What, you want in? Some of us are taking bets."

"I've lost enough on the Players, thanks," I say, throwing a look to the black water below, and the wall rising out of it. Despite its name, the wall wasn't built high to keep the Players out. It was built *low*, sealed with Eleutheraen gold to ward off Players. I've heard rumor that the Cut gained its name because they dug so deep that they accidentally severed Theatron in two.

I hope it does run that deep. That it's enough.

The gate groans open, and Jak takes several exaggerated steps backward to offer me an extra-wide berth. Everyone acts scared to *catch what I have*. Like the Player magic that poisoned me will simply leap into anyone who gets too close.

I ignore him and tug my coat tighter as I pass over the other side of the footbridge.

The District of Dionysus greets me with a strange mix of activity—some shoppers make panicked last-minute purchases, while others seem to be putting on a show of indifference to the news, like the world didn't shift under the weight of a single announcement—or maybe that's just denial. It isn't hard to spot the exuberant Playhouse worshippers flocking into shops to purchase offerings of jewelry and fine wine. Though *that* isn't particularly new.

I cast a sideways glance at the news racks as I go, full of sensational headlines about the Playhouse's looming return:

500-YEAR TREATY ENDS, TERROR BEGINS; WILL THE PLAYHOUSE BREACH THE CUT?

NO NEW AGREEMENT REACHED WITH PLAYERS; NORTH BRACES FOR ATTACK

PLAYHOUSE TO RETURN TO DISTRICT FOR FIRST TIME IN 15 YEARS: WHAT WE KNOW SO FAR

"SPOTLIGHT FALLS ON PLAYER JUDE!" bellows a newspaper hawker over the piercing whistle of the nearby Diolkos Railway.

Enormous, marble statues of famous Players line my path as I breeze past a man trying to barter a playbill signed by the entire cast. Across the street, another woman rivals him, selling copies of the Playhouse treaty.

I duck low while passing the courthouse, just nearly taking an elbow to the face, but my eyes graze over a few of the signs as I round the corner.

NO PLAYERS

Our world is not your stage

The protests have spread almost as quickly as the Playhouse's announcement.

I feel eyes on me as I pass by the most recently erected statue, built in honor of their Lead Player, Jude Stepharros. Face chiseled to sharp angles, hair so artfully tousled it almost looks as if it wasn't made of stone. It stands some twenty feet tall at the center of a rippling fountain, rare gems and coins cluttering the water below his carved sandals—offerings. A dreadful waste, if you ask me. I consider dipping my hand in the water to swipe a few, but I've heard doing so can invoke all sorts of terrible curses.

I can barely afford the curse I have.

"*Riven!* Riven Hesper, you come here," rasps an all-too-familiar voice that catches me mid-step. I turn. The words don't come from the statue, mind you, but from the man propped against its base.

Haris. He's dressed in the same garish robes as always—a discarded costume from the Playhouse that he claims was as red as the auditorium curtain when he snatched it, though with time it's faded to the same gray as everything else. I can't recall a time I've seen him wear anything different. Once, when I brought him an old change of clothes my brother left behind, Haris looked at me like I'd suggested stripping off his own skin.

"Hi, Haris," I say, wrestling my bag from my shoulder. "I was just looking for you."

Haris may be a Playhouse fanatic, but he's also just about the closest thing I have to a friend, the only person around here who doesn't call me cursed. In fact, he's under the bizarre impression that I'm *blessed* to have been touched by a Player. Granted, the rest of them assume I was deemed unworthy, and that's why the monster's golden blood is slowly killing me. Maybe they're right.

As far as Playhouse worshippers go—*Revelers*, we call them—Haris is hardly the worst I've encountered.

He smiles, revealing rows of even teeth as he whispers, "It's *coming*, Riven."

Pity fiddles at my heartstrings. Every performance he attended—thirty-two, he claims—is written on his face. The same telltale sign of every Reveler: a filmy coating of gold over each pupil.

During one of the Playhouse's tours, Haris *literally* followed the theatre as it traveled from city to city. On foot for hundreds of miles. At night, he camped outside its gates, leaving the Players expensive offerings with every last bit of coin to his name, including the deed to his house.

And worse, he couldn't help it; Haris was never marked.

"I can hear them," he whispers, grinning wider and raising his most prized possession: a hand mirror. He prays to the Players through it daily. "They're coming *home*."

If I wasn't marked, I'd probably look and talk just like him.

"Oh, I've heard," I mutter and glance up from rifling through my bag. "That's why I'm here—I brought you something." Now, where did I put it...

Most days, I bring Haris whatever food I can hustle out of the house without too much notice—he's often so absorbed with thoughts of the Players it doesn't occur to him to eat. Today, though, I brought him something even more important.

"You'll take me to it, won't you? You'll come with me," Haris presses, eyes narrowing. "You and me, we're different—but you understand, don't you? Friends understand."

"The Playhouse isn't even here yet," I remind him, and spot the shine of a thin chain gleaming at the bottom of my bag. *Ah! Found it.*

Pinching the chain, I extract the pendant and approach him.

"*Please*, Riven!" Haris wails, stretching his hands out to me. The sleeves of his robes fall back, revealing the loose skin of his forearms, sagging off the bone like bread dough. Puffy, pink-white scars spell out *JUDE STEPHARROS*. I swallow back the bile that rises in my throat. We're both victims of the Players, just in different ways.

"It's finally coming *home*," he pleads.

"Here," I say, and bend to offer the pendant dangling from my fist. "This is going to help keep you safe—wear it if you go near the Playhouse. Especially if you see one of them, okay? I got it from the Merchant Ring. It's pressed with Eleutheraen gold and should—"

At the word, his face twists with rage, and I barely have time to react before he lunges and grabs hold of my wrist so quickly that I cry out in surprise, the pendant clattering to the ground.

"*Take me to it!*" he keens. "Bring me to the Players—" His nails dig into my skin, and I gasp.

My wrist breaks mercifully from his grip, and I stagger backward, falling on the stone.

My skin crawls like spiders are skittering over my body. I think I might throw up.

I hate being touched. *Hate* it. I always have.

Catching my breath, I get to my feet again and study my palms. The pale, waxy color is already bruising a deep purple. *Damn it.* Bruises, sprains, everything takes longer and longer to heal these days—if not just failing to heal altogether. Like the poison has made my body forget how.

Wiping my hands over my coat like I can shake off the touch, I turn to leave. I still have another stop to make before I get home, and even I know better than to hang around the District after dark.

But as I gather myself, I throw one more concerned look over my shoulder at Haris, who coughs and settles his filmy gaze on me. Then grins wide as he raises that hand mirror. Like he knows something I don't.

"It's coming home, Riven."

Act I: Scene II

I nearly sigh in relief when I finally reach Aletheia's Chronicles, a bookstore wedged between a candlemaker and an antique store claiming to sell old props once used onstage by Players. It's also the only shop in the District that sells the texts I'll need for my first semester at the Orkestrian Academy.

"No, *no*! Out with you, Riven," shouts a man with thick glasses and lightly tanned skin. He moves from behind the counter as soon as the door clicks shut behind me. "Leave and take your curse with you."

"Hi, Sebastian!" I chirp, weaving between tables stacked high with tomes.

"Gods help me," he mutters, running a hand through his hair. The old man was raised in the North, making him one of a small handful of marked people still living in the District. "The Playhouse returning any moment for the first time in fifteen years, and now the work of their hands wanders into my store. And a thief, no less."

I frown. "I brought it *back*," I defend, pulling a leather volume from my bag and plopping it onto the counter between us.

"This is a bookstore. Not a library." The owner narrows his eyes at the leather cover. "Who's going to buy something touched by your hands?"

"Maybe they shouldn't," I argue, tapping the cover. "*This* is useless." It contained next to godsdamned *nothing* about Craft, much less what to do if one finds themselves poisoned by it.

I hand over my Orkestrian Academy acceptance letter. "But never you mind it. I'm here for my school materials, and I need to be quick about it."

Sebastian scowls, pinching the corner of the letter like he's afraid to brush my skin. Then he adjusts his glasses and looks it over in disbelief. "They're letting *you* into the academy?" His eyebrows shoot up.

I bristle. "Lucky for you, the semester starts next week. I'll be on a train to Orkestra and far away before you know it."

He shakes his head, almost looking sad. "I happen to have friends in the Healer Quarter, Riven." I stiffen at this. "Rumor is you won't even live to see next month."

The words nearly wipe the smirk right off my face. I've been seen by probably every healer North of the District, to no avail. No one knows how to undo what the Player did to me. No one even knows what's *wrong* with me.

I clear my throat. "Then I invite you to dance on my grave when I'm gone," I respond, flashing him a toothy grin.

"Studying to be a healer, are you?" he mutters to himself, looking over my letter. "Can't say I expected that from the likes of you."

I imagine that's why no healer has any idea how to help me.

A mortal cannot fix what an immortal broke, a healer once said. But this hasn't deterred me from scouring every book I can get my hands on for solutions.

I figured long ago, if I want answers on how to reverse whatever is happening to me, I'll need to find them myself.

With another shake of his head, Sebastian disappears into the back of the store with my letter.

A bell dings over the door, and I turn to spot two girls entering the store. I swallow, averting my gaze. They bustle between narrow walkways beneath wall-to-wall oak shelves, and I turn away, spotting several other patrons I hadn't noticed huddling in a corner, comparing quills.

"Yes, the dead Peacemaker's daughter..." one of them whispers, eyes flashing up at me, then darting back to their companion. I tense, shoving away the sinking feeling in my chest. Apparently, even the imminent return of the Players isn't enough to entirely drop interest in one of the victims of their work. Gritting my teeth, I focus hard on the wood paneling of the floor, pulling in slow breaths like Galen always tells me.

"Cursed, I heard—" someone else utters. *"By that Player who*

broke free and attacked the..."

"Taller than I thought. Did you know her brother..."

"Gods, she's ugly. Why do her eyes look like that?"

Anger ignites like a match in my chest as I touch the tips of my fingers to the half-moon creases that ring my eyes, wondering what they *do* look like. And deciding it's probably best I don't know.

"You pay first." Sebastian returns with an armful of books that will probably fracture my spine to carry home. I dump the money my brother sent on the counter and pile them into my bag, turning to leave.

"Do you think they'll give her a roommate?" My eyes flicker to the whispers of another group of students, who seem to be putting as much distance as possible between themselves and me without leaving the shop. But I have a sharp ear.

"Gods help whoever that is. I heard—"

"...looks like a godsdamned corpse."

My blood heats as I track the speaker of the insult—a boy with rusty-brown hair and glasses. An Eleutheraen mark glitters on his collarbone.

He's marked, like me. Which means he can't lie. No marked can.

North of the Cut, we all bear identical symbols of protection, burned into our skin with the same Eleutheraen gold that can kill Players. A vow to truth and a shield against the lure of the Playhouse. It protects our bodies from Players and their lies. But likewise, anyone with an Eleutheraen mark cannot speak an untruth of their *own*, either.

He means what he said. That I look like a corpse.

But it isn't the distaste flashing across his face that makes my blood roar in my ears.

It's the flash of fear in his eyes when I stare back a beat too long. Like the magic that Player poisoned me with makes me just as dangerous as them.

As I shove the door open to leave, a familiar ice seeps over my bones, and the Player's whispered promise plays across my mind.

Come with me, she said. *Come with me or you will suffer.*

Leave it to me to find the only Player true to their word.

Act I: Scene III

By the time I reach the Dionysian Records, my lungs feel like they're full of pine cones. Aunt Cassia will be inside the archive temple—but at the moment, I'd prefer to sulk peacefully alone.

I drop onto the lowest step of the temple to rest, dragging in sharp breaths. From here, the slope spills out into the District below, washed gold by the last sliver of sun.

Stretching my legs, I peer over my shoulder and up the steps at the statue of Dionysus towering from the top of the temple. I nod at the dead god politely. He doesn't nod back. Statues rarely do.

Some people still pray to the gods for rescue. I stopped doing that a long time ago.

Dionysus is dead. I don't think help is coming.

At best, I think, the gods are cruel for not intervening. At worst, they're cowards for abandoning us with the Players. Though I've heard rumor of places far across the sea that found themselves plagued by monsters even worse than ours.

And right now, I just want to yell at *someone*. A statue will do.

"If you were going to bleed out, did you have to do it in Theatron?" I ask Dionysus. "Surely there are nicer mountaintops to die on."

Dionysus's long, chiseled arms do not move, eternally stretched out to the world. I take it as a shrug.

"Please don't be insulted," I tell Dionysus while studying my nails, which have started turning a funny gray color over the past few weeks. "If I bled out on a mountain, I probably wouldn't have expected monsters to come out of *my* blood, either."

Dionysus does not laugh at this, unmoved as a harsh wind blows through the columns and down the steps.

"One of your Players caused *this*, by the way." I gesture vaguely at my crumbling self, not that I think Dionysus would care. "It didn't start out so bad. Some nausea. Headaches. A bad case of influenza, the healers thought."

Then came the aches that dwelled deep in my bones. A chill that settled over my skin unchanged by layers of wool or the heat of a fire. A tiredness eternally unsatisfied by sleep. No amount of nourishment added a thread of muscle to my bones.

The Player's poison leeched the life from my flesh. I shudder, remembering her golden blood all over my hands.

I didn't truly start to panic until the aches and pains dulled, though, overtaken instead by a vengeful ice that blustered through my veins like a winter storm and made my bones seize like frozen branches.

My body seems to have descended into the afterlife and left me behind.

As if to prove that point, the ground suddenly sways, dips beneath me, and my stomach lurches. I clutch the steps, my nails scraping the stone. *Am I dizzy?*

No. It's the ground. The ground is really rumbling, shaking like it's about to tear open.

A strange darkness rips through the clouds overhead, spreading like ink in water.

The world trembles again, and this time, shouts rise from the nearby Merchant Ring.

My heart thuds against my ribs as my gaze darts down the hill to the District.

Golden light blooms in the center like the rising sun. I wince, choking on a sweet, cloying tang in the air that tastes vaguely of perfume.

Move. I should not be here. The thoughts come in fragments.

Then I see it.

A sinister palace rushes up from the soil as if emerging from Hades itself. Its white marble towers tear free of the earth, roots dangling, clumps of dirt cascading down tiers that must span fifteen stories.

Hundreds of enormous columns glittering with bands of gold surface next, lining the center dome like soldiers standing guard, a haze of pale dust billowing in their wake. At its top, the carved shape of a crow, its marble wings stretched in eternal flight.

The Playhouse.

It's returned. Today.

Now.

I should be frightened—I know this from my upbringing. The sight is unnatural and unholy, stealing the breath from my lungs. An intense draw to the Playhouse that I attribute to years of rage blankets my mind.

For a strange moment, all is silent. The world seems empty, void of anyone or anything aside from me and the entity that ruined my future and stole my father's. Its glowing stained glass windows peer back at me in the distance like the golden eyes of a beast.

What did you do to me?

A heartbeat later, chaos fractures down below. Worshippers from South Theatron race toward the Playhouse like moths to a flame, shrieking with glee. Meanwhile, those who bear marks scatter back toward the safety of the North's wall, screaming at loved ones to follow.

"Riven!"

I startle at the sound of my name. Aunt Cassia flies down the steps of the archive temple, waving for me to stand, but even she pauses to take in the sight, frozen until she calls, "On your feet—*now*."

The urgency in her face has me scrambling to push myself up, stumbling toward the steps after her.

But halfway there, I don't know what possesses me. I can't help but glance back—in time to see another burst of buttery yellow light. Warm wind breathes across my face, curling through the cool air.

The Playhouse doors have opened.

"Ladies and gentlemen!"

The voice is not human. It's thunderous, beckoning, and everywhere all at once. It shimmers across the clouds and rumbles in the ground. Somewhere, a thrilled audience of Revelers shriek greetings. In their joyous cries, I make out a name: *Silenus.*

The Playhouse director.

He scares me almost as much as the Players. In some ways, even more. My hand hovers over my coat pocket, where my father's golden knife hides.

"Thank you for joining us this fine afternoon!" Silenus's voice thrums low, a rich baritone that strangely reminds me of a grandfather clock. It must project halfway across the city. I almost think I can feel it inside my own heart.

My mind goes to the solagraphs in the District Museum. Silenus is always pictured the same way: a head of thick white hair, fair skin, elegant spectacles, a fine suit. Smile lines etched into a face that has not aged in hundreds of years.

And always, *always* in his hands: a small leather-bound book, pages that emit a warm, soft glow. "The Script," it's called, an item long suggested to have belonged to Dionysus himself. I can't imagine anything less than a god's treasured possession could give Silenus the power to direct the Players.

"Wonderful people of Theatron, it is always a privilege to be amongst old friends. But none of us are here for sentiment, I understand." He laughs softly, but it seems to echo through the sky.

My legs cramp as Cassia and I fly up the steps to the temple, and I push myself to keep going.

"Such wicked rumors lately." A sigh. *"But the Playhouse is most happy to negotiate a new agreement with our friends in the North as our revered treaty comes to an end. But! In exchange—"*

I can't catch my breath. My lungs burn.

"We expect utmost cooperation as we hold our most beloved tradition here in the District, one that was so unluckily disrupted last time."

At this, Cassia freezes. My mind races. *Beloved tradition—*

"We are proud to announce a casting call—and a Great Dionysia!"

My heart stutters, shocked as an explosion of cheers rocks the District.

A casting call.

The words send a shudder through me. I don't know much about casting calls, only that they involve a mortal taking the place of a Player. *Becoming* one. Through the most brutal and violent of means, should they win—part of a five-day festival known as the Great Dionysia. A massive spectacle, during which the Players are released from the Playhouse and allowed to roam freely.

Cassia whirls, her eyes widening.

"Perhaps a new Player stands amongst us here today," the director calls. *"We hope to see you all later this evening for this most exciting opportunity."*

A great cracking sound splits the air as the Playhouse doors slam shut.

If anxiety were a person, I think it would look a lot like my aunt Cassia right now. She made us wait inside the Dionysian Records for several hours before she'd so much as entertain the idea of letting me go home, claiming it would be safer once the Revelers are inside the Playhouse for the casting call and not causing trouble outside of it.

Then again, if I devoted as much time as she does to studying Theatron's darkest corners of history, of what has happened and what *could* happen again, I might be anxious, too. But Cassia says our best weapon against the Playhouse is our knowledge of it, devoting her life to protecting what historical records the Players failed to destroy.

"Let me take you home," she says. "While the Revelers busy themselves with all this casting call foolishness."

My pride wants to be stubborn about accepting the arm she offers, but the ice twisting around my stiff spine wins. I loop my arm through her sleeve, just this once.

As we depart the Dionysian Records, my eyes stall curiously on a set of oak doors that remain forever locked. Unlike most,

I know what sleeps beyond them: empty storybooks. Thousands, robbed of their words, their contents devoured by the Playhouse.

Which is for the best. Stories are nothing but lies. Tools of manipulation for Players.

"Gods damn it all," Cassia mutters under her breath, taking in the empty streets. The Revelers are nowhere to be seen, and anyone North of the Cut has clearly made themselves scarce.

"I'm pretty sure they already have," I point out. "What do we do?"

The question feels vague and awkward under the circumstances. The papers have speculated of the Players' return to the District for ages, long before their bulletin confirmed it, but a *casting call*—

It doesn't make sense.

"Absolutely nothing," Cassia replies, like the answer has been waiting on her tongue for a while. "We knew they were coming. Stay home, stay away from mirrors. Let the Players have their bloodbath. It's no business of the North."

Unless the Players will *make* it our business. They've been confined to South Theatron for nearly five hundred years, an agreement they were forced into. And they haven't risked coming this close to the Cut in over a decade.

"I don't see how a building itself can move." It doesn't seem possible.

"It can't. But buildings are also *built*," Cassia replies glumly. "The Playhouse never was. It just appeared around the same time as the Players." She shakes her head. "One big illusion, if you ask me."

I think for a moment. "What if the Players try to cross the Cut—"

"Let's not dwell on what is not yet a problem."

Not *yet*. A half-truth. But I've played mental gymnastics with my mark for as long as I've had it. I can *think* an untruth to myself easily enough. On occasion, I've written out a few lies just to see if I could. But every time I open my mouth to speak a barefaced lie, the words never seem to find my tongue.

And right now, there is something Cassia is trying to avoid admitting.

"While I do *not* approve of you traveling into the District alone," Cassia begins, running a hand over her slicked-back hair. New threads of white peek out of the auburn. "I have something to show you."

She peers down the quiet side street we turn onto, her eyes narrowed at the dimming light. Then, she extracts what looks like a faded solagraph from her pocket.

The Player depicted in the image has a sharp grin and silver-blond hair that tumbles down her back. Searing eyes that look like they might burn through the paper.

My shoulders slump. I've probably studied the Players almost as obsessively as Cassia has and don't recognize this one. Much of my childhood was spent immersed in their histories, a means of distraction when kids my own age stopped including me in their games. In a strange way, the Players' faces are as familiar as those of old friends.

Loneliness does strange things to your brain.

"This is Player Iris—one of the cast members executed in Syrene," Cassia explains. "It's been suggested that some of the cast could have escaped the destruction—if *she* is the one who poisoned you, it's possible that—"

"That's not her." I shake my head, picturing the guilty Player's face. "I know what I saw."

The only thing more infuriating than being cursed by a Player is being cursed by a Player who *doesn't exist.* I should know. I've studied every gold-encrusted inch of the Playhouse's history, searching for answers in its chronicle of lies. I have learned the faces of all its remaining cast members.

There are five Players left.

The Player I saw as a child—whoever she was—is *not* among them.

There's no record of her. Then again, there's no record of someone being *poisoned* as I have, either. Only cases of minds tormented with never-ending songs, or claims of madness evoked by Playhouse performances.

My curse, though—this strange, slow decay that rots me from the inside out—it's an anomaly. One that Player is *surely* responsible for.

Come with me or you will suffer.

Cassia frowns, slides the picture back in her pocket. "I'll keep looking, Riv."

I drag a hand through my hair and laugh bitterly when a few brunette strands fall right out, floating to the ground. That started happening about a week ago. "Yeah," I say. "Me too."

Act I: Scene IV

"Is that you, Riven?" calls my mother's voice, a hint of apprehension in her tone. Like she hopes it's anyone *but* me.

I sniff the air as I kick my boots off in the hall, suspicious of the scents of fried cabbage and braised rabbit. My mother does not cook dinner. Or anything, for that matter.

My eyes fall on the stack of three envelopes that must have arrived while I was gone—but one stands out from the others. The envelope is too rich, too expensive.

My name is scrawled over the back, the seal of the Orkestrian Academy stamped in navy blue over the front.

Before I can break it, my mother's laugh burbles from down the hall, sending a chill along my spine. She has both emerged from her room and is *laughing.*

A second, lower voice answers my mother's, and my eyes widen.

Stuffing the letter into my pocket, I hurry down the hall, a smile stretching across my face. "Galen?"

"Riv!" my brother calls back.

Galen has our aunt Cassia's wolfish grin and our mother's chestnut hair. He makes no move to greet me, aware I enjoy hugs about as much as I enjoy having my nail beds ripped out.

"*Two* coats today," he comments, one eyebrow raised at my attire. "Isn't that one mine?"

"It was," I say with a grin. He left his old jacket after his last visit. It's far too big, but thicker than my own.

The gold scar below his left eye stretches when he smiles. While my injuries from encountering a Player sank deep beneath my skin, Galen escaped with a two-inch scar that turned him into the stuff of legends at school. Proof that he "fought a Player and won."

"What are you doing here?"

"Imposing on Mom for dinner at the moment," he answers.

Ah. That explains the cooking.

Our mother rolls her eyes in his direction as she sets a plate on the counter, though even her feigned annoyance at Galen looks more like admiration. She's doted on my brother since I can remember.

This doesn't bother me. I like being doted on about as much as I like being touched. Still, I've never gotten used to the peculiar way our mother's eyes go anywhere *except* me. Like I'm a ghost she can't see. Occasionally, growing up, I'd catch her staring, lips pale. Then she'd just shake her head. *You look so much like your father is all*, she'd say before going back to pretending I don't exist.

Galen always watched these interactions with his lips pressed together. *Don't mind her*, he'd tell me. *She just misses him.*

I think all of Theatron misses him. An emissary of the council, my father was the North's hope—our best shot at peace. That peace shattered the moment a Player threw his body from the Playhouse and left his blood to dry on the marble steps.

The Playhouse fled from the violent uproar that followed, and it hasn't returned to the District of Dionysus—or ventured near the Cut—since.

Until now. And I'm guessing it's not interested in *peace*.

"Have something to eat, why don't you?" Galen slides his plate toward me, probably to draw attention away from the fact that our mother only prepared dinner for one of us. "If you're going to be taller than me, you might as well eat like I do," he teases, though I only have my brother's height beat by an inch as of this year. While Galen's built like one of the massive statues in the District, I'm all overly long limbs and—well, that's about all I know.

I push the plate back toward him, my stomach uneasy thanks to the palace of monsters that arrived this afternoon. "You're home early," I prompt.

"Business in the District. Seems like I got here just in time." His expression tightens. "The Playhouse requested an audience with the council as soon as it arrived."

Galen only graduated a year ago and was immediately granted a position on our mortal council's board of advisers. It's no secret that everyone expects him to fill our father's role, to somehow mediate a new treaty to keep the Playhouse from the North, now that the old one is finally coming to an end.

Like clockwork, our mother excuses herself and vanishes upstairs. She always does when the Playhouse enters a conversation. Or when I enter a room.

My brother watches her go, the worry plain on his face.

I stare at him, stunned. "You mean…you *saw* them?" I whisper. "The Players?"

"From afar—one of them." He keeps his voice steady, but I know Galen too well. I sense the quiver of fear beneath his tone. "The council met with the director and Lead Player after they arrived. Said they wished to negotiate the terms of their *casting call*."

"Did you?" I ask, leaning in. "Negotiate?"

"What was there to discuss?" Galen laughs, but the sound is dry of any humor. "He's as violent as they say, you know. Player Jude. Snapped a guard's neck for stepping too close to Silenus. Announced he'd do the same to anyone who dares disrupt the casting call tonight. Said any talks of peace would wait until after it concluded."

"Gods," I say under my breath.

For creatures with such great egos, it must be deeply humbling for the Players to be governed by the mortals they once ruled over. To *need* us. Players require worship, attention. They rely on it to survive the way we mortals require food. Otherwise, they might as well wipe us all out.

But if they're denied an audience altogether, gods know what they'll do. Players are dangerous when they're angry, but they're godsdamned *lethal* when they're bored.

"You know, everyone keeps looking at me like I'm Dad." Galen shakes his head at the absurdity of it. "Like I should know how to bargain with these monsters like he did." He shakes his head again, leaving the rest unsaid.

Desperate to change the subject, I unfold the mysterious letter from my pocket and show it to Galen. "Any idea what this is?" I break the seal, but stall at the startled look he gives me.

"Riv," Galen begins slowly. "That's partly why I came home—to talk to you." He looks like he's about to tear the letter from my fingers. "I hoped to beat the notice here, but—"

My gaze drops down, and I scan the first line.

Riven Hesper: We regret to inform you that upon further inquiry...

"What is this?" My voice comes out sharper than I meant. Dread freezes like a block of ice in my chest as I blink, willing the words to change. To vanish.

"They've revoked—" I swallow, my tongue dry. "They revoked my acceptance?"

But why? The semester starts so soon. I already bought my passage to Orkestra—

I exhale. I know *why*. I can read it all over Galen's face.

"The university board..." Galen trails off. Like he isn't friends with the whole godsdamned board. He was the Orkestrian Academy's golden boy for four years. And before him, our father. "Questions were raised about how safe your attendance would be."

Safe for me," I ask through my teeth, "or safe for the other students?" I mean the words, but I don't mean them to come out of my mouth with the ferocity of a lightning bolt. "Which is it?"

Cursed by a Player. The words have followed me since I was a child. Like the Player's magic—*Craft*—that poisoned me is going to spontaneously spread to anyone who gets too close. The same questions were raised in grade school until I was eventually placed on a bench on the far side of the classroom. Sometimes I felt like one of the Player statues in the District: watched from afar and rarely addressed directly. It gave me ample time to debate which is worse: to be abandoned by society or to be famously hated by it.

The former, I've decided.

"Both," he admits.

My heart cracks, exposing the simmering coal at its center.

"Who." My voice is deadly calm.

Galen stills. "What do you mean?"

"You said *questions were raised*," I force out. That's half the truth. My eyes flicker down to the Eleutheraen mark at the base of his throat. I bet if Galen could lie to me, he would right now. "*Who* raised them?"

He presses his lips into a thin line, the truth on his tongue. "I did, Riven."

I stare back frostily, daring him to go on.

"And I was right to. The last time I saw you, you looked—"

"What?" I interrupt. "Go on. Say it."

He averts his eyes. For a moment, I wonder if he's frightened of me, like the neighbor's children who throw pebbles at my window. But when he meets my gaze again, his voice softens. "Riven, please. I know this was important to you. But you're worse off now than the time before—and the time before that. And *now*..."

I stare down at my hands, trying to see what he sees. Long, bony fingers. Gray nails. Dark veins pucker from my wrists. About a month ago, my skin started fading to a pale stone-like hue, not dissimilar to the underbelly of a fish.

"No," I say in blunt response.

That Player *doesn't* get to take this, too. The Orkestrian Academy is a door to a life different from this one. With a new home. And access to the greatest library in Theatron, with probably my best chance at finding answers to what's happened to me.

Answers to *why* it hasn't happened to anyone else.

Maybe even a chance to be recognized on my own merit. Not *Galen's sister*. Not *the dead Peacemaker's daughter*.

"We need to be honest about what's happening." Galen's tone is steady, firm. Infuriating. "Whatever...*ailment* this is—"

"Poison. You were there. You can call it what it is."

"*Clearly*, it's serious," he concludes. "You'd be too far from home, not to mention exerting yourself. You may only worsen faster—" He takes a breath. "I'm just not sure it's a good idea anymore, Riv."

Anymore. The word echoes in my head, like a seal on my fate. *Anymore* sounds final.

Anymore sounds like the Player from ten years ago has won.

I shove the thought down as soon as it surfaces. If I make *one* decision for myself, it will be that a Player doesn't get to finish me off.

"I am not helpless," I bite out, but the words taste sour. *Yet*, my mind adds. "I'll take care of myself—"

"Riven, you are not *capable* of taking care of yourself." Galen immediately winces, like he wishes he could pluck the words out of the air and put them back in his mouth.

Blood rushes to my head, eyes falling to my brother's mark once more. He believes that.

The possibility that he's right only enrages me further.

He pulls in a breath, then utters, "Stay here. I spoke with Mom—" I huff a laugh. Our mother has been counting down the days to my departure as eagerly as I have. "Please—at least until you get better."

Until. As if I'm not dying a little faster each day.

Like a godsdamned corpse. The insult rings in my ears.

"This isn't fair, Galen," I seethe.

"The world isn't fair," he answers. "No one chooses the hand they're dealt. Leave fate to the gods and their whims. It bows to no man." I cringe at the reference to a phrase we all learned in school. *Fate guides the feet of the willing and drags the heels of the defiant.*

"I don't believe in fate," I say. "Certainly not a fate written by gods who abandoned us. Was I *fated* to be poisoned by a Player?" I ask, daring him to agree. "Was *Dad* fated to be ripped apart by one?"

His face hardens, both of us equally shocked at my words. We don't bring up our father's death.

"It doesn't matter. This conversation is over," Galen says, standing.

"No!" My raspy voice shoots out of my throat like an arrow, startling both of us. It ricochets off the walls. There's an abrupt creak upstairs, like my mother has shot to her feet.

Too much, I scold myself. My fingernails bite into either side of my chair. Galen's silver gaze hones in on me. "What?" I snap, failing to reel my voice in again.

"That temper, Riv," he says softly, shaking his head. "If you don't get control of it, that anger will be the death of you."

When I say nothing, Galen moves for the hall but pauses at the door. "I'm sorry, Riven—I really am. And I mean it." I don't meet his eyes. Galen pushes the door open. "If we figure out how to... *reverse* whatever this is, I'll take you to Orkestra and enroll you myself."

With that, he's gone.

I give him a full three-minute head start before I tug on my boots and follow him.

Act I: Scene V

I have *never* been in the District alone at night.

It feels different, vulnerable. Like I'm running through the street naked, shaking the frost from my bones.

I'm deep in the District before realizing I can hear the echo of my own feet pounding against the stone. On either side of me, I notice dark windows and boarded-up storefronts, illuminated by blinking limelights that hang over the street. In all my visits across the Cut, the District has bustled with activity, the market bursting at the seams with busy shoppers and peddlers selling their wares.

Tonight, it's deserted.

No one is here to stare or call me cursed. No one to skitter away like I'm a rabid rodent.

It's godsdamn *liberating.*

It occurs to me I don't actually know where Galen went. But whatever speech I had for him is long forgotten as I march up to one of the abandoned booths.

Those, please—yes, the ones on the shelf there, I mouth, imagining myself buying a sack of potatoes, a loaf of bread. All by myself. Like a normal, *uncursed* person. *How much? Oh, sure.* I'd nod and then reach into my pocket for—

Something skitters in the dark behind me.

I whirl around. A rat? Must be—

Nothing.

My stomach twisting, I step over discarded bits of paper and wood. The words "No more Players" and "Our world is not your stage" are inked across several—ghosts of protests from earlier today. Anyone from North Theatron has clearly surrendered their objections to the casting call to hide safely behind the Cut and out of the District tonight.

Like I should, too. This is silly, being out here alone. *Dangerous.*

But gods, it feels good.

A swell in the air swarms my mind, dampens my focus. I scrunch up my brow, struggling to put a label to the noise. It thrums deep in the ground, crawls up my legs, and digs its hooks into my chest. My feet stagger forward to the bizarre sound—long, drawn-out rhythms that weave together like...

Music?

A prickle spears up my spine.

I've read about music. It heralds the presence of Players. Music is what Players used to summon the Dancing Plague—an inexplicable phenomenon that made thousands of people dance in the streets like puppets. They danced, they danced, and they danced. Then they promptly stopped dancing.

Not because they were tired, but because they were dead.

The Playhouse, I think, enraged. *That's* what's responsible for this. For me. All of it.

My feet move faster toward the sound, anger fueling my resolve. The growing ache in my feet only eggs me on until I'm at the end of the block and turning the corner into the very heart of the District.

The Playhouse is a sight to behold up close. A behemoth of gold and marble bursting with light. Shadows in the shapes of expensive gowns and delicate wreaths flutter just behind paned glass. Chatter and laughter claw at my ears.

The casting call, I think with a chill. Thousands of Revelers will have crowded into the Playhouse tonight, risking life and limb in hopes of becoming the next Player. Gambling their lives for power, fame, beauty, and *immortality*.

I stare down at the cold, translucent skin clinging to my hands. For a moment, it doesn't sound entirely outrageous.

But there it is again, that strange rhythm—*music*. It spills through the cracks of the Playhouse doors, down steps that shine like wedges of starlight. But there's something else, too. Woven deep into the melody of plucked strings and the steady hit of a drum, I hear a *voice*—full as the moon and sparkling just as bright.

The voice reaches around my wrists and tugs me gently forward.

This is music? The descriptions I've read have been vile. Like a sinister snake that slips through your ears and eats away at your mind. *This*, though—it doesn't match the taunting cries of the Underworld I imagined.

It sounds like the clinking of stars. The flicker of a warm candle. The whisper of a loved one.

I like it.

I startle at my own thought, unsure where it came from. *No. No, I don't.*

The massive Playhouse gates gape open at me like a smile. The voice, otherworldly and enchanting, beckons me forward, bringing me to the threshold.

Stop here, I tell my feet.

A soft breeze brushes my cheek. The pearly Playhouse steps gleam like an open pool of moonlight.

"What did you do to me?" I ask the Playhouse out loud. It doesn't answer, the voice gone.

That's not good enough. I ball my fists.

"My life would be different. If it weren't for you," I add, louder, "I would be a normal person. With *friends.* I would probably talk to fewer buildings." My voice is far too loud. "People would call me by my *name.* And they wouldn't treat me like I'm a rabid animal. And my own mother wouldn't be frightened of me. So, tell me!" I'm shouting now, waving my hands. "Tell me what you did! *Tell me—*"

"What have we here?"

The voice startles me so badly, I jump and—too late—clutch Galen's coat at the collar to cover my mark.

A figure, cloaked in black, emerges from the darkness. A blessing. Of all the things my shouting outside of the Playhouse could have summoned, I'll take a stranger in the dark over a Player any day. My boldness forgotten, I scurry back like a mouse. "Who are you?"

He steps in the light, his face hidden behind a Comedy mask—

popular among Playhouse fanatics. A horrific smile is carved into the bronze.

My heart starts to hammer.

"Did I see a stain there on your neck?" I don't know the voice, but I know he's much bigger than me. My hand creeps to my inner coat pocket where my father's Eleutheraen dagger stays tucked away, just as a second figure appears behind the first. This one behind a Tragedy mask. I take in the overstated frown, my breaths coming quicker.

"What is a marked doing outside the Playhouse tonight?" Tragedy Mask asks.

I draw inward and keep my mouth shut. *Who are they?* Overzealous fans from the South, taking it upon themselves to patrol the casting call?

"Well, go on, then," a third voice chimes in—feminine this time. I spin around, finding another Comedy mask, silver and scraped at the edges. That exaggerated smile sends a chill up my spine. "Tell us."

My eyes fall to the blade in her hand.

Fuck. I've read about this. Revelers who target and slash through Eleutheraen marks to honor the Players. A story broke months back about Playhouse fanatics sacrificing some marked soul on a Dionysian altar.

What was I *thinking*? Venturing out here at night on my own—

"Did you not hear me, girl?" she repeats.

My mouth opens, closes. *I'm lost!* I think frantically, but the words won't form on my tongue. I can't lie. "I—I'm..." My eyes flicker up to the Playhouse.

This isn't how I'm supposed to die.

I recoil from the thought, unsure why my mind jumped to it so quickly.

"What, here to audition?" The first Comedy mask roars with laughter. "Well, girl. Has no one told you? A marked can't audition." He's right. Eleutheraen marks are an insult to Players and their egos. The man takes a step forward, but I can't back up anymore—not with the woman behind me. "Nasty consequences for that, actually."

With no option left, I bolt, throwing myself forward. But my sly attempt to dive between them and into the nearest alley is intercepted when one grips my arm, nearly ripping the bone from its socket.

The pressure feels like a door slammed on my shoulder, crushing it. I yelp and thrash like a wet cat as they drag my body forward through the Playhouse gates.

"Come, we can do a little play," one of them jeers. "You can be the lead."

They're taking me to the Players.

My knife. My knife is in my pocket. If I could just reach—

I flail, curling down and clamping my teeth over one of their hands as hard as I can.

A violent force collides with my side, the air punching out of my lungs as one of them shrieks, "The little animal *bit me*!" and drops me like a sack of potatoes.

Something is wrong, I realize, unable to breathe. I don't even know who's hit me. All I know is my lungs feel like they're full of shattered glass. *My ribs. They crushed my godsdamned ribs—*

Then I hear it again. That voice—a song that flutters in the wind like a bird—slows the commotion to a standstill. To my shock, my attackers stop advancing on me, dropping their hands to their sides. I stare up in confusion as their bodies freeze.

The voice sings on, spellbinding and overwhelming. My eyes dart around, searching for its owner as I crawl away at the speedy pace of a sick turtle. The stone feels like sleet beneath my fingers.

When I peer up, I see three flashes of silver emerge. Blades.

They're going to kill me. I claw frantically at the ground, dragging myself across the stone. My lungs feel like they're caving into my chest as I scream for help, but no sound makes it out of my throat.

Strangely, the sting of their blades never comes.

In fact, when I dare a look, they're all staring blankly at one another instead.

Then, like a dance, all three lift their faces high to the sky in perfect unison. The voice sings on. Trancelike, my attackers raise their blades.

Each to their own throat.

It happens so quickly, I don't even know to scream—not until they all drop to the ground with scarlet smiles carved into their necks. Dark pools of blood creep across the stone toward me, illuminated by golden light, which is spilling through the Playhouse doors.

Doors that are now open. Between them, a long, dark figure. His shadow stretches over the landing as he steps through the entrance.

"Ah, a latecomer. Welcome!"

Not much is known about the Players, only that the first ones came from a well on top of Mount Eleutherae, a peak that overlooks North Theatron like a beacon. But even less is known about the man who pulled them out of it.

Silenus Darstellar. Director of the Playhouse.

He's not the sort of man you'd expect from the likes of the Playhouse. He doesn't have the golden eyes or the monstrously exaggerated features of a Player. His eyes are a soft blue, hidden behind a pair of silver spectacles. In fact, he looks altogether *normal*, wearing a suit as black as his hair is white and a smile that glimmers with pride.

He's *smiling.* Doesn't he see the blood?

My breaths come in pitiful wheezes, each one an icicle piercing my lungs.

"For your sake," Silenus says on his way down the stairs, *far* too spry for an old man. "I hope this late entrance is no indication of your onstage timing."

Gods, he thinks I'm here to *audition.*

The ridiculous notion of making a run for it flies across my mind as the director approaches, stepping cleanly over the dead bodies like they aren't there. I slam my palms to the stone, wincing as I push onto my knees, holding my side and bending low at my waist. I think I'll break in half if I straighten any more.

"Please, please, none of that!" Silenus says a little too kindly. "My Players don't mind such displays of admiration, but it isn't necessary for an old director."

The assumption sends my hands into tight fists. I consider the odds of strangling an immortal director and winning.

He thinks I'm *bowing* to him.

That anger will be the death of you, Galen's voice reminds me.

The gates may be only a few feet behind me, but I'm on Playhouse grounds now. I'll die right here if I'm discovered.

I clear my throat and slowly, agonizingly, force my spine straight.

RIVEN: "Hello." I don't mean for the word to come out like a gasp.

The director tilts his head, curious. For a horrifying moment, I wonder if he recognizes me. Sees my father's face in mine, like so many do. I've read that Players rarely recognize the faces of mortals, too tied up in their own vanity. I wonder—hope—whether the same applies to their director. Whatever he is…human or deity or perhaps some unholy mix of the two.

SILENUS: "Apologies for the inconvenience." His eyes drop to the bodies behind us. "Nuisance, the lot of them. They tried the same thing inside only an hour ago. Slaughtered four auditionees before Titus threw them out! Nasty business, the whole thing."

My eyes widen at the casual reference to Player Titus. Could he have been the voice I heard? Silenus is not a Player, so I doubt it could've been his. Though whatever power he wields must be unfathomable.

A power that may very well rest in the book he casually pulls from his suit pocket. My breath freezes in my chest at the sight. *The Script.*

The director makes an amused *hmm* sound in the back of his throat as he consults the book, while I gawk at its gold-rimmed edges, at the ethereal glow that flickers from its pages like a sunrise.

A mortal cannot fix what an immortal broke. The healer's words ring in my ears.

As the director plucks a pen from his suit pocket, a notion of immeasurable foolishness hits me.

If that book has the power to control the Players, surely it can undo the curse of one.

SILENUS: "Well, you might as well come in." He looks up, his smile a little too generous. "The show's just about to start, you know."

No! I think, panicked. I can't go in. He doesn't know I'm marked. What happened to my attackers would be *merciful* by comparison to what they'll do to me inside.

RIVEN: "I—" *I can't*, I want to say. *Get out of this. Get out of—* "I'm hurt!" I wheeze a breath. *Send me home.* "I'm—uh—in no condition to—"

SILENUS: "Pity!" He doesn't sound all that pitying. "Well. I'll leave you to it, then. Should you change your mind, I'm sure one of my Players can stitch you up inside."

And I'm sure I'd rather dive headfirst into my own grave, I think.

With that, Silenus glides back into the Playhouse, vanishing through the doors, though they don't close behind him. They stay wide open, waiting.

Gathering my common sense, I turn to leave, but my first step draws several curses from my lips. My feet wobble beneath me, unsteady.

It occurs to me I'm more than a *little* hurt.

I grip the golden gates to steady myself, and they burn beneath my palms. I won't make it home like this. I won't make it two blocks. The only thing that stings worse than my ribs is my pride.

One of my Players can stitch you up.

I look back to the doors, open and overflowing with golden light. Hesitation holds me in place. I need more than just my ribs stitched up. My breaths come quicker, my eyes fixed on the Playhouse.

A mortal cannot fix what an immortal broke.

Don't, Riven, Galen's voice whispers in my head. But for a moment, all I see is the Orkestrian Academy. All I *feel* is freedom that I'll never taste if I can't find a way to reverse this poisoning.

I stare at the Playhouse, streaming with sunshine in the dead of night.

In my mind, I picture that Script. My fingers release the gate.

If I do this, I'll need to be quick. Stealthy.

The first stair twinges. The second one outright hurts. The third makes my lungs feel like they might explode.

"Fuck it," I say out loud. This poison is going to kill me anyway. Galen knows it. Cassia knows it. I know it. We just don't say it.

And I will *not* die without having tried everything.

For the first time in a long time, I utter a prayer to any of the gods who are still listening. My heart pounds relentlessly, but as I reach the top step, I almost think my feet start to feel lighter, like my bones know a remedy awaits somewhere inside this godsforsaken house of lies.

The soles of my feet land in rhythm with the music as I force myself across the marble landing, right up to the Playhouse doors. My mark pulses, hidden beneath my jacket, feverish now, like my heart is in my throat. The Eleutheraen gold in my blood knows better. *I* know better.

I'm not sure if it's in my head, but I hear it again—that voice, carried by the wind, calming and strangely reassuring.

"Sorry, Galen," I whisper.

I hold my breath and step into the Playhouse.

Act I: Scene VI

What lies beyond the Playhouse doors is a palace fit for the gods. The moment I step through them and into a luxurious antechamber, I feel watched. Like a curtain has been swept aside, an audience waiting just within. Maybe because of the faces—a vast arch of them, soaked in gold and leering at me in agonized frowns and delirious grins that twist around the frame. Comedy and Tragedy. The decorations meld into each other, like actors trapped in the walls, seeking a way out.

They seem to stare at the clock that looms on the opposite wall over the door, an enormous, cracked structure of marble, veins of gold painted over the damage. The floor is just the same: sprawling and gilded to disguise the fractures. Like the Playhouse itself has selected a costume for the evening, doing its best to conceal all the horrors that have played across its floors.

But when I peer up, I gasp.

It takes several blinks before my eyes start to adjust to the shocks of color sprawled across the ceiling—of brilliant blue and deep scarlet, of pops of emerald and touches of vibrant purple. It's so overwhelming that my eyes sting, and I duck my chin before making out what the painting depicts.

I've never seen so much color—*true*, undiluted hues of it—in my life.

My heart thuds in my chest as I go for the golden curtain ahead, hanging beneath the arch of faces and leading out of this antechamber. My fingers brush the heavy velvet, and it parts like water at my touch.

And casts me into another world.

A ballroom awaits on the other side, stretching endlessly into a haze of flickering candlelight and flowery perfumes. In step with the swell of music, mortals float by, their faces blurring together in a dreamlike way that eerily reminds me of the arch.

They're everywhere. Mortals from South of the Cut here to audition, draped in expensive gowns of chiffon and tunics of delicate silk they probably spent their last bit of coin on—all of it the same drained, drab gray cast over all of Theatron. They glide by like silvery ghosts with shimmering eyelids, heels scraping the marble. Their painted lips are a far cry from the shades of red boasted by the curtained-off arches in the corners.

The director is nowhere to be seen and, to my relief, neither are any of his five Players. Just Revelers desperate to catch their attention with varying degrees of absurd dancing, like their very lives depend on each exaggerated word and movement.

Script, I chant in my head. Somewhere between the doors and here, a plan took shape in my head. A really, really ill-advised one. *Find the Script.*

My eyes lock on a luxurious set of stairs on the other side that leads up to a dais. Before I can think better of it, I edge into the crowd, dodging between heels and elbows.

Surely, the director will be auditioning everyone separately. Maybe in a private room. If I find a place to hide, I can catch him off guard—

Someone brushes my sleeve, and I yelp. There are too many people, too close.

Suddenly, I am on the other side, breaking free and scurrying up the steps to the dais before diving through the shimmering curtain just beyond it.

I land on my knees on the other side and groan at the discomfort. The ache in my ribs seems to pulse louder than the music now; I clasp my side and count my breaths, taking in the empty corridor and shaking off the repulsive touch of strangers.

Right or left? Doubt shrouds my shoulders, unsure.

I toe the rich carpet like a scared cat, my path lined by elaborate paintings of Players, alive and dead. For a short moment, I let myself study the scenes depicted in them, fascinated by the colors. They must be from plays—I spot one of a wedding ceremony, another of a family at dinner, a third of a grotesque execution by hanging. The Player who holds the rope has her head thrown back in laughter.

It's hard not to stare. We don't have records of any of the Playhouse's stories. We don't have stories in all of Theatron. They're dangerous, banished, just like music. Stories are just one long *lie*, strung with deception.

A voice splits the silence, radiating with power and shaking the edges of the gilded frames.

It does not sound human.

TITUS: "Gods, they're annoying!"

Horror grips me, my eyes sweeping around the corridor for a hiding place until I spot a large statue of a Player. *That'll do.* I scamper across the hall, skirt behind the statue just in time to see a golden-eyed being round the corner.

My education instantly sets a name to the Player's face: Titus. He's all brawn, with massive shoulders and warm brown skin. A few strands of black hair fall loose across his proud expression as he saunters down the hall, the rest of it tied back at his neck with twists of silver. When he smiles, he shows all his teeth. The image of a wolf nudges my mind.

MATTIA: "You've barely spoken to a single auditionee yet, Titus."

A second Player, her voice sonorous, smooth and whispery like the hiss of a snake. She moves like one, too, carried by the sway of her hips and gliding like she's skating over water. I take in her sharp gaze, steady shoulders, and dark-brown skin that glows like a harvest moon. Elegant braids are styled over her head to reveal emerald earrings that dangle from her earlobes like tiny chandeliers.

Player Mattia. The oldest Player on record.

My heart hammers at the sheer size of them, towering at least a foot over me, with long, toned limbs and brilliant gold eyes. They file before the curtain I just came through, lingering at the entrance like beasts about to be released from their cage.

Gods, what am I thinking? This *is* their cage. I've just stepped into it.

My eyes sting from the soft halo that shivers around their skin, like they're stars that have come loose from the night sky and fallen right into the Playhouse.

ARIUS: "They may surprise you yet, Titus. Casting calls bring in all kinds."

My gaze shifts to a third Player rounding the corner. He's lithe and willowy by comparison to Titus's brawn and most certainly the tallest of the bunch, with fair skin and deceptively soft eyes. Arius works on tying back the golden-blond hair that flows nearly to his waist. While Titus's tone crackles with the spit of fire and Mattia's thrums low, like the rattle of the earth, Arius's voice carries like a mild wind.

He seems too gentle. Too harmless, like a dove.

But I know a *dove* could not do what Player Arius has done. A dove did not make an entire city laugh until their vocal cords tore and split. Player Arius specializes in the comedic arts. He might actually be more violent than the other two.

I hold my breath, easing closer to the statue and peeking between the space of its marble waist and elbow.

The wolf hollers a laugh that makes me jump.

TITUS: "Why bother learning their names? Odds are whoever makes it through will be blood on the stage before this is over."

I draw inward at the words, frightened on behalf of the fools who are actually *auditioning* for this. It's taking all of the self-control I have not to make a panicked dash for the hall.

ARIUS: "You're terrible. May Hades give you no rest."

TITUS: "If he's half so handsome as they say, may *I* give *Hades* no rest."

ARIUS: "Fine. Then a long life in hell, I pray you."

MATTIA: "Don't bother. The gods do not listen to the eternally damned prayers of *actors*."

I hold in a scoff. I'm pretty sure the gods have stopped answering prayers altogether.

SILENUS: “Ladies and gentlemen!” The director’s voice booms behind the curtain, resonant and overpowering the surplus of chatter. The crowd quiets into a restless standstill. “Welcome to the Playhouse. I hope you’ve all had a chance to get acquainted?”

There he is. My eyes lock on the curtain, imagining the director—and that Script—on the other side of it.

Nervous laughter burbles from the crowd in response. While I can’t see them, I imagine a sea of nervous expressions, each desperate to impress a Player or to catch the eye of their elusive director.

“So many lovely faces in our casting call tonight!” Silenus’s speech continues, slightly muffled behind the curtain. “But I warn you, I do not choose my Players on beauty alone. It is rarely the most beautiful, the most talented, the loudest—though of course our casting calls bring all of these and more!”

Dizziness fizzles in my head. I squirm impatiently, willing the director to call his Players out, *away* from here. Then, when he retreats through this corridor alone, I’ll grab my knife and—

“But rather, it is whoever draws the eye,” Silenus explains. “Take it not personally, my friends—actors are born! Not made.”

I wrinkle my nose at that. It feels impossible to believe these creatures were ever *born*, mere mortals who won the casting call by killing the Players who came before them.

They don’t look like they were ever human.

PARRISH: “There you are!”

I perk up at the new voice—a girl’s. It sounds young, accompanied by the soft chime of bells.

Down the hall, she emerges. Player Parrish is smaller than the other three, with hair like raven feathers, deliberately messy and shorn in sharp, chocolate-brown layers around her neck. There’s a youthful bounce to her step that sends all of her many anklets and bracelets jingling.

Parrish’s statue in the District unsettles me the most, always laden with an array of odd objects, ranging from marriage bands to loved ones’ ashes, thanks to rumors that she hoards rare items.

A mouse, I dub her. A greedy one.

PARRISH: "Say, where is Jude?"

The wolf, Titus, shrugs at her question. "Combing that pretty hair of his, probably."

SILENUS: "Five of you will remain with us after tonight to compete for a role in my cast, and so we *must* be selective. But enough of this! Allow me to introduce you to our honored stars of this evening."

The audience hollers a response, and relief washes over me. Once the last Player is out, I'll wait by the curtain. My hand dips into my coat, curls around my Eleutheraen blade.

I can do this. Surely I can take an old man in a fight.

SILENUS: "Please welcome our Comedians: Players Arius and Parrish!"

My ears ring as thunderous applause echoes, the dove and the mouse stepping through the curtain. I count two remaining Players awaiting their entrance.

Their Lead Player *is* missing. There should be five altogether—

Never mind it. Maybe their Lead Player is on the platform already. Once these two are gone, I'll wait by the curtain. Silenus has to come back this way at *some* point—

SILENUS: "A warm welcome for our Tragedians: Players Titus and Mattia!"

The last two, the wolf and snake, step through the curtain, met by another round of earth-shattering applause that shakes the walls.

As soon as Mattia is out of sight, I bolt up to the curtain, hovering there, waiting. My heart has begun to pound in my ears, fear seizing the breath in my chest.

Come on. Come on out, Silenus.

SILENUS: "And a round of applause for our Lead Player and Mimic, *Jude*!"

A question mark forms in my mind as the audience applauds, my gaze darting around the empty corridor. I let out a shaky breath. No Lead Player in sight. He must be on his way through a different entrance.

Curiosity brings me closer to the curtain. I've seen so many posters that I can't help but wonder what the infamous Lead Player looks like in the flesh. My fingers make the *tiniest* slit in the fabric to peek through.

I glimpse an applauding audience—and confused, expectant faces.

Where is he?

"Why are we hiding?" whispers a voice behind me.

I yelp and, before I can think better of it, jab my elbow backward as hard as I can. Then wince when it meets something solid.

Whoever I've hit does little more than grunt and mutter, "We'll work on the greeting."

Cursing and holding my elbow, which is radiating sharp darts of pain down my hand, I look over my shoulder.

And find myself face-to-face with a pair of violent golden eyes.

Act I: Scene VII

Compliments! Three compliments. Pay a Player three compliments and they'll leave you alone.

The rule comes back to me with ease. It was drilled into my head around the same time I learned how to read.

That said, it doesn't matter, because I have nothing nice to say. Even if he is admittedly the most staggeringly beautiful person I have ever seen.

Jude Stepharros. Lead Player of the Playhouse.

I grip onto my common sense before I can reach for my knife and start a fight that I most definitely will not win. Their director is one thing. But Jude, like the others, stands at least a foot taller than me—and I've been regarded as comically tall my entire life.

My second thought is that if I *were* to take him in a fight, I'd pierce one of his eyes first—which are glowing and golden and lined with kohl. And watching me like I'm live entertainment.

Probably because I've been staring in stunned silence for about thirty seconds now.

JUDE: "So, you *are* hiding, then."

My gaze flutters longingly to the hall, where a smarter woman would have escaped moments ago.

Growing up, I always fantasized about this moment: fearlessly facing a Player. Confronting whichever cast member cursed me. Reaching for my knife and plunging it through the Player's dark heart. But I don't feel fearless, and my hands are not reaching for my knife.

I feel *small.*

SILENUS: "Always intent on making an entrance of his own, isn't he?" The director's voice booms on the other side of the curtain as the audience hushes to an amused titter. "Now, if you please…a warm welcome for our Lead Player, *Jude*!" he tries again.

"Well, don't look so scared over it." Jude pouts at me. "It could be worse. I, for instance, am terribly late."

The crowd screams the Player's name, as if this will magically summon him. He makes no move for the curtain.

JUDE: "You know, I looked just like you at my audition—nervous and all. Better dressed, though." His golden eyes look me over as I pray to the floor to open up and swallow me whole. "But anyway, it isn't so bad. Do you know what the trick is?"

I have a feeling he's going to tell me whether I respond or not. He hasn't seemed to notice I'm inching backward or that my right hand has crept into my coat toward my blade.

JUDE: "Take three deep breaths like this— Gods, you're standing like I've got a knife to your throat. Try sitting down? Here."

Before I can say anything, Jude sits himself down and politely pats the ground next to him like I'm a lost puppy. Meanwhile, the onlookers outside have taken to chanting his name.

This is their vicious Lead Player? I imagined sharper teeth. Maybe an evil cackle.

Jude blinks up at me. "Well, I'm not going out there if you don't sit first."

It occurs to me that if he *doesn't* go out there, someone is liable to come *get* him.

I quickly sit down across from Jude, crossing my legs the way his are and keenly avoiding his eyes, staring instead at the dark copper of his hair, which flickers like candlelight at the ends.

Jude looks like he does in his playbill solagraph, with smooth olive skin and tousled hair that probably took an absurd amount of styling to look intentionally messy. One dark eyebrow is arched just slightly higher than the other in amusement. He wears far too much jewelry for one person.

JUDE: "Good! I'm Jude, by the way." As if I don't know exactly who he is. I mouth nasty insults at his statue each time I pass it in the District.

I glance nervously toward the closed curtain as the crowd cheers louder.

"Oh, that? Never mind it. All right, like this—" He rests his forearms on his knees, inner wrists to the ceiling.

I tightly cross my arms over my rib cage instead but wince at the discomfort.

Jude closes his eyes. "Breathe in and picture what you're frightened of."

I breathe in and picture him.

After holding his breath, he adds, "Now breathe out and picture what you want."

I breathe out and picture that damned Script. And maybe a gag to shut him up.

This is not helping.

He peeks an eye open.

JUDE: "See? No need to be nervous. Between you and me, this crowd is nothing but a pack of weeds with only a handful of flowers to pluck." He pauses, stares me up and down. "Maybe a few thorns, too."

RIVEN: "I'm not auditioning!" The words fall out of my mouth before I realize my mistake. I shouldn't say *anything* to him. I can't lie.

JUDE: "Oh?" He tilts his head, curious. For the first time, he seems to take in the rips in my jacket, where my attackers tore it. The holes in my boots. "I *see*. Have you come to rob us? You don't look like you've had a full meal in—well, I don't know. I don't think it's normal for a person's cheekbones to stick out like that."

The director's voice cuts through the applause.

SILENUS: "Our Jude, he...he *does* like to make an entrance, yes? Perhaps if we cheer louder!"

The audience obeys, and Jude sighs dramatically, pulling himself to his feet. I follow.

Then, to my horror, he plucks a golden ring from his index finger, motions for me to hold out my hand, and drops it into my palm.

JUDE: "Tell you what. Why don't you steal this from me? And go find yourself something to eat. The food is free, you know." He makes it three steps before pausing and throwing a look over his shoulder. "And for the record, even if you aren't auditioning, you most certainly *are* scared. Would you like to know a secret?"

I say nothing.

Jude shrugs. "The best actors always are."

Then he just saunters off through the curtain.

SILENUS: "Well, look who it is!"

The crowd bursts into a final surge of roaring applause.

Snapped a guard's neck for stepping too close to Silenus, Galen said.

I've been seen. It's time to abandon this plan before Jude spots me again. Surely there's a better place to take Silenus by surprise, away from Jude's eyes. An office belonging to the director, maybe...

Dressing rooms! I've read Players are particularly territorial about their dressing rooms—their director would have one. Wouldn't he? And he'd be alone, away from his Players.

I stare at the golden ring in my hands. It's so warm, it almost hurts to hold, with a flat surface that carries the inscription *Finders Keepers.* Which oddly feels like a threat.

I pocket the ring anyway. I don't know what the going rate for a Lead Player's ring is, but I imagine it's enough to take the burden off Galen and pay for all the school materials I could possibly need when I'm well on my way to Orkestra.

"To our next Player!" Silenus shouts, followed by the clinking of chalices.

I take that as my cue to move as fast as I can, and trust my intuition to lead me to the dressing rooms.

Act I: Scene VIII

Unfortunately, my intuition is a godsdamned liar.

Or the Playhouse is one big labyrinth of winding reds and golds. Frustration plagues my sense of direction as I shuffle past two ballrooms and yet another rehearsal room, finding myself at the bottom of a staircase with opal railings that feel like they've been dipped in sunlight.

I take the steps at a pathetic crawl, groaning and cursing as needed, my mind set even more firmly on that Script. I did not slip out of the clutches of the Lead Player only to turn around and limp home now.

If that Script has the power to control Players, *surely* it has the power to fix what one of them broke. The "how" of the matter might take me a minute to figure out, but one problem at a time.

The steps land me in a spacious common room surrounded on all sides by twisted candelabras that flicker softly and walls of glowing amber. After a lifetime shivering from the inside out, tolerating frosty days and icier nights, I hate to admit the warmth is welcome.

Crimson chaises circle the hearth, where flames roar beneath an ivory mantel carved with coiling serpents. I snatch a poker from beside the hearth, just in case.

Still, I can't shake the feeling of being watched.

Vanities poke out of an adjacent wall, cluttered with old playbills and vivid swatches of makeup. Bits of gold and coin lie carelessly beside discarded silk scarves and extravagant jewels.

Gods. They hoard all of this for themselves? I've never seen so many valuable items at once.

I pocket a few coins and one silk scarf as I go, cringing at how loud my steps are on the marble in the cavernous silence of the room.

Three halls bleed out of the common area. The first is marked by an exaggerated frown carved overtop—Tragedy, I reckon.

The second hall carries the opposite symbol, a dramatic, frightening smile for Comedy.

The third holds a feathered mask over its center, no expression on its face. Mimicry, the Craft of all faces.

A breath of relief fills my chest. *The dressing rooms.* They must be. The director must have one nearby.

I stumble past Tragedy's hall, each breath filling my lungs with a strange, perfumed incense hovering in the air.

A flutter of movement to my right startles me, and I whip defensively toward it. There's no one—just a great expanse of mirror that begins at the floor and blossoms into the ceiling where it swirls into reflective slats of gold. And right before me is…

Me.

I gasp. The last time I remember seeing my reflection, I was a child—and Galen was dragging me away from the glass.

Embarrassment pinches my heartstrings. Growing up, I conjured my own ideas of my reflection. That I have my father's features. Cassia's stern brow. Maybe the alert, sharp eyes of my brother.

I was wrong.

Two sunken eyes stare back at me, lapsed deep into my skull like a cadaver, ringed with ghostly purple and marked with the hungry edge of a starved animal. Where Galen's skin is tanned from work and travel, mine is translucent like the underbelly of a whale.

Player Jude's comment about my cheekbones rings true. They're hollow and gaunt, caving into my face like a canvas stretched too thin. My lips are white as wax.

I look like I've just escaped a coffin. No wonder people are frightened.

"Like a corpse." I repeat the insult to myself, unable to deny it now.

My throat tightens as I lean closer, pressing a hand to my

face and cursing the tears rapidly trying to escape the eyes of my reflection. They come anyway.

This is what I look like?

This is what that Player all those years ago did to me?

I clench the poker tighter, willing to smash the reflection to bits. *No.* It's time to focus. I can mourn the death of my own absurd fantasies later.

Besides, now I'm pissed.

The hair on my neck stands, a sudden shift in the air. My ear itches at the sound of footsteps and, before I can think better of it, I dart behind the largest of the chaises.

The steps grow louder, closer, clipped and even. Then they halt.

First comes the clatter and shuffle of items on the vanity. I breathe as quietly as humanly possible, wondering if whoever it is has noticed a few select items missing and wishing my sticky fingers hadn't shoved the evidence into my pocket.

My hand curls tighter around the poker, weighing if I should risk staying hidden or accept my fate and lunge at whoever has taken to strolling casual circles around the room, *whistling.*

The steps come to a sudden stop, and the room falls sickeningly silent.

"You can come out now," says a distinctly familiar voice.

Shit.

Gritting my teeth at the tone, I guiltily rise from my hiding spot, still clutching the poker. A tall, imposing figure blocks the exit at the other end of the room, arms crossed.

"I give you my ring, and you steal my scarf." Jude shakes his head, makes a *tsk*ing sound in his throat. "Rude."

RIVEN: "You—you *followed* me!" Suddenly, the room feels smaller, shrinking inward as the Player's enormous presence dwarfs it.

JUDE: "If someone walked into your house and started acting suspicious, wouldn't you follow them?" He raises one eyebrow as punctuation.

Well. Fair enough.

He tilts his head. "Say, is that a bruise under that eye or did you get a little too ambitious with my makeup as well?"

Damn it, I think, unable to tell if he's toying with me and has already realized what I am: a marked. With every intention of stealing from the Playhouse. I move away from the mirror, subtly wiping my eyes.

Jude's smirk wilts. "You're crying." His eyes drop to the poker in my hand. I must be quite a sight. "How about we put that down, yes? Titus stabbed me with one once, and it was hell to pull it out."

I breathe unsteadily, wide-eyed and brandishing the poker between us like a sword as he steps farther into the room. I'm not fooled. Jude carries himself with the lazy elegance of a cat, but there's an edge in his movements that betrays something far more lethal.

JUDE: "Okay, in his defense he was drunk." He shrugs. "And I was holding the other poker. I might have challenged him. I don't remember. The Prop Master took away our swords, and we were feeling creative."

I don't dare move, watching him like I've got an arrow trained on his head, studying the calculated deliberation of his steps. His hands are empty of any weapons—and probably just as capable without them.

JUDE: "All right, something easier, then." As if bored, he falls gracefully onto the embroidered armchair behind him, his tailored costume of black brocade clinging to his frame like a second skin as he throws his boots onto the table. "What is your name?"

RIVEN: "Do you know me?" It comes out like an accusation, hoarse and desperate. Paranoia plagues my mind as I glance back at the mirror, unsure if anyone could recognize my father's features on my ghastly face, much less a vain, self-absorbed Player.

Jude bursts into laughter, a rich sound that ricochets, like the whole Playhouse laughs with him. "Love, *one* of us is famous, and it is not you. But fine!" He throws his hands up. "She has no name.

We'll leave a blank little space on the playbill for you."

It's an effort to unclench my teeth. "I *told* you I'm not here to audition."

"Yes, *that* much is clear." There's a cruel, catlike cleverness that I don't like at all hovering just behind his gaze. "But it doesn't change the fact that you've made me *terribly* curious. Now, let's try this again." He draws out each word. As if that will distract me from the way his eyes have begun to glow. His voice deepens, almost melodic. "Put. That. Down."

The air tightens, then relaxes around me. My hand yearns to release the poker; that's all I want in the whole wide world. To release this weight from my grip—

My mark seizes beneath my collar in hot, angry pulses, protecting me from what's happening. *Craft.* He's trying to use Craft on me.

Furious, I drop the poker of my own accord and go for something more effective.

Jude barely has time to blink before I lunge. It's good he's sitting, because his full height would have made it impossible to slip behind him and press my blade to his throat.

To his credit, he doesn't seem surprised—until the gold of my blade grazes his skin. Players do not fear death. They're trained in the deathless arts, a Craft that renders them nearly immortal. Except against one weapon—the one I'm holding to his neck.

Something in the way he sharply inhales tells me his skin recognizes the Eleutheraen gold. I've imagined holding this very knife to a Player's throat many times, but my hands never shook this badly in any of those fantasies. We're facing the mirror, and I don't like that I look more scared than he does.

RIVEN: "Try that again, and I'll slit your throat." I mean it but hope he can't hear the tremor in my voice.

JUDE: "I'll have you know I've talked myself out of worse." His breathing is ragged. "Hell, I've talked myself *into* worse." I cut off his laugh by pressing the blade in a little closer, inhaling the sharp scent of citrus and hyacinth that lingers on his skin. "Hurt me and four Players will be ripping the flesh from your bones before you take another breath," he says, steely. His eyes slide from the knife to meet my gaze in our reflection. "Not that there's much there. Didn't I tell you about the food downstairs?"

RIVEN: "Stop. Talking."

JUDE: "And besides." His tone softens, the pitch rolling low like thunder. I don't hear whatever he says next. I don't even understand the words. I'm too focused on the sudden warmth shivering up my arms and the curious way my knife loosens in my grip. "You aren't looking me in the eye," he goes on in a voice that wraps effortlessly around my mind like silk. "Someone taught you that."

My eyes flash back to our reflection just in time to see his hand, glowing gold with Craft, reach for mine.

Three things happen at once. First, nausea, deep and dizzying, bursts through my head as his hand grazes my wrist.

Second, Jude's eyes shoot up to mine, dark with confusion.

Third, my blade clatters to the floor as we both scatter to opposite sides of the room.

I panic, eyeing my blade on the ground between us and clutching at my throat, the Eleutheraen mark, hidden beneath my jacket, burning. Jude swears loudly and steadies himself on a marble beam, wrapping an arm around his stomach as if it is persistently trying to expel its contents. He gasps a breath and speaks to me through gritted teeth.

"You're *marked*," he spits, announcing it like it's a death sentence—which it is.

SILENUS: "Jude?"

He jumps at the director's voice, his attention snapping to the hallway.

Meanwhile, I make my move and dive for the blade. But when Jude's shoulders tense, I raise one hand, shoving the knife into my pocket to indicate I do not wish to fight to the death just yet.

And unfortunately, the nearing steps have me rethinking whatever half-baked plan I was harboring. My mind tries to do the math: me, marked. One Eleutheraen blade. A Player who knows both of these things. The director on his way through the door.

My window of opportunity to steal that Script is rapidly closing.

A similar calculation runs clear across Jude's face. Whatever conclusion he's come to, I know it can't be good. He marches forward, grips me by the sleeve, and hauls us both into a run down Mimicry's purple hall while muttering, "*Don't* make me regret this."

Act I: Scene IX

The story goes that Players used to capture humans just to drag them around as their own personal audience, sometimes tearing their eyes out to carry in a jar after the humans' legs finally gave out. And the mortals would go willingly, their minds too blissfully numbed with Craft to notice what was happening. I'm pretty sure Haris would beg for such a fate.

But I *am* marked, and I know what's happening to me. Suddenly, I'm a child again, dragged away by a Player. The thought sends my heels digging into the ground in a panic. Jude stumbles, the alarming strength of his grip nearly ripping my arm from its socket and making my ribs sear with the strain. He spins around. "Do you *want* to die?"

RIVEN: "I'm still deciding."

SILENUS: "Jude?"

Jude hurries faster down the corridor, dragging me along as I curse at him; his long legs are impossible to keep up with. Even through my sleeve, his touch burns and sends my skin crawling. The pinch in his brow tells me it hurts him, too.

There's a blur of golden lanterns poking out of a dark plum-colored passageway, then a sharp turn, and a mahogany door he shoves open with his shoulder. I catch myself on the wall as we pummel through it.

The door shuts with a creak, like it hasn't been used in a while.

Pain radiates along my spine as I straighten and take in my new cage: a smaller oval-shaped room, elegant and draped in lush velvets and walls of silvery brocade. Pristine violet drapes are drawn tight above a vanity with a tarnished gold mirror.

This space feels personal. Not only by the hairbrush on the side table, stiff with age, or what looks to be sleeping quarters down a narrow corridor, lit by candelabras that cling to either side.

And not even by the distinct smell of lavender perfuming the air.

But rather, by the crowning centerpiece of the room: a portrait hung over the fireplace. The woman in the painting is all doll-like porcelain features with rich brown curls. She's wrapped in crushed velvet, her diamond-shaped face and dazzling eyes piercing me through the chest. A deep shade of mauve stains her lips, one that I bet matches the tube of lipstick standing guard on the vanity.

Anyone in Theatron would recognize her. Gene Hunt was the Playhouse's renowned Lead Player, before the catastrophic performance that ended her career and life in one blow. Patrons claimed she fell mad, breaking character and screaming nonsense at the audience, warning them to run.

Moments later, she died onstage. No deathless arts were used to prevent it.

Jude Stepharros was the mortal auditionee who replaced her. My eyes fall on him, trying to picture this monster ever being human as he paces the room, one hand pressed to his temples. "We don't have much time. Tell me your name."

Time for *what*? I narrow my eyes, more and more suspicious.

JUDE: "Your *name*."

RIVEN: "Call me Alistaire." A statement. Not technically a lie. My grandmother's name is the first to come to mind. I'm not about to give him mine.

Jude frowns. "Is that your real name?"

I bite my tongue. "No."

He exhales, annoyed. "*Fine.* What shall Alistaire's family name be?"

My eyes dart to the painting. "Hunt."

"Hunt?" He gestures wildly at the portrait of the dead Player, Gene Hunt. "Endless names in the world, Alistaire, and your mind can't conjure one outside of these walls? Gods, I'm doomed."

My brow lowers at that last part. "What?"

A knock at the door sends my hand flying to my Eleutheraen blade. I point it up at Jude again. "Get me out of here."

He returns a cold, easy look, arms hanging indifferently at his sides as the doorknob rattles. "If I were you, I'd put that away."

The door cracks open, and in a move I *know* I will regret, I sheathe the knife in my pocket. Something tells me I won't be getting that Script away from Silenus with Jude around.

SILENUS: "Ah, there you are!" His head pops in, and he pushes the heavy door all the way open. My heart hammers furiously.

JUDE: "Sil! Do you know, we've been looking everywhere for you."

The director turns a curious, hesitant smile my way.

SILENUS: "Well, who have we here? I never forget a face. We met earlier, yes?"

JUDE: "Alistaire, meet Silenus." His voice is bright and cheerful despite the menacing glare I'm shooting his way. "Our director."

SILENUS: "Sil! Please, call me Sil. Silenus makes me feel ancient."

I scoff. "Well, historical records would imply you—"

"Sil," Jude interrupts, coughing. "I'm glad to hear you've already met Alistaire."

The director's eyes wash over my tattered clothes and oversized boots. "Yes, Alistaire...?"

"Hunt," I say, hating myself. And thankful he didn't ask *my* name.

"Hunt." The director's eyebrows shoot up, eyes flickering to the portrait of Gene Hunt. "We lost the last one of those we had. Any relation, I wonder? Perhaps that's why you look familiar." He tilts his head, examining my face.

I stare murderously back at Silenus until Jude steps slyly between us. "I was just showing Alistaire her rooms."

SILENUS: "Oh?"

RIVEN: "What?"

Silenus's kind gaze turns scrutinizing as Jude clears his throat. "She's a...natural." For an actor, he doesn't sound very convincing.

The director tries and fails to hide his surprise. He looks at me again, closer this time, as if waiting to see if I'll wither away or drop dead right in front of him. And suddenly, it doesn't matter that I shouldn't care for the opinions of a monster like Silenus. The shock on his face stings.

"Jude," Silenus begins, quieter this time. "I thought perhaps you'd like to speak with a few of the auditionees I selected—"

JUDE: "Why waste my time? My mind is made up."

About what?

SILENUS: "I—I guess it's no trouble, then." His eyes finally tear away from me and land on Jude. "I only came to let you know Mattia is about to dismiss the crowds."

"Let her!" Jude says a little too quickly, coming to stand beside me. "I've chosen my contender for this year's Great Dionysia."

Act I: Scene X

TEN YEARS AGO

"Twelve!" cries a girl whose name I can never remember. "Twelve Players."

"Correct," says Professor Ariti, striking *XII* on the board. "We believe twelve Players rose from the well on Mount Eleutherae upon Dionysus's vanishment. How many remain today?"

"Five!" another classmate volunteers. "None of the originals, though."

On the sheet beside my textbook, solagraphs of Players glare back at me in black and white. I stare at them, puzzled.

None of them match the Player I saw yesterday.

"Indeed." Professor Ariti turns back to the board. "At one point in time, each of the Players you see onstage today were *people*, just like you." The teacher drones on, her voice like a distant horn over the fresh, roaring pain between my collarbones, where my new mark sits. "Mere mortals who killed a Player and became one in turn."

I wish that the hour were up, that we were switching to mathematics. My pen goes through the paper, scrapes the wood of my desk, and the ink smears.

Or maybe the ink isn't smeared at all, I realize, as the edges of my desk begin to blur. I blink rapidly until it clears.

"However," she goes on, "Craft is not free. Craft *costs.* Which is why, should you ever find yourself in such a situation, pay your compliments and pray they leave. *Never* make a deal with a Player, no matter their offer."

Everyone's eyes find me, question marks dotting their pupils. They all seem to have heard about the Player who spoke to me yesterday. Everybody wants to know what happened. What she said. If I made a bargain with her.

I don't think compliments would have made the Player leave. She wanted me to go with her.

Several people in black-and-silver uniforms showed up to our home to ask me questions afterward, and none of them seemed satisfied with my answers.

The teacher clears her throat. "Think of Craft as a trade," she adds. "For memories, for heart, and for soul. For morals and for values. For *humanity.* The Players have each murdered, lied, and traded every mortal aspect of their being for what they are now."

My vision stirs. The nurse said I'd be good as new within a few hours after Galen and I left with our new marks, but that was a whole day ago and I'm beginning to suspect she was wrong.

I don't think mine healed right, but I'm too scared to check.

I blink at my hands, which have felt cold and strange since yesterday, ever since the Player's blood—

"Who can tell me about the Cast Trade?"

Not me, not me, not me.

"Riven?"

I mutter one of the swear words I learned from Aunt Cassia and blink upward, realizing my forehead has made contact with the desk. "The trade, Riven," Professor Ariti prompts as the class snickers. "Why did the Players sign into a treaty with mortals?"

My mouth moves to form the words, recalling the details from my memory cards. *Trade* seems like a stretch.

"Because a Player was captured," I answer weakly. "Silenus traded peace for the life of his Player. The captured Player was returned alive, and in exchange, Silenus signed an agreement to tour only South Theatron for five hundred years."

My head reels. I mean to add that in a decade's time, that treaty will be up. That *this* is why they train us for encountering Players, because our world will plunge into chaos when they're freed, if the wall can't hold them.

I mean to say all of this, but the room has suspiciously begun to tilt.

Someone screams, but I can't tell who it is as the classroom fades to groggy shades of gray and black. And in the distance, a pair of golden eyes, watching.

Act I: Scene XI

"No deal," I hiss at Jude the moment Silenus excuses himself. I watch the door shut behind him longingly, that Script still somewhere in his pocket.

Jude stares down at me. "What are you talking about?"

I huff a breath, unsure what game he's playing at. I can't fathom why Jude would choose me as his contender, but he's one of the Players. The *Lead* Player. Silenus's second-in-command and supposedly the keeper of the Playhouse's magic.

His reasons are not good; I'm certain of that.

"Whatever *this* is." I gesture vaguely at the dressing room around me. "Players always want to make a bargain. *No* deal."

His smile turns coy. "A bargain would imply *you* get something out of this." He strides across the room. "Come. You'll be expected in the arena—then at the cast party."

Fear cuts into my veins. I'm marked. I *cannot* enter this casting call, even if I wanted to. I'm not even convinced I could get back up if I sat down right now.

I panic. "Wait!"

Jude crosses his arms over his broad chest, taps his foot dramatically.

RIVEN: "I—" I wince, bracing myself and hating the words I force out of my mouth. "You have a voice like velvet. The copper of your hair is more beautiful than even the papers give you credit for."

Jude blinks. "What?"

RIVEN: "You're twice as handsome as the other Players."

Jude's mouth falls open.

I breathe, angry and humiliated. "That's three compliments. Now let me *go*."

JUDE: "The Three Compliments Rule is a myth." A note of

pity pinches his tone as my face hardens. "They still teach that? Just like the North to believe something so foolish. Sweet words cannot satiate Players. It's kind of you, though, considering you can't lie about them. *Do* say more! I'm curious."

My face burns with embarrassment, and I think back to the other things we were taught in school, unsure what else could've been a myth. "Open it," I growl, pointing at the gold-encrusted mirror braced on the wall. "You *know* I'm not qualified for the competition. I know Players travel through mirrors. Open the mirror and *let me out*."

JUDE: "No." He shrugs. "The casting call has closed, and I'm bound by contract to the Playhouse. I can't summon a portal out."

RIVEN: "Then just *do* it!" The shriek leaves my voice exhausted. *I'm* exhausted. Clearly, this is some sick form of live entertainment to him. I try to scrape more vicious words from my throat, but the tone that escapes is small. "Why are you dragging this out?"

JUDE: "Do what?" To his credit, he feigns confusion well.

RIVEN: "Just tell them I'm marked and get it *over* with."

He hollers a laugh and shakes his head. "Oh, *Alistaire*. I didn't trap you here to kill you." His tone drops, quiet as the tick of the old clock as he steps closer, like a shared secret between us. "You're here because I need you to *win*."

Win.

My mouth forms several words before landing on: *"What?"*

A Great Dionysia only ends in one of two ways. One, the mortal manages to kill the competing Player during the final performance, seizing fame, immortality, and power for themselves.

Or two, more commonly, the mortal's remains are scrubbed off the arena floor.

I guess triumphing in such a grandiose performance is too tempting for creatures that delight in blood and ego. Cassia says this is why all the original Players are gone, their lives eventually lost to their own hubris, their places taken. Every Player in the cast today was once mortal.

Even Jude.

"Whichever contender makes it to the finale will compete with me," he says. "*You*, love, are here to ensure there's no match in the arena. Once all the contenders are gone—"

"Dead," I offer helpfully.

"Once you're the only one *left*," he rephrases, "*then* I tell Sil the truth. That you're marked! That you don't qualify. Sil won't want the bad press—there's already so much tension with the North. He'll send you away quietly, believe me."

RIVEN: "*Believe* you?" He must be kidding.

JUDE: "The Great Dionysia will be forfeited. I'll hold my place as Lead Player, and *you* can go home." He steps back and takes a low bow, peeking up to offer me a roguish grin.

Jude hasn't chosen me in *spite* of being marked. He's chosen me *because* I'm marked. And probably the only marked within a mile of the Playhouse tonight.

My eyes narrow. "I thought it was an *honor* to kill in the arena." Isn't that why Players throw their gruesome festival anyway? Every Great Dionysia builds the Lead Player's reputation. Some theorize each kill makes them stronger.

And for some reason, he wants out of it.

My mouth drops open, a mocking grin pulling at my lips. "You're *scared*, aren't you?"

"Dear heart, I fear one thing in life, and it is not death." Jude's own smile strains at the edges, like some dreadful thought has caught him off guard. Come to think of it, he hasn't stopped smiling once this entire conversation. "I have reason to believe someone in this Playhouse wants me dead."

"Yeah. Me."

"Unfortunately," he goes on, "the only way I can ensure a *fair* match in the arena is if there isn't a match at all. Just a little favor, you see. Do we have a deal?"

A *deal*. Only a Player would make this sound like anything other than a *hostage situation*.

I'm not sure what possesses me. My hand grips the hairbrush

from the vanity, brings it over my head, and hurls it at Jude with all my might.

It bounces pitifully off his shoulder. He stares at the brush as it clatters to the ground at his feet. "I'm relieved you've chosen to be mature about this."

Before he so much as looks up, I launch at him, blade aimed for his eye this time.

Jude curses and grips my armed hand like he's swatting a fly, lifting me right off the ground until I'm eye level with him.

"Okay!" he relents as I kick viciously at his legs, his touch burning through my sleeve. The Player's eyes flicker nervously to the clock, then back at me. "A trade, then! There must be *something* you want. Money?"

"No." Rage and exhaustion weave into the refusal that comes out of my throat as he begrudgingly sets me down, my ribs searing. "I don't want your godsdamned—" My voice breaks, and I cough violently into my elbow, lungs wringing.

When I pull away, the ice from my lungs has wrapped its way around my throat.

Jude tenses, steps back. His eyes scan me up and down, uncertain and seeming to take me in for the first time. A revelation dawns plainly on his face. "You're unwell."

I clench my teeth, ball my fists.

He nods. "Dying, then."

Some desperate part of me responds to those words. I never say them out loud.

His eyes narrow in suspicion; a warning threads his tone. "Why did you come here?"

I try to lie, pointlessly open my mouth to make a claim about stealing prized stage props or something. But my tongue won't form the words. The truth falls out. "I wanted to find...I wanted the—" I know I'll regret this. "Script."

Jude's eyes nearly bulge out of his head. "The *Script*?"

RIVEN: "I'm not sick. A Player—a Player hurt me when I was young. Poisoned me, I think." Even as I say the words, my jaw aches. There's a crushing, heavy feeling in my chest, like I can't breathe.

Jude walks a circle around me, the disbelief plain on his face. "A *Player* did this to you? A Player couldn't have—"

I cough, and he jumps. "You can..." I hate myself for the words. "You can help me? You can get me the—the Script?"

"*No.* If you value your life, you'll leave that cursed book alone." He mulls the words over a moment. "But yes," he says finally. "I can help you."

It exists. An antidote exists.

"Do this one thing for me, Alistaire." Jude's gaze locks on mine. "And I promise you will safely return home. Healthy."

Never make a bargain with a Player. The lesson from my childhood battles my ego as I consider. There's a catch. There *has* to be.

RIVEN: "I—"

JUDE: "We'll work out the finer details later." His gaze dips to my throat, like he can see the mark beneath the top buttons of my coat. "Including what to do about *that*."

Do about what? My *mark*? What does he mean—

To my horror, Jude turns and presses his palm to the oversize mirror on the wall beside us. My heart stutters at the way the glass ripples, swirling beneath his hand like water.

RIVEN: "I thought you couldn't conjure a portal—"

JUDE: "To *outside* the Playhouse. Within it, yes."

Our reflections sink into the glass, replaced by a shadowy hall that definitely looks haunted.

He gestures at the mirror—the *portal*.

"For both our sakes, don't say one word to anyone down there." He plucks the blade from between my fingers and catches my wrist when I lunge for it.

RIVEN: "Give that *back*—"

"Not a good idea for you to be swinging this around. You might hurt someone!" He winks, a lock of copper falling across his kohl-rimmed eyes. "There'll be plenty of time for that later."

I ball my fists, moving away from the mirror, but Jude catches my elbow, and I sneer, “Wait, wait, this is not what I—”

JUDE: “Think of this as a little introduction!”

RIVEN: “*No*, no—I’ve changed my mind. Now give me my—”

Before I can finish the sentence, Jude hurls me into the glass.

Act I: Scene XII

G*alen will never know what happened to me.*

My heart races as I find myself in a long, dim passageway. I whirl back to the mirror, but the glass swallows up the image of Jude, and he's gone. When pounding on the glass and screaming insults doesn't summon him back, I give up. No one, especially Jude, is coming to save me.

With a deep sigh, I drop my fists and turn. The only path forward is a flat, dark tunnel lined by mirrors.

Did I really think myself so smart? That I could march into the Playhouse and leave just as easily?

My vision adjusts, and I spot the shadowy outline of a swaying curtain at the end of the hallway. I creep forward, Jude's offer still taunting me. *Do this one thing for me, Alistaire, and I promise you will safely return home. Healthy.*

Players always lie. But what if—*what if* this one isn't?

The possibility of this being some sort of elaborate execution occurs to me as I part the curtain. I'm a marked. On Playhouse grounds. They'd be within their rights to do whatever they want with me.

Beyond the curtain, an arena awaits, pitch-black but massive judging by the echo of whispers and vague shapes of high dome walls.

Movement to my right sends my hand for my knife—but it isn't there.

Damn you, Jude.

"Gods, I hate waiting here," whispers a raspy, feminine voice on my other side.

A sound like thunder cracks overhead, and I wince as white light blooms around me. In each of the pocketed arena entrances, an illuminated figure stands. There isn't time to determine anything beyond that they all look like they belong here, striking and beautiful and, well, presumably *unmarked*.

We're not on the Playhouse stage. At least, I don't think it can be—it doesn't look like any of the solagraphs I've seen, save for the cracked marble at my feet. I'm standing on a low, circular platform, rings of tiered seating rising up around me.

The arena. Players have fought to the death here.

Pulling in a shaky breath, I count six entrances to the arena floor, including where I just emerged from—but one looms larger than the others, and it's empty. Overhead, the Playhouse symbol hangs in polished gold—a cracked mask, with one side stretched into a delirious grin and the other wilting into a tragic frown. An arrow piercing through both.

The other auditionees all seem to find me at once with similar baffled expressions that read: *Why is that one here?* I wince away from their eyes, backing closer to the curtain.

A second crack resounds with the beat of a drum. The Five Players file onto the raised platform towering directly above us, their places in the podium ring framed by gleaming white columns, each overlooking their contender.

Then comes a thunderous roar of applause from every corner. Incandescent limelight flashes, revealing faces in the audience, so many I can't begin to count. They all blur together: eager eyes, wide smiles, open mouths gleefully screaming the names of Players. Revelers.

Heart pounding in my ears, I steal a glance at the podium ring above me, my loathing gaze locking on Jude.

He winks.

SIL: "Ladies and gentlemen!"

The voice fills the amphitheatre as applause crashes in around me. The director marches through the sixth entrance and into the arena.

SIL: "Congratulations! You should all be proud. A round of applause for this casting call's auditionees!"

His words somehow carry over the waves of applause as he

announces each name. My mind is buzzing too loudly with anxiety to note them, but I cringe when he calls out *Alistaire Hunt*.

This feels too real now. It was foolish to even consider Jude's offer.

And I have a terrible feeling it's too late to get out of it.

As the cheers settle, Sil moves on. "The five of you were handpicked. You each have someone to thank for that."

The other contenders share grateful glances with their respective Players. I duck my chin to glare hard at the ground instead.

"All that said, tonight marks your final chance to leave," he goes on.

This catches my attention, and I look up to stare at the director.

"No one leaves the Playhouse beyond tonight. You'll each find a contract in your room, to be signed by tomorrow. The Playhouse leaves the District at midnight."

My mouth pops into a smile. Jude will have to slice my hand off before it picks up a pen and signs that contract. Though, given the Playhouse's reputation, I decide not to give him that idea.

"Now! A few ground rules." The strangely comforting timbre of Sil's voice takes on an edge. I listen closely. In all my time studying the Playhouse, I've come across mentions of *The Rules*, but they aren't actually listed anywhere.

"Rule one!" Sil announces. "*Never* wish an actor good luck. You might as well wish disaster on all your castmates."

Hints of laughter flutter at the edges of the arena. Noticeably, none of them come from the mouths of Players. I raise an eyebrow. From my understanding, this is little more than an old theatrical myth—a superstition.

"Rule two," Sil continues. "*All* Players and auditionees alike are to *stay out of the dark*. Whether a rehearsal room, stage, or even your own dressing room, *never* enter a dark space in the Playhouse. Follow the lights. The Playhouse is a different place after hours, and our Stage Manager doesn't take kindly to those who disregard the rules."

Wish everyone good luck and make my escape after dark. Got it.

"Finally, and consider this the most important," says Silenus. "*Never* break the fourth wall. For your safety and for others."

A tinge of frustration clouds my mind when he doesn't elaborate. The fourth wall is referenced in several historical accounts of the Playhouse. None are clear about what it means.

Silenus nods approval at the lack of objections. "This year marks a Great Dionysia festival."

TITUS: "Make it a good one, everyone. Last time didn't go so well."

The heckling Player shrugs when the rest of his cast pins him with iron stares.

My brow falls as I draw the connection. The last Great Dionysia was canceled when a Lead Player—*Gene*—died onstage two nights before the finale. With one less Player in the cast, Jude, an auditionee at the time, won her role by default after stepping in to save the performance.

That last performance is memorialized in the District Museum, a chronically overcrowded exhibit. I managed a square look at it once, though. It's a massive thing, framed in gold. In the solagraph, a faded rendering of Jude kneeling at the edge of the stage, a limp Player clothed in silky layers of white cradled in his arms like a dove. His mouth is parted open, singing her into eternal sleep.

Realization dawns on me. Jude's mentor died in his arms, and he took her place. He's *never* competed in a Great Dionysia. And it seems he still *really* doesn't want to if he's trapped me here to get him out of it.

I peer up at him. He doesn't look back, but a muscle feathers in his jaw.

What are you hiding?

Sil clears his throat. "Over the next few weeks, the Player who selected you will put you through a number of trials to measure your strengths in three areas: Compulsion, Reality Suspension—"

Titus interrupts with a proud holler. *The deathless arts*, my mind translates. Could *that* help me? Is that what Jude meant?

No. It doesn't matter. At this point, I'm lucky if I can get out of here with my life.

"—and Mimicry as we embark on a three-week tour. You will train closely with your mentor." I cringe at the thought. "Of course, it does you good to gain the favor of the audiences you perform for. But I urge you to remember, this is a casting call, and the winner will be decided upon by myself. So bring me your best."

I'm going home, I assure myself as a nervous, hollow feeling churns in my stomach. Sil will undoubtedly eliminate me first if I *do* stay and take Jude up on his offer. There's no way around it. I don't belong here.

"Should one of you—by my selection—survive to see the finale, you will compete against my Lead Player."

Eyes swivel in my direction. Then above me, at Jude. Whoever wins will face him.

"Kill my Lead Player in the arena, and you have a place in my cast, and all the Craft that comes with it." *Immortality*, he means. *Beauty. Power.* "And in turn, your mentor becomes our next Lead Player."

The other Players stand a little taller and prouder at this reminder. Jude's freedoms, his prestige, his power—it all falls to whichever one of his castmates trained his killer.

I wonder how he sleeps at night. I don't think I would.

Granted, maybe that's why he's trapped me here.

ARIUS: "Sil, you make it sound so *serious*." The Player's gentle eyes drift over the arena, at us. "There's some blood, darlings, but it's a great party."

TITUS: "And besides!" He leans forward, bracing massive forearms on the ledge. "Maybe one of you doe-eyed runts will manage to oust that pompous ass."

There's a round of distinctive gasps as Titus targets a particularly arrogant smile at Jude.

JUDE: "Perhaps a demonstration, then, Titus!" The room startles when Jude's voice strikes the amphitheatre, the pitch glassy and commanding. It's the first time I notice the lyrical clip of a

Syrenian accent, a territory west of the District in North Theatron.

Interesting.

Jude leans forward, the rings on his fingers gleaming under the spotlights as he grips the ledge and challenges, "I'm sure any one of them would be thrilled to scrape what's left of you from the stage floor."

Titus huffs. "Good, it'll give you an opportunity to earn your fucking place." I raise an eyebrow. *Also* interesting. "Besides, it'll take the rest to mop up your tears once you've lost so much as a button."

JUDE: "This *vest* is worth more than your—"

MATTIA: *"Enough."* The oldest Player smacks her hand down on the railing, calling order back to the room and silencing both of them. To be fair, if I'd spent hundreds of years listening to such drama, I'd probably be fed up, too. "Save your bickering. You can threaten each other later."

Then, to my horror, Titus's gaze flicks down to me. "Unless *that* one wins. More complicated that way."

I'm about to open my mouth to ask what exactly happens if *this one* wins—but Sil answers before I need to.

SIL: "Yes, if...Alistaire—" He clears his throat, like he still can't fathom that I'm here. "Should Alistaire be our winning contender and *not* wish to challenge her own mentor, she may challenge a different Player for their place instead."

I almost turn to shout at Jude and ask why the hell he wouldn't choose someone who might stand a *chance* in this competition, if his contender could just challenge a different Player anyway.

But I answer my own question first.

If his contender is strong enough to win, they're not going to want just any role. They'll want the Lead Player's role.

And he wants out of this.

When the chuckles in my direction dissipate, Sil delivers the last of his speech: "You can all worry about what's ahead later. For now, I suggest you get acquainted with your castmates. Let the show begin!"

Act I: Scene XIII

The Playhouse departs at midnight.

According to the clock, that gives me two hours to convince Jude to let me out of his bargain before the Playhouse vanishes from the District and takes me gods know where.

"You'll be expected at the cast party," he says flatly as I emerge from the arena, leaving me to ponder how the hell he changed clothes so quickly, exchanging the tailored black suit for a wide-sleeve shirt and wine-colored vest, dramatic flairs of gold at the neckline to match the ring through his nose.

I watch the gilded walls longingly as we go, eyes peeled for an indicator of where we are, of where an *exit* might be. Didn't I already pass through this way? Part of me suspects the Playhouse is teasingly shuffling and rearranging itself. Like it knows I'm scheming a grand escape and has taken to taunting me with its labyrinth of winding corridors.

JUDE: "Let's play a game: I'll talk and you nod, yes? We can make you the quiet, mysterious type."

RIVEN: "I don't like parties." At least, I don't think I do. I've never actually been to one.

JUDE: "Shocking! You seem like such a social butterfly."

SIL: "Jude!" The director turns the sharp corner ahead, his gait too young for his age. My eyes lock onto his left suit pocket, imagining the Script beneath it and weighing how I might snatch it on my way out. Jude seems to think I'll combust into ash if I touch it, but Players are liars.

"There's been a situation." Sil's eyes flicker my way as he approaches. "A word with my Lead Player, please. Privately."

Perfect! I'll slip away while they're talking—

A second thought slices through the first.

Unless I'm the situation he's referring to.

"Nonsense! There are no secrets between Alistaire and me." Jude tosses a meaningful look my way that conveys he isn't foolish enough to let me out of his sight. "What's the trouble?"

Sil sets his jaw. Arguing with Jude must be commonly regarded as pointless, since the director doesn't bother trying. "Someone slipped into the casting call earlier tonight—a pretender."

My heart drops to the floor. I'd bolt if Jude didn't right then clamp an iron hand around the back of my jacket. The heat of his palm feels like it might singe the fabric. "A pretender, you say."

SIL: "It would seem our old friend Dorian sent one of his imposters in again."

Just barely, the tension eases from my chest. He doesn't mean me.

Jude twists his lips, his humor gone. "Of course he did."

Dorian. The name clicks at once. Dorian is a myth of a man, a bounty hunter of Players, probably funded by the Players' richest enemies. A vigilante legend North of the Cut and a disgraced god killer South of it.

SIL: "I've sent Parrish to deal with it, but—"

Jude barks a laugh. "*That's* a nasty way to go. Poor soul."

I shudder, wondering what Player Parrish is doing to the spy. And for that matter, what the Players would do to *me*.

"But I think it best to cancel the cast party," Sil goes on lowly. "Dorian rarely sends only one of his little assassins. Who's to say there aren't more lurking about?"

A *network* of Player bounty hunters? Hope blooms in my chest at the thought as I try to school my expression.

Jude's grin tenses at the corners. "The North already do their worst to keep our curtain closed. Why should we let their threats ruin a good party?" With that, he ushers me away and calls over his shoulder, "And tell Parrish to clean up the mess this time when she's done with the spy."

As soon as we're out of earshot, Jude murmurs, "I saw your face. You know that name."

"Of course I know it," I respond smugly. "Dorian has killed two cast members." I find that hard to believe, though—that one man could assassinate two Players. A single Player has taken out entire armies. "He's called the Playhouse Bounty Hunter."

Jude frowns. "And he's raising more of them. Sends one of his sheep into the Playhouse to be slaughtered every once in a while, pretending to be an auditionee or even a patron in the audience. One tried to attack Arius at the stage door not too long ago."

We come to a set of steps that lies just beyond the dressing rooms. "Stop walking like that. They lead to the rooftop, not a guillotine," Jude mutters after me. I walk even slower in response and hear a scoff as we climb the flight of stairs.

The rooftop glows silver in the moonlight. A great dome shades the terrace, braced upon a colonnade laced together by an ornate railing and gloved in emerald ivy. Torchlight dances between each set of opulent pillars, illuminating a gathering of plush armchairs and sofas.

Three Players drape over the seating like spoiled royals. Across the terrace, their respective auditionees have taken to picking at the feast off to the side like little birds. My eyes widen at the dishes piled with more food than I've ever seen in my life—sweet melons, fresh figs, and aged cheeses arranged on silver platters beside trays of roasted meat.

Four or so shadowy figures, clothed all in black, attend to another table, arranging luxurious displays of honey cakes and fruit tarts. But before I can glimpse any of their faces, they exit silently as ghosts, vanishing down the stairs. Stagehands?

I look to the tables and push off my hunger. It's late, inching toward midnight. I need a plan.

Unless I accept his offer—

I wince, shaking off the thought.

"Jude." I hate how desperate my voice sounds but push on. "What will it take for you to let me out of this?" My soul, probably.

Jude crosses his arms, armlets winking in the moonlight. "Interested in a *second* bargain to undo the first?" He leans back onto the railing, looks at me. "There is nothing you could say to convince—"

A horrible wailing assaults the night, and my gaze jumps to the ledge behind Jude.

Down below, thousands of dismissed auditionees smother the gates, weaving their fingers through the bars like the dead reaching from their graves. Faces—*so many*—stretch with agony, like departing from the Playhouse is the most treacherous fate imaginable.

It occurs to me that I don't know how the auditionees were selected while I was snooping around. Did they audition? I certainly didn't.

TITUS: "Stop *crying*!" The Player's voice strikes the night like thunder. He leans back in his chair, drinks deeply from a gold chalice. "At least the lot of you can leave. Be grateful."

I raise an eyebrow at the odd comment, but the wailing only grows louder at the acknowledgment of a Player, their voices searching for a way up to us like little monsters clawing out of hell.

Jude rolls his eyes. "Don't worry about them. They'll get over it. Now, listen closely." He gestures to the cast from afar, to where one of the auditionees is approaching the Players with the caution one might use to approach a vengeful god. Which, I suppose, the Players aren't all that far off from being. "The other auditionees are *not* your competition. Worry about the Players. And *especially* about Sil. The ones who go first are usually whoever he finds the least amusing."

At Jude's prompt, I study the cast as their searching gazes rake over the unnerved auditionee. One of them asks a question I can't hear.

RIVEN: "Shouldn't *you* be over there?"

JUDE: "And leave you here to plot and seethe by yourself? Never."

I scowl.

"Now, that loud one is Titus," Jude murmurs as the burliest of the Players leans back into his seat, looking at the others like a king regarding his loyal subjects. Titus is frequently cast as such. His herculean arms stretch wide over the sofa, knees spread so as to take up as much space as possible. As if on cue, Titus throws his head back and laughs, a hearty baritone that pulses in the marble.

One hundred and ninety years in the Playhouse, if I remember right. Titus specializes in Tragedy, and the deathless arts with it.

JUDE: "Do *not* challenge him. Doesn't take losing well. And that there is Mattia—"

My gaze falls to the woman beside Titus, who casually stretches the longest legs I have ever seen over his lap. She's all supple curves, wrapped entirely in jade diamonds that cling to her like a second skin. Her jawline might have been carved by the gods themselves. While the other Players favor their cosmetics, Mattia's face is bare, save for a clean slash of maroon lipstick. Like anything more would only obscure her beauty.

I shrink inward, wishing I'd never seen my reflection. Embarrassment presses against my skin like ice. They're all so *beautiful—*

"The oldest Player," he says. "Close with Titus—and about a hundred times more lethal. Keep your distance; few are fortunate enough to *not* fall in love with her."

I wonder briefly if he's speaking from personal experience as Mattia dangles an empty cup at Titus and asks him to refill it in a tone so sultry, *I* nearly volunteer to do so.

RIVEN: "Are they…together?"

JUDE: "Gods, no! Sil forbids it, doesn't like us getting attached." I blink, surprised at the brevity of the remark as Jude throws a bored look at the gates below. "Most dalliances are kept to whoever interesting shows up at the stage door."

Well then.

"Last year," he goes on, "a woman impaled herself trying to scale the gates, all to bring Mattia a *rose*. Whole mess." Jude jerks his chin toward his cast. "Anyway. You see the man across from them? That's Arius."

My eyes go to the slender, golden-haired man with an overly friendly smile, who crooks a finger at another two auditionees, motioning them over.

"Seems nice, doesn't he? He likes to think so, too. But remind him he isn't a saint, and you'll see how quickly he becomes a demon."

"Was he really a healer?" I ask, noticing the decorative purple glass bottle Arius pulls from his pocket, which looks more like perfume until he brings it to his jaw and sprays the mist into his throat.

Jude nods. "One of the best, he claims. Better poisoner, though. Probably took a hundred lives before he ever came here."

My understanding is that's *why* Arius came to the Playhouse—a last resort to escape hanging after being caught helping those who asked him to poison their abusive partners. Some sources suggest he got carried away and extended his little hobby to whoever irked him. He didn't have much to lose.

"Oh, and if you hear him sing, plug your ears. He's known for his skill in Compulsion, particularly during—"

"The Battle at Melpomene Shoreline," I say numbly. In my head, my eyes sweep across a page detailing the massacre. "He sang a song so convincing, an entire army marched itself off a cliff." I sniff in disgust. "They say the Players went down to the shore later to collect the bones and turn them into props."

Jude chuckles. "You know, I think we might still have some of those in the prop room."

The wheels spin faster in my head. I need to get out of here, bargain or no bargain. *But how...*

"Let me do the talking. Focus on making a good impression," Jude murmurs as we approach the Players, where the next two auditionees seem to be undergoing interrogation. I vaguely note that they're obviously siblings, a boy and a girl with the same black eyes; fair, narrow faces; and icy blond hair.

Part of me strangely longs to speak to them, ask why they auditioned together when they both can't possibly leave as two. Or at all.

I scold myself and look away. I can't be *that* desperate for friends.

TITUS: "Enough! We get the idea. You both have *dreams.*" He rolls his eyes and waves a hand. "Dismissed. Go make friends." His voice drips with condescension. "Or don't. I don't care."

"That was rude, Titus," chides Arius as the siblings scatter, his words welding together like soft, spun sugar.

"*Boring* me is rude," Titus retorts.

Jude nudges me forward, a few paces away from the Players now. "Like I said," he whispers in my ear. "Let me do the talking."

He wants me to stay quiet, to do as he says. Because he certainly wouldn't want me to…

Embarrass him.

An idea ignites in my head.

Players are vain creatures. Prideful. Ego is everything.

I turn to Jude. "Yes, Titus *is* very big and frightening!" I yell loudly. "I would be scared of him, too!"

Not technically a lie. Only an implication.

If eyes could kill, Jude's would have turned me to ash several times over as every head turns in our direction. Titus bursts into uproarious laughter. Before Jude can so much as open his mouth to defend himself, I veer a sharp right and march over to the closest banquet table.

Maybe he won't be as keen on keeping me if I'm a giant thorn in his side.

JUDE: "Alistaire, *where* are you go—"

I glare daggers at him while sliding a rather large platter of expensive-looking spiced truffles off the table edge. The porcelain shatters loudly.

Jude swears, prowling forward as I go for a wine basin next, toppling that over, too.

Right onto his shoes.

Now he looks ready to *throw* me off the terrace, but before my parade of chaos can continue, a voice calls out, "Arius, you're in my chair."

Player Parrish jingles when she walks, charms of silver fastened around her wrists and ankles, a girlish spring in her step.

And rust-red stains on her palms, which she wipes on her pleated cream dress.

I don't need Jude's commentary to know she has one of the bloodiest histories of them all. Parrish bounces over to a chorus of *Where have you been?* As an answer, she presents a box from her pocket and pops it open.

My jaw drops, revulsion churning in my stomach.

Inside the box are several…*bloody teeth*?

"I needed to retrieve a place to put these!" she chirps to a series of rolled eyes and groans.

ARIUS: "Gods *above*, Parrish." He scoots a seat away from her. "You can't keep telling auditionees this is a requirement for Playhouse entry."

I'm going to be sick.

PARRISH: "They aren't *from* an auditionee." She pouts at her cast. "But imagine how lovely they'll look with the rest of my collection in my rooms!"

TITUS: "Don't take this the wrong way, Parrish, but I wouldn't enter your rooms if my own fate were trapped inside."

My mind grazes briefly over what I've read of Parrish. In the arena, she made her opponent's death slow, pulling them apart in pieces and threatening to give them to spectators in the audience.

She laughs like a crow, anklets tinkling as she plops down next to Arius, who busies himself with combing his fingers through that golden mane of hair. "They're from the imposter. Sil said I could keep them."

Imposter. I straighten, remembering Jude's comment about Dorian's *"sheep"* being slaughtered—spies sent in under the guise of auditioning. My blood runs cold.

I'm marked. The daughter of the dead Peacemaker. *What will they do to me if they find out*—when *they find out…*

A hand pinches my sleeve, ushers me away from my mess. "Now," Jude growls. "What will it take to get you to quit destroying things and act like a civilized person?"

I return a lethal glare. "Release me from the bargain."

PARRISH: "Have I missed anything exciting?" She scrunches her nose, smattered with freckles that shimmer like stardust.

TITUS: "Yes, indeed!" He studies his nails. "Jude's little hyena in the corner has been the most entertaining part of the night. We think she might try and kill him next."

All the Players turn to me, and I clutch the railing.

"*Speaking* of," Titus prompts with a wolfish grin. "What have we here, Jude?"

Does he recognize me? I wonder and immediately regret calling attention to myself. *Can he see my father's face in mine? Can he have been the one who killed—*

"Were none of the breathing auditionees good enough for you?" Titus's tone turns cruel. "Whose grave did you rob to drag *that* into the Playhouse?"

I grind my teeth. Like the others, Titus is devastatingly handsome, and the comment strikes a chord.

"Watch your mouth, Titus." Jude marches forward, shoes squelching with the wine I spilled. He points at me. "Sweetest girl I met in my whole life, on my honor."

Titus snorts. "What *honor—*"

"This way, Alistaire." Jude motions me forward, a warning in his eyes.

I make no movement and spit in his direction.

Arius chokes on his wine. "Gods, what have you done to the girl, Jude? Anger in that one."

"*Anger* is an actor's best asset," Jude defends, flashing a smile.

"Indeed." The steady voice comes from Mattia. The oldest Player watches me with interest now, which I gather is a bad thing.

Resentment bolsters in my chest. Paranoid, I look away, more and more certain she knows who I am. Her cutting tone. The searching way of her eyes.

"Allow me to prove she's the gentlest little fawn you've ever laid eyes on," Jude announces, then turns to me. *"Be nice,"* he utters, seething. "Act normal."

I pinch my eyes at him. "No."

"My, you *are* ghostly, aren't you?" Parrish calls as Jude throws me a biting smile that clearly reads: *Walk.* I return one I hope conveys: *You too. Off a cliff.*

TITUS: "Is one ghost in the Playhouse not enough for you, Jude?"

Jude stops cold beside me.

"Ghost?" I ask stiffly, defying Jude's order not to speak.

PARRISH: "Gene Hunt's ghost! You have her old dressing room." She makes a *tsk* sound when my jaw drops. "You haven't told her, Jude."

Ghost? She can't be serious.

"You can have that portrait removed if you like," offers Arius while I pin a new look of shock and betrayal on Jude. Behind him, Parrish volunteers to keep the dead Player's portrait in her rooms instead.

"There isn't *actually* a ghost," Jude says before I can ask. "Just a myth. Gene is dead."

TITUS: "They say your name is Hunt as well? Why, what are the odds?"

ARIUS: "Jude, feed this girl before she passes out."

RIVEN: "I don't want—"

MATTIA: "Why are you here?" Her voice slices through the flurry of conversation.

The group falls silent at her accusing tone. Mattia keeps one eye on me, her maroon-painted lips pressed together, sending a shiver through my blood. *She knows.* And she's daring me to acknowledge it.

"I..." I search for something to say. A lie. But nothing surfaces, my tongue bound to truth.

Titus stands to a full, terrifying height that rivals Jude's. He cocks his head, and a few strands of dark hair fall loose across his face. "Well, Alistaire?"

ARIUS: "Leave her, Titus."

TITUS: "I'm feeling rambunctious, Arius. I want to play."

Jude leans onto the back of one of the couches, crosses his

arms. "Play with an audience. She isn't an option."

"The world is my audience, and I'll not settle for less," Titus says through his teeth, then turns to me. "Tell me, Alistaire! Why are you here? Because it certainly isn't to win."

My heart hammers furiously as Titus saunters closer, until I'm enmeshed in the cloud of rich perfume he must have bathed in. Jude is throwing me wide-eyed looks that scream, *Answer the damn question.*

How did my father do this? Walk into a cage with these monsters and negotiate *peace* with them. I can barely keep my legs steady.

Craning my neck up, I meet the sparkle in Titus's gaze, sizing me up with the curiosity of a cat that's just spotted an injured mouse.

Don't look a Player in the eye, I remember with startling clarity and drop my gaze.

Titus laughs. "What, do I not hold enough interest for you?" He clicks his tongue, offended. "Impolite, I say. Sour expression, too. Won't you smile at least?"

"Fuck off," I growl, then immediately panic.

What the hell possessed me to say *that*?

Jude's eyes widen as he quickly pushes off the couch. Titus's narrow.

Gods, Galen's right. My temper is going to get me killed.

Titus's fingers play at the blade at his belt. Jude's posture suggests he's about to pounce between us. "I could force you to cut yourself a whole new smile if I wished."

The disturbing images of my attackers outside who did *exactly* that flash through my head.

Well. This is it, isn't it.

Then it all seems to happen at once. A splinter of gold, like a shooting star, zips through the night behind Titus with a *whoosh.*

Titus's smirk goes blank, his face full of shock, then rage, then agony as a scream erupts from his throat, the sound gut-wrenching and visceral as he crumples.

Confused, I stumble back as my eyes fall to the ankle he's clutching.

To the shaft of an arrow sunken into the flesh above his heel, like a needle in a pincushion.

Chaos fractures the stillness.

I yelp as something collides with my back, knocking me to the ground, before registering Jude has pulled us both to the floor and is shouting at the other Players to follow suit.

Gold pours from Titus's ankle like sunlight as he shouts every curse known to man. I frantically scoot away to carve space between the injured Player and me as Arius dashes across the terrace, kneeling. In soft tones, Arius instructs him to stay still, but Titus only howls louder when he wrenches the arrow out.

In the corner of my eye, auditionees rush messily for the stairs.

Escape. While Jude's distracted. Hastily, I crawl for the stairs, the ice in my ribs feeling like splintered tree bark from the fall.

"Alistaire." I peer over my shoulder at the sound of Jude's voice, where he helps Arius tend to Titus. "Are you all right—?"

"Jude?" Arius interrupts, face white with worry as he extends the arrow in a clutched fist.

I study the golden tip. Eleutheraen gold, based on Titus's reaction. Whoever shot that arrow shot to kill.

For a moment, the Players don't seem nearly so invincible.

Jude unravels a crude note looped around the arrow and scans it with annoyance.

ARIUS: "Would you hold still? You'll make it worse."

TITUS: "Get off me. I'll hold still when the bastard who shot this is—"

"Dorian. One of his followers, probably," Jude concludes, crumbling the note in a fist. A smug smile tugs at my lips. Apparently, not all of Dorian's hunters came *inside.* "Take this to the Prop Master and get Sil to kill the lights." He hands the offending arrow to Mattia, who throws a concerned look at Titus before vanishing downstairs.

I watch her. With my knife gone, that arrow could be *very*

useful for coaxing Jude out of this bargain and going home.

"I'll cover us." Jude's tone sours. "Get Titus inside, and everyone meet me at the gates." He spares me a glance before adding, "We're departing a little early."

The smile falls off my face as the Players file for the stairs, Arius and Parrish carrying Titus between them.

No. *No.* The Playhouse can't leave until I get out—

I turn to plead my case once more, but Jude is on the move, irises glowing, as if someone has struck a match in each pupil. Gold pulses through the veins in his neck, through the hands he raises, crossing the terrace.

Then it begins: a great fog, too thick to find the stars above. It smothers the night, the entire Playhouse, in a vaporous wall. One by one, torches flicker out.

Then nothing—just the wailing of dismissed auditionees clutching onto the gates below in mist and darkness.

"Come now," a voice says, and I startle to find Jude has reappeared behind me, his face back to normal. "Those arrows aren't known to miss more than once."

For my sake, I decide he's exactly right.

Once I get my hands on that arrow, I won't miss.

Act I: Scene XIV

JUDE: "Frankly, Alistaire, I don't know what's riskier at the moment. Moving the Playhouse while someone's out shooting Eleutheraen arrows at our heads or leaving you here to brood by yourself. Unfortunately, I must take both risks. Please be good."

He narrowly slams the dressing room door in time to avoid being hit by the vase I've hurled at his head.

It shatters and falls to the ground in pieces. On the other side, the lock slides shut. Of course this place would have locks on the *outside* of the doors.

I'm left with little more company than Gene Hunt's portrait. She just stares and stares like she knows something I don't.

"I'm not signing that contract!" I shout through the locked door. "Do you understand? The deal is off! I'm leaving. *Tonight*." But his steps are already gone.

I turn to the empty oval room, breathing hard.

My plan was to be out of the Playhouse before midnight, Script in hand. Instead, I'm locked inside while the Players move us to gods know where.

It strikes me that lifting this curse won't matter if I'm trapped in here for good.

How did this all go wrong *so* fast?

First, I go for the dresser, yanking open the chestnut drawers and throwing them to the floor. No key of any kind. There isn't one hiding under the mantel or sewn into the delicate silk throw pillows, either, which I didn't necessarily need to tear apart, but I'm in a mood. I go for the purple curtains next, flinging them from their hangings. I'm on my way down the corridor to shred the bedroom next when I pass that long mirror off to the side.

With a huff of anger, I storm up to my own feral reflection.

"Home," I growl at the glass, keeping my eyes on the floor.

"Do you hear me? *Take me home*."

Nothing happens. I heave a breath, panic whirring in my chest as a *crack* alerts me to the Playhouse doors opening and sends my feet hurrying to the window.

Outside, the Players gracefully file around the Playhouse, aside from Titus, who limps furiously from his injury and seems to be cursing every other step. Jude's wall of black smoke billows at the gates, his illusion blocking the cast from anyone's vision—or weapons.

Impossible. Buildings cannot be moved.

But as my nails dig into the windowsill and flecks of gold fall from it like stardust, I feel less certain the Playhouse is a proper building at all.

I watch helplessly from my window as all five Players seem to ready themselves to move the theatre and take me with it.

Then the floor sways beneath me, the window glass starting to rattle.

Jude's eyes flicker up to my window, locking with mine.

He grins.

And the Playhouse slowly sinks into the ground.

"You know, I find myself asking," begins Jude, leaning in my doorway. His hands are closed around an ornate silver box. "My, doesn't she have a lovely profile from all the way outside? And I can see it so well because—oh yes, of course. She's torn the curtains to shreds!"

Ignoring him, I slice the letter opener I unearthed in one of the drawers through the last of my bedsheets. That makes twenty-seven strips between them and the curtains I wrestled from the rods, plus the towels I gathered from the closet. I glance up at Jude. "Your room is next." Then I go back to tying two ragged pieces together, silk fraying in my hands.

JUDE: "You are *remarkably* destructive for someone with the frame of an injured hummingbird." He stalks after me but startles several steps back when I swing my letter opener at him.

RIVEN: "This little bird is on her way *out*." Fluttering my fingers at him in a wave, I throw the room's glass doors open and skitter out onto the balcony I discovered beyond them.

JUDE: "Gods, *stop*. They'll see you—"

Outside is a city that is *not* the District. Not that I can glean much of it in the dark—only mountains in the distance and the crash of nearby waves.

And hundreds of faces smothering the glowing Playhouse gates below.

They shriek a greeting at the sight of Jude chasing me onto the balcony, but the screams quiet into confused whispers when I loop the end of a silk sheet over the marble railing and start tying what used to be towels around my torso. I'm ready to launch myself over the ledge when a strong hand grips my makeshift halter and throws me back onto steady ground.

"You will be a *pile of bones* if you try that."

I swear and catch my balance on the railing, pondering how hard it might be to push Jude over it.

JUDE: "I sincerely thought keeping you alive would be a matter of protecting you from the other Players, but clearly we have to add *you* to the list." He turns to the crowds. *"Leave."*

His voice travels with the warmth of the wind. A glassiness drapes over the faces below and, without another word, they disperse.

We've most certainly moved deep into South Theatron, then. No one is marked to resist his Compulsion. Those below belong to the cult that worships these monsters.

"Where are we?" I demand, certain I don't want the answer.

"Koilon. The coast."

My heart sinks. We're hundreds of miles from the District. A marked is less likely to get executed here and more liable to be hunted for sport until they find their way to the unfortunate place of a Dionysian altar.

"But..." I shake my head. "But *how*?" I wave my arms at the crowd as they dazedly scatter, wondering if any of them have a clear thought in their heads. "How can a building move?"

"The Playhouse is not a building," Jude protests, like this is common knowledge. "It's a *set piece*. And the world, our stage. Set pieces can be moved wherever I wish to perform." He shrugs. "The Playhouse is more illusion than material. The 'moving' of it all is mostly just for spectacle."

I glare at him, still confused.

Jude gestures to the doors. "Why don't we talk about this inside?"

"I'd like to see you tr– *Hey!*" I shout as Jude plucks my makeshift rope off the floor like a leash and prowls inside, dragging me with him.

Below, the ground shakes with the gong of an old clock striking midnight. I picture the one I spotted in the Playhouse foyer, encased in white marble.

Overhead, the lights dim. Jude throws a nervous glance at the candles as they flicker. "We don't have much time, so I'll make this quick. First, you're meant to sign that." He points to a slip of parchment on the vanity, and my eyes widen.

I *know* I shredded that contract into tiny pieces fifteen minutes ago.

I pause to look around. The remnants of bedsheets I destroyed no longer clutter the floor. The curtains are fastened cleanly back in place over the window. "No," I breathe, running to the closet and throwing it open.

There, folded and stacked neatly where I'd found them, are the towels. A frustrated, strangled sound escapes my throat as I rush back into the room, only to find my makeshift rope has disappeared, too.

Jude shrugs. "The set doesn't like being messed with."

A strange, soft murmuring emanates from the vanity mirror behind Jude. I jump, pointing an accusing finger at the glass. "And what is that? Why is it making that noise?"

JUDE: "Prayers. Not everyone is as unwelcoming as you vile creatures beyond the Cut."

I stare at Jude, then the glass, unsure which I trust less. I shouldn't be surprised by this, but it's horrifying to see in action. "You...you can actually hear those? Through mirrors?"

Haris will be thrilled.

JUDE: "I— One thing at a time, yes?" He sets that thin box on a chaise between us, popping it open to reveal an arrangement of silvery gauze and tinctures, half of them encrusted with jewels. It doesn't look like any healer's kit *I've* ever seen. "I stole this from Arius while he's off mending Titus. It won't be long before he misses it. Sit down."

RIVEN: "Why?"

JUDE: "Because you've been holding your ribs like they're trying to escape you since you got here. Clearly, something is broken. I need you alive, and at this rate, a medium-size wind might turn you to dust."

Stubbornly, I stomp over and sit, mostly because my body is begging for rest. Jude kneels and fiddles through the case, his rings producing a series of delicate, metallic clinks as he squints at the various handwritten labels, distinctly giving me the impression he does *not* know what he's doing. Especially when he pops the lid off one bottle, sniffs it, and gags.

Hopefully Arius doesn't keep his poisons with the rest of his supplies.

"So," he says. "I don't suppose you've considered my *extremely* generous offer."

"No more than climbing the catwalk and plunging to my death."

"That would be merciful in comparison to what they'll do to you." I watch his hands with distrust as he unfolds a flat cloth and tips a glittering salve that smells like spring flowers onto it. He looks at me pleadingly. "If I put this near your ribs, is it going to cost me a finger?"

"I'm not some rabid animal," I hiss.

"Well, I'd hardly call you domesticated."

I scowl and pull away on instinct, but the jerk of movement deploys a searing ache down my side. The pain wins.

Pinching my shoulders together, I swallow my pride and peel all three tattered layers halfway up the left side of my torso. The mirror tells me my ribs are nauseatingly visible beneath a sheen of ungodly bluish skin. I scrunch my eyes shut to avoid my reflection and brace myself.

Something warm presses against my ribs, and I startle, expecting the salve to be cold, for the hand holding it to be too forceful. Instead, it's light, feathery, like the flicker of a candle.

I blink my eyes open, and Jude is watching my expression. Probably worried I'm going to try and claw his eyes out.

He's less intimidating when kneeling at eye level, his features softer in the dimming light. This close, I guess it's easy to see what the world obsesses over, a devastating sort of beauty that puts his statue in the District to shame. One of those faces built for the stage, all sharp and dramatic angles, curved lips that seem permanently tilted up in a grin. A long, straight nose offset by a delicate ring.

It's no wonder they warn us not to look Players in the eyes, gilded and brilliant and ready to hypnotize an audience. I've noticed they all seem to come in different shades, though. Parrish's, sparkling like a jewelry box of rare amber. A terrifyingly close look at Titus's reminded me of a volcano, burning and roiling.

Jude's, though, glint like sunlight through storm clouds.

Realizing I'm staring, I throw my gaze to study the floor. It feels absurd admiring Jude, maybe wrong. He'd probably laugh, say something cruel and pitying.

"I know you don't believe me." His voice cuts through my thoughts. "But I don't plan to hurt you. I need your help, Alistaire. The other Players are going to spend the next three weeks training their champions to be lethal and gifting them much of their Craft to do so. If you let me, I'll give you mine." He lets out a breath. "I never wanted to be Lead Player. It's a death sentence."

A death sentence. In spite of myself, my resolve softens. I know how that feels, for death to hang over your shadow.

The salve prickles along my skin, and the soreness dwindles—it's probably some sort of pain sedative. But this isn't what startles me. It's that, as he ties the bandage taut, the sharp, cold splintering in my lungs dissipates, that mysterious ice dislodging from my rib cage.

I gasp a deep breath, and—and *warmth* fills my lungs.

Stunned, I lift my chin, savoring the strange, comfortable feeling that weaves between my ribs. "The rest of me now—" I don't mean the words to come out so ragged, but I don't care. "I—I mean, *thank you* but...I need you to fix the rest of me." In the wake of some of the ice relenting, my resistance is magically forgotten. "You wanted a deal, didn't you? Then reverse this—whatever it is. *Now.*"

The candles sputter again. Several go out entirely. Jude swears and goes for the matches on the mantel. "We're past curfew." He lights one of the candelabras that hover over the hearth. It goes out again just as fast. He gives up, looks at me.

As the last candle dims, all I see is the golden hue of his irises, which are more frightening in the dark. "In your time here, keep away from the shadows. You'll notice the lights in your bedroom are always on, even when you sleep— *Out!*" He grasps the last candle, rushing its light to a corner where a thick shadow emerges from the darkness in the shape of a long, taloned hand, like a monster waking. "*Patience*, love! We'll just be a moment."

He isn't talking to me. I move away until my back meets the wall. *What is that?*

Sil's warning comes to mind. *All Players and auditionees alike are to stay out of the dark.*

"Nyxene. The Playhouse's Stage Manager," he says, and I realize I asked my question out loud. "She is one of many reasons to *not* break the rules. There are things that move in the Playhouse after dark that mean you harm."

"What is she? A...a guard for Players?"

"Players hardly need guards," he says, indignant. "Alistaire, because you're...you, I think I need to state this bluntly, and hear me when I do: Nyxene protects Sil above all else. Do not—*ever*—lay a hand on Sil. She will rip the marrow from your very bones."

I return a look of reasonable confusion and utter horror until he elaborates. "She's here to keep things in order. But she's godsdamned violent about it."

Any wild ideas I had about getting that Script away from Sil slip further out of reach. Jude may be an actor, but I don't get the sense he's lying about this.

I inhale sharply as the darkness shirks away from the light. Satisfied, Jude sets down the candle and straightens as if nothing odd has happened.

JUDE: "Do you mean it, Alistaire? I'll help you, and you'll keep our deal? You'll see the casting call through to the end?"

Yes. I feel the word on my tongue. *Yes, I will. And then I'll go to school; I'll get a job. I'll have a home and friends, and I'll find a place in this world just for me.*

"Okay," I whisper. "If you—if you *can* fix me, I'll..." I swallow, taking in the cage around me. "I'll see it through."

A chill rolls down my spine at the slow grin working its way across Jude's features.

"Lovely," he says in a smooth tone, one that gives me the impression Jude is used to getting what he wants. Then, strangely, he goes for the fireplace.

Confused, I watch as he plucks an iron from the mantel and pushes the hot coals around. "This may hurt, by the way."

"This may—" I lower my brow, tasting unspoken context in the air. "What?"

He straightens from where he's crouched by the fire, iron in hand. "You'll never make it through the competition marked."

He wants to destroy my mark. My vow to truth and protection against the Playhouse. The mark that keeps me from becoming like the Revelers who spend their days worshipping the Players.

The mark that keeps *me* from bowing to *Jude.*

The thought sickens me, and I press my back to the wall, pointing at the door. "Get out."

JUDE: "Now, Alistaire, let's not be rash—"

RIVEN: "Now. Go." My next words turn into a shout. "And don't *ever* suggest that again—"

JUDE: "There's stage combat tomorrow. You cannot use our Craft or suspend your reality with that mark. You'll *die.*"

RIVEN: "You do realize—" I lower my voice to a hiss. "My freedom means nothing outside these walls with a ruined mark." I'd be more ostracized than I am now.

JUDE: "There must be something you want—"

RIVEN: "Something more than my *life*?" I grit my teeth. Even my curse isn't worth that. "What do *you* want? What will it take to let me out of this?"

Jude's smile is paper-thin now as he stands slowly. "The gods themselves could plead your case at my gates, and I would not open them. You will not leave this Playhouse as long as I live."

The words set a chill in the air.

RIVEN: "Leave." The word comes out as a whisper but fills the room as if I'd yelled.

JUDE: "Perhaps sleep on it—"

RIVEN: "Gods, I said *leave.*" I snatch the letter opener and turn to chase him away this time, though Jude is already halfway out the door and barely manages to save his toes when I slam it after him.

I press my back to it, breathing until my vision adjusts to the dying light. Though it's still easy to see my problems doubling tenfold in front of me.

So long as he lives.

I won't just have to escape Jude. I'm going to have to kill him.

But Jude has underestimated me, too. I've spent my entire life studying the Players. My father gave his life to ensure they stay caged inside this theatre.

And Jude has no idea who he's let into the Playhouse.

Act I: Scene XV

"Show me Galen Hesper," I beg the hand mirror I discover on my nightstand.

Jude was right about the lanterns in my bedroom—they stay on. Oddly enough, I can't seem to control any of the lights, but there's just enough to find my shadowy reflection in the small mirror. A reflection I will *never* get used to.

The mirror darkens and swirls, murky. Nothing happens.

Any chance of making a deal with Jude vanishes from my mind as I realize something else: If he finds out who I am, whose daughter I am, I won't be the only one in danger.

I need to warn Galen.

"Galen," I try again, but still nothing. If Players can hear prayers through the mirrors, there *must* be a way to speak to the outside world.

As I slam the mirror back down, swearing, it occurs to me—Galen hates mirrors even more than I do. Growing up, he shattered every last one we owned and threw out the pieces. My brother won't be anywhere near one.

Another stroke of bad luck. I grit my teeth, about to fling the damn thing across the room when a murmuring stirs at the edges of the glass. It hums around my hands as I grip the mirror, like secrets shared between old friends.

A new idea takes shape in my head—along with the image of a small, cracked mirror, one I've seen a hundred times, never in the hands of a family member but in the hands of…

"Haris," I whisper to the mirror, moving forward, picturing his face. "Show me Haris."

The glass brightens and shifts cheerily this time, as if welcoming a request it can grant. Then it goes black.

Through the mirror, I hear the muffled sounds of weeping. The whoosh of Theatron wind. A distant horn of the Diolkos Railway. The sounds of the District.

"Haris?" I call into the darkness. The weeping on the other side stops. "Haris, it's me. It's Riven."

Nothing.

Then, quietly, "Riven?"

"Yes!" I call with relief. "Yes, it's me!"

Silence pulls between us. Then light washes across my mirror, and Haris's weathered face fills it, his eyes wide as dinner plates.

I'm not sure how much time I have. The words fall out of my mouth at record speed. "Haris, I need you to listen to me. I'm in the Playhouse and—"

"THE PLAYHOUSE!" You'd think I just told him I stumbled across a lifetime of riches. Awe fills his face, his scream drowning out my frantic explanation. "It's *gone*, Riven." He rakes his fingers down the glass, as if trying to claw his way through it. "The Playhouse is gone. *Vanished*."

"Haris," I hiss, desperate to shut him up before someone hears. "Stop it. Quiet down."

"Show me the Players!" he shrieks. "Show them to me, Riven. *Show them, show them, show—*"

Maybe this wasn't a good idea. "I'll make you a trade! I'll make you a trade, Haris," I call over his wailing.

Gods, I'm making all *sorts* of deals tonight.

"I'll bring you something. I'll bring you—uh—" I dip my hand into my pocket, fishing out Jude's Finders Keepers ring. I pinch it between my fingers and show it to him. "This! This belongs to Player Jude. It's yours if—"

"Jude!" Delirious joy fills his voice, his eyes widening, his gaze turning hungry as he watches the ring in my fingers.

"This is yours on one condition." I try to keep my voice steady, but it's shaking now. It may be paranoia, but I can't escape the feeling that Jude could be listening in on every word of this. "Haris, I need your help."

Act I: Scene XVI

By morning, I have the beginnings of a plan. A bad one, but a plan nevertheless.

It begins with tracking down that rogue gold-tipped arrow from last night.

As the sun rises through stained glass windows, I discover a pair of scarlet pants about a hundred times nicer than the ones I wandered in with, along with a silk blouse that laces at the sides. Both look like they might have been neatly folded before being tossed through my mirror and landing in a heap on the floor. Along with a note.

I borrowed these from Mattia until we get you to the costume wing, so for both our sakes, please do not cut them up. And ditch that shabby jacket. You're embarrassing both of us.

After proudly donning my jacket over the blouse, I head for the door, but I catch myself sticking my legs out in front of me a few times. I've never worn color before and can't seem to stop looking at the vivid hues of red. Something about it makes me feel guilty, so I pull my gaze upward, awkwardly ignoring the unsigned contract on my vanity on my way out.

I discover the other auditionees already in the common room, at last putting names to their faces and wishing they'd stop looking at mine like it scares the daylights out of them.

The siblings, who I learn are twins, are called Thyone and Phileas—championing Players Parrish and Arius respectively. According to both, their Reveler uncle turned them out and warned them not to return unless one of them was dead and the other had acquired a role in the cast.

Titus's chosen champion introduces herself as Tig, a strikingly tall, willowy girl with umber brown skin and curly hair. She makes it known several times over that Sil himself spotted her from the crowd and insisted Titus audition her last night.

Then there's Mattia's champion—Linos, a boy with a quiet, commanding presence and tanned, broad shoulders. He shrugs when asked about his upbringing, mentions he has siblings and something about Players' salaries.

Guess I'm not the only one who showed up out of desperation last night.

We're all about the same age, and that's where the similarities end.

But I am far more concerned about what *they* all share in common, since at some point between last night and this morning, their eyes brightened, gleaming almost gold.

I'm *certain* the twins shared the same cold black eyes just yesterday. This morning, both glitter in a way that unsettles me. Linos rarely looks up, but I caught a flicker of it in his, too.

"Y-You're all—" I stammer. They startle, and I realize it's the first time I've spoken to them. "Your...eyes?" That isn't the question I meant to ask, or a question at all. I'm not used to being included in conversations. One of the twins cocks her head, confused.

THYONE: "Of course. Didn't you do a Craft binding last night?"

Gods above. Do I even want to know?

RIVEN: "Uh—a Craft binding?"

THYONE: "With your mentor."

I'm going to kill Jude. "What?"

PHILEAS: "An exchange—borrowed power during the casting call."

TIG: "You didn't think they'd make us compete as mere mortals, did you?"

Wait, Jude *did* say something about that last night—that the other Players would gift portions of their power to their chosen champions. *If you let me, I'll give you mine.*

There's the smallest, *tiniest* chance I should have asked for clarification before screaming at him to get out.

The doors open, and the other auditionees file out. I follow them through.

The dining hall welcomes us with a clatter of silverware, the scent of fresh fruit, and a dozen ornate tables perched alongside a wall of glass that looks out to a beach.

Immediately, there are two things I don't like about the scene outside.

One: the water. Jude was right—we've moved so far away from the District, we're on the damned coast. The tide is coming in, dark waves slapping against high, sharp rocks in the distance.

The clouds are just as foreboding here as they are in the North, an ominous haze rolling over the black sea. This is not what fogs the enormous glass panes, though.

It's the second thing I hate about the dining hall: Hundreds of thin, desperate faces surround us from the outside, their eager breaths clouding the glass. Revelers. Their clammy hands push against the windows, reaching for us. Some of them stumble over one another just to get a look. Most of them don't even seem to blink, their eyes hollow.

Is *this* what life is like in South Theatron? A frenzy of obsessive Playhouse fanatics, wasting their every thought and breath on the Players? Is that what *I'd* become without my mark?

TITUS: "Well, if it isn't *Alistaire*! We were just talking about you." I jump at the sound of my alias and almost drop the fruit I was spearing onto my plate. Titus leans back in his chair at the Players' table, where they all cluster like a gathering of overdressed swans. He points a fork at the windows. "Get used to it. I know it feels like being in a fishbowl, but truth is, they're the ones who can't help it." He smirks wickedly. "How'd you sleep? See any ghosts?"

RIVEN: "No ghosts." I answer the second question instead of the first. Because the *truth* is I think I slept better than I've ever slept in my life. No thanks to Titus, whose groans and declarations of vengeance toward whoever shot that arrow could be heard anywhere in the Playhouse.

This morning, though, the only sign of his injury is the slightly bulging heel of his left boot, probably bound in gauze beneath the leather.

TITUS: "Disappointing." His smile falls. "If you see her, tell Gene I still have her earrings and that I won't be returning them." Without awaiting a response, Titus goes back to warning his castmates he'll be making up most of his lines tonight, as he's not bothered to review the script.

My eyes narrow. There are only four Players in the dining room.

"Where is Jude?" I ask Arius a little too urgently as he passes. *And what the hell is a Craft binding?* I almost scream.

His fair brows draw together. "Heard him arguing with Sil this morning." Perhaps noticing the unabated terror I fail to prevent from crossing my face, he offers a reassuring smile. "I'm certain he'll be back soon. He argues a lot. I'm sure you've noticed."

My hands clutch the plate I'm holding so hard, I'm surprised it doesn't crack.

He's gone to turn me in. I refused his deal and now...

I try the dining hall door and find it locked. *The hell? I just came through here—*

ARIUS: "Is everything all right, Alistaire?" He tilts his head as I yank on the handle with all my might, his mane of golden hair falling to one side. "Here, why don't you find somewhere to sit, and I'll go check if—"

I ignore him and storm over to the empty table in the corner, where I can at least keep one eye on the door. Worse comes to worst, I bet one of these table legs could break the glass panes. The Revelers outside will panic, causing a distraction and giving me a chance to—

TITUS: "Watch the council go and blame us for it! It's a *casting call.* This is just what happens."

He crumbles the newspaper on the table in a fist and tosses it, just close enough for me to subtly kick it under my table and snatch it up. As I flatten the article out beside an empty plate I have no intention of filling, I listen to the Players.

ARIUS: "One of their temples burned to the ground, Titus." The legs of his chair scrape the marble as he seats himself at their table. "Their council was taken underground."

What? I stare at the crashing waves beyond the crowds outside, wishing I could see home.

PARRISH: "All this drama isn't going to help Jude's case for opening the Cut." She drags a fork over her plate, a line forming between her brows. "Their rulers will take one look at the damage to the District and refuse treaty negotiations with him."

MATTIA: "Pretty sure *Jude* already refused negotiations with them." She spears a strawberry. "Not diplomatic like Gene was, that one. I bet you my best jewels this ends in blood."

TITUS: "Why wait for them to open their wall? I say we just go. Perform in the North for those who will have us and bury those who won't."

My eyes widen at their words, and I keep one ear out while turning my attention to the report.

12 DEAD, declares the headline. ***HUNDREDS INJURED AFTER CASTING CALL MAYHEM. PLAYERS FLED.*** Below the words, an image that vaguely resembles the District is printed in black and white. Fallen columns, tufts of smoke, ash, and ruin.

Is this what all those dismissed auditionees got up to in the District after we left?

My teeth clamp together. If the District fell under attack after our departure, there's a chance my brother was called in to help manage the destruction.

I wonder if Haris got my message to Cassia, if help is already on the way. Never in my *life* have I had to rely on a Reveler. Now I'm at the mercy of one.

And a Player. The Lead Player.

ARIUS: "You think Sil will let you sacrifice half our audience, Titus?" He shakes his head in answer to his own question. "You must be kidding."

Why are they talking so casually about crossing into the North? They *can't*. They can't cross the Cut. We're safe from Players in the North.

We have to be.

TITUS: "The North is full of self-righteous zealots who've publicly shamed us with their marks. They're practically immune to our Craft. *Killed* how many of our own? Tell me how you expect to win them over."

MATTIA: "We won't." Her voice is bold and resolute. "We won't win the North, not while territories like Syrene still stand. It's time to give up that fantasy. Their so-called resistance threatened our cast yesterday." She looks pointedly at Titus, who grimaces.

My gaze flickers up at the mention of Syrene. Its people have a long and bloody history with the Players, beginning with the forging of the treaty and ending with a nasty dispute over the placement of the Cut.

Titus scowls. "So what would you have us do?"

MATTIA: "We take them by surprise. Before they dip their blades in Eleutheraen gold and come *here*. Give me six days, and I'll bring you the North on a platter."

I fight to hold still as the horror of Mattia's words settles in. I've always been taught that Players kill for three reasons: a threat to their cast, a blow to their ego, and, on *rare* occasion, for pure spectacle. It occurs to me the North as a whole could fall into all three of those categories, if they refuse the Playhouse entry now that the treaty is up.

ARIUS: "So long as there's a chance of you getting skewered with an Eleutheraen spear, Mattia, I wouldn't count on Sil letting you out." Some of the tightness in my chest releases. North Theatron isn't defenseless. We have Eleutheraen gold.

PARRISH: "Or any of us." She sets her chalice on the tablecloth. I almost think she looks sad. "Ever."

TITUS: "I say we just cross and tour. The threat is mild! Our schedule isn't public, and their armies will never move fast enough."

Tour? Schedule? They can't possibly mean to perform in the North before—

"Good morning!" calls a rich voice, muting the conversation as Sil sidles through the double doors. Outside, the Revelers break into hollers and applause. "I hope everyone is well rested?"

The director's eyes hover on me just a second too long before he continues. "Pardon the interruption, but it's a full day ahead. Everyone is dismissed to costume fittings and will report to the auditorium immediately after for an assessment in stage combat and Reality Suspension."

The deathless arts. I assume that's what Jude meant when he said he could help me. I press gently at my ribs, which somehow healed miraculously during the night. But it's that single warm breath that filled my chest, the way that ice seemed to melt and dislodge from my lungs that I can't seem to shake. My mind fixes on it, on the moment I step out of this Playhouse and leave the lingering consequences of my curse at its gilded doors.

With another pleasant smile, Sil turns and vanishes the way he came.

"I've never died before," chimes Phileas at a neighboring table, a peculiar sparkle in his eye.

Died? Wait, isn't the whole point not *to—*

"Can't be much worse than living," jokes Tig, though I notice she set her fork down rather quickly.

The dining hall begins to clear out, and the queasiness in my stomach starts to feel like a ball of lead as my mind flips through everything I've read on Craft over the years. Maybe the deathless arts *can* help me, but I would do well not to forget their main purpose.

Death.

Act I: Scene XVII

"They must have every piece ever worn in here," says Thyone, moving between costume racks ahead of me. Her brother, Phileas, pinches expensive suits and elaborate dresses as we go.

"Do you think we'll get to wear these?" Phileas asks with wonder in his voice.

I hope not, I think, eyeing a particularly gaudy contraption with a train the size of my bedroom at home.

The costume wing is a yawning golden chamber, two stories up from the dining hall, jam-packed with thousands of opulent fabrics and colors hanging upon long, mahogany rods. One wall is stacked high with bolts of silk, gossamer, leather, and velvet. The opposite is lined with mirrors and pedestals. In between, a frightening display of mannequins dressed in costumes.

Even the mannequins are built to the Players' muscular statures. My mind wanders once more to the *test* ahead. One Jude is certain I won't survive.

"When do you think we'll see the prop room?" Phileas wonders aloud.

I'm wondering the same thing. I need to get my hands on that Eleutheraen arrow.

"Touch someone else's prop, costume, or otherwise, and you'll have to answer to *me*," replies an elegant, humorless voice. I look up from the red coat I've been pocketing a gold button from to see a tall man with a broad chest and large framed glasses. "Or the Prop Master. And I promise you, Marigold is scarier."

Noted.

CICERO: "You can call me Cicero. I'm one of your costume designers." He eyes the three of us. "They're sending you in groups? Oddly considerate for the Players. All right, come along."

I cough, lowering my voice as I follow the costumer. "If one of the Players—" I pause, choosing my words carefully, sidestepping a lie. Jude sent that arrow down to the Prop Master last night. *Marigold*. "If one of the Players asked me to retrieve something from the Prop Master, how would I do that?"

Cicero stops short, turns. The pure and utter alarm etched into his expression is decidedly not comforting. "Marigold? Now, which of the Players did you anger so badly to deserve *that* fate?"

So the stories *are* true.

"She's real?" Thyone pipes up. "Is she really more beautiful than the Players?"

"If you value your life, you won't let the Players hear you say that," Cicero says with a harsh laugh and continues down the aisle. "She was human once, I'm told."

The most beautiful woman in Theatron, according to most books.

Or she was a few hundred years ago.

"What…what is she now?" I try to ask casually, though the nervous, high pitch the question comes out in doesn't do me any favors.

Cicero turns and raises an eyebrow at me. "I promise you don't want to find out."

Before I can push for answers, he ushers us onto the pedestals, his lips immediately returning to their pressed expression whenever he stops speaking.

"*You're* going to be a problem." He pinches one of my shoulders buried under Galen's jacket, and I cringe. "What is this supposed to be?" He flicks my collar. "Take it off. How do you expect me to measure you?" He waves a finger between the twins. "You two, as well. You think I have all the time in the world? Dionysus have mercy."

I fold my arms protectively over my chest. My mark itches in warning under the top button of my jacket.

If anyone sees my mark, I'm done for.

CORA: "Give them a break, Cicero." A woman with a low

bun of perfectly silver hair and a long, pointed nose appears at his side. "He's right, though. We might as well fit you for a potato sack measuring you in this."

Another costume designer, then. "I—uh," I start as Cicero brushes by to wrap a measuring tape around Phileas's neck.

"Shy, Alistaire?" teases Thyone, already halfway undressed.

The silver-haired woman laughs. "There are no secrets in the theatre, especially when it comes to costume changes." I take a defensive step away from her. Cora's head tilts. "Dear, there are *plenty* of things to be afraid of in the Playhouse. I'm not one of them," she adds more pressingly. "At least this coat? It's very large on you."

"Cora?" sings a familiar voice. Emerging from a row of sapphire-beaded costumes is Jude. "I hate to be a bother, but have you seen the atrocious stitching on my combat uniform? I refuse to be seen in it."

Exhaustion falls across her face. "Again?" she asks.

"Yes, that was my thought as well," Jude says primly as the woman throws down her measuring tape and hurries off through the maze of costumes, muttering about Players and vanity. For some reason, I expect Jude to stay and tell me how to get out of this before someone sees my mark. But when he sweeps back through the costume wing after the silver-haired woman, I guess I shouldn't be surprised he exclusively came to complain.

On my own, then. Though I'm not plotting my grand escape for more than thirty seconds before the silver-haired woman returns. "Heron is on it," Cora calls to Cicero, who rolls his eyes and mutters something about tearing all the stitches out of Jude's uniforms so he can't complain about them anymore.

Without pretense, the woman tugs at my jacket. She doesn't look surprised when I pull away from her with a scowl and, to my shock, says, "It's *me*, Alistaire."

Her eyes flash gold, then dull back to gray just as quickly. My mouth falls open. "Jude?"

The silver-haired woman—*Jude*, apparently—nods. Before I

can ask questions, he turns my shoulders back toward the looking glass, and I'm not sure if I cringe more at the touch or at my reflection.

JUDE: "Arius tells me you're desperately missing me. I'm so sorry to deny you my presence this morning, but I've been out bargaining for your life."

I whirl around, horrified. "You told Sil."

"Not to be morbid, Alistaire, but if I told him, you wouldn't be here in one piece right now. Say, I risk my neck borrowing one of Mattia's costumes for you, and you insist on covering it up with this?"

I hug my arms over my jacket. "It's too big anyway," I say and kick a leg out to emphasize where the scarlet fabric bundles at my knees. Though maybe I've grown a little fond of the color.

"Well, your new costumes will be too big as well if I can't measure you." He reaches past the mirror and snags what I can only describe as a glorified nightgown hanging behind it. "It's a slip. Same as they're wearing." He nods to the other auditionees. "Be quick about it."

I snatch the flimsy excuse for fabric out of his hands as Jude steps away, but taking off Galen's jacket feels like discarding my armor. Somewhere, a few costume racks away while I change, Jude complains loudly in the costume woman's voice to Cicero about how "poor Arius's performance was in last week's show" and that "Sil really should have given that role to the far more talented Lead Player."

By the time he returns, I'm making poor attempts to arrange my hair to cover the mark at my neck and pondering what the hell the point of a slip even is.

JUDE: "*Stop* wincing away from the mirror. They only do that North of the Cut."

I reluctantly shift back to the glass, palm angled over my mark while Jude plucks a measuring tape from a sewing box and cinches it around my shoulders, calling measurements to Cicero.

"I can get you out of this part. But I won't be able to help you in stage combat. Turn this way." The tape wraps around my ribs next, and Jude stills, looking a little sick. His eyes flash up to mine, down again, and then, gritting his teeth, he calls more numbers out to Cicero, who swears loudly at the measurement.

I shrug off the strange reaction, focusing on what must be a *perfect* imitation of the costume woman. Everything down to the beauty mark above Cora's lip is intact. "Did you—" I'm not sure how to ask this. "Hurt her? Cora?"

Jude blinks up at me with Cora's face. "Are you asking if I've skinned a woman in less than thirty seconds? That would take me at *least* ten minutes to do." Finding no humor in my face, he rolls his eyes in a distinctly Jude-expression. "No, Alistaire, I did not skin anyone. It's called Mimicry. You'll learn it, too, if you survive today. Which you won't, at this rate."

I've read of Mimicry, but like Reality Suspension, the North doesn't have an inkling of what it entails. From the stories, I was inclined to believe the worst.

RIVEN: "Jude, what is..." I throw a suspicious glance at Thyone, paranoid someone will hear. "What is Craft binding?"

Jude raises an eyebrow. "Something you *cannot* do with that mark of yours. Oh! That reminds me." He reaches into his back pocket and places an item in my palm. "A gift."

I examine the small silver blade between my fingers as he goes on. "I asked Sil to shift the assessments. You don't stand a chance if Reality Suspension is first, which it is, since he refused me. So, when you slash the seal of your mark, do so with *that*—it's prop metal. Shouldn't hurt as badly, and certainly better than that atrocious gold blade you were waving around—"

He snatches his foot away from my aim, barely in time as the blade comes down hard, spearing through the wooden pedestal. I straighten, lean forward, and whisper, "Make another mention of slashing my mark, and I'm taking one of those pretty golden eyes."

"So you think they're pretty?" Jude asks wryly. I frown. "If you get yourself killed, it's on you, then. If not only for your sake, but for—"

RIVEN: "For what? Yours?" I restrain the laughter catching in my throat. "Let me be clear, Jude. We might have a bargain, but I don't care what happens to you."

I startle, confused by the twinge in my throat.

JUDE: "You know? I'm starting to think you don't like me much. And everyone likes me. I'm *delightful*."

RIVEN: "I hate you."

Jude's costume slips, gold bleeding through the gray eyes. Abruptly, he goes back to measuring, and a brush of skin draws a yelp from both of us. "*Why* does your skin always feel as though it's been dunked in ice chips?"

"Why does *yours* always feel like hellfire?" I spit back.

He stares hard at me for a moment, then at my mark. "You *don't* hate me."

Gods above. He's so used to being adored, he can't handle this.

RIVEN: "Jude, I'm not sure how many times we have to go through this, but I can't lie to you. I do hate you. I hate this place. I hate all of it." There again—that strange twinge.

Jude shakes his head at me, smile recovering, with too many teeth this time. "What is the difference between love and hate? Just that one is the sweeter of passions. It's a fine line in the theatre." He allows me no time to respond before vanishing back into the tunnels of clothing racks, leaving me to gather my jacket.

But when he's gone and my anger cools, I peer at the blade and press a hand to my mark, starting to suspect only one of us will make it through the day.

Act I: Scene XVIII

Already I know this will end badly.

Unbearable layers of leather cling to my skin, laced up my back. I blame Jude for the clumsy measurements as the buckles on my gloves catch again. We march to the tune of Arius's heavy boots as my eyes search for an exit that doesn't exist, on our way to a challenge that Jude insists I won't survive.

They usher all five of us auditionees down a dimly lit hall, through a narrow door, and up some steps. "This is the right wing of the stage," explains Arius ahead.

I can see the stage clearly from here, a massive white platter that rounds in front of the audience, melding into a secondary rectangular platform near the back. A brilliant red curtain is held at bay by golden rings on either side. Beyond the stage, a sea of empty velvet seats stretches farther than my eyes can see. There must be thousands.

TITUS: "Welcome!" His voice booms throughout the auditorium as he and Parrish enter from the opposite wing, met with a thunderous greeting from the other auditionees.

Titus looks excited, which I decide is not a good thing.

TITUS: "Come now, gather round!"

My foot hits the stage, and a shock like lightning cuts through my ankle. It isn't necessarily unpleasant; rather, an almost effervescent feeling shivering up my calf. I shake my ankle until it goes away.

Mattia charges across the platform, a merciless double-ended blade in her grip. She tosses it to Titus as if it weighs nothing.

TITUS: "Stage combat often ends in Reality Suspension. You won't use it for all combat on the stage. But when you need it—" He swings the blade over his head, the sound slicing through the air and raking along my nerves. "You'll want to know what the hell you're doing."

"Think of this as a trust exercise," Parrish says. "You've all had the chance to do a Craft binding now, so follow the rules, and you'll be just fine."

Well. *That* doesn't bode well for me.

Parrish's gloved hands reach for the leather belt strapped at her torso, retrieving two thin silver knives about the length of her arms. She moves across the stage, having exchanged her skirts for a flare of black gauze that flutters cape-like behind legs that move with the sharp speed and precision of a spider.

TITUS: "You'll need to know Reality Suspension for certain types of performances, mostly Tragedies. Remember, Comedy is not the antithesis to Tragedy. Everyone endures suffering, hardship, loss. Everyone dies."

PARRISH: "Some of us just know how to have a good laugh about it." She winks.

Hold on. What does that—

TITUS: "First, a demonstration! Watch closely."

Uncertain, I take a few steps away and collide with someone at my back. Whirling, I find Jude, his olive skin looking rather pale.

JUDE: "*This—*" He nods at Titus and Parrish, who have begun to walk cool, calculated circles around each other, the former adapting to a noticeable limp on his left side. Jude lowers his voice. "Is why that mark is going to kill you."

My heart starts to thud in my ears.

TITUS: "What *is* Tragedy? Why does it exist?" His voice reverberates off each slat of marble, coming back tenfold. "Mortals are simple creatures. Fewer things grip hold of an audience like the inescapable reminder of their own shared fate. Their eternal quest to understand what the journey toward the end *means*." He's speaking to us, but his eyes never leave Parrish, apparently his opponent now. "Reality Suspension is not something you *learn* to do. It's something you learn *not* to do."

PARRISH: "You make us sound lazy." Her head tilts, childlike. "Stalling?"

Without warning, Titus brings the blade down in a swift blow, scarcely missing Parrish's head. She ducks, striking for his torso with one of her blades, laughing at his attempt.

RIVEN: "Jude." My voice comes out in a whisper as Titus runs at Parrish. Those are *real* weapons. "What is happening?"

He doesn't answer, his eyes following the fight unfolding before us.

This doesn't look like mere stage combat. They're trying to kill each other.

TITUS: "Don't turn your back on your opponent. Reality Suspension requires at least two bodies—if one of you dies onstage, your life has to temporarily go somewhere *living*. So for Dionysus's sake, hold eye contact." He dodges one of Parrish's strikes. "This is why we do Craft binding. We're all connected on the stage, and one life will depend on the next. If you can't trust your partner, you're as good as dead."

I glance up at Jude. I am extra dead.

Titus jabs Parrish with the center hilt of his weapon, forcing her back. Showing little reaction to what looked like a hard blow to her hip, she rolls onto her feet. One of her blades goes flying as their shadows waltz across the stage, Parrish's anklets jingling with each step. The blade clatters on the ground beside the curtain as she shifts, wielding the other cleanly like a sword, her expression one of mere annoyance.

TITUS: "And if the script says you're *done for—*" Titus corners Parrish to the edge, the orchestra pit looming at her back. He swings again, and everyone gasps, excited. This time, Parrish doesn't block; her feet are a smidge too slow. Titus lunges and swipes his good foot behind her ankle. She lands on her back with a huff, her second knife sliding away from her grasp. He wastes no time springing over her.

There's an unmistakable, intimate second of shared silence between them, their eyes meeting, fusing. Parrish doesn't look frightened. In fact, I think I catch her sticking her tongue out at him mockingly.

TITUS: "Then you calculate the moment you fail *exactly*." His gaze narrows. "And you don't fight it."

Titus utters a word under his breath that I think only Parrish can hear. Then, without hesitating, slides the blade clean across her throat.

Act I: Scene XIX

"*That,*" declares Titus, pointing the wet blade at each of our stunned faces.

My heart hammers against my chest as my eyes drift to where Parrish's throat used to be, gold spilling out on the marble. Her eyes are turned toward the spotlights, glassy and distant.

No, no, this is *wrong*.

TITUS: "That is what you want. Shock your audience. No matter how many times they see it, they will never be immune to death. Which is why *you* must be."

She isn't dead. Certainly not.

I swallow, suddenly unable to feel my feet as I grip hold of the red curtain to steady myself.

This cannot be Reality Suspension. It *can't* be. This is just...

Death. *Murder.*

Lost for words, I look to Jude, waiting for an explanation. Something. Anything.

He doesn't look back.

Titus throws his weapon to Mattia. "We'll return shortly." With that, Titus scoops up Parrish—her *corpse*—and saunters for the wings. "You're in good hands. And if this is your mentor"—he lifts Parrish's limp body up, and she looks so light, so *vulnerable*. There and gone in an instant—"I promise to return her shortly."

But there's something different to his walk now. What had been a lazy, catlike stride shifts into a stagger, like he's carrying an invisible weight draped over every inch of his being.

Meanwhile, Mattia looks right at me and moves. I tense, not even having time to react when she swings the blade at Jude's neck.

In a breath, he catches her arm and forces the blade back on her so hard, the silver slices into her bicep.

Mattia pulls back, an easy laugh parting her maroon-painted lips as she clasps a hand to the slit in her arm, where gold has begun to bleed. "Don't ever underestimate your opponent," she announces to the group.

Jude flashes her a grin. "Ruin this shirt, Mattia, and you won't get the chance to."

"You'll all be dismissed to rehearsal rooms to train with your mentor," Mattia announces, gold seeping between her fingers. "We hope to see you alive at dinner tonight. Unless anyone is eager to try now."

She means it jokingly, I think.

"Your first death is the hardest, don't worry," Arius says, as if it's *comforting.*

"This way, Alistaire," Jude says quietly, nodding to the wings, which lead back into halls of rehearsal rooms.

I frown. "I thought you weren't going to help me."

"I'm not. I *can't* if you're going to be stubborn about it." He lowers his voice. "But at least I can make it quick."

Make it quick.

I can't think straight. Panic paints little dots across my vision until it numbs, turns red as rage. There's blood on the stage. A body carried away. And what I *thought* might be my saving grace—Reality Suspension. It isn't some deathless curse breaker.

It's a sick, disgusting *stage trick.* One that I can't even perform.

When I look around, all I see are arrogant, ego-driven Players, just like the monster who ruined my life. One of them, or maybe all of them, is responsible for killing my father. But he didn't back down from the challenge of these monsters, even though it cost him everything.

Rage boils under my skin at the thought. I will *not* be quietly executed by a Player.

Especially not by Jude.

That anger will be the death of you, Galen's voice repeats once more. But that anger is curling hot and quick beneath my skin, throttling the fear in my bones. *Bottle it up and keep your mouth shut, all right? Use your head. Never open your mouth when you're angry.*

As auditionees prepare to disperse, I open my mouth. "I volunteer."

Act I: Scene XX

I regret the words as soon as they leave my mouth, but I'm committed now.

JUDE: "No she doesn't—she does *not* volunteer!"

He's still yelling after me as I storm to the prop armory I saw them pull weapons from. My audience breaks into conspiratorial chatter, and Mattia tracks my movements as if only now noticing I'm here.

Jude's voice pitches higher as he chases me backstage. "She's just being *silly*! Natural Comedian, this one."

Actually, I am not a natural *anything*. I don't know shit about fighting a Player. In fact, a couple of years back, before the worst of the slow poison took hold, I got my ass royally handed to me by a couple of Revelers after wandering too close to the southern border in the District. They entertained themselves by trying to force a lie from my mouth. Galen came to my rescue with the scolding of a lifetime on his lips.

After that, Galen refused to let me enter the District at all, even by his side—unless I could beat him in a fair fight. Unwilling to give up my freedom, I spent the next three months trying, more bruise than skin and increasingly pissed about it.

But I did. I broke four fingers that never healed correctly, but I beat him in a fight. Once.

This is, apparently, enough to fuel the unhinged confidence that has my hands running over the selection of blades and axes hanging in the wings.

Now that I think about it, though, I'm pretty sure Galen let me win.

Oh gods. He *definitely* let me win.

Jude speeds up, hot on my heels, whispering, "Alistaire, you've made your wish for death *abundantly* clear. But let me speak plainly: Parrish's body is dead, but *she* will be fine. You can't do that—to suspend your reality, you have to be able to *leave* yourself." He reaches for my wrist before I can grab the dory spear, and I jerk it away, offering him a scathing look instead. He goes on. "That mark is like a lock. *On you.* You can't escape. Your body will die, and so will you."

My stomach turns, and I force a shrug.

RIVEN: "You heard them. This is practice for stage combat as much as it is your atrocious Player magic—Reality Suspension—whatever it is." I select a dagger from the armory, my voice shaking. "What makes you think Mattia'll win?"

"What makes me think she'll—" he repeats, as if unsure he's heard correctly, staring at me with a sort of beseeching horror. My knees snap as I charge back onto the stage. "A dagger?" he scream-whispers after me. "Grab a damn sword, at least, Alistaire!"

I don't announce that my arms aren't strong enough to swing a Player's sword. This will have to do.

Mattia's brow falls as she takes in my dagger. She levels a look at Jude that seems to read, *Really?* while I head for the center of the circular platform and turn, silent. Waiting. The whispers of auditionees hush as Mattia approaches me the way one might approach a gravely injured animal that needs to be put down. Cautious but pitying.

The realization of my mistake arrows through me. Up close, it's easy to tell how much bigger Mattia is. Her shoulders are corded with lean muscle from years of training—and that cut on her arm already seems to be healing rapidly. A tooth the size of my palm dangles at her neck. Legend claims Mattia ripped that tooth from a beast sent by Artemis herself.

I look to her blade, wet with blood. This Player wrangled a beast sent by the gods with her bare hands. A mortal with a dagger and a big mouth must be an insult of a challenge by comparison.

Mattia closes the remaining space with a rudimentary swing, as if testing to see if I'll move or if I really am suicidal.

She looks mildly surprised when I dodge her blade and mimic

the counterstrike I've watched Galen do about a thousand times. But I miss her entirely, clumsily swinging at her torso.

Turning, Mattia slashes the blade down toward my armed hand. I throw the dagger up, just barely shifting to catch it before it can clatter to the ground. That singular movement leaves me exhausted, cold gripping at my bones.

"You've taught her well in a short time, Jude," Mattia remarks.

I glance in Jude's direction, out of breath and annoyed that he should get any credit. But he isn't watching the fight at all. His eyes are focused above. I track his gaze past the golden box seats and over the highest balconies, where a spindly series of bridges crisscrosses along the theatre in a maze.

Then I see what he sees. A wisp of white, racing over us on the catwalk at otherworldly speed, like a—

Like a ghost.

When I look back down, Jude is on the move, sprinting backstage.

Something strikes the back of my knee, sends me toppling forward with a shout of pain.

"Ali, get up!" shouts an auditionee who seems to think we're on a nickname basis.

I vaguely register that the sole of Mattia's boot has granted me this surprise trip to the floor. My vision spins. She's advancing on me, clearly bored with pretense.

Pain pinches the bones in my fingers as I grip the dagger for dear life. I can't do this.

"Get *up*, Alistaire!" someone shouts. I don't know who. "Do you want to die?"

Anger beats in my pulse. *Do I?* I won't survive this stage trick, this Reality Suspension, if I lose this fight. Not with this mark. Not without whatever "Craft binding" is. The others will.

No, I decide. I don't. I don't want to die.

My eyes flash up at Mattia advancing on me. I *certainly* don't want to die at the hands of a Player.

Galen's voice shouts in my head. *No big movements. When*

someone comes at you, it doesn't matter how strong they are.

I shoot an ankle out and snag her shin, swearing at the pressure on my knees. My defenses aren't impressive by any stretch. Just quick and clumsily unpredictable. Maybe because I don't know what my next move will be, either.

All that matters is how smart you *are. And gods, Riven, you are smart.*

I don't want to die. In fact, I *really* want to live.

Jude shouts something from above, and it draws Mattia's eyes. She peers up to the catwalk just long enough for me to lunge onto my feet and slice my blade across the muscles of her stomach.

The Player doubles over and swears, gold bleeding through the leather where I've cut her. But her eyes are ablaze, burning through me. With no warning, she pivots, pushing and swinging and cornering me to the edge of the platform, finally unleashing her true skill.

Skill I am in no way, shape, or form prepared to combat.

Jude shouts something again. Galen's voice is yelling at me to strike. But I don't know how to strike, how to fight. I skitter backward like a cornered dog.

In a frantic, last-ditch effort, I aim my dagger for Mattia's neck and throw it as hard as I can. She moves, and it clatters pathetically to the floor, leaving me open and defenseless.

This isn't how I die. The words slam into me like a tidal wave as Mattia raises her weapon.

Jude screams again, and I hear it this time: *"Éxodos!"*

The world flashes black, then white.

Then there is no color, no sound, no nothing, like reality has drained itself from my world. Like time has stopped.

I raise my eyes to the catwalk and have only enough time to see a wisp of white disappearing on the other side of it, the ghostly figure vanishing.

Jude stares down at us from the bridge, his expression frantic.

Right before the chandelier overhead falls toward the stage, Mattia and me in its path.

Act I: Scene XXI

TEN YEARS AGO

"She's having a strange reaction to the gold," says a woman's voice. "It's eating away at the flesh."

I wake, thinking I must have gone my entire life with this awful throbbing sensation at my throat. It hurts too much to think of anything else. Whispers of memory nudge at my mind—my classroom, Professor Ariti. I was supposed to answer a question when the room went dark.

Now I'm on some sort of cot. Shadows talk by the door, hardening into the shapes of people. The second voice belongs to my brother. "I'll take her home. Please don't tell our mother."

"How are you feeling, Riven?" says a third voice. I shift my gaze to a pair of bright hazel eyes at the end of my cot. He appears a few years older than Galen's twelve, and he's neatly packing what might be healer supplies into a bag, the clasp of it catching on a wad of cotton wrapped around his hand.

"Bad," I answer without thinking, my new mark diluting any untruths that might have softened the word. "Who are you?"

"Sometimes marks don't take cleanly. I'm the person who gets called in when they don't." He offers me a wink. "Take care, Riven." With that, he pats my hand and stands to leave.

My attention stirs back to my brother and the school nurse in the doorway.

"Has she?" the nurse says, voice unsteady. "Was she exposed to that—"

"Whatever you're insinuating…" Galen's answer is too hushed to catch the rest. But my mind fills it in. *A Player.*

The nurse shakes her head. "If *any* sort of Craft may have entered her blood—"

I think back—the Player's golden blood all over my hands, sinking into my skin…

"Nothing to worry about here," interrupts the hazel-eyed healer. "Just a bad reaction. Let her rest and send word if it gets worse." With that, he leaves before the nurse can object.

My fingers twist at the bandage woven tightly around my neck. The pressure is uncomfortable, so I pull at it—

"Riven?" Galen calls, pushing past the nurse. "Riv, don't touch it!"

He bats away my prying hands and clumsily adjusts the bandage. Squinting at the lights, I recognize Galen's silver eyes hovering over me.

"My throat hurts." My mind is unable to focus on anything else. "And I'm cold."

"It's an allergy." Galen blows a lock of chestnut hair out of his face, throwing an anxious look at the door. "We're going home."

No! My mind spins. We're supposed to practice the Three Compliments Rule today in class. I've already thought of four for Noah. And a few insults for other classmates.

"Can you stand?" asks Galen.

A strange feeling builds hotly in my chest. I pin my lips shut, looking to the door, where the nurse watches me like an escaped animal. Galen reaches for my shoulders and pulls me upright, startling when I violently pull away. "Riven?" His eyes cloud. "What's wrong?"

I know the things I am supposed to say: *"I'm scared. I'm hurt. I'm hungry."* Things that would make Galen nod and say, *"Let's get you home."*

But I can't tell lies anymore, and the feeling is bubbling up my throat.

"Riv, what is it?" Galen presses.

I blink. "I'm *angry*."

Act I: Scene XXII

At first, I think I must be floating. Until someone sets me down.

"Move that table out of the way, will you?" Jude's voice, echoing somewhere in the darkness.

It occurs to me I cannot breathe.

"Gods," says another voice. Titus? "Do you really think an auditionee could've gotten up there and cut the—"

"It wasn't an auditionee," answers Jude. "Something worse. Thanks, Titus. You can go."

"You sure? I can stick around. First death's the hardest." A pause. "Bit of a fighter, isn't she?"

"You have no idea. Don't waste your time; it'll be a while. She's stubborn as a bull."

Boots pad across the floor, followed by the click of a door shutting. There's a dip beside me on whatever cushiony thing I'm on. Too cushiony to be an altar. And so far, no one is leaning over me with a blade to cut my heart out. This is good news.

Something cool presses to my collarbone, and I gasp, stars piercing my vision. Pain too all-consuming to be real explodes in my lungs and zips through my shoulder. I try to reach for it and wince.

"Stop, you're making it worse," says Jude. But the pressure eases slightly. I drag my eyelids open and make out his blurry silhouette. The dimming lights form a halo around him. There's a cloth in his hand covered in blood.

Mine, I think. That's unfortunate.

"Don't—touch me—" I rasp, squirming away.

He pauses. "Are you serious, Alistaire?" He throws the cloth down. "I've seen a lot of people die and a lot of people pull through, but none so determined to hang in the balance. I *am* trying my best, but it's rude to push away someone trying to help you."

"It's rude to drop a chandelier on someone," I seethe, but the words turn into a cough that feels like blades raking across my lungs.

"I didn't drop a chandelier on anyone." He drags a hand through his hair. "Someone else did, though."

All the auditionees were onstage. Titus was off somewhere in the wings with Parrish. The rest of the Players were on the platform.

Who, then?

I narrow my eyes. "I don't believe you."

"I don't believe what I saw, either, so that makes two of us."

I try to lift my head to stare at what I imagine is a large, gaping hole around my shoulder by the amount of blood on the cloth. But I can't. Something jerks in my chest, sudden and instinctual. Like a bird fluttering around inside the cage of my ribs, searching frantically for a way out.

Jude must notice something is wrong, because he nods and almost rests a hand on mine before thinking better of it. He sits back, shaking his head. "That's you—your life is trying to escape to wait out the worst of the physical damage."

I narrow my eyes at him.

"It wants to escape someplace safe so your body can die," he clarifies. "*That* is Reality Suspension. To fool death long enough for it to pass over, to suspend your reality *before* it comes. We're Players, not healers."

This isn't how I'm supposed to die. The thought pounds through my head with a vengeance. I did not make it this far to give up now, injured at the hands of a Player. Dying under the eyes of another.

RIVEN: "Show me—show me how to do it. *Now.*" My demand ends in another vicious cough. He gives me a pitying look.

JUDE: "You can't suspend your reality. That mark...it works like a seal. It keeps us out, but—"

RIVEN: "It keeps me in." I choke on the tinny taste of blood. *What's happening?*

Jude sighs—I must have asked out loud. "It pierced you. I think your lungs might be collapsing. I'm not sure."

It? It. Mattia? I remember her running at me, lifting her blade—

"Mattia?" I cough again, a rage even deeper than the pain filling my head.

"What the— *Lie down*," Jude orders as I try to haul myself up, finding it also a very bad idea and collapsing onto what I realize is the chaise in my dressing room. "And no," he says. "Not Mattia—not exactly. The edge of the chandelier hit you. Mattia took the brunt of it."

"She's dead?" I blurt, hopeful.

"For the meantime," he says with a shrug. "We're actors. We live a thousand lives, but we still die at the end of each one of them."

I remember the world flashing, color draining. Jude had called out a strange word.

The bird in my chest makes another breakout attempt, and I gasp. "What did...you do?"

JUDE: "I suspended Mattia's reality. And did my best to suspend yours, but..." I try to muster the energy to look confused, but truthfully, I just want him to keep talking to distract me. "Think of it as a pause in the show. A moment backstage." He shrugs. "It's time that doesn't exist."

So, even if Mattia is dead for now, the moment she died doesn't exist. A moment to fool death. My heart sinks. She's alive, then. Or will be when the magic wears off.

The bird throws itself against the wall of my chest again, weaker this time. Dying.

I'm dying.

The wrongness is overwhelming.

Then my hand is grasping furiously at my throat, at the high collar of my shirt concealing the mark beneath. "Get rid of it," I wheeze. "Get rid of the mark." I am *not* dying here. I'll live out of sheer spite if I have to.

Jude's eyes fix on mine, uncertain as I reveal the swirls of gold. They seem to squirm, burning hot and ice-cold at once, like they know something bad is coming.

"You're sure?" he asks, eyes flickering between mine and the mark at my throat.

No, says Galen's voice in my head. Fainter now.

I nod, startled as the bird in my chest shudders, no longer trying to escape. Then Jude isn't there anymore. Though I hear him shuffling around somewhere a few feet away.

"One condition," he says, reappearing and setting something down just beneath my right hand. It feels like paper. He wrestles my palm open and presses a pen into it. "Sign it."

The contract. Every curse I can think of rolls through my mind.

"You're unbelievable."

"Come now, Alistaire. You have the only thing an actor really needs anyway."

I scoff, glaring at him. "And what is that?"

He offers what I think is an attempt at a comforting smile. "Not a thing to lose."

I groan, but another scorch of pain sends my hand writing my fake name wherever he's settled it on the page. Then the paper is gone and so is Jude. I hear what sounds like coals being pushed around. My vision fades in and out. I can't seem to properly move my other hand and vaguely recall the not-too-pleasant feeling of it smacking onto the marble stage.

"Let me be clear, Alistaire." When Jude returns, there's an iron in his hand, the edge of it burning orange. His words seem a great deal more dangerous while holding it. "Turn on me, or try to hurt my cast, and I will kill you myself."

I don't need to be fully coherent right now to know he means that.

"Don't look away, all right?"

I nod, numb, and focus on the sinister gold of Jude's eyes against every instinct I have. I almost think they soften but quickly dismiss the thought. I'm delusional from pain. "Right. Good. Focus on me."

Never look a Player in the eye, warns Galen's voice.

"When your mark is gone and the Craft takes hold—"

"Player magic," I hiss with disgust, one eye on the iron sizzling too close to my neck.

He clears his throat. "Don't think of your body as dying, yes? Just, uh…sleeping. Think of this as a very intense nap."

"You are the least comforting person I have ever met," I mutter.

He breathes. "First death's the worst. I promise."

The scalding heat of the rod presses into my skin. I'm not sure if I scream. I'm not sure of anything. My world narrows to a boiling warmth flooding my every muscle, to the heat of Jude's palm curving around the back of my neck, to those bright golden eyes that seem more like stars as everything darkens.

Something is wrong. I try to gasp, but the next breath doesn't come, the air not reaching my lungs. The space between my heartbeats stretches wider, *quieter*, and it hits me that I'm too late. Too late for this Reality Suspension trick. That unsealing my mark didn't work—

That bird in my chest makes one final retreat as Jude speaks a strange word. And finally, it breaks free.

ACT II

Act II: Scene I

Someone is singing, soft and quiet. It's a familiar, melancholy melody my mind itches to recognize.

No, that can't be right. I don't know any songs. Singing is banned in the North.

I feel breath in my ear. *"He's onstage. Hurry."*

My eyes snap open. Whoever whispered the words isn't there when I turn my head. Maybe I imagined it.

Slowly my vision clears, tracing intricate patterns of gold leaf across the ceiling. If I'm dead, the underworld looks suspiciously like the Playhouse.

Confused, I search for the edges of the chaise I remember being laid on. My hands grasp cool layers of silk instead beneath a thick duvet. The firmness of the chaise has been replaced by a soft mattress.

I bolt upright, taking in the sleeping quarters of my dressing room, the four-poster bed. Embroidered throw pillows are piled around the dark wood bed frame beside a nightstand presenting a full glass of water. A footstool has been left to the side of my bed. It's empty.

Did I drag myself in here, delirious from pain? After—after...

Somehow, my feet find the ground. A blistering sensation brings my attention to the bandage pressed between my collarbones. It doesn't take more than a moment to remember why. What I've done.

A second cast is wrapped over the wrist that snapped when I fell, though it doesn't hurt at all. How could that have healed so quickly?

There's a line of ink scrawled across the cast: ***Go back to bed.***

I nearly catch myself laughing before the seriousness of the situation takes hold. But the thought of my betrayal to the North is unbearable. So I focus on the second most crucial issue at hand: I need a weapon. And if I can't get to that arrow yet, I need to find my father's knife.

In an instant, I'm across the room and out the door, skidding into the vacant hall, buttoning my jacket up to the neck like hiding my ruined mark will somehow undo what I've done. There's a surge of applause somewhere in the distance. A performance tonight. Jude will be onstage, away from his dressing room.

Which is next to mine and unlocked, apparently. Awfully trusting of him.

Or at least, that's what I think until I swing open the door and a thin slip of parchment lodged behind the PLAYER JUDE nameplate floats to the ground. Suspicious, I pick it up and read:

I said go back to bed, Alistaire. You won't find it. Nosy.

Chaining the door shut behind me, I quickly discover he's right.

My knife isn't in any of his suits or the sleeves I rip off them. It isn't underneath the floorboards I pull up and toss into the fireplace. It certainly isn't in any of the little makeup bottles I spill all over his vanity.

I'm writing a few choice words in eyeliner over his mirror when my eye catches an old playbill hanging on the wall behind me.

There, beside it, I see something—framed by fan letters signed with crimson lips. Jude is overly sentimental, I decide, examining the wall of memorabilia. But between a tattered playbill and a dated call sheet, a tour schedule is nailed to the wall. It's old and out of date by years. But if he has this one, he *would* have the current one, right?

I dive for his dresser and then the vanity drawers, rifling through them as I replay Titus's comment this morning: *Our schedule isn't public, and their armies will never move fast enough.*

But if the North *did* have their tour schedule…

My hands grip a newer page printed delicately with cities and tour dates for *this* season. This is it. With a little "aha!" I pull it from the drawer, and my attention snags on the newspaper clipping hiding beneath.

I *should* run. I have the tour schedule.

But something about the angry way the newspaper clipping

has been frayed at the corners, with several words viciously underlined, piques my curiosity.

COUNCIL RULES: CHILDREN NOT EXEMPT FROM MARKINGS IN THE NORTH, EXTENDS TO DISTRICT WALLS

It's dated ten years ago, when marks widely took root in the North, a preventative measure as the expiration of the treaty grew closer. The article includes comments from key council members, talk of extinguishing deception in the North and protecting our youngest members of society from trained liars—and preventing them from being lured in by the temptations of the Playhouse.

Thunderous applause echoes from the auditorium again. Curtain call.

A thought occurs to me, and I shove away the newspaper clipping. My eyes flicker to the mirror, only long enough to press my palm to it and whisper, "Galen Hesper."

Please, Haris, I think, desperate as my palm meets the cool glass. What are the odds he actually delivered my message?

It happens faster this time, the glass swirling. "Galen?" I ask the glass limply as it darkens.

While I wait, my eyes flicker to the top of the mirror—to a message written in a line of crusted brown lipstick that I didn't notice before.

If not in this one, then in the next, it reads. A prickle walks down my spine as I compare it to Jude's message on my bandage—a sharp and vicious cursive. Then I glance back at the writing on the mirror. I'll bet a fan wrote it. Maybe one of the "dalliances" he mentioned.

The thought of a fan being in this room sends a pinch of annoyance between my shoulders. *Jealousy?* No, definitely not. I have no reason to—

"Cassia!" my brother's voice hollers in the distance, hard and frantic and pulling me from the distraction. "Cassia, it's her!"

The darkness on the other side gives way to dim, flickering light as what looks like a curtain is pulled away from the other side. Wisely, they kept the mirror partially covered.

My brother's quicksilver eyes peer back at mine through the glass as the curtain falls.

Thank you, Haris, I think, relief blanketing my panic for just a moment.

Galen doesn't look himself. Dark rings line his normally bright eyes. He's wearing the same pressed shirt as yesterday—only now, it's wrinkled and battered. He looks like he hasn't slept since I last saw him. Which feels like ages ago now.

"Galen," I say in a whisper, throwing a look over my shoulder. "It's me—"

"Prove it."

I startle. His voice is colder than steel. He doesn't sound like my brother at all. Behind him, Cassia materializes in what I recognize as the old study in her home. I can tell by the carved shelves lining the walls, thick with books I begged to borrow growing up. I look to Cassia, shocked.

"You heard him," my aunt prompts, a little softer. But her face has paled white.

They don't trust that I'm me. My eyes dart around. I'm standing in the dressing room of a Player, one who specializes in Mimicry.

I look down at my clothes, covered in blood. My own, but they don't know that.

Why *should* they trust me?

I swallow. "I'm your sister." His expression is unchanged. "I—I *hate* it when people touch me." Galen's face softens just slightly. My mind scrambles for something convincing. "For my twelfth birthday, you wrote and mailed letters from my entire class wishing me well." He'd have gotten away with it, too, if I hadn't recognized the slanted *T*s of his handwriting and asked him directly. Unable to lie to me, he'd confessed on the spot.

That does it. His expression breaks, his lips parting in disbelief. Aunt Cassia lets out what sounds like a small cry on the other side. "The Reveler wasn't lying," she says, more to herself than me.

I definitely owe Haris that ring.

"We thought you went missing in the riots." Cassia's voice shakes when she talks. "The District went to hell after last night when the Playhouse vanished early—and Galen, we—"

"Do they know?" Galen's tone slashes through Cassia's, sharp and angry.

I don't need to ask what he means: my mark. Do the Players know I'm marked.

Resisting the urge to press a hand to the collar of my jacket, to show them what's happened, I clear my throat. My oath is broken; I'm no better than a common liar now. They'll never trust me again.

"Just—" I pull in a breath. "Just one. One of them knows."

"Which one?" Galen presses. "Tell me who took you. Which Player?"

I flinch. None of them are *good* answers, but I have a feeling some names are worse than others in this case.

"Riven—" he begins again.

"Their Lead Player," I admit quietly. "I've been put in their casting call."

Finally, the reaction I expect. A mask of unabated disbelief. I track Galen's vision from the dried blood flecked on my cheek to the cast that reaches my hand. Like he can somehow see through the jacket concealing scars that should have been fatal. By the laws of nature, I should be dead.

"What's he done?" he says. "If he tortured—"

"No, *no*," I interrupt, the dark possibility humming in the silence between us. I remember the year Galen went through *that* part of his training after graduating, taught to endure Player interrogation methods in the devastating case of capture. It's required of anyone of his rank—of anyone who bears information the North would *not* want the Players getting their hands on. Especially when he can't lie about what he knows.

Galen refused to speak of it when he returned home.

"This is from something…e-else," I stutter, omitting the *I got hit with a chandelier* of it all. "He—he promised he could reverse what happened to me if—"

"He's lying," Galen says flatly before I can explain. "They lie, Riven. They aren't like us."

I hide a wince. *I'm* not like us, either, now.

But he's right. I made a bargain with a liar. Jude probably has no intention of holding up his end of the deal—if he even *can*.

"Your Eleutheraen blade," Cassia urges. "You have it?"

I shake my head, swallowing my frustration. "It's gone."

Galen swears under his breath. "I'll get you out, Riven. I *will*," he says. "But first, I need you to listen to—"

"No, I need *you* to listen," I interrupt, speaking quickly. I'm not sure how much time I have until Jude returns and notices his tour schedule is missing. "I think the Players are going to cross the Cut or try to, at least—"

"He told you that?" Cassia questions sharply, her face blanching white.

"I'm holding their tour schedule." I skim the list in my hands. "They intend to cross the Cut in two weeks' time," I say, reading off the order of cities before stopping myself short and picturing the arrow that sliced through Titus's ankle. "I don't understand. Why risk it? Most of the North is marked. There's no audience for them there."

The conversation in the dining hall this morning comes back to me.

Tell me how you expect to win them over.

We won't.

"And why a Great Dionysia? Why *now*, when they're years early—" My heart drops as I look back to the tour schedule. "They're planning to cross the Cut right before the festival starts."

The Great Dionysia festival lasts five days. *Five days*, during which all the Players are released from the Playhouse and allowed to roam freely.

They're just biding their time until the treaty is up and the Great Dionysia begins.

And if the Players are after revenge, it'll be slaughter.

Something in me counters the thought. Players don't inherently *desire* bloodshed. If they did, they'd have killed everyone by now. Every mortal loss is one less patron in their velvet seats. They're after something else.

I'm missing part of this picture. I'm certain I am. But until I know what it is—

"Take their schedule to the council. Maybe they can use it so that the North will know where to place their forces—and be ready to defend the Cut if the Players try to—"

"We'll fight, but we won't win." Galen speaks up, breaking his silence. His voice is devoid of emotion, resigned. "None of this is news, Riven. We know what they mean to do."

My jaw tightens. The North succeeded in barring the Playhouse from entry once. Why shouldn't we do it again?

"What do you—" My brow falls. "What do you mean? If you send word now, the North can begin pooling its resources of Eleutheraen gold—"

"Riven, the North doesn't *have* Eleutheraen gold." Galen looks me in the eye, and the grim certainty there rattles me to my core. "We haven't for years."

Act II: Scene II

"What?" I whisper into the mirror. In the distance, I hear applause.

We're running out of time.

"Our access point to the well has been drying up for years."

No mortal can reach the heights of Mount Eleutherae or the Eleutheraen gold that pools at its top. But beneath the mountain, it runs deep underground throughout the North.

Or it *did*.

Galen is staring like I'm as good as dead. "The miners began reporting diminishing lines of Eleutheraen gold ages ago." The acquiescence of his tone only startles me further.

I stare back in disbelief. Eleutheraen gold is our only defense against the Players. It's always been a part of my world, used for marks, for dipping weapons.

"It's a bluff?" I say, shocked. "Our defense is a *bluff*."

The North is built on truth, yet our greatest protection hinges on the Players believing a *lie*. A half-truth so thin, we wouldn't even be able to deny it if asked. I heard the Players say it just this morning: Our Eleutheraen gold is all that stands between them and taking the North for themselves.

"Not *entirely*," Galen whispers. "The North has continued markings, but what's being sold on the market is diluted at best. New markings aren't done with pure Eleutheraen gold anymore."

A half-truth. *Technically*, Eleutheraen gold is being sold. It's just watered down.

"I don't know how effective it is," Galen admits. "Even parts of the Cut aren't pure."

Our infallible wall is flawed.

Cassia doesn't look even mildly surprised, her eyes low, head down.

She knew, too, then.

The Players may be able to cross the Cut. And we can't fight them off.

My escaping the Playhouse will mean nothing. There will be nothing left to go home to. There may be *no one* left if they have their way.

"That Player who has you has refused any talks of peace until the Great Dionysia." Galen shakes his head. "If the wall falls, there's little to stop them." He locks his gaze on mine. "We may not see the light of a new treaty. We have no leverage to bargain with."

And the North will be back at the mercy of the Players all over again. Even today, Syrene's streets are said to be red from the original Players drenching their land in so much blood, the rain couldn't wash it away.

"Leverage," I whisper to myself. *Leverage.* "Wait—but we *do.*" I lock eyes with Galen, a horrible idea materializing before my eyes. "Me."

Cassia looks up, her eyes flashing to Galen.

"No," he says, resolute. "What matters is getting you *out* of—"

"But I can help!" I press, trying to sound more certain than I feel. "I can get leverage."

"Galen," Cassia tries again. Her face is meek, but I see the calculation behind her eyes. "The things she could learn may be invaluable to—"

"And risk the Player realizing whose family she comes from?" Galen raises his voice. "She is a *child*, Cassia."

"I am *not* a child," I grind out. "Dear gods, Galen, I am only *four years* younger than your twenty-two!" Besides, I've survived this long. I fought a Player and lived to see another day. Clearly I am capable.

In fact, this may be the best chance I have to prove it. How could the council *not* pardon my ruined mark if I deliver them everything they need to stop the Playhouse?

The possibility gleams like a shiny trophy in my mind. I

wouldn't be Riven-cursed-by-a-Player. I wouldn't even be Riven-the-dead-Peacemaker's-daughter anymore.

I would just be Riven. I could finish what my father started. I could do what he couldn't.

People won't be afraid of that Riven. There'll be a place for that Riven.

A stinging sensation brings my attention to the place my mark used to be. I have a score to settle with Jude now.

Maybe I can do both at once.

The hairs on the back of my neck stand up. My ear has grown familiar with Jude's deliberate, quick steps. He's closing in on the hall. I'm out of time.

And my mind is made up.

"Get a message to the council for me," I say, snapping my gaze up to Galen. "Tell them to ready a new contract for the Playhouse to sign, one that details every ban on the North and the Cut imaginable. The Playhouse is to surrender their every right to perform in the North."

Cassia stares at me like I've grown a second head. "Their director will never sign—"

"Would he trade one of his Players' lives for it?" I ask urgently. "If the North had one of the Players as collateral. Would Silenus make a trade? Peace in exchange for the life of his Player. That's how the first treaty was forged."

Even Cassia steps back at this. "Riven, to capture a Player would mean—"

"Do *not* entertain this, Cassia," Galen says firmly, anger falling across his expression as he turns to scold me. "Whatever you're thinking is *not* worth—"

"But it worked once!" My grade-school memory cards flicker through my mind. "A Player was captured and traded in exchange for peace." It kept the Playhouse out for five hundred years. Why couldn't it keep them out for five hundred more?

The door, which I've chained shut, shakes. I hear Jude on the other side. Along with furious mutterings that sound suspiciously like, "My kingdom for a moment's peace from that woman."

I swallow, lowering my voice to a whisper, studying their tour schedule, calculating the dates.

RIVEN: "Tell the council to prepare to make a trade with the Playhouse in Syrene. I'll meet them there." I breathe, glancing toward the door. "And I'm bringing their Lead Player."

I push away from the mirror, banishing the connection before Galen can respond.

For the first time, the roar of rage in my head sounds more like applause.

I've just barely stuffed the tour schedule back in the drawer and slammed it shut when the chain on the lock snaps.

The door awkwardly creaks open, Jude waiting on the other side, arms crossed. His eyes take in my destruction with a single bored glance.

JUDE: "You know, I was about to do the silliest thing and look for you in *your* room." His eyes land pointedly on me. "And then I asked myself: *Where, oh where, would Alistaire be?*"

RIVEN: "I was just leaving." My eyes stall on the quiver of arrows secured to his back and the uniform stitched carefully across his broad shoulders.

JUDE: "*My*, Alistaire. Don't look so scared. This is just a costume from tonight's show. I haven't come to personally execute you." There's a cut below his eye, bleeding but healing rapidly. "We almost lost that girl, by the way. The boy's sister." I picture the twins. "No true knack for Reality Suspension, that one. They're cleaning up the stage now."

Nausea rises in my throat at the casual declaration, and I wonder what horrors the auditionee might have been subjected to onstage. Jude strolls into his room and begins loosening the golden armlets from his forearms. I unintentionally let my gaze flicker to the drawer, then to the mirror, paranoid.

JUDE: "Speaking of Reality Suspension, you're all...here, yes?"

I narrow my eyes, ignoring the scorching pain at the base of my throat. "*Most* of me made it."

"Well, that part couldn't be helped. I meant up here." He taps a finger at his temple and drops his weapons in a pile on the floor. "Memories and all, you know. Reality Suspension can be...messy. And your mind was so—"

"What?" I ask, suddenly at attention. "What about my mind?"

Jude's eyes widen, like he said something he didn't mean to. For once, he struggles to find words. "Reality Suspension, it can offer a...glimpse of sorts, into your—"

"A glimpse?" I ask, barely tamping down my rage. "Inside my *head*?"

"It's not like looking at a finished portrait, Alistaire! Just small corners of one. Loose pieces of a larger puzzle. People's minds are complicated places. You—you *feel* it more than anything."

Does he know about Galen? Who my father was? Does he know my *name*—

"What did you see?" I demand. "Or *feel*," I add, accusing. And he called *me* a snoop.

But for once, Jude doesn't quip back, doesn't hurl my own mocking tone back at me. I glare daggers at him, but his own gaze is unreadable—no pity there, not even judgment. "I'm sorry, Alistaire," he says, tone too controlled in contrast to my outburst. "Truly." For what, he doesn't say.

And I don't ask. I'm skilled at matching anger for anger, insult for insult. I don't know what to do with apologies, though.

My shoulders drop a little, the embers of my rage burning out.

"Anyway." He clears his throat, recovering. "I only meant to tell you Sil is *sorely* disappointed over you missing tonight's performance."

"Just wait until he hears I won't be at any of the other ones, either," I dodge, diverting my attention to the bookshelf at my back. Anything to avoid looking Jude in the eye will suffice. I pluck a trinket off the shelf, examining.

A frustrated exhale. "Sil wants you tested across Crafts, under his eye. I've kindly volunteered to do the honors. Your little stunt with Mattia earlier today caught his attention."

My mood darkens. "I don't want it."

JUDE: "Well, you have it. And worse, you have Mattia's. Honestly, Alistaire, you should know by now never to go for an actor's most vital organ."

I hesitate, trying to remember where I aimed my knife. "Heart?"

Jude frowns. "Ego. But we'll worry about that later." He wanders to a cream-colored settee, throwing his long legs over the coffee table. His boots have blood on them. "And I'd put that down if I were you."

I ignore him and pop open the wooden case I've plucked off the shelf. Inside, between folds of purple silk, lies a small vial filled with a substance the color of rosewater, its silver cap twisted into the shape of a serpent. "What is this?"

"Poison of Echidna," he explains, taking his rings off one by one and placing them on a side table. "Rarer than Persephone's flowers in the winter. Incapacitates you so quickly, you don't have the breath to suspend your reality. Even Titus won't go near it."

My hands freeze around the box. "Why do *you* have it?"

JUDE: "It was a gift. From Syrene's ruler to yours truly. A promise of sorts, you might say." He chuckles under his breath. "Would've been outright *rude* if I hadn't sent him something back."

RIVEN: "What did you..." Syrene is perhaps the North's *most* hostile territory to the Playhouse. Three Players were executed there before the Cut was completed. "Uh, send?"

JUDE: "My regards and my knife in the hands of his mistress." He smirks. "You'd think those in such high rank would bother checking where their loved ones spend their time. She was a fan."

I close my jaw, which had fallen open. I remember learning of the sudden death of Syrene's ruler in school not too long ago. He was succeeded by his daughter under suspicious circumstances. "You convinced his mistress to...kill him?"

"I asked *nicely*." Jude's eyes glow, as if to emphasize how he managed that. "Anyway, we have a deal, Alistaire. You've garnered

Sil's attention now, and we need to talk."

I stare at the poison. Too bad Jude is no use as a bargaining chip if he's dead. Otherwise, it might be handy. "I don't want to talk. And I'm *definitely* not going to train with you."

Whatever endless supply of patience that runs in Jude has apparently, at last, been exhausted. His boots hit the floor in quick succession as he stalks toward me. And with each step, I'm almost certain the room shrinks.

I whirl, steeling myself and whatever nerves haven't been fried by the past twenty-four hours as Jude swiftly closes the distance between us, a look on his face that makes me think my cooperation is no longer a cute, optional bonus.

The box is plucked out of my hand.

"Hey," I snap, temper flaring as Jude reaches over my head. I glance up in time to see him place the poison on a ledge out of my reach. My back digs into the hard edge of the bookshelf, but there's no more room to move as Jude braces his free hands on either side of me, close enough to notice the warmth that radiates through his costume.

"Sil's attention is a *good* thing," he says. My gaze darts away from his, focusing instead on the green jewel hanging from his ear. "Sil may let us choose our contenders, but he's the one who chooses who stays. If he dislikes you or, worse, gets *bored* with you, your stay here will end."

Warnings shout through my mind, but I press my shoulders back. I've despised being so tall most of my life, feeling like my existence takes up too much space in any given room. But craning my neck to meet Jude's eyes, I find myself wishing I were taller. "What, that old man will kill me?" I challenge.

"He'll make me do it," he returns bluntly. I grind my teeth together before opening my mouth, about to snap that I'd like to see him try when he adds, "And I fear I may even begin to miss your vicious mouth and incomprehensible need to reorganize my room."

My brow pinches, my mind scrambling to analyze whatever

I misheard. That almost sounded like a...*compliment*? No, not quite. But my mouth opens and nothing comes out.

A slow, knowing grin widens on Jude's mouth. "Alistaire, love, I don't think I've ever seen so much color in your face."

The entire room is suddenly deprived of air, and what's left of it is scented with whatever citrus and hyacinth perfume Jude probably dunks his clothes in. "What do you—" *No, don't ask that.* "You aren't mad?"

He glances down at the carcass of what used to be a silk throw pillow and the scattered feathers trailing across the floor. Lightly kicks at the ones between us. "I've learned not to get attached to things," he says dully, then turns that gaze, which is starting to feel like one of the stage lights, back on mine.

"What are you—" Apparently, there are no clever words to be found in the shrinking space between us. "What are you staring at?"

"I was trying to work out if a creature like you has ever admired someone in her entire life." Jude tilts his head, amused, studying me with an intensity that makes me want to vanish into walls. "Do you fancy me, Alistaire? Go on, answer. We need to make sure you can lie."

My defenses shoot high, right hand going protectively to my throat. To my horror, no words find my tongue. My mark is long gone, and still, the simple deception of *no* feels like pushing a boulder uphill. "I think you're heartless and spoiled and violent—and have far too much power for one person."

Jude's smile stays perfectly in place. Widens, even. "That isn't the question I asked."

He's mocking me. This must be entertaining to him.

"Lie to me," he presses.

My lips glue themselves shut while I wish him a slow, painful death with my eyes. "Not until you tell me where my knife is."

"Long gone," he sneers, his voice barely more than a whisper. "Fine. Something easy. How about we start with something true."

"There will be *nothing* left when I am through with you."

The words come so fast, they startle me. Jude straightens, even takes a step back. In the candlelight, something that almost looks like hurt flickers behind his eyes. It's gone too quickly to tell. "And now," he says, the words strained. "A *lie*."

I open my mouth. "My name is Alistaire Hunt."

Jude's eyes light up with relief as he shouts, "Ha!" and claps. I choke on the deception. My blood feels like it's on fire. The room opens up, cooler as more space carves between us.

"I'm going now," I say weakly and head for the door.

"Alistaire," Jude says. I turn. "You got the Reality Suspension you were so curious about. And a taste of the Craft you so love to loathe. How do you feel?"

My mouth drops open, and I clamp it shut before I can tell him the honest truth.

Because I feel...*better.* Like some of the weight has lifted off my shoulders.

But it's not enough. Not *nearly.* Not while that familiar ice still seeps into my bones. It hits me with a devastating note of finality: Reality Suspension, a tentative death or not, failed to banish the poison from my veins.

I turn to leave.

"Wait," he calls, and I pause again. "If you—if you hear anything strange tonight, stay inside, all right? Don't leave your room."

I don't bother asking why. I doubt he'll tell me. "Good night, Jude," I say warily.

"We can make it through this, Alistaire," he says, like we're *allies.* This competition may pit me against the other auditionees, but I'm certain we both know who the real battle is between.

My eyes lock on to the quiver of arrows he laid on the floor. Props. Normal arrows. Useless against a Player.

I hide my grin and the plan forming behind it.

That Eleutheraen arrow that was shot at the Playhouse is still here somewhere.

And suddenly, I know exactly how I will deliver Jude to the council, *and* how I will escape the Playhouse.

Act II: Scene III

The screams begin thirty minutes before curfew, ricocheting through the halls like shattering glass.

Don't leave your room, Jude said. As if I'd listen.

I'm not sure why I thought the candelabra over the hearth was my best weapon of choice, but there wasn't much time to think on it. Tearing the door open, I burst out of my dressing room, brandishing the heavy fixture.

And I'm not the only one. Outside, my fellow auditionees—Phileas, Tig, and Linos—peer nervously from their doors that pocket the hall, dressed in expensive silk nightclothes for bed.

Except one of us is missing: Thyone. Phileas's twin sister.

Barefoot but still fully clothed due to the *other* plans I had tonight, I ease into the hall.

Jude flings his door open, hair tousled, jewelry gone, shirt half buttoned, like he'd been readying for bed when the commotion began. I don't have time to register much else before he catches my elbow. "Alistaire, *wait*." His eyes aren't on me; they're searching the hall. "You don't want to see what's about to—"

Thyone's door soars open, crashes against the wall. Through it, Player Arius hauls the auditionee's thrashing body out by the elbows. Behind him, Silenus.

The director pauses, taking in the mixture of curious and terrified faces.

SIL: "*Good night*, everyone," he says pleasantly over Thyone's cries and carries after Arius, who is now pulling the girl toward the common room.

Why is Arius dragging her like that? She's his contender—

"Wait, *wait*—" the girl shouts. Her screams shatter into wailing.

At the cry, I break from Jude and bolt down the hall, wishing I had my Eleutheraen knife. But by the time I peer behind me, the other auditionees have vanished to hide in their rooms—except Phileas. He looks after his sister with a sort of anguished indecision, his knuckles gripping the doorframe so hard, they've gone white.

Then his gaze flickers to mine, reaching a decision. He shakes his head and shuts the door.

What the hell? What is happening—

The other Players haven't bothered to leave their rooms at all. Except for Jude, who catches up to me. "Alistaire, don't watch—"

But I've already reached the end of the hall, where Sil is standing casually by the fireplace, cleaning his glasses. Meanwhile, Arius is holding Thyone's arms down to prevent her from escaping. The Player's expression tells a different story, though, the panes of his face constricted and grieved, like he can't bear what he's doing.

Sil barely takes notice of my presence, or Jude's, as he pulls that strange book from his pocket. The Script. He flips it open, runs his pen down the page, like he's looking for something to cross out. "I do apologize for the inconvenience," he says to Thyone, whose indiscernible cries echo from the amber walls to the marble floors. "My Playhouse only has room for one new actor, and cuts are necessary. You understand."

Cuts? Gods, no—wait—

She bolts, almost breaking free from Arius—

And lunging at Sil, the tips of her fingers barely brushing the Script as he sharply jerks it from her reach.

Her cry vanishes mid-shout like a light flickering off the moment her hand makes contact with the book. She falls to her knees and blinks several times, her eyes blank, confused.

Sil shakes his head, mere disappointment crossing his face. Jude's warning plays through my mind. *If you value your life, you'll leave that cursed book alone.*

Before I can register what's happened, Arius's strong hands close around Thyone's head, his fingers digging into her white-blond hair.

Her eyes, still gleaming with gold, find mine, her mouth open in a plea, but nothing comes out. She doesn't quite look scared—she looks...*confused.*

She's a Reveler, I try to remind myself. A Playhouse worshipper from the South. She signed up for this on purpose. *Right?*

At the moment, though, she just looks like a person.

I run forward, my heart dropping through the floor as I bolt at Arius—

He snaps her neck. One swift, violent motion.

Then it's over. I stand, cold and still and shaken as Arius scoops the girl's body into his arms and follows Sil to the stairs, like nothing at all has happened.

Sil smiles politely in passing, tucking that book back into his pocket. "Good evening, Alistaire. Jude."

I turn to Jude as they leave, my body numb. My vision swims, drifting over the walls as if they'll have answers. "That...that was Reality Suspension, right?" My breaths are coming too quick. My head feels light. "He was *testing* her—her skills in—"

Jude is already shaking his head. "It's how eliminations are carried out in the Playhouse. Like I told you." His voice, usually so steady, sounds like a thread stretched too tight. "It's a casting call. Whoever the director thinks is right for the cast..." He trails off. "We choose our contenders, but Sil chooses who stays."

I can't breathe. It's common knowledge that auditionees don't leave the Playhouse. But—but I never imagined seeing it in action, that it would be so—

And Jude wasn't lying about the Script, then. I don't know what happened to Thyone when her hand brushed that book, but I know I don't want it to happen to me.

But why? I stare at a scuff mark on the marble, where the heel of Thyone's shoe had dragged. *Why not just let her go? Send her away from the Playhouse? Why* this?

I look up, as if I'm going to find comfort in the eyes of a *Player.* They probably revel in this horror.

At the moment, though, Jude doesn't look like he's reveling

in anything. His jaw tightens, that blithely aloof expression of his almost cracking at the edges, and I realize I asked my questions out loud. “Don’t look for meaning in everything, Alistaire.” He turns to leave. “You might find it.”

A moment later, he’s vanished down the hall.

Fine. He can go to bed. I have work to do.

And it starts tonight.

Act II: Scene IV

A second night in the Playhouse is two nights too many. Luckily, I won't be trapped much longer. Provided I survive this. Well, and provided I can find it—or *her*, I suppose.

The Prop Master of the Playhouse: Marigold.

The first shadow comes five minutes to midnight, fast and delicate, just like the one Jude chased away yesterday. Nyxene: a ghostly Stage Manager checking that her actors have properly gone to their beds.

A finger of shadow reaches under my dressing room door, as if to scold me for being awake.

I hold my breath, watching, my feet at the threshold of my sleeping quarters.

There are things that move in the Playhouse after dark that mean you harm, Jude warned. But I imagine they can't mean me any more harm than *he* does, so.

My eyes track the last of the dying candlelight on the mantel beyond my bedroom, waiting, waiting...

Somewhere below, the great Playhouse clock resounds its midnight call, thrumming beneath the floorboards. Curfew.

The hot coals in the fireplace are dimming, dimming...

Gone. Dark.

Satisfied that I'm in my bedroom, the Stage Manager, at last, retreats—presumably to check on everyone else. Which should keep her busy for a few minutes.

I bolt through the short hall, across my dressing room, and for the door, slipping through and shooting down the corridor in the dark.

Then, pressing a guiding hand to one wall of the common room, I run.

My memory has always been sharp. Entire chapters I glimpsed

in history books sometimes stay lodged in my brain for ages.

But tonight, there's a specific section I mentally mull over in my mind. *The Playhouse: A Captivating History of Craft and Horrors, Vol 2.* Chapter Sixteen. *All items belonging to the Playhouse either come from, or are to be examined by, the Prop Master.*

That Eleutheraen arrowhead that was shot at the Players—Jude told Mattia to give it to the Prop Master. Probably to be dismantled.

And I need it to get out of here. I'm leaving, and I'm taking Jude with me.

By the time I reach the first floor, the cold is eating me alive. The Playhouse, normally bursting with warmth during the day, is colder than the bottom of the ocean at night. My breaths form little ghosts at my chapped lips.

The Prop Master resides in the deepest crevice of the Playhouse. Most sources suggest the monster dwells at the bottom of the Labyrinth Steps.

I glimpse the stage as I pass through the wings, an eerie yellow light hanging over it. A ghost light. I've heard they leave them on to keep away the spirits, an old legend. My mind briefly flutters to Gene Hunt before pressing on.

Shivering, I set my jaw and inch into the murkiness of the twisting backstage maze until discovering the south tower. After what feels like an eternity searching, the tightness in my chest eases as I finally reach a door that reads PROP ROOM, barely legible by moonlight.

It opens to a stairwell and a set of narrow steps that spirals down. Moonlight skirts through slats overhead, illuminating the Labyrinth Steps.

Well. Down I go.

The stairway seems to wind on endlessly. I'm not sure how much time passes, but at some point I pass a landing with an ornate sign indicating a corridor that leads to the arena, which sits under the stage. I ignore it and continue down.

Desperate to distract myself, or maybe to prepare myself, I sift through the pages of my mind until coming across the words of *The Prop Master's Tale.*

They called Marigold the most beautiful woman in Theatron, I read mentally. *But fearful that she would grow old and her beauty would fade, vain Marigold climbed Mount Eleutherae before the first Players emerged.*

I descend lower into the dark, my ankles sore from the cold. But the farther I go, the more unbearably icy it gets.

The beauty Players possess still belonged to the well back then. When Marigold stared into the well of Dionysus's blood, it reflected the most magnificent version of herself, twisted with Craft.

Stumbling over an uneven step, I curse. It's even frostier now, and my shoulders ache. My body begs me to turn around.

I ease my mind back to the story before the cold wins, picturing the words. But the deeper I go, the more certain I am that the quiet humming emanating below is not in my head. I breathe heavily, force myself to keep going.

Greedy, Marigold stayed there for months, unable to look away from her own beauty, until one day, she fell into the well.

I gulp a breath of cold air. Marigold felt less threatening when she was a page in my textbook and not dwelling at the bottom of these steps.

She emerged monstrous, gold clinging to her skin, her eyes, her hair. She has not aged a day since.

I pause as I hear the lilting notes of an eerie lullaby echo through the stairwell.

A chill skitters down my spine, and it's an effort to keep myself going. One, two, three more steps, and my ankle hits the final one. I walk across the small landing to the outline of a door, a quiet rustling on the other side.

I hold my breath and lower my grip to the golden handle, continuing the story.

When the first Players emerged from the well, Marigold's obsession shifted to them instead. She searched down the mountain for the Players, dragging away unlucky passersby to check their eyes for gold—and tearing them out if they were not.

Praying the hinges won't creak, I inch open the door, and the scents of cinder, beeswax, and paint rush out.

Inside, the warmth of blessed light kisses my skin. I might be inside an underground cage with a monster, but at least I can feel my toes again.

The brilliance of the well left Marigold's vision poor and damaged, but seeing her devotion to the Players, Silenus took her into the Playhouse.

My surroundings quickly overshadow my relief. I'm being watched. Not by a person, or even a monster, but by the walls—painted with thousands of detailed golden eyes. Some, a pale yellowy shade. Others, burning with deep hues of orange. A few are almond-shaped, others hooded. Still others are round as coins with spiderlike lashes.

One pair, oddly enough, emerald green.

The flickering oil lamps cast the illusion that they're blinking at me.

It's so warm in here, I find myself unbuttoning my jacket.

Since then, Marigold has crafted every prop onstage, asking nothing in return, only that she can reside in the same quarters as the Players.

The next thing I notice is an easel and the striking oil painting of Jude staring back at me. It sits below a set of glass wind chimes, which seems odd in a place with no wind.

I avert my gaze to a golden statue in the corner, then to a silver lyre leaning against a delicately painted tree. Lastly, to a shelf of skulls—which I *hope* are props—flanking a music box that plays merrily along.

My shoulders sag. I'm not sure why I expected the Eleutheraen arrow to be neatly stored in a glass case at the center of the room or something. This place is a mess.

A furnace blazes in one corner, where several long broadswords hang over a workbench of blacksmithing tools. Thick webs enmesh the ceiling. I make a face at the rather large spider spinning down to my right.

Then the golden statue moves. It's not a statue.

I duck behind the canvas of Jude.

"Player?" the Prop Master asks sharply. No, not sharply. *Desperately.*

She may have spotted me, but then I spot something, too, when I peek around the easel.

There, hanging at her hip, is the dismantled arrowhead.

I am *not* leaving without it.

The arrowhead swings as she rushes forward.

Gathering my courage, I ease out from behind the canvas but stay in its shadow.

Marigold is smaller than I thought she would be, shorter than me, with skin the same gold as her lips. Tight coils of thick hair are dried stiff around her shoulder, shimmering with Craft. A carefully tailored dress patched with dozens of different patterns, materials, and colors clings to her waist.

Her eyes fix on mine. Or at least, I think they do. A haze of gold hangs over her pupils, too, but there's a warm brown color peeking out at the edges of her irises.

There's no denying—she's striking, almost devastatingly so.

"Player," she breathes.

Thank the gods. Her vision really is poor.

"Yes," I whisper and wince. That's my second lie tonight. "I've come to collect my arrowhead. Thank you for holding it for me."

Her hands grip the arrowhead at her hip. "A gift. From Mattia," she hisses, revealing a golden tongue and teeth. "Dangerous for you Players. For me to keep you safe."

Well, she does have a point.

"Sil has sent for it," I lie. That makes three. "I'd hate to tell him you've disobeyed a Player. Are you so ungrateful for your position here?"

Her eyes widen, and she snatches the arrowhead from her hip, thrusting it toward me. "Take it!"

Don't mind if I do, I think, stepping forward and reaching my hand out to clasp the object.

We both seem to notice my mistake at the same time. Me, when I glimpse the mirror leaning on the wall behind her and notice the jacket I stupidly unbuttoned. And Marigold, when those cold eyes land on the blistering remains of my scorched mark peeking out from under the bandage at my throat.

Her hands tighten around the arrowhead just as I grasp it. "Marked," she whispers with disgust.

Well. I guess her vision isn't *that* bad.

My eyes flicker to the painting of Jude as the naivete of the legend hits me.

She paints. She makes the props. She can see just fine.

Marigold tugs the arrowhead back with alarming strength. But I'm stubborn, and so I go with it, flying forward and finding myself closer to a mythical monster than I ever wanted to be.

"Oh, this? Just stage makeup!" I squeak. Four lies.

Marigold stares at me the way one would expect an ancient monster you're trying to gaslight would stare. *Definitely* not blind. Her eyes examine me, narrowing as she opens her mouth. I've been so focused on her teeth being gold that I hadn't noticed they're also sharpened into little points. This is easier to observe when they're two inches from my face.

Something bites into my side, and I shriek as she extracts what I can only describe as tiny daggers for fingernails. "Mortal," she sneers.

The crisis council in my head panics and starts tearing open old files for any helpful information. Weaknesses. Bargaining tools. *Something.*

Her dagger hand aims for my heart now, and all I can think is the little Reality Suspension trick Jude did earlier would be handy right about now.

Jude. My eyes swivel past her, where the striking painting of him rests on the easel.

"Jude sent me!" I shout in a panic. Something softens in her eyes at the name, so I run with my fifth lie. "With a message. I can prove it."

"Jude," she repeats, her grip on me loosening just a little, and I free a hand.

Another passage from the text comes back to me, and I grab hold of it: *As Prop Master, Marigold is known to hoard beautiful things.*

I dip my hand into my jacket pocket, extracting the golden Finders Keepers ring Jude gave me when we first met. "Here," I rasp, holding it between us as light bounces off its surface. *Sorry, Haris.*

I mentally make a note to swipe more jewelry from Jude at my earliest convenience. It can't be *too* hard to snatch one of those rings he leaves on his vanity.

Marigold covers a gasp with her hand but doesn't reach to grab the ring.

I push my hand out farther. "He told me to give you this…as a token of his love."

Six lies now. It feels easier.

Her eyes flicker down to the ring again as she lowers her hand, a gleeful smile pulling at the corners of her mouth. "Jude," she repeats, giddy this time. Or as giddy as a monster can be, I guess.

"He wishes to wed," I add for extra sparkle. "He'll send for you soon."

I'm not sure she hears me. But she drops the arrowhead, which I catch as she tugs the ring from my fingers and examines it carefully between her sharp fingernails.

Meanwhile, I take my cue to leave. I'm backing toward the door when my eyes catch on something heavy and golden strapped at her ankle, secured to the wall.

A chain. A *golden* chain. The Eleutheraen gold still in my blood sings to its neighbor. No wonder she never leaves this cave. She *can't*.

As I make a hasty exit for the stairs, I decide I'll be paying Marigold another visit.

"Don't tell anyone about this, and I might even bring you the finger that ring came from," I call over my shoulder as I shut the door behind me, this time not lying.

Because if that chain can hold Marigold, I'll bet it can hold Jude.

Act II: Scene V

No one mentions Thyone's absence in the dining hall the next morning. I glance more than once in the direction of her brother, wondering at the relaxed way he eats his breakfast, like his sister wasn't brutally murdered a mere twelve hours ago.

Huddled at my private table in the corner, I fight to keep my eyes open. I'm not even sure how I dressed myself this morning. After discovering a myriad of costumes miraculously sized to me in my closet, I ripped the least offensive one from the rack: a white chiffon contraption with a high collar that I personally think is more ribbon than dress. But at least it covers the bandage at the base of my throat. Cicero apparently works fast.

I'd say the dress feels a *bit* much for breakfast, but Mattia is draped across a wingchair in a floor-length ballgown embroidered with rubies. A jeweled diadem is pinned into her blue-black hair. Her bright eyes fly across the heavy book in her hands, her skin gleaming more luminous with golden light when she reads, red lips mouthing the words silently.

She plops the play on the table, resigned.

MATTIA: "Sil is going to kill me. I can never remember my lines for this one."

TITUS: "Don't worry over it. I don't even remember yesterday's rehearsal!"

MATTIA: "That's because you were *roaring drunk*." She emphasizes the point with a disapproving frown.

TITUS: "Better roaring drunk than murderously sober." He blows her a mocking kiss.

I yawn again from my lonely table, reaching for my cup of tea. I may be dead on my feet, but I have the first piece I need for my plan: The arrowhead is stashed behind the old clock in my dressing room.

Once I figure out how to retrieve that golden chain, I'm out of here the moment the Playhouse lands in Syrene. And so is Jude, whether he likes it or not. I have a trade to make.

Exhausted from my little excursion last night, I rest my head on my palm and twist my waist to gaze out the windows in the dining hall. The Playhouse is hedged on a cliffside overlooking crumbling sandstone buildings overgrown with ivy and cracked gray streets below, which means we must have moved again.

I heard an auditionee say we're in Diazoma now, which is yet another area of the map I did *not* have on my bucket list.

A shock of copper hair flutters in the corner of my vision. I pull my gaze from the window as two overly full plates are set on the table. I don't bother to lift my head from my palm.

JUDE: "Alistaire, do you know the most *peculiar* thing happened this morning when I went to pick up my prop box for this evening's show from darling Marigold?"

Jude slides the food I didn't ask for in my direction with two fingers and invites himself to sit down across from me, dressed head to toe in black today, several thin gold necklaces layered across his collarbone.

I pluck a grape from the fruit on the plate and pop it into my mouth. "Oh?" I inquire, innocent.

JUDE: "It would seem I am to be wed. She's understandably very excited about the whole thing. But as I'm sure you can imagine, breaking off an engagement with one of Theatron's most feared creatures was not first on my list this morning." He leans forward, burnished hair falling into his eyes. "You wouldn't know where she got my ring, now would you?"

"Ring? Oh, I don't know," I say virtuously, plucking a pastry from my plate. "Maybe I dropped it somewhere."

"Mm-hmm. Well, don't you worry. I've explained to her that you and I are *madly* in love and that I shall never love another. Unless, say, something terrible were to happen to you." He gives me a deadpan look and weaves his fingers together on the table—it would appear the signet ring has in fact found its way back to his own hand. "I don't recommend venturing down there again. I can't imagine she'll take so kindly to you twice."

I mutter a curse and mentally cross out tonight's plan to use a lock of his hair as a bargaining chip. Not that I had a plan on how I was to acquire *that*, either.

"Have you slept since yesterday, Alistaire?" He asks the question like he already knows the answer.

Ever since Reality Suspension—since *death* tore that birdlike thing from my chest—I haven't dared to sleep.

The pastry turns bitter in my mouth, and I place the rest back on my plate. Jude reaches over, shaking his head at me and placing it back in my hand.

We both seem to notice it at once, that touching doesn't hurt anymore. That shock my mark sent through both of us at the slightest brush feels more like a faint skitter of electricity, new and strange but not unpleasant.

I pull back and drop the pastry on the plate again.

The sleeplessness must be written under my eyes, because Jude clears his throat and says, "Your life isn't going to escape you while you sleep. Reality Suspension doesn't happen by accident."

I lift my tea, which has gone cold. "Reality Suspension, it's—" I search for words but come up empty-handed. "Wrong."

"I agree, but some of us would rather be wrong than dead." I roll my eyes, and he goes on. "Anyway, eat. We don't have much time."

Oh gods, what *now*? "For what?"

Jude tilts one corner of his mouth up and says, "For me to train you! You're onstage this week."

Act II: Scene VI

A spotlight claps on overhead as we cross the stage. The auditorium is empty, our steps echoing into the abyss of scarlet seats as I follow Jude to the center platform.

"Watch your step," he says. "There's a trapdoor there at the center of the stage. I've fallen through it twice by accident."

RIVEN: "I'm not performing in one of your wretched shows."

He turns to face me.

JUDE: "I can't put you onstage at all until you do a Craft binding."

RIVEN: "Whatever that means, I'm not interested."

JUDE: "You're tethered to reality. That mark may be gone, but there's still enough Eleutheraen gold in your blood to give you away onstage." He shakes his head, and a cuff of silver peeks out at the top of his ear, between tousled locks of dark hair that fall into his eyes.

Yeah, I probably wouldn't have been able to knife one of those hairs for Marigold no matter how subtle I was. I bet he counts them before he goes to sleep.

JUDE: "Craft binding is a loan of power. A link between your life and mine. I'm going to teach you how to create a bridge to that Craft—between you and what you will become."

Become?

He takes a few long steps back, until there's a wide berth between us. He gestures at the emptiness. "This is the gap. Imagine it as a bottomless abyss, and that you, as you always do, *desperately* want to reach me—more than anything in the world."

RIVEN: "I think I'd rather fall into the bottomless abyss."

JUDE: "*This* gap is what you face when going into character. But we can't reach across such a gap, now can we? You need a *bridge* between actor and character. The tie between reality and story. It makes everything else possible—Mimicry, Compulsion. Without a bridge to summon those things across to you, what are your options? Your Craft would have to jump back and forth over the gap. And you're already exhausted as it is."

I frown. "I'm not playing a character *right now*."

Jude grins. "Alistaire, we are all of us playing characters. Even when the character is ourselves." He gestures between us again. "But *without* a bridge to close this gap between reality and story or the energy to jump across it..." He looks down at me and arches an eyebrow as if to say, *Go on. Guess.*

I don't.

JUDE: "You *fall*."

The words echo off the stage, striking a nervous, hollow feeling in my stomach. Maybe breakfast wasn't a good idea.

RIVEN: "And if I simply don't create a bridge across this imaginary gap?"

JUDE: "*Not* imaginary, Alistaire. If the Playhouse identifies something that doesn't fit in a scene onstage—reality, for instance—it eliminates it. Craft—" I balk at the word. *Player magic*. "Craft is the thing that cloaks you, a lifeline that connects us onstage. So if your Craft cannot reach you and something *unplanned* happens—" He carelessly slides a finger across his neck to indicate *lights out*.

I roll my eyes. "I seem to have survived your Reality Suspension just fine without it."

"And you can consider yourself lucky I managed it," he says, frowning. "That's the difference between carrying someone across a bridge and jumping over a cliff with their weight on your back. That wiped me out for the rest of the day. So, for my sake, let's try, yes?"

Well. If he's going to make me feel *guilty* about it.

JUDE: "Repeat after me." The air grows warmer, the ground thrumming beneath us. "*Methexis.*"

There's a rising warmth beneath my feet, the marble heating as if the stage has just woken up. It brightens around me, shimmering gold and white. With little fight left in my tired bones, I shut my eyes, bite my tongue. The word tastes strange, though I can't place why. *"Methexis,"* I repeat.

The center of the stage feels like it's sinking beneath me, and I tense.

JUDE: "Good. Now open your eyes."

When my eyes flicker open, I swallow a scream.

I'm still standing in the auditorium. Everything is the same—except the stage itself.

Beneath my feet, the marble now looks like glass, sleek and translucent. Under the clear floor is a tumultuous sea of shadows, dark and wild.

I tear my gaze from the darkness beneath, looking to Jude across from me.

The glass is different where he stands. Amid the roiling shadows beneath him, a luminous tendril of gold rises upward. Its glow cuts through the darkness like the line of an anchor thrown into the ocean, and Jude is the ship. The light ends at his heels, a thread that sews his flesh to the stage.

He steps forward, and the tendrils of gold follow him beneath like strings on a marionette.

RIVEN: "What is this?" My voice echoes back a hundred times over. I clap a hand to my mouth.

JUDE: "A place the audience cannot see, just outside the bounds of reality." In its departure from reality's restrictions, Jude's voice takes on a thunderous edge, reverberating off every nonexistent slat of marble. He gestures to the roaring sea of darkness churning under the glassy stage.

Then I see it. Through the darkness, what seems like miles below: *light*. Brilliant and gold like the sun, like the threads holding on to Jude. It can't reach me, and I can't reach it.

"Craft," I say to myself. My eyes shoot up. "This is yours?"

"I'm its keeper. Craft is what connects the cast; we channel it from one another. It's why a Player can't be brought back if they fail to suspend their reality during an onstage death—your life has to *go* to another Player, through the binding." *Craft binding.*

"Craft isn't a matter of quantity," he says, curling his hand into a fist. Below, threads of gold respond, drawing closer to the surface, humming with power. "You can think of it as a weapon. A blade is only as lethal as the hands that wield it."

I'm probably going to regret asking this, but I say, "How do you wield it?" I can't seem to take my eyes off the gold swirling below the stage. It almost seems to be alive, *breathing.*

"All Players have a driving force, a motivation that binds them." Jude's steps stop short. "What is it that drives you, Alistaire? Picture a desire. Follow that thread."

Something tugs in my chest. I'm pretty sure I desire to reach those coils of gold at the bottom.

Cautiously, I lean down to press my palm to the stage.

Just as quickly, a sizzling pain of warning grabs at my throat, seems to choke the air from it. Below, the gold dives deeper into the shadows. I flinch and skitter back, ready to bolt into the wings.

Jude utters something, and the real world solidifies again, the white of the marble flooding back over the stage and disguising what lies beneath it.

My blood freezes cold, pulses that awful ice through my entire body.

Jude studies me with pressed lips. "You'll endanger both yourself and me if you let that happen onstage. Reality is slippery. You'll fall right back in if you lose your focus like that."

"Oh? I'll suspiciously die onstage, then. Like Gene Hunt," I pant, fuming. The convenience of her death has prickled my mind since the Players brought it up. I gesture broadly at the stage. "She was Lead Player and just *forgot* to suspend her reality for her own death scene? Conveniently leaving her role open for you?"

Jude looks at me like I've slapped him. "She didn't *forget*, Alistaire—"

RIVEN: "Then why did she die?"

SIL: "Did it on purpose! Haven't you heard the stories?"

We both startle as Sil wanders down the center aisle. "Drank a glass holding as much poison as it did wine. Right onstage, too!"

Sil shrugs, climbing the steps of the stage. "Her death wasn't even scripted. She didn't suspend her reality. Wildly unprofessional of her! Talented girl, incredibly. Too dedicated for anything to be done, though."

There it is, that cold politeness again—the same that accompanied his visit to Thyone last night. Like death itself is little more than an inconvenience to his theatre.

Wariness overcomes Jude like a shroud as he sets his eyes on Sil.

SIL: "It has, of course, given birth to endless rumors. 'The Ghost of the Playhouse'! Spirits and nonsense. Many now believe a Player *must* be killed in the arena to die a true death, or else haunt the halls of my theatre." He sighs. "But Gene, disappointingly, didn't die in the arena. She died right where you're standing."

I shudder, unconsciously taking a step back. I've heard the story—everyone has at some point—but never much thought about it. I was always more concerned with what followed Gene's final performance: my father standing from the audience as she died and running like mad for the exit. His body being found on the Playhouse steps only moments later.

Then, as if Sil had just finished commenting on the weather, he turns to Jude. "You're approaching Alistaire's Craft binding all wrong." The director's gaze turns on me, assessing. "I hate to hear how much trouble you're having after such a bold performance in stage combat yesterday."

I casually tuck my hand over my shoulder, covering my throat in a way I hope doesn't look like an injured bird.

SIL: "What Jude often forgets is that not all actors are in *want* of something, nor will they do anything to get it, and therefore build a bridge to it. *Some* actors, you see"—he claps a hand on my shoulder that nearly sends my fist into his face—"are not building a bridge in pursuit at all! Alistaire, what *is* the common thread among all actors?"

Jude's face grows apprehensive, like he doesn't want Sil to answer the question.

SIL: "You are all running from something. And it is almost always the same thing you are made of. So, tell me! What are you running from?"

Cold indignation courses through my expression until Sil chuckles.

SIL: "Close your eyes, Alistaire."

"No."

Sil's gaze widens in surprise, and Jude's in warning. I'm left to wonder again why Jude seems so scared of him.

The pivot of Sil's heels sets my nerves on edge as he walks circles around me, studying me through those silver spectacles as he taps his chin.

SIL: "Has anyone ever told you you're angry, Alistaire?"

My brother's warning returns the question. *That anger will be the death of you.*

RIVEN: "What is that to you?"

SIL: "I'm not going to ask you *why*."

Disgust pulses beneath my skin as Sil pauses before me, raises his hands, and presses his thumbs over my eyelids, closing them.

SIL: "I want you to use that thing you are made of. *Use* that anger." He removes his thumbs from my closed eyelids. *"Methexis,"* he prompts, and reluctantly, I follow suit.

I open my eyes as the marble washes away and find myself staring back into the glassy abyss of the stage.

RIVEN: "I still don't see a bridge." Just those roiling shadows below.

SIL: "Of course you don't. You can't see something that hasn't been built. So tell me, what are you running from? What angers you?"

Craft. Players. The Playhouse, I think urgently. *Jude.*

Nothing happens, save for an odd twinge at my throat.

"So reluctant!" he clucks. "Tell me, Alistaire. Why do you so love your sorrow?"

I present a detached, ignorant smile, though ice has begun to grip me at my core. "What is that supposed to mean?"

SIL: "You aren't just angry. That's surface-level." He gestures to the stage, where that raging sea crashes beneath the glass. "You'll need to go a little deeper than that."

Suddenly, I wish Jude was not here. I wish more that Sil wasn't staring at me like he knows my mind inside and out.

My mask of indifference slips as Sil's relaxes into a sort of *aha!* "You *love* it," he concludes. "You don't lack emotion. You're *obsessed* with it. You let it fester." He's grinning like a fox now. "Someone has taught you to suppress quite well, I think."

Galen's voice passes through my mind. *Too much, Riv.*

SIL: "Your bridge is not made of pursuit, nor escape, but of both." He walks another circle around me, faster now, heels clapping against the glass. "The source of all you dwell on—it's completely on *this* side, isn't it? Above the surface, in reality. Because reality is painful, and pain is familiar."

RIVEN: "I don't know what you're talking about." I don't owe him truth. *Of course* reality hurts. Of course it's familiar.

Reality is unfair. If it weren't, I never would have encountered that Player all those years ago.

SIL: "Then prove me wrong."

JUDE: "Sil—"

The director cuts him off with a dismissive wave.

SIL: "Look below." There's a smile in his voice. "You can run from this anger you harbor. You can lock it away. Or you can *use* it. Leash it and make it do your bidding."

RIVEN: "I'm not angry." My voice shakes.

I am angry.

SIL: "All my Players are angry. But more importantly, they are all *something*. Often, not what you would expect. Titus, for instance. He lives and speaks and moves out of fear. My darling Parrish's bones are racked with envy. Arius, always seeking to mend the world around him because he cannot mend himself. And Jude here—"

JUDE: "Enough, Sil. She understands."

I am angry. I am angry.

SIL: "Do you want to know a secret, Alistaire?" His voice rises, echoing. "That anger you feel. That bitter thing wrapped around your heart. It may not be directed at what you think."

A dam I didn't realize existed rumbles in my head. For a moment, I think I know what's coursing on the other side of it. The thought vanishes.

But the anger doesn't.

I am angry. I am angry. I am angry.

"Stop pushing back," Sil roars, his voice now pounding in my ears. "You're angry, Alistaire! Be angry!"

I am angry—

The thought ceases, and something else fills the space.

I am alone.

The dam in my head breaks. It floods my senses, washes over my skin until it feels like it's on fire. The feeling spreads, sinks into my heels. But Sil was wrong—it's too much to leash or contain. It fills me with the urge to run, to bolt from the stage.

But when I try to move, the weight in my heels is too much, and I fall. The palms of my hands crash into the glass stage, so violently that it cracks, and I brace my body to plummet into the watery sea of darkness below.

But the fall never comes.

Instead, my palms sense something warm. I crane my chin up, and the glass doesn't look so dark anymore.

Instead, a multitude of golden tendrils crawls out from beneath the stage, like a sea beast with a thousand tentacles.

"Bind it, Alistaire." Jude's voice. "Now."

I draw on the feeling, and the tendrils reach up, summoned, wrapping around me, weaving and locking together. Gold seeps into my hands, my clothes, my feet. Craft rises fiercely to the surface, everywhere, seeking a way in.

Before I can stop it, before I can *think* to, I let it.

Craft washes over the platform, brilliant and warm and gold, the gap of darkness closed. Every beat of fury locked away for years pulses through me, reaching up my wrists, my calves.

"Extraordinary," Sil marvels from somewhere behind me.

For a moment, it feels like I've been traveling a thousand nights only to catch a sunrise.

"A bridge," I hear myself utter, feeling those threads of gold pulse with power. A thread not just to me—those same tendrils connect to the place Jude stands. Elsewhere in the Playhouse, the same Craft must follow the other Players, a shared web that sews their cast together.

The Players. Right. This is a loan of power. This is something to *not* get used to.

A hand lowers into my vision as I try to pick myself up. I stare at it for a moment, follow the arm up to Jude, and then grasp it, my legs shaky as he pulls me to my feet. "On three, yes?" Jude says and counts down.

"Methexis," I say with him.

The golden stage, the Craft below—it vanishes, disguised beneath reality once more.

I blink dazedly at the spotlight, feeling the hot press of Craft all over.

The world has changed in a short time. It's brighter now. Every sound echoes and chimes, every step and movement holding new intention and meaning. Everything is amplified and beautiful, exposed. And *color.* There's so much color.

Something has changed—something that feels like it can't be undone.

Worse, I'm not sure I want it to be.

SIL: "How do you feel, Alistaire?"

Warm. The word comes to mind unsolicited, some of the coldness in my veins dissipating.

And something else, too. The frosty ache in my limbs eases, just slightly, like someone's reached inside and spread a salve over the worst points.

"I don't—" I still at the unfamiliar sound of my own voice in my ears. The pitch isn't different. It's just...*more.*

For a moment, the Player's curse feels less like an impossible glacier and more like a sheet of ice that I'm holding a candle to.

I take a step forward, but my legs feel strange. Stronger. Things I never paid mind to, like where I pause for breath when speaking, how many steps I take in any given direction, feel oddly relevant now.

"I think that..." I struggle again to wrangle my voice. What is *happening*? Why am I so *loud*—

"Alistaire?" At the sound of Sil's voice, I turn to face him. He looks surprised.

And Jude is no longer there.

I turn to see Jude's hurried steps toward the wings, his back to us.

SIL: "Well, would you look at that. You were right, Jude!"

At Sil's words, Jude makes a brief look back and—

He's...*crying.*

Then, as fast as he left, Jude is gone. Sil claps a hand on my shoulder, and I catch my reflection in his eyes. My heart stutters at the image.

SIL: "You're a natural, Alistaire."

Act II: Scene VII

"That's *my* fucking line," shouts Titus, storming out of the wings half-dressed and pointing a long finger at Parrish. In his other hand, he waves a script.

PARRISH: "Well, *you* weren't here to say it." She smiles snidely while Arius releases the illusion around us with a tired sigh, the set melting back into the stage. "Honestly, I'm shocked you know which lines are yours anyhow. You can read?"

TITUS: "I was trying to find a new costume." He glowers. "Mine looks like it just went through several performances of *Gods' War*. I'll bet you Cicero ravaged it with a blade on purpose. He never liked me."

Damn it. I thought that costume belonged to Jude.

It's been three days since the Craft binding, all of which have been crammed with rehearsals and brutal stage combat lessons with Jude that have left me too exhausted and sore to think straight—which is new, strange. My muscles are *sore*.

Not numb, and not *cold*. I can feel them again.

It doesn't matter, I tell myself. I'll be out of here as soon as the Playhouse lands in Syrene, and so will Jude. I just need to figure out how to wrestle that Eleutheraen chain away from Marigold.

So long as I can stop the Great Dionysia. Stop the bloodbath they're plotting.

PARRISH: "I think I'll sing my lines instead, Sil."

SIL: "You will not." He cleans his glasses. "Alistaire, from your entrance? We'll go from the top."

Indeed, my little bridge demonstration awarded me not one but *four* speaking scenes. But since I refuse to read their cursed scripts, learning my lines devolved into several repeat-after-me sessions with Jude that rendered us both frustrated and storming out of rehearsal.

"Did you do something to your face, Alistaire?" Titus mutters, passing close behind me. "It looks different. Nicer, though, so there's that."

I suggest that he do something about his face, too, and he barks a laugh on his way out.

SIL: "Let's run it from the beginning. Where is Jude?"

"Primping in the Greenroom, probably," Mattia mutters and goes back to picking at her nails with a prop dagger. "This is a stumble-through at best, Sil."

The Greenroom. Another part of the Playhouse I've read about and have yet to discover.

SIL: "The worse the dress rehearsal, the better the show!" He flashes a forced, encouraging smile. "Someone fetch Jude, please."

The sharp scent of hyacinth warns me first. "Whatever you're plotting, I hope it doesn't involve that axe you keep staring at." Jude appears at my side with a look of patient suffering and calls out, "Here, Sil."

He's changed into a finely tailored black jacket, trousers, and a shirt he's unnecessarily left half unbuttoned to show off gold markings he no doubt made some poor stagehand paint on.

"I count that four costume changes in one rehearsal," I mutter at him as the lights go down.

"Oh? Do you have a favorite?" he asks, adjusting the cuffs of his jacket.

"Do any of them come with a gag?"

"Didn't know you were into that."

"Hold for lights!" calls Sil, running a hand through his white hair and leaving a few raised at odd angles. If he's stressed over *this*, I wonder how he'll react to his Lead Player going mysteriously missing in a week's time.

Above us, a stagehand adjusts the glaring limelight. I squint, trying to catch a glimpse of who aims it. I know they're *there*—I've spotted half a dozen stagehands setting the banquet tables, moving props, adjusting the curtain. But I can never seem to get a square look at their faces.

SIL: "And go."

I brace myself, brushing my fingers across the fabric that hides my mark. It burns each time I set foot onstage. Worse since the Craft binding.

"How's that healing, by the way?" Jude asks while we wait for our cue.

"*Healing*" is a stretch. Last I peeked under the bandage, an alarming gold film had begun forming over the wound, festering in the shape of the iron Jude used to burn through it.

"I'm *not* going out there tonight," I say, ignoring the question. "Rehearsals are as far as I go." It's bad enough my mark is gone. I'm no better than a common liar now. But I will not be *worse* than one. "Performance is unnatural. One strung-out and outrageously public lie. It's *wrong*—"

JUDE: "*Life* is a performance." Our cue is called, and he moves for the platform, whispering over his shoulder, "You might as well be applauded for it."

Between hasty rehearsal breaks, I scavenge the dining hall for anything I can get my hands on. Somehow, I'm still starving when Parrish comes to retrieve me. She promises to have a stagehand deliver more food to the dressing rooms, or else cook me her very favorite snack if she can "catch the ingredients." I gently decline the offer.

"Get dressed," Jude calls as I enter the wings, throwing a linen garment bag zipped over an elaborate costume in my direction. He's dressed much the same: loose white shirt, tailored black pants, black boots. Stitches of gold leaf thread his neckline, and scarlet stones hang from his ears. "The rest are already backstage. You're going to be late as it is."

"I'll get you back for this," I grumble, dread churning in my stomach at the sound of audience chatter just beyond the curtain. I reassure myself no one from the South will recognize my face—its similarity to my father's—from so far away onstage.

JUDE: "Yes, I'm sure you will. The walls of my dressing room tremble with fear at the sound of your step."

I slip behind the screen used for quick changes and make a point of raising my middle finger over it before donning the costume: an ensemble of white, accented by notes of gold and crimson.

"I'm sure any of the three auditionees you *haven't* slaughtered would be proud to take my place." I pull the blouse over my head and fiddle with the thick belt that goes with it. Then I jam my feet into the knee-high leather boots that have about a thousand laces.

"They'll each have their shot onstage. Just as what's-her-name did the other night."

"The *dead* one?" I offer helpfully, then stomp around the divider, trying and failing to button the tiny wrist cuffs on my sleeves.

Jude looks me up and down, pausing at the boots and the cords I opted to wrap across my knees. "Did you even *try* to lace them? You'll trip over your feet onstage." His own (properly laced) boots clack sharply across the floor. With a shake of his head, Jude sweeps one foot back and swiftly kneels. I yelp and nearly fall over when he tugs my leg up and sets my boot on his knee, undoing what *I* thought was a very nice bow.

I ignore the way my pulse trips as he steadies my calf with one hand to undo my clumsy lacework with the other. I'm nervous about going onstage, that's all. And half shocked he isn't complaining about dirtying his costume with the heel of my boot.

JUDE: "I should leave these untied. Maybe it would slow your scheming."

RIVEN: "Are you trying to get kicked in the face? I have a great angle here."

Jude smirks up at me and mouths, *"Dare you,"* while pulling the boot laces taut.

My heart stumbles over itself again as Sil calls out, "Ten

minutes!" from somewhere in the hall.

"You'll be fine out there," Jude says, mistaking my nervousness for stage fright. "Three deep breaths, right?" He peers over his shoulder before continuing, lowering his voice. "Rehearsals are different—those are done cold, without much Craft. It's too demanding on us to cast those sorts of illusions without an audience during run-throughs." I cringe. I forget this is what they *feed* off of. "The auditorium may seem larger, too."

"What, it's grown since rehearsal?" I ask with an incredulous laugh.

"The Playhouse draws its strength from its audience. A theatre grows weak without them," he says, avoiding the question. "It's going to feel more...intense out there."

"If I didn't know you any better, I'd say you were worried." I try to sound careless, but I don't believe me, either. He snaps the buckle in place at my knee and sets my foot back on solid ground.

"You should be. This is a hell of a role for Sil to throw you into." Jude reaches for the other boot and looks up at me. "My character will take the brunt of what happens out there, but it isn't going to be pleasant. Hold close to your bridge, yes? Just in case."

"Fine." I cross my arms. "Wouldn't want to make you *burst into tears* again."

I never did learn what made him so upset the other day. For someone determined I learn all this Craft, he seemed awfully emotional over my making progress with it.

He stills, pausing his work. Breathes once, then quips, "Not all of us are terrified of emotions, Alistaire." He buckles the other boot and sets it down before standing and heading for his place in the wings, calling over his shoulder, "And cover up those purple circles under your eyes before going out. You'll frighten the children."

I ignore him as he stalks off but still grapple with a pod of creamy, pale liquid on one of the vanities, making awkward attempts to smear it under my eyes without the help of a mirror.

"No, no! Not like that," Parrish's young voice calls,

accompanied by the jingle of anklets as she passes through with perfectly lined eyes and carefully painted lips. "Don't smear it; you'll get streaks all over your face! You *dab* the color on. Like this, see?"

Parrish taps below her eye and gestures for me to imitate, hiding her chuckle when I poke myself in the eye instead and reconsider suffering a look in the mirror. "Didn't anyone teach you how to do this?"

"I—I, uh," I stammer as she picks up a pinkish powder and begins swiping it over my cheekbones. With so few mirrors North of the Cut, cosmetics require a second set of eyes to apply. The idea of asking my mother for help, of asking her to look directly at me, was out of the question. Besides that, there isn't much pigment in such things outside the Playhouse anyway. "No, not really."

"Well then, I'll have to do. Jude's no use at this. Lines his eyes like a sailor," she mutters. "There! Beautiful."

Parrish offers an encouraging smile before vanishing down the corridor, leaving me to puzzle out the idea of *beautiful* and *my face* in the same thought. I turn the slightest glance to the mirror to examine her work—and gasp.

Not at the makeup but at the scrawl of amber gold that crawls beneath the ochre of my irises, there and gone in an instant. The makeup palette in my grip clatters to the floor, and I clap a hand over my mouth. Craft. Player magic.

Not only that but—*my reflection.* For a moment, I don't recognize it. There's *color* in my face. My shoulder bones aren't sticking out like my skin is a sheer curtain anymore. And something looks...*different.* I can't put my finger on why. Something has changed.

The Craft binding is responsible, no doubt.

"Five minutes!" Sil's voice.

"Don't worry yourself, Alistaire!" Arius calls, interpreting my panic for stage fright. A funny expression falls across his face as he pulls that throat spray from his pocket on his way to the wings. "You look different."

"I— Parrish helped me…" I gesture vaguely at the makeup but don't dare look at myself in the mirror again.

He shakes his head once. "No, not that, I think."

"Places!" Sil shouts.

Moments later, I'm sipping shallow breaths of dread as Arius leads me backstage, where murmurs from the audience stir on the other side of the curtain. *Thousands of Revelers*, I think nervously. *How did I end up here?*

SIL: "Welcome, welcome! Dear patrons, we are honored to present to you a tale of old, in celebration of our most beloved treaty's impending end. Let us not forget how it was formed! Tonight, we perform for you Act One of *The Cast Trade*—"

I tune out the uproarious applause as Silenus introduces the show: a brutal reenactment of the trade between the Playhouse and mortals that started the treaty five hundred years ago, when Silenus traded peace for the life of his captured Player. No doubt this performance is designed to evoke pity for the Players.

But all I can think about is how warm the stage feels when I step onto it, how guilty that makes me feel. And that strange inkling of Craft, squirming around my pupils, warming the place behind my eyes.

"Methexis," I breathe, feeling my bridge lock into place beneath me, but my mind stays focused on the big picture: on capturing Jude. On delivering him to the council and stopping the Playhouse's terrifying plans for the North. Of getting back to Cassia and my brother. I almost have all the pieces. I just need to hold out a little longer.

Then the curtain rises, and the world fades away.

The boom of applause shifts into the slap of rain and thunder. Smoke fills my sinuses, though I thought I smelled perfume a moment ago. I blink down curiously as the white marble beneath my feet cracks, mud and dirt bleeding through until I can no longer see the floor.

It occurs to me I cannot remember my name. Come to think of it, I don't have one.

Above, the voice of a god falls from the sky, offers explanation to a vicious conflict unfolding between black-and-silver uniforms wielding rudimentary weapons, and the rest—golden-eyed Players clad in white and scarlet.

I move through the world, the beat of a drum pulsing in my blood. Every word that falls from my lips doesn't feel like a line but like a part of me. Each movement deliberate, intentional.

I gasp as I exit stage left, my entrance finished. My mind grapples for reality. On the platform, Mattia and Arius have broken into a violent argument that I'm only half certain was scripted.

Tig, Linos, and Phileas crow lines from the chorus, then disband and pass me as they flee into the wings.

"How are you doing?" Jude asks over my shoulder, and I jump. He's drenched from the rain onstage, hair falling over his face in dark tresses. The shoulder of his costume is torn.

"I'm fine," I say, not sure that I am. This isn't how rehearsals felt. "Are you stalling?"

"Absolutely, I hate this scene," he whispers. "And between you and me—" He shakes some of the water dripping from his sleeves. "I've never cared for Tragedies." Then he moves for his next entrance.

The scene onstage shifts as Jude stumbles onto the platform, throwing furious looks over his shoulder as Titus's character pursues him, wielding a golden blade. I know it's paint—not *real* Eleutheraen gold—but even *my* heart clenches at the sight as Jude ducks, dodges, and forces the blade back on Titus so hard, he nearly slits his throat as they toss carefully rehearsed lines back and forth.

Eventually, Titus's character gets the high ground and succeeds in hitting him on the back of the head. Something twists in my chest as Jude's dragged away while the crowd shrieks and wails.

This is just a performance. And even if it weren't, I would *not* care.

But I decide I'm with Jude on one thing. I prefer the Comedies over this, by far.

A crack of thunder summons me for my next cue. The world vanishes. Whatever magic blooms on the stage sucks me in as time moves in strange spurts of battle and heated conversation. My name slips my mind again.

Then someone knocks me out, too, and everything blackens. The stage lights come up—

No. Lightning. Flashes of it illuminate the canvas tent around me. Mud cakes my boots. There's a man on a bench beside me, blond, brown-eyed, oddly familiar. He repeats questions I won't answer. *Where are my other castmates?* he asks. *What are our weaknesses?*

I say something he doesn't like, and he answers with a blade aimed at my throat.

A shock of pain rolls from my neck to my heart. *My mark.*

My bridge to Craft severs, seems to drop right through the floor, out of reach.

As if awoken from a dream, my consciousness jolts me out of fiction, reality pressing hard on my skin.

I'm onstage. This isn't real. The warmth of the stage fades, ice dissolving the bond between the performance and me. I recognize the Player beside me, holding a prop knife. He hasn't hurt me with it. It's just Arius. *Arius—*

My heart freezes painfully in my chest. I can't breathe.

The fourth wall shatters. Whatever strange shield prevents actors from noticing—*realizing*—an audience is there is gone. The eyes of the audience are everywhere, blinking, beginning to clear, to realize this is a performance.

Downstage, Titus and Mattia fire lines of dialogue at each other. Between them, Jude is watching me in abject horror. A word falls from his mouth, and warmth presses on my skin once more, clouds my mind. The stage vanishes. I'm in the tent again. I can't remember why I'd thought of the name Jude. It doesn't sound familiar.

Exit! It's time for me to leave. Impossibly drawn to a strange passage leading out of the tent, I run. I'm almost out, almost offstage when—

I freeze. My eyes fix on the arrow trained on my heart, tracking its razor point up to the woman aiming it. A stranger.

Her eyes are wild and wet. Gold trickles down her neck from a wound on the side of her head, nestled in tresses of rich brown that fall from her scalp in gnarled tangles. Most disturbingly, the skin of her arms and hands is ripped open, revealing flecks of gold beneath.

The woman stands under a curtain of darkness a little ways off. *She's in the wings*, I think, curious and confused. But the thought is fragmented, colliding with reality.

None of this is so frightening as the fact that she looks *so* familiar.

The stranger seems to mouth something to me as she releases the arrow. I don't catch what she says—a hard shove from my right knocks me to the ground.

Then I'm coughing, my lungs filled with smoke and the scent of blood in the air as I take in the riggings above. I'm backstage.

Embracing the ice-cold arms of reality, I register the shouts of the audience as the principal roles battle across the platform. Vaguely, I remember this is a scene; it ends in a dramatic standoff between the two leads.

I roll onto my side, searching for the woman who shot that arrow—the stranger. She's gone.

Jude is yelling something that sounds like *Stay here!* as he runs back onto the stage. I blink up at the ceiling, confused and disoriented. My head hurts.

The hairs on the back of my neck stand to attention. I'm offstage, but the feeling of being watched hasn't left me. Lifting myself, I steal a glance into the darkness of the wings and go still.

Two bright, menacing eyes watch me. A dirty, torn white dress hangs on a tensed figure. She reaches a hand out to me, hooks a finger in my direction.

I do not believe in ghosts. But the woman from the portrait in my room has climbed out. She's cornered me here.

Gene Hunt.

The dead Player brings a finger to her lips as if to say, *Hush*. Then flutters back into the dark like a pearl in the ocean.

ARIUS: "Alistaire!" He flies into the wings, casting a bloodied blade into the prop armory. "Are you all right? Jude saw, too—Gods, I haven't seen that happen in ages."

When I look back to the hall, Gene Hunt is gone.

RIVEN: "I— What?"

ARIUS: "My friend, you nearly broke our illusion!" He scratches the back of his neck anxiously. "How did you manage it?"

MATTIA: "What the hell was that?"

Mattia tears backstage, the other Players at her shoulders. I can see every single gold vein in her neck. By the thunder of applause outside the curtain, I surmise the show is over.

Somehow, according to the clock, six hours have flown by.

"Who did that?" she demands again as Arius peers sidelong at me, concern constricting his soft features. "Who broke the illusion?"

Some quick math brings me to two conclusions: One, no one else noticed the dead Player aiming arrows at me from backstage. Two, they most certainly *did* notice me break the illusion when Arius brushed my ruined mark.

TITUS: "Interesting that you assume it couldn't have been *you* who made a mistake, Mattia." He works on the straps that bind two broadswords to his back. "But by all means, accuse one of the auditionees who've been here less than a week of somehow doing so."

Before Mattia can question further, Jude strides into the wings. Judging by the blood running from his temples, Titus hit him awful hard onstage. "Calm yourself, Mattia. It was my fault. I slipped." He throws a warning look at me. *Don't say a word.*

Mattia watches him, flabbergasted. I pretend not to notice Arius staring between Jude and me, open-mouthed.

MATTIA: "Why did you run offstage?"

TITUS: "Run offstage? He tackled poor Alistaire to the ground; didn't you see?"

JUDE: "She forgot to exit on time. Very clumsy of her."

I turn my eyes toward the skene that stands at the back of the stage. There, ingrained in its side, an arrow—the one Gene Hunt aimed at me.

The moment breaks at the clapping of hands. Sil emerges from the dark corridor. "Well done, everyone!" His mild-tempered smile simmers into something else—a stiffness to it. "Jude, a word?"

A collective dread shrouds the other Players at the director's tone.

ARIUS: "There was a lot of chaos onstage, Sil—and a long time since we've performed this piece. We all might have slipped a bit."

Mattia moves to argue, but the director cuts her off.

SIL: "Were one of you to slip, it is my *Lead Player's* job to preserve the illusion *before* an audience glimpses anything beyond the curtain. Correct, Jude? And gods above, running offstage like that."

Mattia's face tightens. "*None* of us slipped. Something cut through it."

"And who could have done that?" Sil gestures to me. "Perhaps a new, inexperienced actor? Come to think of it, I don't see your contender, Mattia." He feigns a glimpse around the wings, and I find myself looking around, too, trying to remember what happened to the others onstage. I can barely remember what happened to myself. "If I'm not mistaken, it *was* Linos who fled the wrong side of the stage early and took the whole chorus with him, wasn't it?"

Mattia says nothing, baring her teeth. But her eyes land on me, and they stay there as Sil turns for the hall, yelling, "Curtain call!"

over his shoulder. "And would someone *please* collect the damned chorus?"

I don't know what overcomes me. My mouth drops open. "It was Gene Hunt."

Sil stills, along with the Players. Jude's eyes are pleading with me.

Slowly, the director turns. "Alistaire, I do hope you aren't in the habit of blaming deceased Players before admitting fault. That was an awfully late exit you made." He glares at me, waiting.

"Jude saw her, too. She was *here*—she was backstage and—"

"I have no idea what you're talking about," Jude says coldly, expressionless. "I made a mistake. The illusion slipped."

Sil and Jude look to be locked in a silent debate until the director mutters, "Curtain call. All of you," and vanishes down the hall. Where I *know* Gene Hunt stood just moments ago.

In my time in the Playhouse, I have gathered that Gene Hunt is a great many things, and none of them is *dead*.

Act II: Scene VIII

The stage door flies open, and the screaming from the Revelers begins.

Even from where I'm crouched on my balcony, peering between the marble balusters, I have to cover my ears.

Fine. Jude is right. I'm a snoop. But it's better than being alone in my dressing room with Gene Hunt's spooky portrait.

Sil's head peeks out. Then the cast: Mattia and Titus first, with humble words of thanks that don't seem very humble at all. Parrish and Arius next. Finally, Jude, with a dramatic bow. Each cast member is greeted with louder screams than the last.

I can't help but cringe at the way spectators reach over the golden barrier, so many Revelers—so many hands grasping, *touching.* One succeeds in grabbing Mattia's hair and is dealt a merciless fist in return. It only seems to egg the offender on, though.

Arius scribbles across playbills shoved into his arms, and someone kisses his hand, weeping loudly, when he tosses them back. Sil thanks the crowd for coming.

A particularly pretty-looking girl with a thick blond ponytail and the sort of nose that belongs exclusively on a porcelain doll has fought her way to the front of the barrier. And is batting her eyelashes at Jude.

Predictably, he's enjoying the attention. Arius must have tended to most of their stage wounds, but the cut on Jude's head is still noticeable when he leans down for the girl to convey in his ear whatever she's trying to shout over the crowd. He nods, feigning humility behind a dazzling smile, a hand to his chest. *Her* hand has found its way to his arm.

Realizing my jaw is clenching, I force my attention to Titus, who is doing godsdamned *nothing* to console the man breaking into hysterical sobs at his knees, declaring eternal devotion. Another Reveler tosses what must be her life's savings in jewels at Parrish's feet. Parrish gleefully kicks them around on the floor and asks if the Reveler brought anything more interesting.

When Sil signals it's time to go in, the crowd surges violently forward, jealous fans in the back pushing their way to the front. Obsessive moths to the Players' golden light.

That girl Jude is talking to lets out a high-pitched squeal as someone shoves her back, hurling her into the barrier. Fine. Maybe she'll go find another place to—

Jude decides the way to remedy the situation is to pick her up and set her on the *other* side of the barrier, beside him.

My mouth falls open. *Not* that I care. I don't even notice the way he places a hand on her shoulder and seems to ask if she's all right or the way she giggles and thanks him.

In fact, I care so little that I go inside and only half slam the door behind me.

They come for the next auditionee minutes before curfew; the lights in my room have already begun to dim, flickering and dying.

They're coming for me this time. I hear the approach of Sil's step, closer to my dressing room with each stride. He knew it was me who messed up onstage.

I whirl, search my room, and dive for the Eleutheraen arrowhead I stashed behind the old clock. I'm at *least* taking one of them down with me.

The steps freeze right outside my door, two polished black shoes. Sil's familiar old sigh.

The dead bolt slides into place.

The shoes leave.

They take Linos instead.

Act II: Scene IX

"Something's different about you." Cassia's eyes scrutinize me from the other side of the glass as I sway in front of the mirror, hanging on to the edge of it for balance. I've managed to communicate with her through my mirror every few days, the process a bit easier each time I try it. Which is unsettling in and of itself.

"Well, for starters, I haven't slept in..." I count on my fingers. "Six-ish days?" I try to joke, but my aunt doesn't smile back. I can't sleep. When I *do* drift off, I'm harassed by dreams full of golden eyes and red curtains. Sometimes worse.

"And your voice..." Her brow falls; the distinct crackle of my voice has been sawed down, its rough edges vanishing almost entirely. "What's happened?"

"Nothing," I lie. It's wildly easy now. "Have you heard from the council?" I ask.

"Your message was delivered. Galen refused to tell them where the information came from, though." Cassia clears her throat. "Syrene's ruler has agreed to assist in the trade. If they succeed in crossing the Cut."

And somehow, someway, *I* will have to turn Jude over myself.

I will, though. *I have to.* I have to stop the Great Dionysia—stop the slaughter the Players are planning.

"I'll bring him," I repeat. "The council will have all the leverage they need to strike a new deal with Silenus and force the Playhouse back out before the Great Dionysia. I just need something to restrain him." Like that chain around Marigold's foot.

"Riven," she begins. "I went to the Dionysian Records after we spoke. There isn't much information on him. Whoever he was when he was mortal is...murky." She takes a breath, looking uneasy. "But one source suggests he hails from Thymele."

The name immediately rings a bell. I stare silently back at Cass, a picture beginning to paint itself. "Oh."

Thymele doesn't exist anymore, a small territory at the border swallowed by Syrene's army years ago, so that the wall could be sealed.

Several Players were killed during its fall, publicly executed during the ambush.

And now what was once Thymele is just part of Syrene.

"Jude would have been a child at the time," Cassia says, looking down at the tome in her hands, as if to confirm. "How he managed to escape is anyone's guess."

"So he has a vendetta against the North," I conclude, blunt.

"Wouldn't you?" She meets my eyes. "War is an ugly thing. Our side of the Cut is far from innocent."

We stare at each other for a moment. A confusing twinge of sympathy clashes with my anger. I shove it away.

Jude might not just be on an ego trip, and it only confirms my worst suspicions. He's too proud, too calculated to simply want *out* of the Great Dionysia. He's lying. He's planning something.

He's after vengeance. And he's going to make the Great Dionysia his stage for it.

And somehow, this involves me. There's something here I'm not seeing.

"Have you heard from Galen?" I press. "You didn't tell him about—"

"*No*, of course not." Cassia's voice hushes, and we don't say the rest out loud. That my mark is ruined. Useless. Cassia expected as much but was nevertheless devastated when I admitted it to her several days ago. "Your brother has gone for help," she admits.

"What do you mean?" I whisper sharply into the mirror. I don't want Galen any closer to this impending disaster of a trade than he has to be.

"He reached out to an old contact your father had. To help track down Dorian."

Gods. "The Playhouse Bounty Hunter?" It's impossible to

imagine my brother, an adviser to the *council*, turning to reckless vigilantes for help. Dorian and his hunters refuse marks—both to easily traverse South Theatron in pursuit of the Players and to outsmart one if caught or captured. "Of course he did. Of *course* he doesn't trust I can do this on my own—"

"Riven," Cassia cuts me off. "He just wants you home, alive. We *all* do."

I'm not sure there will be a home to return to if Jude gets his way.

"I have the arrowhead," I say, even more determined now to prove Galen wrong. Prove all of them wrong. "I just need something to restrain Jude. He's strong, but there's a chain bound around the Prop Master's ankle. If I can just figure out how to fool her into letting me—"

"Riven," she breathes. "If you're going to be downright *foolish* about this..." My aunt shakes her head, debating whether or not to give me this next bit of information. "Jude will be most vulnerable in costume. He won't be as alert while in character. It's the best time to catch a Player off guard."

In costume.

Costume. I need a *costume.*

"Cass," I say, a smile forming on my lips. "Do you know I've just had the best idea?"

"I *told* you I saw her up in the fly tower." Jude sounds angry. "She cut the chandelier's hangings."

"You're *certain* you saw her backstage last night?" Sil's voice responds.

I breathe quietly, assuring myself I am no eavesdropper. Jude's voice just has a way of carrying.

Particularly when my ear is pressed against his dressing room door.

"Nearly plunged an arrow *right through*—" Jude's voice rises, and Sil hushes him. "Do you see this? I don't *have* much longer."

"Stop talking about it," snaps Sil. "You'll only make it worse."

"Speed up the casting call. At this rate, I won't be able to move the Playhouse past the Cut. Much less compete in the Great Dionysia."

"I've been plenty lenient with you, Jude. I'll *not* have you going off again and—"

The button of Galen's old jacket scrapes against the door when I press too close, and I panic, bolting back to my room with all the subtlety of a frightened horse. Jude's door swings open, and innocent pleasantries trade loudly between Sil and Jude.

I make it a whole four steps before my own dressing room door swings open behind me.

JUDE: "Funny thing just now." I feign surprise at seeing him.

RIVEN: "Is the funny thing that you still don't know how to knock?"

JUDE: "I was having a conversation with Sil, and I could have sworn I heard your sneaky little feet scampering away just outside my room."

I stick a foot out and point at it. "Actually, they're a very normal size."

Jude ignores me and heads for the floor-length mirror. "Come, I want to show you something. It'll give us a leg up for the competition." Pressing a palm to the glass, he summons...

A very dark stairway, from the looks of it. Awesome. I never grow tired of these.

I plant my feet. "Is your little blond friend from last night coming along, too?"

My eyes immediately dart to the window, and I consider throwing myself out of it. *Why did I say that out loud?* I don't even know if that girl was let into the Playhouse after all his flirting at the stage door. Not that I'd be shocked if she were. And *not* that I'd care.

Jude's brows shoot up, but his surprise is subsequently replaced by a slow, widening grin. "*My*, Alistaire." He crosses his arms, the mirror forgotten as he leans against the wall. "Are you *jealous*?"

A mortifying second of panic passes before I remember I can lie. "Nope."

Am I? I hope not. Somehow, at some point, Jude has begun to tangle into my thoughts like a gnarled branch.

And I think he can tell.

His mouth twists in a knowing smirk that I consider tossing a footstool at until he nods and says, "Guess I'll have to try harder, then." And steps one foot through the mirror. "Oh, and if you could avoid letting Sil know about showing you this, I'd appreciate it."

Then Jude's gone. I unclench my teeth, curiosity burning a hole through my resolve.

I follow him through the glass.

"Welcome to the Playhouse Archives," announces Jude, descending what feels like the one thousandth step. I throw another nervous look over my shoulder. We passed Marigold's door and the creepy humming beyond it about ten minutes ago.

I cling to the railing and sip shallow breaths, ice snaking through my limbs from the hike down. Still, as I shift my weight from foot to foot and stretch my ankles, I feel a hint of pride at my newfound resilience.

Whether or not I care to admit it, I'm stronger now than I was when I first set foot in the Playhouse.

The white marble railing guiding my hand shifts the deeper we descend, from polished, to ancient, to bonelike, fissures threading its side and gold filling in the gaps. A cool breeze carries the scent of aged parchment and the soft rustle of pages.

Beneath our feet, the stone levels out.

A cavernous labyrinth sprawls before us. Marble depictions of Players border a path to a series of polished staircases that serves the gap between floors. Every tier stacked with walnut shelves and presenting thousands of…

Books.

The rustling, and what might be whispering, comes to a halt—like the ghosts wandering the library have noticed visitors.

"Is someone down here?" I call out, and Jude shakes his head.

"It's them," he says. When I return a puzzled look, he goes on. "The books. They only want your attention. They get excited when someone visits." He gestures to the shelves. "Every story ever told is in these rooms."

A rush of excitement rises in my chest, my eyes darting from shelf to shelf. The books begin their chorus of rustling again as I hurry forward eagerly to examine their spines. I love studying—I have since I was a child. It's where I feel at home, deep in knowledge and history. Things that are already written and done, because they're free of uncertainty.

It almost looks like how Galen described the Orkestrian Library. *But better.* Bigger and filled with thousands and thousands of tomes bound in gold, silver, and bronze.

Except the Orkestrian Library is filled with historical texts. Sciences and languages and mathematics. And *these* books are full of…

RIVEN: "*Every* story?" Anger simmers in my tone. "So it's true, then. The Players stole them from Theatron."

Some recreations used to be locked away for historical record, but Cassia says those are liable to vanish, too, full with ink one day and empty the next. Writing stories is forbidden anyway. Punishable, like singing.

It summons Players.

JUDE: "They *belong* to the Playhouse—"

RIVEN: "What about those?" I point past Jude's head to a cavernous alcove of empty shelves looming eerily vacant by comparison to the rest.

Jude tenses. "Those aren't available to us anymore."

RIVEN: "Why not?"

JUDE: "We don't know. There used to be more Players. Each death takes a toll on the Playhouse."

The stories just *vanished*? "Where do they go?"

He frowns. "Probably back to the mortal world, to be abused and told poorly."

That gentle rustling murmurs from the shelves again. Like spirits pacing the labyrinth. *Ghosts*. Gene Hunt flutters across my mind. Not a ghost. *Alive*.

Or alive enough to try to kill me, at least.

JUDE: "Here." He plucks a book from the shelf and gestures to a dark mahogany table, but I stay where I am, watching distrustfully. "Whatever that question on your lips is, you might as well ask it."

RIVEN: "Why did you pretend you didn't see her? Gene."

He saw her, too. I *heard* him tell Sil he saw her.

Jude blinks at me, unmoving. I stand my ground but let my gaze drift to the golden ring pierced through his nose instead. Looking Jude in the eye sometimes feels like staring directly into the sun.

JUDE: "Gene's dead. Died in my arms. I remember it well." He shrugs. "I don't know what we saw. Now, please. Can we sit?"

I don't believe him. But his apathetic expression tells me I'm not getting any more information. Stubbornly, I ignore the seat beside him and instead drop into the red velvet chair on the other side of the table, where a fireplace sputters embers at me.

JUDE: "I'm assuming you haven't held a story before."

RIVEN: "Does your atrocious script from yesterday count?"

JUDE: "The one you refused to read? No, it doesn't." I roll my eyes. "And that's why we're down here. I can't have you raising Sil's suspicion any further than you already have. We'll start with this."

He leans across the table and presses the book into my hands. It's leather-bound and warm with golden lettering. *The Last*

Spring. He taps the cover. "Do you know this story?"

I swallow, glaring at him. "I don't know any stories." Most of the myths we have access to are regarding the Playhouse and generally presumed factual. History. "We don't live on *lies* where I come from." I try to thrust a sharp edge into my tone, but it comes out softer than I mean it to. That's what we're taught. Stories are all lies. Harmful and ugly and manipulative.

But in spite of the angry sting dancing up my throat, I don't put it down. My thumb rolls over the cover. They *are* lies, aren't they? Stories are just one deception after another.

JUDE: "None?"

RIVEN: "When the first Players appeared from the well and took all its Craft, the storybooks were wiped clean, too. You *Players* swallowed the words and only passed them on to other Players."

A question mark unintentionally tacks itself onto the end of my sentence as I take in the shelves around me. Suddenly, I can't help but wonder. If stories belonged to us before the Players stole them away, doesn't that mean there was a time when mortals like me held them, read them?

Were they bad then, too?

"Well, this story is based on history, so maybe it'll be easier for you." Jude reaches across the table and flips the cover open in my hands. "Go on," he encourages. "Read."

The book feels warm. Alive. *Good*.

After nearly a week in the Playhouse, *I* feel good. Better than I have since I can remember.

I focus on the first line, hearing it in my head, but it feels heavy on my tongue. "Once—once there was..." I stop, frustrated, and start over. By the third time, I slam the book shut and let my chair's legs screech against the floor as I move to leave.

"That was good, Alistaire! That was *good*," Jude calls after me, turning in his seat. The air in my lungs feels heavier, but something stirs inside. Something that *wants* to read, just a little more.

I pivot on my heel. Jude hasn't moved, sitting patiently.

Curiosity nudges at my mind.

"Why?" I ask.

Now he extends a hand heavy with golden rings. I stare but don't take it. There's a deep white scar etched into the top of his palm, running all the way to his wrist. I wonder when he managed to find the wrong side of an Eleutheraen blade. Players' skin won't scar by any other means.

"Because I have the most interesting theory." He redirects his hand to the seat beside him, eyes glimmering. "And I'm not often wrong."

I throw one more look at the exit. I *know* better. Being down here is dangerous. Story is dangerous. *Jude* is dangerous. Whatever envy I might have harbored over his behavior at the stage door last night was a fluke. Even if I *were* some beautiful, mindless Reveler, I would know better than to fall for Jude's charms. In fact, I'm lucky I'm not. Clearly, she caught Jude's attention, and I wouldn't want that.

Furiously reassuring myself of this and feeling very justified over it, I march back, this time for the chair beside Jude.

He flips the book open again, placing one half in my hands, and I start at the crackle of energy that jumps from its pages. Like the book has violently awoken, recognizing the touch of a Player. That funny feeling squirms in my chest again when he braces one palm on the back of my chair and leans in to read with me.

JUDE & RIVEN: "Once, there was a god named Hades, brother to Zeus and ruler of the Underworld—" I cough, my voice lagging behind Jude's. He was right, though—I know parts of this. "Hades would often venture up to the earth to watch Persephone, daughter of Demeter, tending her flowers in a field. Persephone sang a song so irresistible, Hades fell madly in love."

Jude taps the lines below. "And of course, you know how the song goes."

My mouth turns dry. "I— No, I don't—"

JUDE: "Then I'll teach you."

RIVEN: "I can't."

JUDE: "Why not?"

RIVEN: "I don't know how to sing."

Jude blinks a couple of times, as if not believing me. "They don't even allow you to *sing*?"

RIVEN: "It summons Players." I once saw someone lose their tongue for it as punishment. "Surely you must know some of this—you're from Syrene—"

JUDE: "I am *not*." His voice lashes the air so suddenly, it startles us both. It occurs to me too late that I shouldn't admit I know of Jude's history. He presses his lips together, apologetic, and quietly adds, "I'm from *Thymele*—when it was still Thymele. Not Syrene."

It's true, then. No wonder he hates us.

"But you weren't—you weren't a Player back then," I utter uselessly. "It's not like you were *hunted*; the North would never—"

"Such moral high ground, you and the North have!" Jude laughs, a bitter edge to it. "When I was small, this group came to my parents' home one day. *Begged* us to take them in, and we did. They waited until nightfall to make their attack."

He describes the ordeal with little more interest than he'd discuss rehearsal.

"I don't remember all of it. They bound us—me, my parents, my little sister—forced Eleutheraen gold down our throats: to *cleanse us*, they said. Then slit my family's necks." He shrugs. "Similar attacks across the city heralded the end for Thymele, long before your armies came. But please, tell me more about how much holier the North is than the rest of us."

Silence stretches between us for a moment. "How did you escape?" I ask quietly.

"I don't know." Jude stares at the table. "It feels like I shouldn't have. But I did, alone."

Alone. For a strange moment, the word slices through my anger.

I hate Players, I remind myself. *I hate Craft. I hate—*

None of these thoughts are enough to stop my hand from

reaching for Jude's before common sense can catch up to me.

Jude goes still, eyes flickering to the place where my palm rests over his rings. Probably a breath from laughing and pulling away. So I do it for him, wrench free to tuck my hands into my lap before I can embarrass myself further.

He catches my hand instead and tugs it back, as if to argue with the thought, fingers closing firmly around mine. I can't help but notice the sharp pinch of his Finders Keepers ring pressing into my skin, gleaming warmly in the light.

Jude might be horrible. Violent. A Player. But Cassia might have been right, too.

There's no winner in war, and the North is far from innocent.

"I'm sorry," I say, alarmed by my own words—that I mean them. I'm not sure why. *I* didn't hunt down his family or force Eleutheraen gold down his throat.

Guilt drapes over my shoulders. I'm going to do something *much* worse to Jude.

Can I? I'm suddenly not as sure. He doesn't look like an evil, emotionless monster in this light. He looks lost.

But monsters can look lost, too.

I succeed the second time I try to pull my hand away, and Jude clears his throat.

"So, no one's taught you how to sing."

I shake my head, desperate to get out of here all of a sudden. Somewhere far away from Jude and the heavy guilt building in my chest.

JUDE: "Mimic this sound." His eyes shift, simmer to a brighter gold when he casts a soft, entrancing hum from his throat. Reluctantly, I try.

The note falls flat, cracks right in half. Then turns into a string of curses that sends Jude hollering with laughter. "Well, you might try breathing first. Again, yes?"

He takes a dramatic inhale for me to mimic and repeats the note. I follow suit, and the sound feels smooth in my vocal cords, strong and easy. Jude's pitch goes up, and mine shadows. Then back down, and I follow again. "There! Good!" he applauds, and in spite of myself, I laugh, the corners of my mouth pulling up for the first time in I'm not sure how long. Something loosens in my chest. I feel ridiculous, in a nice sort of way.

A peculiar expression crosses Jude's face. "You know, Alistaire," he says, head tilting, "I'm not sure I've ever seen you smile before."

Just like that, my chest tightens again and I stiffen, defensive. "What of it?"

But Jude just loosely shrugs. "It was worth the wait."

The selection of quips and insults I was preparing to hurl back at him shrivels. That almost sounded like a compliment. I think I'm supposed to say *thank you*.

But Galen's stern warnings to *never* sing chime through my head instead, and I tense. Plucking the little book off the table, I go to return it to the shelf. That's when I catch a peek at the spine and the words printed finely at the bottom, below the title:

Acceptance of Change

I look where Jude pulled the story from: a shelf with a large *A* engraved over it. Below it, more labels on the spines of each book.

Admiration, Agitation, Amazement, Amusement...

They go on and on. "Jude," I say, quiet. "Say this is not what I think it is."

These stories are organized. By their intended evils and manipulations.

When I turn accusingly back to him, Jude's jaw tightens. He lifts his head proudly. "We're Players. We're the keepers of story, and we use them to—"

"That's not your *right*!" I shout, voice clapping against the stone ceiling. "It's true, then." My eyes spin around the library, catching gold plates dotting every inch of it. "The audience doesn't stand a chance. You *choose* what they feel. You manipulate our thoughts and emotions until—"

JUDE: "Why do you assume the worst for how we use them?"

He makes a sweeping gesture around the shelves. "Don't you think we'd have taken ownership of the entire world by now with access to this many stories if we wanted to?"

"Who's to say you haven't tried?" I snap, pointing to where my mark used to be. The mark that used to protect me from manipulation like...

My eyes fall back down to the book in my hand. "Are you using it on me—right now? To make me feel—"

Jude stands quickly. "No. *No*, Alistaire, I wouldn't—"

RIVEN: "How many of these stories do Players know?"

JUDE: "I— It depends. I think Parrish only knows the ones she likes. Titus rarely follows the scripts anyway..."

RIVEN: "And how many do *you* know?"

Jude chews his lower lip. "Lead Player has to know all of them."

Do you know where the word "actor" comes from, Riv? The memory of Galen helping me with my coursework as a child comes back with startling clarity. *It traces back to the same root as "hypocrite." Players costume their words just as much as their faces.*

I turn my eyes to the shelves. Too tall, too many to count. All of them full with glossy tales, words coated in sugar to soften the manipulation of their magic. The vileness of Craft.

Jude steps toward me, but I back away. "It doesn't matter how you use them," I say. "This is power no one should have. *Least of all* creatures like you." With that, I head for the stairs.

"You'll be relieved to know that you'll be home soon, Alistaire."

The cold shift in his tone freezes my steps on the stairs. I turn.

"What?" I say.

Any remorse has vanished from his expression, replaced by that usual bored aloofness. "That treaty your council so loves. That keeps us out." There's something in his eyes I can't read as he tilts his head. But I don't like it. "They tracked its expiration rather poorly over its five hundred years."

How wrong? It ends in four days when the Playhouse crosses into Syrene and I can—

I inhale, measuring my next question carefully. "And *when* does it end, then?"

Jude raises his chin. "It already has."

Act II: Scene X

"I know it! I know it!" squeals Parrish as Titus swaggers elegantly back and forth on top of the long banquet table. "You're Sil!"

TITUS: "And we have a winner!"

ARIUS: "Only because you cheated." Arius pins him with a withering glare as Titus slides into the seat and throws an arm over Mattia's shoulders, which she immediately shrugs off. "We said no Craft in charades."

TITUS: "Far be it from me to break the rules, Arius!"

ARIUS: "Your hair is still white."

Titus twists his lips, hair fading back to black. "Oops."

I pick from a bowl of candied plums by the railing, somehow hungry again after storming as far away from the Playhouse Archives as possible, which turns out to be the rooftop.

Jude lies, I remind myself. He lies all the time. He's lying about the treaty, too. It doesn't change anything. My plan will still work.

TITUS: "Alistaire, get over here! You fight like a Player. You might as well drink like one." Reluctantly, I wander from my corner. "You wouldn't happen to know where our least favorite prima donna is, would you? You two seem awfully close these days."

I return a tight smile before remembering Jude specifically asked me *not* to tell anyone about bringing me to the Archives. So I say, "He was showing me the Archives. Probably still down there."

Arius chokes on his wine. "The *Archives*?"

PARRISH: "Bound to learn the hard way about auditionees, that one. At best, they die." She looks at me. "At worst, they don't."

TITUS: "Won't matter. My girl Tig will see the light of the arena. You should have seen her in rehearsal today"—he gives me an unapologetic nod—"no offense, Alistaire." Then turns back to the group. "Jude can count his days. His crown is mine."

Bored of hearing about my impending doom, I drift back to my candied plums and ignore Titus's boasting.

"You're looking...well, Alistaire."

I nearly knock the bowl over spinning around, alarmed—mostly because the words came from Mattia. Gods, how does she *move* like that? She could give Nyxene's shadows a run for their money.

My brow knits in suspicion as I question both why that's been said to me several times now and if that's Mattia's subtle way of indicating she recognizes something about me. Or rather, about my father.

Keen on not finding out, I turn my face to the city beyond the ledge and change the subject. "Must be strange, moving from one place to the next all the time."

To my surprise, she joins me, leans her sculpted brown forearms onto the ledge, and sets a silver chalice between us. "Depressing, more like," she replies smoothly. "We've been through every inch of this side of the Cut and hardly ever glimpsed any of it." She brings her chalice to her lips and drinks, leaving an echo of maroon lipstick on the silver. "I came from this city at some point, I think."

"At some point?" I ask, taken aback by the bitter edge cutting her tone—and still not trusting that Mattia came over here for a mere casual conversation.

"I haven't walked those streets in hundreds of years. I had four sisters back then. Gone now, of course." She shrugs, expressionless, blue-black braids falling over her shoulder. "If I *could* leave, I'm not sure I could even tell you where our old home is, if it still exists."

"Why are you telling me this?" That was probably rude to say.

Her bright eyes flicker in my direction, then back to the city below. "You surprised me the other day. I didn't think you had so much fight in you." She seems to be speaking to herself as much as me. "Almost reminded me of my first day in the Playhouse." I raise my eyebrows, and she adds, "Don't get it twisted; you're a terrible fighter. But you're excellent at pretending to know what you're doing, and that'll get one far in the theatre." She drinks again. "*Awful* at pretending you want to be here, though, so I'm guessing Jude has something to do with that."

I tense, searching over my shoulder in case the others heard. "I don't know what you mean."

"Sure you don't." She twists her lips, seeming deep in thought for a moment. "Be careful of Jude. All he knows is winning."

"Why are you—" A vase shatters. Behind us, Parrish has challenged Arius to a duel.

Mattia looks out at the city. "I no longer have a stake in this," she answers without needing to hear the rest of my question.

I fall silent. Her contender, Linos, is gone. *Eliminated.*

"All I'm saying is if you do find an out—" Mattia almost winces, like it's difficult to force the words from her lips. "You should take it." She turns her eyes to her cast, suspicious. "I don't know what he's up to, but I have my eye on you. I suggest you don't do something stupid, or Jude and his drama will be the least of your problems."

I'm going to take a wild guess and say abducting their Lead Player indeed falls under *"something stupid."*

JUDE: "You all might have the decency to at least *look* thrilled by my presence." Mattia startles, and all of us turn to where Jude is standing at the stairs. "Much as I hate to break up a party, I need everyone to meet me downstairs." He points at me. "*Not* you, Alistaire."

"Why not?" I say, insulted.

"Because I can move the Playhouse or I can keep you out of trouble, but I *cannot* be expected to do both at once."

The smile melts off Titus's smug face. And mine. "Move? We just got here," he argues.

JUDE: "I've heard stirrings in the mirrors. From the North."

Titus snorts. "You mean for me to believe you stopped staring at your own reflection long enough to listen?"

JUDE: "They've been tipped off." His eyes swivel briefly in my direction. "Our tour schedule has been compromised. They know we mean to cross the wall through the District and settle in Syrene in nine days' time. So we're moving across the Cut tonight."

MATTIA: "The Revelers of Diazoma won't appreciate our time with them being cut short for the sake of *Syrene*."

JUDE: "We aren't going to Syrene. That's where they expect us. We'll go east and move the Playhouse through the Paraskenia border."

"What?" I blurt, panic spilling into my veins.

No. *No*.

Titus blanches. "You can't be serious, Jude."

JUDE: "Sil made the call."

My plan crumbles before my eyes. I need more time. And I promised I'd deliver Jude when we crossed into the North, when the Playhouse arrived in *Syrene*—

Titus sticks one foot out and points at it. "*Sil* wasn't the one who got lanced by a godsdamned Eleutheraen arrow."

"If we're lucky, they'll get your mouth this time," Jude calls, exiting. "Downstairs. *Now*, Titus."

At night, the Playhouse shines like the sun as the doors shriek open. The crowds hovering around the gates cry desperate welcomes to the Players filing out.

I watch from my dressing room's high window, alone and sick to my stomach as Jude calls out, "Good people of Diazoma." They fall still at the unmistakable pitch of Jude's Syrenian accent, listening carefully. "I am afraid we must take an early bow. You can blame our friends in the North."

The audience dissolves into wails, like each word of Jude's announcement has sliced into their flesh. The sound is so awful, I'm tempted to cup my hands over my ears.

As the other Players spread out, Jude doesn't move, looking to the distance like he can already see the barrier from here, its limestone strong and towering and running deep into the earth.

Strong enough, I pray. Though I don't think anyone is listening.

"Perhaps you will meet us there when the wall is gone," he announces, the dark timbre of his voice soaring over their cries.

The ground mists, unsteady and unsure of itself. A thick black fog rises around the Playhouse, ready to whisk it away. Ready to breach the Cut.

I close my eyes as the Playhouse descends into the mist like a sinking ship.

The Playhouse is more illusion than material, Jude said. *The "moving" of it all is mostly just for spectacle.*

A deceitful illusion. But surely, one too enormous to cross a divide built with Eleutheraen gold.

Galen's admission comes back to me.

Parts of the wall were never sealed with pure Eleutheraen gold.

A horrid, splintering sound fractures the air, like the ground is splitting in half.

But I know it's not the ground. The sound came from far, far away. From the Cut, pushing back against the Players and their magic.

The Playhouse stills before shaking violently. And when I dare to open my eyes, we aren't in the heart of Diazoma anymore.

All I can see is limestone running in both directions, webbed with veins of Eleutheraen gold carved into swirling symbols. The wall.

The mist thins where it presses up against the threshold of the Playhouse, right at the Cut's border. The golden gates press into the limestone, emitting a violent screech as dark water from the moat seeps over the Playhouse's sparkling terrace.

I grip the windowsill, banging my knee and cursing when the Playhouse jolts.

The wall outside prevails, sturdy and immovable, as if to say, *You will not come through this way.* But I see the cracks threading up its face, accompanied by a wretched snapping sound.

Squinting through the mist, I make out the line of Players down below by the glow of their skin, their hands raised. Mattia swears loudly while Titus shouts, *"It's that damned wall; I told you it's..."* I try to listen, unable to make out the rest.

But for a moment, I almost relax. The Playhouse can't cross after all. I won't *need* my plan. The North will be safe from—

Jude prowls up to the golden gates and throws them open, where they slam into the limestone wall beyond. The Playhouse feels slippery beneath my hands as I grasp onto the purple curtains to steady myself, but they tear like tissue paper. The candles around me blow out and relight themselves frantically, unsure of themselves.

The Players are holding us in limbo—somewhere between what is real and what is not.

Below, Jude flattens his palm to the wall, upon those ancient engravings filled with Eleutheraen gold.

He shrieks so horribly, I have to avert my eyes—but not before catching something.

I narrow my gaze. Jude's left foot is inches across the Playhouse's border, where the gates meet the outside world, water from the trench washing along his shoe.

Past the confines of Playhouse grounds.

Mattia calls something to Jude, but I can't hear what it is over the screams that have begun to tear through the air—not from the Players. From *people*. Though I'm not sure if they're on this side of the Cut or on the other. Maybe both. And then I realize *why*.

The Eleutheraen gold veins in the wall are pulsing with light, heating.

Melting.

A labyrinth of cracks dances up from the place Jude's palm is pressed, like lines on a map. Molten gold bleeds from the crevices, those ancient symbols becoming empty, ugly smears on the limestone. The wall groans loudly.

I shut my eyes, cover them with my hands. I don't want to see. I don't want to know.

The sound of limestone crumbling crashes through the air.

And when the world finally, *finally* falls still, I blink my eyes open and dare a single glance through the window. But I already know the Playhouse has slipped out of one place and into another.

Into the North.

It's over.

Behind the Players, who all look ready to drop from exhaustion, a violent fissure yawns open at the Playhouse stairs like a cracked vase, curling into the foundations of one of the towers. A toll for crossing the Cut.

As the Playhouse settles in unfamiliar territory, and as the black mist begins to clear, I can at last grasp what I saw: Jude's foot sliding past the threshold.

Jude is able to leave Playhouse grounds.

And the realization hits me all at once, with dread, that he *has*.

Act II: Scene XI

"Let's have a flood, right here in this room." Sil paces around me, but I'm still panting from the last ridiculous illusion he made me cast, which involved setting all the curtains on the windows ablaze. Sweat beads on my forehead.

It's been one day since the Playhouse crossed the Cut into Paraskenia, and the city outside has been silent as death.

Hiding. *Waiting*. For me. To do what I promised.

I have to get Jude to Syrene, where the Playhouse was *supposed* to be. And I have to do it today.

RIVEN: "No." Casting illusions has become second nature. I've endured learning Reality Suspension. And Compulsion—the art of embedding a thought in someone's mind—comes easily to me, as it turns out. Though I've learned it either cannot be used on Sil or it's forbidden.

But there's still one skill I *need* to get out of here. "I said Mimicry. I want to learn *Mimicry*."

The director raises an eyebrow at me.

Today marks yet *another* day Sil has dismissed my attendance from rehearsal to observe me one-on-one. Thankfully, he opted for a rehearsal room over the stage—a big, empty space with lattice gold wallpaper and oval windows overlooking a mountainous skyline. I hope I never set foot on that stage again.

And I hope at some point, saying that won't feel like a brazen lie.

SIL: "Mimicry is an advanced technique, but of course, we can give it a—"

Jude slips through the mirror behind him with a yawn and a stretch.

JUDE: "I move the Playhouse over their *impossible wall*, and you give me an early call time? Cruel even for you, Sil."

SIL: "Jude! Just in time. Alistaire here would like to have a go at Mimicry. Show her the ropes, will you? Greenroom is probably easiest for it." With a polite wave and a promise he'll "keep an eye on us," Sil vanishes through the door.

When he leaves, I ask, "What *is* the Greenroom?" The Players mention it often in passing, but I haven't spotted any clear doors or signs that might lead to it.

Jude is already strolling back toward the mirror, summoning a portal through the glass, stopping only to raise a suspicious eyebrow at me. "You *want* to learn Mimicry?"

I search for an excuse. "I'd rather practice that than Reality Suspension."

He shrugs as if to say, *Fair enough*, and steps through the mirror. The lights of the rehearsal room shut off as soon as he does; reluctantly, I follow.

And nearly jump out of my skin when I find what's on the other side.

The Greenroom is hardly a room at all. It's a funhouse of reflections, walls entirely made of mirrors. Red—not green—ceilings, oddly enough.

And no door.

"This is the safest spot in the Playhouse," Jude says while I try to conjure what could be *less* safe than being trapped with a Player in a room that has no exit. "No one can get in or out of here without Craft."

I search frantically for somewhere to rest my gaze that doesn't contain myself. There are mirrors *everywhere.*

RIVEN: "Why...why do we have to practice here?" Out of places to cast my focus, I look to Jude. "We could go back to the stage." I'd even prefer that over this.

"You can't put a costume on *onstage*," he taunts. "Everyone would see!" Catching the barest glimpse of my reflection beyond his shoulder, I scrunch my eyes shut as he prattles on. "Perception is the heart of Mimicry. We're never who we appear to be." My eyes might be closed, but I can hear the smirk in his voice as his steps move behind me. "Even you, *Alistaire*. Now! Look up."

My jaw tenses as I squeeze my eyes shut tighter, shaking my head. Anything to avoid looking at the glass.

Warmth flutters at my shoulders. Jude's hands guide me forward, closer to the mirrored wall, no doubt. I dig my heels into the floor, let my back press to his chest. "I think maybe I've changed my mind," I say, squirming.

There must be another way around my plan. A way to execute it without Mimicry—

There isn't. I know that. If there was another way, I'd have found it.

Jude chuckles, the sound rolling through his chest. "You'll run at Mattia with a dagger, but *this* frightens you?"

"I can learn Mimicry somewhere else," I argue, letting my eyes fall open but keeping them trained on the floor. "In another room—"

"If you're going to put on someone else's face, you'll have to get used to your own first." The cool metal of Jude's rings grazes my neck where his knuckle hooks under my chin, tugs it upward to face the glass. "And there isn't a thing wrong with this one. Look up."

My eyes dart away from my own in the mirror, focusing instead on the place where my head reaches Jude's shoulder and then, cautiously, all the way up to his eyes. I expect him to be shaking his head at me in the reflection, to snidely thank me for not biting him or something as he drops his hand away, settles it back on my shoulder.

Instead, he offers an encouraging smile in the mirror.

I blink a few times, unclenching my teeth. Then, slowly, let my focus fall from Jude to me. But only to my eyes, which don't quite look like mine anymore. The eyes in the mirror widen, larger than they ought to be. A hundred shades of gold web around my irises, the dull brown forgotten somewhere beneath. In the center, my pupils glow with a glittering, sinister light.

They look like Jude's.

Fear coils around my spine at the image, at the evidence of

the Craft binding gleaming back at me, undeniable proof of my disloyalty to everything I was raised to believe. How will it look to the council when I bring them Jude? One Player betraying and handing over another.

No. That's not what I am. I'm not like Jude. I'm not like any of them.

It's enough to send my eyes slamming shut again.

Jude exhales through his nose, probably annoyed and *also* probably late for rehearsal. When the weight of his palm lifts off my shoulder, I'm certain he's frustrated and on his way out. I listen for the sound of his departing footsteps.

Fine. I don't want to learn this stupid stage trick anyway—

I jump when Jude's palm closes over my hand instead, guides it upward, toward my face.

It takes a second to remind myself I loathe it—touch. Ever since I can remember. But Jude's is slow, featherlight; I'm not sure I haven't imagined it altogether. And I'm not about to open my eyes to find out.

The pads of my fingers flutter across my brow under his hand. "Did you know this eyebrow arches higher than the other when you're angry?" he says. I tamp down the urge to tell him *he would know* as his hand guides mine down. "And this little line by your jaw, it tightens when you try to lie to me. You're getting better at that, by the way." Something loosens in my chest, and I startle myself with the small laugh that escapes my throat.

"And here—this mouth." His hand moves, thumb brushing across my lips. The air in my lungs seems to go still. "Absolutely vicious. It's rather lovely when you smile, though." Our hands glide up again, the movement easier, more familiar. The muscles in my shoulders ease, and my mind wanders, curious about the distance between us, wondering what it might feel like to lean into the warmth.

"Your nose wrinkles when you're trying to work out a problem in that frightfully clever mind of yours." His words are closer now, a murmur that tickles my ear. "And then there are your eyes." Our hands still at the crease below my lashes. The hollows beneath don't *feel* as deep as I thought they looked. "They give you away. All your angry little layers, Alistaire, and none of them properly reach your eyes. You might try opening them, though."

Slowly, carefully, I do.

My eyes flutter open and don't dart helplessly to some corner of the room again. They settle on me, on the hollows of my face that don't look as gaunt as I thought they did before. On the nose that seems to fit better now, long and curved. There's a pinkish hue to my lips that matches the color heating my cheeks, where our hands linger.

I tell myself it's a trick of the mirror. Some devious Craft Jude has worked on me in the past moment. The face in the mirror is still mine—just different now. Better. Maybe a trick of the light.

"*These*, by the way"—he clasps my hand a little firmer—"I try to keep an eye on. They're awfully resourceful. And destructive."

I consider snatching my wrist away, tempted to interpret it as an insult. But to my own confusion, I don't want to. I almost smile instead. For a moment, I don't feel so out of place standing beside Jude.

Reality crashes through my mind at the thought. I am standing far too close to a Player, to arms that are capable of unspeakable violence. The very monster I'm supposed to bring to justice—*tonight.*

I wrench away from Jude, and he doesn't try to hold on to me, probably expecting it. He just stares, waiting for me to speak.

"This is a trick," I say under my breath. Jude is all mind games. This is to keep me on my toes, keep me confused, keep me fighting. I'm no use to him dead. That's why he's doing this.

"A *trick*." He looks around, like he's searching for the aforementioned trick. "Alistaire, are you frightened because you hate me or frightened because you don't?"

That's what this is about. He can't stand not being admired by everyone he encounters. This is just a challenge to his ego—

Or, a voice offers in my head. It isn't a familiar one. It comes from some deep, incomprehensible layer of my mind. *Or—*

Before I can think through it, before I can talk myself out of it, I hurry a step forward, stopping right in front of him. Jude watches me back, entirely still and relaxed as I reach up. But my hand isn't as steady as his. It shakes uneasily as the tips of my fingers graze over the curve of his cheekbones, along his brow, his dark lashes tickling the side of my hand. I mimic all of his motions. His face seems more familiar now, in a nice way.

It isn't hard to see why an audience of thousands would fall in love with him from their velvet seats. I imagine it's hard not to fall for his charms; he's crafted from the same stuff as the Playhouse—from beauty, from pride, from that obscure likeability some people seem to be born with.

My palm glides down the curve of his jaw, stays there, out of places to explore but not quite ready to let go. Unsure *why* I don't want to. My eyes flicker up to his, which are still watching me, softer than before. A confusing twinge of something pinches in my chest when Jude catches my hand, lingering and frozen in place. My heart downright begins stuttering over its own beats when he guides my open palm to his lips, presses it to his mouth.

Alarm bells ring in my head. *Loudly.* I jerk backward. I'm not falling for whatever ploy this is—whatever charms Jude unleashes on anyone who stumbles into his path.

"I—" It occurs to me I'm out of breath. I drop my arms to my sides, recovering my common sense. "I'm ready to learn Mimicry now."

Jude blinks a few times, like he can't remember what we were talking about. Then, nodding stiffly, gestures at the mirror. "Right, then." He clears his throat. "First things first. Find your bridge."

I throw him a funny look. "But I'm not onstage."

He gestures around us. "You don't have to be. The world is your stage."

Gritting my teeth but remembering Marigold—and that chain shackled around her ankle—I relent. I need that chain. And I need this plan to work—*tonight. "Methexis."*

A world of glass blooms beneath my feet, and tendrils of gold twist there, reaching for my heels. I tug on my anger, struggling still to banish that funny feeling from a moment ago. It takes a second before I can summon it to the surface, until the warmth of Craft floods through my veins.

JUDE: "Perfect. Now, I want you to picture a face—one deeply familiar, easy to Mimic."

I riffle through my mind, searching for faces. Except, any familiar ones could endanger them.

Maybe sensing this, Jude nods. "Yes, mine is an option." He leans over my shoulder and adds, "No one could blame you." And I internally vow to Mimic him with a big fat nose and crooked teeth once I get the hang of it.

JUDE: "When you look in the mirror, do not see yourself. Imagine you're looking at me. My eyes. My mouth. Speak and hear my voice. Mimicry is all about *intention*. Imagine you know me, inside and out. *Become* me. Let Craft take over, envelop you." He stalls. "The Playhouse will want something in return, though."

There it is. "Come again?"

JUDE: "Think of it as borrowing a costume. The Playhouse expects it to be returned. It will want something of *you*. A deposit—a promise that you'll return what you've taken."

RIVEN: "What *sort* of deposit?"

JUDE: "The longer you're in the costume of someone else, the less you'll remember what's beneath it. You may begin to lose pieces of yourself—your memories, your thoughts—if you wear it for too long."

I study the mirror, noticing the strange way the brunette of my hair has started to deepen, darker.

Redder.

"You mean me," I say. "My memories are the deposit."

"The fade won't begin until you've been in costume awhile. The distant, older sort of memories go first. Then maybe...more important details."

"Always a catch, isn't there."

"Do you know why there are so many mirrors, Alistaire?" he asks. "Because theatre is, itself, a reflection. When an audience sits before us, we're not here to tell them about *us*. We are here to tell them about *them*. A conduit of catharsis, body and soul. So long as you're in the Playhouse, you will always *give* something."

I have to punch down the bile fighting its way up my throat, biting my tongue. A strange, freeing sensation wraps around my limbs. Then I can't quite remember what I'm doing.

From the ground, Craft hums, pulses through me.

JUDE: "You are me."

The words, sudden and spirited, fly from my lips. "You are me."

I force the intention of it into the mirror, braving the face there.

Silence fills my world as I stare deep into my reflection and repeat Jude's voice in my head: *My eyes. My mouth. Speak and hear my voice.*

Warmth washes over my skin and, as it does, my features mold and shift, sharpening.

The spitting image of Jude stares back at me from the glass. With it, though, I feel a strange sense of emptiness. An urgency to remember my own name.

I stare at my hands, at the forest-green sleeves that match the ones Jude wears now. The floor is farther away than it was before when I peer down. There's a tickle at my neck from the brush of copper hair, the texture coarser than I'm used to. My arms feel heavier at my sides, woven with muscle. I reach one up to find the pinch in my nose—a golden ring.

I'm Jude. And the Jude beside me has lost all sense of dignity.

"Look at you!" he yells, clapping his hands and then waving them at the mirror. I'm about to tell him to pipe down, except he's right. *I did it.* Even if he doesn't know it, *this is my ticket out.* My mind lays out the pieces, every detail—each part of my plan until it hits me.

I'm leaving the Playhouse. Tonight. And so is Jude.

A peculiar shadow zips behind him in the reflection. *What was that?*

My eyes widen, and I turn to track the figure when Jude steps in the way, blocking my view.

JUDE: "Incredible, Alistaire! Oh—well, almost. There should be a single freckle *right* here." He taps the left side of my face below my eye.

RIVEN: "Wait—" My voice has dropped an octave, fuller and glassy. "Something is…in here."

JUDE: "A near-perfect imitation! Brilliant. *Brilliant.*"

Alistaire. The name drives a splintering confusion through my mind. My name is Jude—I think? No, that's not right, either.

I catch sight of that odd shadow as it flutters by again, closer. "Something is—something is in here," I try again, more urgent.

The shadow darts by once more, gathering in a single mirror at the center of the room, solidifying into something—into a figure—into—

Before Jude can react, the figure, sleek and quick, slips through one mirror and disappears into the next.

"Hesper," hisses a voice. A voice I'm sure I've heard before. Feminine, soft, *familiar.*

It's so out of place, even Jude momentarily forgets his insistence, venturing up to the glass. "That's not right," is all he says, suspicious.

A flash of white solidifies in the mirror again, no longer a shadow but—

A woman in the mirror, fashioned in layers of white, torn at the hems and sleeves.

She *glimmers*, her skin chipping like paint from her face to her fingertips, gold gleaming right beneath. Her eyes bleed like the sun.

Gene Hunt.

Alive, in the flesh—barely. There's a curious, sad smile on her lips, unlike the mask of unceasing shock Jude wears.

Her hair runs longer than it does in her portrait, curled into shimmering, brandy-colored locks. Several clumps are missing, leaving bald patches on the side of her head. Like a child's doll that's been played with too rough.

I can't move. I've never seen anything so maliciously beautiful.

Somewhere, Sil is yelling, but it sounds distant, muffled, as if through a window, like he's trying to get into the room, but I can't tell from where.

Jude has only the time to incredulously speak the name "Gene" before a vibrant and guttural scream erupts from her lips.

The splintering of mirrors runs in circles around us like broken ice as I clap my hands over my ears.

What the hell is happening?

Half the room shatters, and a sharp, angry storm rains down as we drop for cover on instinct. I shield my eyes, peeking through my fingers at the display of glitter blanketing the ground. Slowly, I look to Jude, then to the broken mirror, empty of any ghosts now as we struggle to our feet.

Then I feel it. A suffocating, visceral presence just behind us.

A searing silence lingers between Jude and me as we turn.

The woman in white is no longer bound by mirrors. She's in the flesh, standing before us.

Gene Hunt. Her eyes are shiny, bobbing between Jude, then me, then Jude before settling on just one—the one who moves to put himself between the ghost and me.

With a final shriek that sends my ears ringing, she lunges for Jude.

Act II: Scene XII

What feels like an arrowhead slamming into my chest tears me from my surroundings and whisks me into darkness.

I stay there, in the dark, feeling far away, tearing deeper and deeper through layers of nothing until—

A woman's eyes, kind and thoughtful and promising. *This is for the best*, I hear as a cup is forced to my lips. I can't feel my hands, bound tight. But I feel the burn of Eleutheraen gold in my throat.

The world blurs again. This time, I shrink inward, like a child. I'm in a brick alley, filled so thick with smoke that I worry it may suffocate the stars above. Rolling over, I shake the shoulder of the figure sleeping beside me.

"Wake up," I say. The voice isn't mine. It belongs to Jude, but younger, naive. "Lukas!" I try again with Jude's childlike voice.

The boy sits up, dazed. "What, Jude?" His eyes widen as he takes in the blanket of smoke around us. His voice trembles. "What's happening?"

Horns blare in the distance, followed by shouts of alarm and confusion. Someone zips into the alley like a shadow, slight and frantic and somehow familiar.

"Get up!" orders the shadow, a girl. Juliet. Her clothes and hands are damp with ash. My chest tightens as I reach for the tattered pack at my other side.

"Leave your things," she urges, pulling Lukas to his feet. "We need to hide."

A chorus of clashing metal resounds in the distance. Juliet tugs at her dirty braid, leading us out of the alley, into the street. "One of the North's armies, someone said," she explains hurriedly as we run. "From Syrene."

Smoke stings my eyes. "Why haven't they called in the Players to help?" I ask.

My boldness shrivels as the ground shakes beneath our feet, what feels like an explosion nearby. A city I know well, suddenly utterly unfamiliar in the red light of slaughter.

"They *did*!" she shouts over the panic.

The streets burn hot, chaotic with disorder and fear. As we run, I look over my shoulder, squeezing Juliet's hand when I spot the army, like an endless colony of ants rushing down the hill in the distance. They spill out from the caravans that arrived yesterday. Caravans that rolled in last night, gifted from Syrene, filled with costumes and food to celebrate the Great Dionysia.

Or so we were told.

"Dionysus," Lukas swears, halting to a sharp stop. *"Look!"*

I do, and the Playhouse is gone, vanished. Fled.

The air still hums where it stood. Then I see what's taken its place, and the breath tears from my lungs.

Juliet's scream cuts through the smoke.

Several stakes blaze ahead, each crowned with a figure writhing in Eleutheraen fire—Players, their skin burning gold, their screams piercing the night.

Something shifts in me as I watch their bodies still, their Craft burning away, given to the sky. The fear around my heart shrivels, collapses in my chest. It hardens into something else entirely.

I mouth a silent vow to the dead Players. Then my feet are moving.

The world blurs again, and everything speeds up. Suddenly, I'm in the Playhouse, Gene leaning so close that I can feel her breath in my ear. "Help me stop this, Jude," she whispers, her eyes wide.

Then I hear a hushed, sharp argument between myself and Sil that ends in a swift decision.

The scene shifts. Gene, running downstage, her voice fierce. *"It's not real!"* she roars at them. "*None* of this! It's not real!"

A tightness in my chest releases when she, at last, collapses on the platform. I hold her under a stage light while she chokes up spots of gold that foam at her lips. The audience watches in awe. They don't remember this part of the show.

Her eyes lock on mine, full of hate. She's fighting to suspend her reality.

I won't let her. I can't.

The world shifts, and Sil stands in front of me now. "Do you see what you've done, Jude?" He's upset. On the verge of tears.

I am, too. I'm terrified.

Another blur. This time, I see the halls of the Playhouse. My feet slow when I notice someone stealing quietly behind a curtain.

Alistaire.

And once again, I feel certain I have seen her face before. And, with even more certainty, that I will never let her leave this Playhouse.

Somewhere, someone is screaming in the muffled way you hear things underwater.

"The damn mirrors are broken—try that one!" Titus's voice, I think.

"Get them out—*now*." Sil's voice.

"She attacked him, didn't she? I *told* you there's something off..." Definitely Mattia.

My muscles feel rigid. Bits of broken glass bite into my skin where I've fallen. I recall strange dreams of a burning city, of an army hidden in caravans disguised as gifts. Players burning upon golden stakes.

Finally, I remember the woman—Gene. The ghost in the mirror and the way she lunged at Jude. She didn't look very dead to me. I remember him barely making out the word *"Éxodos"* before she reached him.

Jude suspended his reality, gave it over to me, casting me deep into his mind, his memories.

He *knew* the woman in the mirror meant to kill him.

Gene Hunt is not dead. But she wants Jude to be.

Carrying two lives instead of one is much heavier. With what feels like the effort of moving a mountain, I turn my head, broken glass sliding beneath my hair. Jude's eyes are open, empty. Blotchy shades of sickly yellow and purple paint his throat.

A large piece of broken glass protrudes from his neck. Gold gushes from it.

Titus's heavy steps approach, and I think I see him point a long finger down at Jude's lifeless eyes. "*Tell me* that one isn't ours."

It occurs to me in a distant, amusing way how easy it would be to end Jude's life right now. This monster who's destroyed cities and lives and trapped me. To catch hold of that little light full of memory and life fluttering somewhere in my mind and crush it—

Are you frightened because you hate me or frightened because you don't?

The thought crashes into my anger, violently derails it.

"Alistaire!" Sil. The director is on his knees, leaning over me. I don't have the energy to look as disgusted as I feel when he lifts my head from the broken glass with the gentleness of a concerned parent. "Alistaire, let him go." Like he knows what I'm considering. "*Please*—let Jude go."

For some strange reason, his plea resonates with a part of me I don't recognize. My eyes flutter open, finding Sil's wide with worry. I let my head roll to the side, where Arius is frantically checking over Jude, extracting the glass from his neck. Parrish sobs just behind him.

I tell myself that Jude is lucky he's no use to me dead. That I need my bargaining chip alive.

I'm so convincing, I nearly believe that's the reason I meet Jude's open, glassy eyes and mutter, "*Éxodos.*"

Act II: Scene XIII

Taking Jude's place onstage tonight was not part of the plan. But then, neither was Gene Hunt coming back from the dead to try and kill him.

My memory swears by the nervous look she gave him, then me, before lunging at Jude with ungodly rage. Gene had been deciding something in that moment. She was confused.

She'd been unsure. She didn't know who was who.

I catch a glimpse of the face I'm wearing in the mirror now—Jude's face still. He hasn't woken up, and Sil doesn't seem to think that he will any time soon. Apparently, I am not very good at Reality Suspension.

If I'm not mistaken, the auditorium tripled in size around the time the lobby doors opened. Or at least that's what it looks like through the slit in the curtain: an endless array of winding seats and balconies stacked in rich reds like a layered cake. I glance over Jude's lines one final time.

MATTIA: "Alistaire is a *novice*."

Her voice booms from the hall as she and Sil rapidly approach. I quickly tuck my script behind a crate before I further prove her point. I *think* I know his lines.

MATTIA: "This is a *lead role*, Sil—and a Playhouse *cast* performance. No auditionees are permitted onstage—"

SIL: "Exactly!" His shout is so loud, I startle. "We're over the Cut now. I won't have news of our incapacitated Lead Player making its way to reporters."

MATTIA: "Jude can still go on tonight. He's *excellent* at Reality Suspension, Sil—"

SIL: "*Unexpected* Reality Suspension is messy at best. Jude is in no shape to perform, and we will *not* appear weak during our first performance North of the Cut."

"No auditionee could have done what—what *Alistaire* did here today," Mattia accuses. "She's conveniently still doing a *perfect imitation*."

SIL: "She appears to have an affinity for—"

MATTIA: "None of *us* can do one this exact, much less for this long."

"Places, Mattia. Now. Alistaire!" Sil calls to me while waving off a furious Mattia. She stalks back into the wings but throws me a look that reminds me of her warning—that she has her eye on me. Not to do something stupid.

And oh boy, am I about to do something stupid.

I clench my jaw at the unfamiliar bite of Jude's teeth and turn to Sil. "Yes?"

From his breast pocket, Sil draws a silvery envelope. The Playhouse symbol seals the flap—a single mask cracked in two, one half grinning wide and the other tilted downward in a frown. A single arrow protrudes through both, binding them together. "You take the role of a Player tonight. You deserve to be paid as one."

A peek inside the envelope makes my hands go numb.

I've never seen so much money in my life.

"And." Sil hands me several envelopes, plain and more tattered than the first. "These are for you. The audience often sends well-wishes to our final contenders."

Final? It occurs to me I've hardly seen the other auditionees since I arrived. I've often felt like the only auditionee here.

Why?

I watch Sil's eyes, certain there's something unspoken between us. Something I'm not seeing. But before I can open my mouth, he stalks down the hall, calling for places.

Parrish hovers at the curtain, peeking through the crimson.

PARRISH: "Full house tonight."

I grimace. It didn't take long for Revelers to follow the Playhouse through the Cut and fill their velvet seats. I imagine every face in the audience as blissfully numb as Haris's and shudder.

TITUS: "I hope you're ready, *Jude*." He waves mockingly as he passes. "A new master of Mimicry on our horizon, perhaps! Do me next, won't you?"

"Come now, Titus," teases Parrish. "I wouldn't wish *your* face on anyone."

My hands file through the envelopes Sil handed me: a shocking series of letters from strangers declaring admiration, love, promises of loyalty, and hopes for me in the casting call.

But when I tear open the final one, I inhale sharply.

"What is it? A lock of hair?" asks Titus, pocketing a prop ring that he uses to propose to Parrish's character in the third act of tonight's Comedy. "Don't worry yourself, Alistaire. I once received a hand in a box!"

Arius whistles from the wings. "We still don't know whose that was."

But it's not a lock of hair. It's a note.

The lights begin to fall. I steady my breath, counting everything I'll need tonight: my Eleutheraen arrow. Marigold's chain. About fifteen minutes during intermission. Jude.

As the curtain rises, I look over the strange note once more, this one different from the others. It's not full of pretty words and delicate scrawls.

It's one line, and in a hand I know well.

I'M COMING, LITTLE SISTER.

—G

Time moves in indistinguishable blurs of story and memory and emotion. Whether it's measured in hours, days, years—during a performance, I'm not sure, and I don't care.

Then it stops moving altogether as I burst into the wings, back into reality's wintery grip.

Someone claps a hand on my shoulder and says something to the effect of, "I'll be damned, Alistaire!" and the name clears my vision.

It takes a moment to remember what's just happened onstage, the way a dream flees from your mind the moment you wake up. We're in intermission.

Sil hurries backstage, clapping his hands and raving about the first act while I quietly excuse myself to get some water.

Then I'm bolting as fast as I can down the hall, rounding the corner and tearing through the door to the Labyrinth Steps. By the time I've scurried halfway down the spiral stairs, I'm still shaking the Craft from my fingertips, and that strange dreamlike feeling that I've lived someone else's life in the few hours I was onstage.

The farther I go, the dimmer the lights get. By the time I reach the landing, spot the door leading into Marigold's prop room, I can barely see the face of my timepiece. It grimly reminds me I have nine minutes before the curtain rises for the second act and everyone notices the lead is nowhere to be found.

I check my hands before knocking on the door. Still Jude's hands, still covered in heavy golden rings, with an ugly scar across my—his—palm.

I hope to Dionysus I'm right about all of this.

I knock.

Act II: Scene XIV

The rattle of a chain precedes a set of wild, unfocused eyes peeping through the cracked door.

"Jude?" Marigold whispers, hopeful. She moves away from the door to make room. Inside, her music box plays cheerily along.

"Yes! It's me, uh, Jude," I say, correcting my pitch. *Gods*, I do a bad Syrenian accent. I search frantically for things Jude might say. "Please hold the applause, I know I'm pretty," I add awkwardly.

Her face is damp with wet trails over the gold of her cheekbones. Curiosity surfaces on my tongue, almost forming the words: *Why are you crying?* And I stop myself long enough to remember Jude has a tendency to make statements and wait to see if someone argues with them. So I clear my throat and rephrase: "You've been crying."

Marigold huffs, bequeathing me an unsettling glimpse of her razor teeth. I'm a lot bigger than her in this form, but that doesn't make me feel much better when she's got nails like unpolished daggers. The chain at her ankle drags when she moves, though it's hard to see it beneath her dress, which is patched from about a hundred different fabrics and patterns. She skulks past the portrait of Jude, still on the easel.

Only now the canvas is absolutely *mutilated*. Like she's dragged those sharp little nails right across the face. The edges are singed.

This may not be as easy as I hoped.

"I've come to free you," I say, but the statement comes out like a question.

Marigold turns abruptly. "Leave the Playhouse?" she hisses in a way that sends alarm bells ringing in my head.

"No! No, of course not," I backpedal but inch forward. "Only from this room—you ought to get bored in this room, yes?" He always does that. Adds *"yes?"* at the end of statements like no one could ever refuse him. "I'll take you to the auditorium, where you can see the rest of tonight's performance."

Her expression darkens, but there's a glint in her eye at the mention of a performance. "He said I'm never to leave this room, not ever." *Sil*, I presume. "Not since I—" Marigold begins to weep. Loudly. *"My dolls."*

I pause. "Okay, is that…a no?"

"I have a contract," she whispers, sniffling and annoyed. Then she narrows her eyes at me. "*You* have a contract."

I hadn't thought about that. Jude would have one. I don't know what it entails, but Marigold gives me the impression that leaving the Playhouse is a no-no. Though clearly, he *can*.

"Contracts can be amended," I say with a shrug and a grin, the way I think Jude would. "Where is yours?"

"With the rest of them, and yours," she says, hesitant.

I blink, not saying anything.

"The stage," she clarifies, like it's the most obvious thing in the world.

"Right! Forgot where I left that old thing," I reply nervously, tucking away this information.

Her brow lowers. "The freckle below your left eye is missing."

Well. Damn it.

I'm about to say something about makeup when she grabs a godsdamned *hammer* off the table and swings at me.

Ducking, I skirt behind the table and push it between us. "Now, Marigold, I'm sure we can talk about this," I say, as if a monster who arose from the ruins of the Eleutheraen well is going to *reason with me*.

Marigold freezes, and I realize my mistake. I'd pronounced the first part of her name "mare" instead of "mahr." "You don't sound like him," she says, showing all her teeth.

Well. It was worth trying to do this peacefully. I fly across the table, foot aimed for her chest, knocking Marigold onto her back while I snatch the Eleutheraen arrowhead from my bag.

I hold it high and bring it down hard on the base of the chain in the wall. It takes Eleutheraen gold to break it—and for once in my entire time at the Playhouse, it would seem I've lucked out. Because this arrowhead wasn't just dipped in Eleutheraen gold, it's outright crafted from it. No wonder Mattia couldn't destroy it herself.

The chain loosens but doesn't break. My luck runs out after that, because when I look up, I notice two horrifying things at once.

One, Marigold's jaw unhinging as she screams and lunges at me.

Two, the smell of lavender and the woman watching by the door.

Gene Hunt observes, quiet as death.

She looks different. Her eyes, which bled gold before, are overtaken with it now, bright and feverish. A glow radiates over her skin, suggesting she's more apparition than flesh, though the skin she *has* is peeling right off. It flecks down her neck, torn away entirely at the shoulder.

The air surrounding her stirs uneasily, as if struggling to hold on to her form.

Then she moves, impossibly fast, as she shoves Marigold away from me.

I'd thank Gene, except she whirls around, wielding…

The striking gold of *my own missing knife* in her hands.

I blink, having only enough time to think, *I should move*, before she lunges.

"Where did you get *that*?" I shout, skittering away. Her blade—*my* blade—sinks into the wall, and the room shakes from the impact of Eleutheraen gold meeting a Craft-based foundation.

Somewhere upstairs, an orchestra sings to life, summoning me back to the stage.

Intermission is over.

Seized by panic—the preamble to all good decisions—I grip the workbench and throw it at Gene just as an enraged screech closes in from behind.

I whirl, reaching for my arrowhead, as Marigold flies at me, shrieking like a vengeful spirit.

Her screech cuts off, vanishing behind her golden tongue. But her mouth hangs open.

We stare at each other, our eyes slowly turning downward where the jagged point of my arrowhead is lodged into her side.

I barely register what I've done by the time Marigold falls back onto the crooked floorboards, dead.

A *very* warm hand grips my wrist from behind.

"I'm *not him*!" I scream, thrashing out of Gene's reach to point my arrowhead at her.

The door shudders. Her eyes go as wide as the clockface behind her. She brings a finger to her lips, as if to say, *Hush.*

I start yelling instead. "I'm not Jude! I'm not him. Believe me, I understand the indisputable urge to shut him up for good, I do. But *I'm not the one you're looking for.*"

The door shakes in its frame again, only this time, fingers of darkness stretch through the cracks like smoke, bleeding across the walls. And with it, an echoing, staccato clicking that makes the collection of skulls on Marigold's shelf chatter their teeth.

Nyxene. Jude's warnings of the gruesome Stage Manager creep out of my memory, sinking into the air, heavy and foreboding.

Ice edges into my veins, then into every part of me, like I've been pushed into a cold bath. Darkness unfurls over the room.

The shadows are Nyxene's first and only warning, Jude once told me. Shadows he said to stay away from by *any means necessary.*

Nyxene is coming. My heart lurches. I'm not supposed to be down here.

And I've killed the Prop Master.

Gene rushes at me, knife held high. Clearly, she has it out for Jude, but on the bright side, Mimicking his form gives me a height advantage. I catch her wrist with one hand and hold my arrowhead to her throat with my other. It catches on a little half-moon necklace at her neck, snapping the silver and sending the pendant clattering to the floor.

I gasp, my grip on her wrist slipping as Gene pushes the blade down toward my eye with unholy strength.

I'm cold. So cold I can't feel my toes, my fingers, or the hand just barely keeping my own knife from plunging into my skull. In the corner of my vision, Nyxene's shadows grow like vines around the room in the shapes of reaching hands—hundreds of them. The door shakes on its hinges once more, Nyxene demanding entry.

The arrowhead in my other hand drops to the floor as I clutch my heart, gasping against the ice seeking a way in. One of Nyxene's shadows stretches far enough to brush Gene, a wraithlike finger of midnight grazing her shoulder.

It's the first time I hear Gene make a sound—a cry as the dagger tumbles from her grasp. I twist free, dropping to my knees to wrap my fist around the fallen dagger. I can hardly feel my legs as I straighten and point the tip up at her. "What do you *want* from me?"

Gene shakes her head frantically, begging my silence. As if I'm doing her any favors.

But the damage is done. The door bursts open, and darkness floods in. Shadows everywhere stretch wider and higher and colder. And with it, a high-pitched shrieking distorted by low, rasping whispers that send my skin crawling.

I fly back into a corner, trying to breathe, but the cold air burns my lungs.

Nyxene: a silent, lethal monster. The Playhouse's guardian that cleanses magic from the stage after shows, that guides patrons out once the curtain falls. That keeps actors in line. Heard, felt, and never seen.

But I see her now, and the sight makes my knees shake. A frigid, solid darkness that reeks of peril and melds into the shape of a monstrous Stage Manager. Somewhere, deep in the midnight mist, I glimpse fierce silver eyes. About twelve of them.

Gene pinches her brow, as if gathering concentration. Her lips part, struggling to form words. Frustration dampens her expression, her hands curling into fists.

Then her eyes snap open, and a single, strangled word escapes her lips.

"Riven."

I shove my back into the corner again, almost dropping my knife. "How do you know my name?" I demand, but it's useless. Gene lets out a furious cry that shakes the lanterns hanging above. She looks pleadingly at me and whispers one more word: *"Script."*

All at once, Nyxene flies at the Player, dozens of shadows racing up Gene's legs and cutting clean through the glow of her skin like butter.

A guttural warning pounds in my ears as the shadows encase the dead Player in mist, otherworldly screams ripping what was Gene into shreds of darkness and gold.

It's vicious, visceral.

And then it's nothing.

As silence rings out like a bell, my mind seizes on her last words, strangled but clear.

Riven.

Script.

Act II: Scene XV

If I were to guess how long it takes me to get back upstairs for the second half of the show, based on Sil's face when I reach the wings: too long.

SIL: "Where in the hells have you been?"

I decide not to tell him I was downstairs slaying his Prop Master or that I was nearly murdered by a dead Player who I assume is now *extra* dead. I also don't tell him that I had to hide in silence for another ten minutes before Nyxene drifted back upstairs.

It took breaking Marigold's ankle with a hammer to get that Eleutheraen chain off, which probably would have taken less time if I didn't have to keep pausing to retch into the nearest corner. Even if Marigold *was* a monster, I can't help but wonder at what point I became capable of this.

But I have it. I have the chain. I'm getting out of here tonight. It's all I can do to hide the excited little skip in my step.

Instead of admitting any of this to Sil, I smile politely and say, "The Greenroom. Napping." To be fair, I *did* go to the Greenroom to drop off the chain in a leather pack, along with a crossbow I snatched from the armory behind Marigold's workbench.

Sil's face says he doesn't believe me. Then he shoves me onto the stage.

After the shadows in Marigold's lair, the warmth of the stage is overwhelmingly welcome. Like crawling under your sheets and falling asleep after a long day. The ice in my lungs dislodges as I speak my lines.

Then they don't feel like lines anymore.

Hours melt into days and then years. Or maybe it's just been a few minutes by the time my world ends with the crash of a closing curtain and the storm of applause roaring outside it. Reality hits like a hailstorm as I follow Titus offstage and the other Players exit in the opposite direction. What looked like the set piece of a brick alley a moment ago suddenly looks more like the wings now.

And what looked like two strangers arguing in that alley are no longer strangers—they're Sil and Jude, standing backstage.

Pity Jude couldn't have stayed dead just a bit longer. That's going to complicate things.

"Fantastic job, Alistaire!" congratulates Sil just as Jude interrupts with, "You need to take my face off. Now."

"What? Jealous she wore it better?" Titus asks, clapping me on the shoulder.

Jude grits his teeth. "You've been in costume too long—Sil, *tell* her. It's dangerous—"

"Our Alistaire looks just fine to me. Don't forget, there's still curtain call!"

The curtain flies open, and from the opposite side of the stage, Parrish and Arius approach the glaring spotlights, shattering the illusion of the show as they whirl into fond farewells.

Titus follows with gracious "Thank you"s before joining the others off to the side.

Mattia crosses the platform next, dropping into a graceful, low bow. The applause slows, confusion stirring at Jude's—*my*—absence.

Sil takes the stage next, and the audience flies into hysterics as he bows.

SIL: "I'm proud to announce we had somewhat of a surprise this evening."

I will the stage to open up and swallow me whole, already puzzling out what's about to happen. Now that Jude's back on his feet, Sil is going to spin it like this cast change was *intentional.*

"Alistaire," says Jude softly and coughs. "Don't take this the wrong way, but you look like hell. And that's really saying something, considering you look like me at the moment."

Instead of admitting that I had a little scuffle downstairs with the Prop Master, I take in the dark circles under his eyes, the sickly pallor of his skin, and mutter back, "And you look like you spent most of today being dead."

SIL: "You'll notice we are short one face on this stage. That of our Lead Player? You see, just earlier today, we found one of our casting call's own was secretly harboring an affinity for Mimicry the Playhouse hasn't seen since the likes of our most beloved Player Atlas."

The audience shouts their approval. I pass over the archives of my mind, recalling Mattia slaughtered Atlas in the arena. I remember this mostly because it's the only match so bloody that, at first, no one thought either survived.

SIL: "So! Just for you, tonight we invited this surprising new talent to share her discovery. A force to be reckoned with in this year's casting call. Everyone, welcome *Alistaire Hunt*!"

The audience shatters into a storm of cheers and whistles as Jude and I cross center stage. The applause stills a little in confusion, unsure who is who until Sil calls, "A perfect imitation, no? Come this way, Alistaire!"

Reluctantly, I resume the long walk off the main platform and into its round center by myself, surrounded on all sides by faces and screams as I nervously descend into a bow. My heart hammers in my ears as I come back up, the sea of eyes dizzying sets of expressions everywhere I look. I have told fourteen lies today, and this is by far the biggest. But I'm almost done. I'll be gone in the next thirty minutes tops.

Jude joins me on the platform and takes his bow, gesturing to me again and then clapping himself. A strange feeling flutters, birdlike, near my heart.

This almost feels...good? No, that's not the word.

Right. It feels right. For a moment, I feel like a puzzle piece, one that's been sitting in the wrong box for years, too jagged for other pictures.

Until now.

Disgust surfaces at the thought, and I shove the feeling away just as quickly.

I turn my eyes coldly to Jude and hope he enjoys his final curtain call.

• • •

Sil orders everyone to change and be at the stage door in twenty minutes.

"Be ready to talk. Smiles, my Players, all of you! Paraskenia's journalists will flood the media with smears by morning." He turns to me. "And, Alistaire, let us see your face once more. Perhaps stop by the Greenroom first and take off this costume?"

Anticipating this, I nod. And shortly thereafter, burst into the Greenroom while the Players return to their dressing rooms to change.

It's empty. The destruction from Jude teaching me Mimicry earlier today is nowhere to be seen. The mirrors are perfectly restored on all four walls.

I guess Jude was right. The set *doesn't* like to be messed with.

It's getting darker, which means I'm not supposed to be in here. I'm supposed to follow the lights back up to the dressing rooms and then to the stage door.

Of course, I will be doing neither of these things.

After extracting the pack and crossbow I stashed behind the costume rack, I stalk up to the mirror and stare into my—well, *Jude's*—reflection. I recall the sound of my own voice, the curve of my jaw, the slightly crooked raise of my left eyebrow. The healing scars beneath my collar. The white birthmark across the right side of my neck.

An intense pressure releases from my skin, the air suddenly cooler. When I blink again, it's my own set of gold-and-ochre eyes staring back, widening as I take in my reflection.

I'm *almost* me. Except new cords of muscle have begun to swell at my legs, my arms. My frame looks fuller, stronger. If my reflection is to be believed, my hair has grown, reaching my shoulders. Hesitantly, I touch a hand to my jaw, longer and sharper now.

Backing away from the mirror, I yank my collar, expecting the wound of my mark to be irritated from the pressure of the Jude costume I wore all day.

But there's no damage there at all. It's healing.

The lights flicker off, and I curse at the dark—

Only, it *isn't* entirely dark. I spin, frantically searching for wherever that soft golden light pressing around me is coming from.

When I realize: It's me. The light is coming from *me*, a flicker of gold radiating just above my skin. That same golden glow that hovers around the Players. It pulses painfully over the place where my Eleutheraen mark once was.

The Craft binding. This is Jude's. His Craft has already sunk into my skin, my veins. My mark isn't there to deter it anymore.

It's time to get out of here. I tighten the strap of my pack back to my own form, but not before checking that my Eleutheraen knife and Marigold's chain are secured inside.

Gripping the crossbow and my single Eleutheraen arrow, I conjure a gateway within the Playhouse like Jude taught me to and plunge through the mirror.

Right into Jude's dressing room. I point my arrow high, right at his heart.

"Hello, Jude," I say.

Act II: Scene XVI

Jude's eyes never leave the point of my arrow. "Alistaire," he says politely. "You know, I've thought it over, and maybe we should institute a knocking-before-entering rule."

"Put a shirt on," I order, praying my face hasn't turned the same shade as the stage curtain at the sight of him half-dressed. His arms are webbed with glimmering veins that thread corded muscle down to the bracelets at his wrists. Intricate gold symbols swirl across his shoulders.

"And—" I breathe, getting a grip. "And grab that cloak on the hook. It might be cold outside."

"Outside." Jude raises a dark eyebrow, amused. "And where are we going?"

"Hands where I can see them," I snap, and he defensively raises both. "We're leaving the Playhouse."

In spite of the hearty laugh he lets out, I see the tension in his jaw, the way his eyes still haven't left my arrow. "Why would I do that, Alistaire?"

"Fair is fair. You kidnapped me. I'm kidnapping you back."

He tilts his head. "You and what army?"

He's purposely leaning his right shoulder forward, but I can see what he's trying to conceal in the mirror behind him.

RIVEN: "What is that? That gash on your left shoulder you keep trying to hide."

JUDE: "Oh? Looking, were you?" I feel my face heat, annoyed as he evades the question. "As you well know, I can't leave the Playhouse, Alistaire. Even if I wanted to."

Liar.

RIVEN: "You can. And you *have*." My eyes move to the deep white scar across his right palm and stay there. Something about it has bothered me since I noticed it in the Archives.

I know how he got that scar.

I know it because I gave it to him.

My mind races back to the memory of that day in the courthouse with the Player, the woman who spoke to me. The Player who *cursed* me. How she'd screamed and wailed when I raked the blade through her hand.

"You just looked a little different at the time," I whisper.

Jude goes still.

RIVEN: "We've met before." I raise the arrow higher. "And you're going to tell me why."

Act II: Scene XVII

The Player who cursed me, who *doesn't exist*, has been right in front of me *all this time*. Just with his own face now.

"News spread about the markings, that the North had begun marking children, too," Jude admits, too calm. "Sil sent me out to the District to verify if it were true. Obviously with a different face."

"Why?" I press, even though I'm certain I know the answer. "Why a disguise?"

"Because, as I'm sure you're aware, I could not go as Lead Player," he says, sounding bored with the conversation.

RIVEN: "So you *can* leave."

JUDE: "Players are not kept in the Playhouse by your human laws; they're kept in by Sil's. Lead Player already has more freedoms, and my contract was...amended."

RIVEN: "You were taken away. I *saw* the sentries take you."

Jude shrugs in response. "Congratulations. You witnessed their very last breaths."

"You *spoke* to me!" I try to keep my voice steady, but my tone is falling off its hinges, shaking with anger.

"That," he says, "you'll have to forgive me for. I have no idea what you're talking about. There were a lot of people around." He raises a shoulder. "I'm honored you've kept your first sighting of me so close to your heart, of course."

"You *cursed* me!" I shout, rage roaring in my head. "Do you have *any* idea what my life has been like? Tell me what you did to me—"

"Nothing! *Nothing*," Jude insists, moving closer and freezing when I raise my crossbow. "I swear, Alistaire. I didn't hurt you."

He's so convincing, I almost want to believe him.

But I don't. I remember *every* sleepless night, and I remember *every* lonely day, getting weaker and weaker.

"You attacked me," I hiss through my teeth. "Tell me *why*."

"Me? Cause a scene? Unimaginable!" Jude rolls his eyes. "I was probably *bored*, Alistaire."

The padding of footsteps and chatter parade outside. The other Players heading down to the stage door. The lights fall around us, candles hushing out one by one.

I pull the arrow back farther. "Call for them and you're done." I cock my head at the mirror. "Portal. *Outside*. Now. Before they notice we're gone."

Questioning him will have to wait.

At last, Jude looks uneasy. "We're in the North. I don't know where the closest mirror will be. It could take us anywhere."

"Guess you'll just be risking it," I hiss.

Jude stares evenly at me and my arrow for a hard minute before abruptly turning to the ornate mirror hanging over the lattice red-and-gold wallpaper. He brushes a hand over its frame, then brings his palm flat against the glass, uttering a few words.

I grab the cloak off the hook and hurl it at his feet. "You'll need that," I say as the glass opens up. His shoulders shake with laughter.

He turns a look back at me, the surge of Craft making his eyes glow like candlelight. "We'll be needing a lot more than that to survive this, Alistaire," he mutters and steps through the portal with me close behind.

INTERMISSION

Intermission: Scene I

I'm not sure I've ever been so cold in my life, and *that's* saying something.

But then, I've never been to Paraskenia. Or in this particular tent, staring at this particular family.

I count an older woman and man and what I assume are their two grown daughters. Judging by their faces, I think they must be surprised to see us, too, until the older woman cries out something to the effect of, "Our *prayers*—they've been answered!" and falls to her knees.

"Aren't you all lucky? I don't usually make house calls," says Jude casually, but he's stiff as one of the costume mannequins, and I'm guessing he's also noticed how cold it is out here.

We're in a canvas tent with four sleeping rolls and a single mirror, from which we've barged through. The air smells of smoke, I think from the remainders of a fire I spot burning to its last coals through the slit of the tent.

"Are you alone?" I demand.

"Alistaire, darling, that's no way to ask—"

This, of course, is when the lot of them notice the arrow I'm pointing at Jude's back. Their expressions fall, shifting rapidly. Before rage can manifest on their tongues, I whisper to Jude, "Make them forget."

He turns and rolls his eyes at me. "I'm a Player, Alistaire, not a magician. Players can put things into your heads, but we can't take them out." He turns back to the family. "You'll hold this meeting dear to your hearts, yes?"

Their eyes glaze over, gold and filmy, all at once. I shiver.

"*So* dear to your hearts that you wish to share none of it," he drawls. "You know how greedy people can be. Would be a shame for someone to come try to take this beautiful mirror from which a *Player* came, now, wouldn't it?"

"No, never, I wouldn't think of it," the man babbles.

"Lovely," Jude says with a nod. "And with that, we bid you farewell, as we must be on our way. Unless you have gifts for us, of course."

It takes all the self-control in the world not to elbow him, so I settle for, "You're terrible," as the family gathers every last bit of food, silver, and a wool cloak from their bags, compiling it in a single pack that they rest in Jude's hands. He returns a brilliant smile and a bow, then proceeds to gallivant through the tent flap, my arrow just behind him.

"That was an awful thing to do," I whisper as we step into the night. We're in the outskirts, and the city isn't far off; I can see the lights. More importantly, I can see the Playhouse.

I've actually made it out.

"They'll be fine. Put this on." He tosses me the wool cloak and adjusts the one I threw at him earlier over his shoulders. "If you shiver any harder, you'll drop that arrow I'm sure you worked *very* hard to smuggle away from Marigold. And I can't begin to imagine how you found that damned knife again."

"Maybe you didn't hide it very well." Since clearly *someone* found it.

Jude ignores me and tosses an apple in my direction. I keep my arrow trained on him and let the fruit fall limply to the ground. He shrugs. "Forgive me for trying to keep you alive until we get back."

I laugh. "*We* are not going back. You think I'm so sweet that I'll just go on my merry way home and then let you return to the Playhouse?"

"Calling you 'sweet' is like calling a mountain lion 'fluffy.' Perhaps true, but also the *least* of your worries if you've gotten close enough to tell."

I breathe in, still shivering hard. But we have to keep moving.

"*Walk,*" I order.

"Where?"

Thick maple trees make up most of our surroundings, but

there's a dark path that cuts through the forest toward the city. Riddled, I'm sure, with similar encampments of Playhouse fanatics crossing through the broken wall.

"The agora. A station. We'll board the Diolkos," I conclude, referring to the railway that runs east to west near the North's border. The Diolkos might get us to Syrene by morning.

"Amazing how you resist the arts of the theatre." Jude stubbornly turns down the path, my arrow at his back. "Being delusional seems to come so naturally to you."

He marches off with a sort of long-suffering dignity that I think only a Player could manage, shivering and throwing me the occasional tragic look to make sure I know he isn't enjoying himself.

But as we travel deeper into the darkness, I feel eyes. Jude doesn't look like a normal person, and even the dark won't do much to disguise his height or glowing irises.

A thought occurs to me. "Sever your bridge to your Craft."

Jude tries to smirk, but it looks more like a wince. "Now, Alistaire, be *reasonable*."

"Do it. Now."

Jude's face darkens as I direct him behind one of the trees off the path. I don't feel bad, really. It doesn't matter what Jude does or doesn't remember. If he's responsible for what happened to me, he deserves worse than this.

"It's harder for a Player," he protests.

"Not a moment to waste, then."

Jude sits in the dirt, rattling off a string of complaints about dirtying his pants, while I quietly prepare to reach for the Eleutheraen chain in my pack. He throws me one last annoyed look before closing his eyes and seeming to focus harder than he usually does. *"Methexis,"* he utters, and a change wraps steadily around his form, constricting the lines of his shoulders and softening the gleam of gold veins under his skin. The copper of his hair, which usually flickers like firelight at the ends, dulls into a dark-brownish color.

While he's distracted, I dive for the thin chain in my pack, looping it tight over his wrists and securing both hands behind his back as Jude barks out a curse at me.

"Gods, Alistaire!" he shouts. "What else do you keep in that hellish bag? Poisonous lollipops for children? Pointed shoes for stepping on small dogs?"

I roll my eyes. Passing through the city with thick cloaks and the quiet clinking of chains hidden beneath is subtler than marching through with an arrow pointed at my golden-eyed companion.

The Eleutheraen chain tightly secured, I drop it and stare at my hands, realizing how uncomfortable it is to hold. Eleutheraen gold isn't supposed to hurt *me*.

"Surprise," Jude mutters glumly, noticing. "You've got Craft in your blood, Alistaire. Haven't you looked in the mirror lately?" With his bridge severed, his voice is about a hundred times quieter, restrained. He almost sounds like a normal person and, when he blinks at me, most of the gold has drained from his irises, leaving a mild shade of hazel in its place.

We pass no fewer than sixteen more encampments before making it to the agora, crossing into the main square, which bustles with activity, though the thick of night has long since fallen.

I expect fights or protests, but for the most part, it seems like anyone who's trickled over the border from South Theatron has stayed near the gates of the Playhouse, where commotion gathers in the distance.

Sil has probably noticed our absence at the stage door.

I push Jude through the crowds, keeping to the side streets while navigating the winding roads, stopping only once to ask for directions. Gathering that we're not from here, the stranger simply spits at us and walks off.

The second time I catch him almost slipping his hands free from the hidden chain, I sharply reroute and dip into the first apothecary I see.

Jude stiffens but clearly knows better than to comment out loud as I point to the scarce shelf of Eleutheraen gold vials and say,

"One will do." It's only a matter of time before Jude schemes his way to escaping, and I'm done taking chances.

It feels fitting, handing over money Sil gave me in exchange for Eleutheraen gold. Though, given the shocking price, it suddenly isn't hard to believe the North is in low supply. I roll the bottle between my fingers, watching it shimmer through the glass.

"And one dilution blend," rasps Jude. He's reeling in his voice as much as he can, but between that and the hood over his head, his subtlety is a hard sell. He had to duck to avoid hitting the doorframe on the way in.

The man across the splintering table sets his hands on his apron, mark at his throat gleaming beneath the dim light of his shop. Finally, he retrieves what Jude asked for.

I turn to Jude. "*What* are you doing?" I whisper.

He glares at the wall behind the counter. "You're planning to poison me, yes?"

"Yes. And?"

"And if you force pure Eleutheraen gold down my throat, you'll kill me *and* yourself and everyone within a few miles of us."

The man returns and pushes a second dark bottle holding clear liquid over the counter. I push the money across the surface and swipe the dilution blend before herding Jude out.

Then I hear it as we step onto the street. Two words pulled from the frantic chatter surrounding us: *Missing Player.*

We need to get out of here. Now.

Intermission: Scene II

"How quaint," Jude comments as I hurry us into the Diolkos station.

I take in the vaulted ceilings clad in stone, the high glass windows dotting the walls. A clock tower ticks at the center of the open space, reminding me that time is a luxury we can't afford right now.

Hurrying Jude ahead of me, I note a series of seven platforms that line the Diolkos railways, their timber tracks laid in stone. Nestled on three of them are enormous carriages that look more like ships to me, their sides polished and reinforced with oak. I follow the thin retractable sails secured to their tops with my gaze, curious how they operate.

I've often wondered what else was lost during the time that the first Players walked freely, maiming and destroying as they wished. But they left the things they liked: printing presses to report on their movements. Limelights to illuminate their stage. Solagraphy to capture stills of their faces.

The piercing whistle of a departing train makes me cringe as we shuffle past the wooden timetable braced over the clock. My first ride aboard the Diolkos was meant to land me at orientation week for the Orkestrian Academy.

Instead, I'm herding a disguised Player to almost certain death while he complains about his shoes being uncomfortable.

"You should have let me change," he says. "Cicero must have sworn vengeance on me while making these boots. If I lose a foot, it's on you."

My own costume boots make a conspicuous clip-clopping sound on the stone as I drag Jude to a small booth across the station and request two tickets to Syrene. The woman behind the counter sorts quietly through a stack of envelopes, though her eyes flip up to Jude more than once. And I do mean *up*.

"Runs in the family," I blurt. "Giants. All of us."

Though it hits me when she smiles a little *too* friendly in his direction for the second time that she isn't concerned with his height. She may not recognize Jude as himself in this condition, but it's done little to hurt his looks. And his charms are apparently not limited to Player magic.

Noticing the attention, Jude snaps his smile into place.

Gods help me. I roll my eyes. And do a very good job of ignoring a weird twinge in my gut when Jude leans into the wall and begins asking the girl if she always wanted to work in a ticket booth, because he "knows a place that might be hiring." I elbow him.

This girl isn't the only one who's taken notice of Jude and his unusual height. And, for the record, mine.

A man with watery silver eyes and jet-black hair has peered in our direction more than once from the second platform. The first thing that registers is just how much I do not like his smile. The second is that he's missing an ear.

The third is that he's still staring.

With the exchange of another chunk of my Playhouse money, I swipe the tickets from the counter and nearly throttle Jude for suggesting the girl wear her hair down more. "What?" Jude asks as we hurry across the station. "If you had big ears, I'd tell you, too."

"Quiet," I snap as we head to the third platform.

"Ticket—thank you," I hear ahead of us. It feels like I'm in a race with my own breath as we move up in line on our platform, until we're called next by a stout man with beady black eyes.

I look over my shoulder, unable to shake the feeling that the man with the missing ear on the platform is still watching us.

Waved forward after presenting our tickets, I shuffle Jude through the steel doors and onto the Diolkos.

"Toward the back—go on," I say, feeling eyes with each passing compartment. I wonder if bystanders can help it or if they just intuitively sense they're staring at a Player without realizing.

Finally, we settle into a small compartment with poorly cushioned seats and gray walls. My mind tugs back to the one-eared man's gaze, and I find myself searching the window for it, not bothering to mention it to Jude, who's been prattling on for the last ten minutes.

"—and if you're going to hold me hostage, it's just good manners to purchase nicer seats—"

"If you don't shut up, I swear I will tie you to the roof where you can't bother anyone."

Jude raises one dark eyebrow at me. "You *swear*? To do something we both know you won't do? Getting awfully comfortable with language like that. That's progress."

I rub my temples. "What will it take to get some silence?"

"Well, for one, I'm starving."

I pull open the pack of *gifts* he stole from that family and throw a piece of stale bread at him, praying it shuts him up.

"Players don't need food much, Alistaire."

My head is pounding now. "Fine. What *do* you need?" I ask, exasperated.

"Attention." He pouts at me.

I groan and drop my face into my hands.

The Diolkos jolts into motion, the station rolling by us as we begin our trek west. I make a point of ignoring Jude and watch the window, still looking for the one-eared man.

"They won't take you back, you know," he says after a little while.

I cast him a side-eye. "The Playhouse?"

"No, the Playhouse would if you play your cards right." His eyes drop to the place where my mark used to be. "The North, though. They'll never take you back with a ruined mark."

A lump gathers at the base of my throat where that ruined mark is.

"They will," I say and try to believe it, "when I stop whatever horrifying spectacle you're planning. The Great Dionysia isn't happening."

Something darkens in his expression. "Alistaire, neither you nor I can stop what's going to happen at the Great Dionysia."

I take that as all the confirmation I need. He's plotting something. "We'll see."

As if a switch has been pulled, Jude's face clears. His smile looks forced now. Cheerful but full of malice. "May I tell you a secret, Alistaire? From one soul to another."

Jude shifts in his seat, as if trying to get comfortable with layers of chains binding his wrists behind him.

"I fear you and I are just the same," he says. Appalled, I search his expression for a punch line as he continues. "Two sides of a shiny coin used to purchase terrible things."

The Diolkos jolts again, and I grip the table between us to steady myself. "I don't see how we're similar at all."

"You don't? I do." He leans forward and lowers his voice. "You can be a great many things, dear heart. But you cannot be fewer."

Galen's voice bursts through a door in my head. *You laugh too much, Riven. You frown too much, Riven. You talk too much, Riven. Too loud, too angry, too much.*

Even at my softest, I am too hard for most people.

For a moment, I wonder if Jude is, too.

"That's enough." I clear my throat and retrieve the two bottles I purchased earlier.

Jude tenses, eyes on the Eleutheraen gold. "Alistaire. Be reasonable."

"For what it's worth, I wish this wasn't necessary." I can't risk him being at full strength during this trade, especially if Galen is there. Gods know what Jude might do, who he might hurt.

"Stop!" he almost shouts when I'm ready to pour the Eleutheraen gold into the second bottle—the diluted solution. "One drop at *most*, or—" Jude shudders. "I know you don't trust me, and you have every right not to. But I am a Player, and more than that could do...bad things. And frankly, you don't have the weight on you to drag me around."

I grit my teeth and use the dropper to squeeze the smallest

drop of Eleutheraen gold into the solution before instructing Jude to lean his head back. He stares stubbornly at me instead. His olive skin has paled to the same shade as the melting snow flying by outside.

"Why?" he says. "If all you want is to get home, why go to all this trouble?"

"I am *far* past only wanting to get home," I hiss. "Do you know how they formed the first treaty, Jude? How they caged you Players to begin with and kept the likes of your cast out of the North?"

Jude grows very, very still, a lethal sort of calm settling over his features. "I'm familiar."

"They captured a Player," I push on anyway. Granted, *that* capture entailed an army. I seem to be doing just fine going at it solo, though.

"They took *three* Players," he corrects, showing all his teeth when he does.

Fine. Maybe I couldn't manage three. Whatever. "The North held them for ransom," I go on. "Then traded them in exchange for the five-hundred-year treaty."

"Held for ransom!" Jude laughs pleadingly. "Gods. They *tortured* them, Alistaire! Took three and traded the only one they hadn't killed yet."

I go still. I didn't know that. "They...tortured them?"

Jude's face darkens. "I'm sure mortals *love* to omit that last fact from the history books. And they didn't ask for a single bit of information from the Players they tortured, by the way," he says. "They asked their questions of the Player they forced to watch."

My hands go cold.

"Which is damned stupid." He falls back in his seat, bored. "Leave one of us alone long enough, and we'll be begging to tell you our secrets just for attention. So!" Jude tilts his head, humor vanishing. "You plan to trade my life for...what exactly?"

I set my shoulders back, gathering my resolve. "I am willing to bet that Sil will do nearly *anything* to get one of his Players back."

"He will." Jude bares his teeth at me. "We all would."

"And I think that includes signing *whatever* contract is presented to him. Maybe an oath to never tour the North or even enter the District again. Permanently this time." I smile smugly. "In exchange, to keep the life of his Lead Player."

Jude's eyes brighten with a dark glimmer. "All the world's a stage. You think I'll give up half of it?"

Not easily, I don't. Admiration. Love. Devotion. It's what Players feed on, a drug they can't get enough of. They'll kill for it. They *have* killed for it.

And the larger their audience, the stronger their power.

Gods know how strong they'll become if they take the rest of Theatron, too.

"Drink up." I lean over the table with the bottle as Jude laughs. The cool exterior he's worn most of today is melting off, giving way to something darker.

"I have been in this position before, you know." Jude stares at me, and there's something like hurt in his eyes that I try not to notice. "You *should*. I shared that with you."

Guilt clouds my mind. I've been doing my best not to think about that—those terrible people who forced him to drink Eleutheraen gold when he was only a child. Not even a Player at the time.

There it is again, that same wrenching sensation from earlier—the wave of nausea that hit me square in the gut at the sound of Marigold's body hitting the floor. *Is this what I'm capable of?*

I draw my eyes from the bottle to Jude, wondering at what point he stopped looking like an immortal monster and started looking like—

Well, like Jude.

"I didn't tell you the full story, though. Do you know what I did to them?" Those people who took his family. He tilts his head at me. "I *waited*," he whispers. "Sent them messages for years, telling them *exactly* when I was coming for them. So they'd know."

I swallow, stalling. "Why?"

"I had a sister. They had a daughter. I thought I'd let them get attached, let them know they'd be ripped from her the way my family was ripped from me. As you said"—he nods at the bottle in my hand—"fair is fair."

There it is. Monster. A vengeful one, at that.

Before he can say more—because *gods*, I don't want to know more—I lunge across the table and force the bottle to his lips. Predicting this, Jude doesn't bother fighting. The rest of the gold drains from his eyes by the time I lean back in my seat. He wavers like he's about to keel over.

"I probably deserved that," Jude mutters and turns to cough. Bits of gold splatter onto the seat beside him, and he's fighting to keep his eyes open. "But for the record, that was a really bad decision."

I lower my brow. "Why?"

"Because we're being followed," he says, groggy. Then passes out.

Intermission: Scene III

My eyes dart between Jude, unconscious on the seat across from me, and the door. I'm suddenly aware of every fleeting shadow beyond our compartment. I overhear a whispered mention in the hall that we should reach our destination by morning, but it's the conversation between a second pair of passengers that has my shoulders tensing up to my ears.

"Yes, a missing Player—can you believe it?"

My heart starts to race. There's nothing I can make out about the woman or her companion through the frosted glass, just that she pauses.

Pauses a beat too long. Her companion murmurs, "Making his way north for vengeance, I heard..." They continue on by, and I can't hear any more.

In this state, I don't think Jude is about to avenge anyone. His skin has faded to the pallor of melted wax, and he only awakens to cough miserably, curse, and fall back asleep. A thin layer of gold is gathering under his eyes and at his lips—which have paled white.

Will they torture him? Kill him? I figured it would be a neat trade, plain and simple. And even if things went poorly, I felt certain I wouldn't care. But whatever happens to Jude—I'll be responsible.

One life for the entire North, I chant to myself. That math has to even out somewhere, right? And I'd have done something good. I'd have a life and a name for completing what my father started. I wouldn't waver in the shadow of Galen's legacy.

The Players started this game; it's not my fault that I have to sink to their level to win it.

None of this eases the remorse crowding my mind.

I turn to gaze out the window but meet my faded reflection in the glass and let it drift back to Jude, wondering if I've lost the right to call anyone a monster. Maybe some monsters are crafted from survival. I think Jude was.

And I'm starting to worry that I do care. I picture myself dragging him to Syrene's capital, delivering him to the arms of guards who will be too rough handling him. Probably throw him into some awful cell to keep him restrained.

My conscience groans under the weight. And I'm almost positive Jude is intentionally looking as sad and innocent as possible while he sleeps just to guilt me.

When his breathing goes quiet, though, I start to panic.

"Jude?" I whisper. Nothing. *"Jude,"* I try again.

There's a shift outside our compartment. Then quiet again.

I press my lips together, hesitating a moment before launching up to pull the drape to our compartment closed. Then I move next to Jude to check for a pulse, pressing two fingers there at his neck.

A shock of cold moves from his skin up my arm. Startling away, I restrain a gasp when I notice a strange, textured pale color on my index and middle finger. I match it to his neck, where my fingers have left a visible spot, the patch of his skin rubbing off on me like faded ink.

My mind conjures the image of Gene Hunt, her skin chipping away like paint on a doll.

My heart pounds wildly, fear sucking all the air out of the space.

"It was down there—that one, I think." The voice in the hall is male and suspiciously quiet. My blood dips a few degrees as two large shadows slip past our door.

"If you want help," Jude mutters, eyes still closed, "you're going to have to undo the chains."

I almost cringe at how relieved I am to hear him speak. At least he's not dead.

But he might be if I go through with this. If I turn him in as a bargaining chip.

No. They won't kill him, I reason. *A peaceful trade. That's all.*

"Not happening." I pull my pack over my shoulders and keep

my ear to the door until I'm sure they've passed. Then, sliding the door open, whisper, "Come on. We're moving."

It takes a solid two minutes to bully Jude into sitting up and another three to get him moving down the hall, in the opposite direction from where I think the men went. He stumbles out of the compartment like a drunk from a bar after last call.

"I suppose we'll just outrun them?" he slurs ahead of me as I shush him. "After all, there are *sooo* many places to go!"

"We're getting off early at the next stop," I snap at him under my breath.

He turns a knowing—if a little delirious—grin at me. "Oh, someone feels *guilty*."

"I just need to think about it a little more. Don't get excited." Damn it. I've never been good at making decisions. But I need to be sure about this—before I hand him over.

"Would you *miss me*, Alistaire?" Jude takes a stumbling step forward, catching himself. "That's very sweet."

"Would you *stop* leaning into the wall like that?" I nudge him down the hall and peer over my shoulder. "Someone will hear you."

"Oh. I'm sorry. Are the *chains* you tied me up with making too much noise?" Jude leans a hard right, loudly scraping the Eleutheraen gold against the bronze siding of the wall, emitting a wretched screeching sound.

I panic. "Okay! *Okay.*" I throw another nervous glance over my shoulder and grab at his cloak, searching for where I've clasped the chain shut and freeing his wrists. "Don't make me regret this," I hiss, piling it back into my pack.

A horrible grin slides up Jude's face, and I have less than a second to realize my mistake before he bursts into a run down the hall.

"You were *faking*!" I call, bounding after him.

"Acting, Alistaire! There is a difference."

Jude is faster than me, and he knows it. Which is probably why he takes the time to drop into a low, graceful bow before skirting through the door into the next carriage with a wink.

I navigate the narrow hall, sparing careful glances over my shoulder as I crash into the next compartment—the common carriage, with long sets of seats lining either side. Most of them are full with strangers, whose eyes turn to me upon my haggard arrival, aside from a few sleeping passengers.

Dread sinks into my bones as I pass each set. Jude could be disguised as anyone if the Eleutheraen gold has already worn off.

I scan the following three carriages for signs of him—a loose lock of copper hair, a golden eye, *anything* that might indicate a clumsy costume in his fatigued state—but for the most part, they all look like regular people.

Until I see a whisper of a familiar cloak down the aisle and make a dash for it—

Only to find Jude's cloak hanging neatly over an empty seat.

My furious expression must give me away, because I sense someone staring curiously in my direction as I drop the cloak and turn—a woman with chopped, light hair and a narrow chin. She smiles just a little too sweetly as I pass, and my ear itches toward a conversation in the passage ahead. Casually slowing by the sliding door, I listen in.

"A moment, sir—I've just received word *mumble mumble* don't mean to alarm you—a passenger *mumble mumble* jumping off the—"

Suddenly, I forget all about being cold. I'm pretty sure my blood is boiling.

Jude is gone.

With any luck, he'll return himself to the Playhouse. Without that luck, I've set a Player loose on the world to do gods know what near a city he's sworn to take revenge on.

As I grip my pack and return to my seat, some senseless part of me chants: *Hunt him down.* But he could look like anyone or anything. I register vaguely that the blond woman is staring at me again as I pass back through to my carriage.

When I reach my compartment, I collapse onto the seat,

exhausted. The space feels extra empty. In a strange way, Jude's absence is louder than his presence.

We probably weren't being followed at all. I was hyper-fixated on anything suspicious, and Jude picked up on it. For all I know, he could have conjured the sounds of that conversation outside our door to make me panic in the first place.

Time feels too precious to dwell on it, though.

Jude is loose and likely heading back to the Playhouse. I could try to cut him off before he reaches it.

Or I could give up the hunt, cut my losses, and go home. I don't know how, but Galen would find a way to fix all of this, ruined mark or not. He'd figure it out. How would I track Jude down again anyway?

Another wave of dread tingles in the back of my head. I *know* how. There's Craft in my veins. *His*. It calls to its likeness through a shared thread. Whether I want to admit it or not, it'll lead me back to Jude.

The compartment door slides open, and I half expect him to march in and sit himself back across from me.

But it's not Jude behind the door.

It's the one-eared man, and he isn't alone.

Intermission: Scene IV

My hands go for my knife.

The one-eared man shows little surprise as he slides into the seat across from me, raising one eyebrow over a set of blue-gray eyes that don't seem to focus on anything in particular. I almost think he's looking right through me. "Eleutheraen gold? Interesting."

Syrenian accent.

His companions—a shaggy, bearded man who my brain labels as their Muscle and the petite blond woman I noticed earlier—file into the compartment, all armed heavily enough that I think twice about making any sudden movements with my blade. I'm cornered and outnumbered.

The woman sits at my right while the bearded fellow slides in beside One Ear, who sets his hands on the table, fingers laced together.

"Dorian. Pleased to meet you." He nods at the Muscle. "This is Basel." Then gestures to the woman. "Eleni."

I'm not sure if my real name or my made-up one is more damning, so I say nothing.

"Tell me," the one-eared man continues smoothly. "Where's your friend run off to?"

A dark possibility rattles me. *Dorian.* The Playhouse Bounty Hunter.

When I don't answer again, he continues. "I could have sworn you had a companion accompanying you at the station earlier." He pauses before adding, "Riven."

My heart leaps into my throat, but I latch on to that simmering anger that's never too far out of reach and ask, "Did you always have one ear or did the other get so bored of hearing you talk, it fell off and walked away?"

What possessed me to say *that*? Half expecting him to backhand me across the face, I start when all three of them burst into laughter.

"Your brother said you'd be stubborn." The blond woman—*Eleni*—grins at what I'm assuming is the sight of all the blood draining from my face.

"M-My...brother?" I stammer, remembering at long last what Cassia said: *Your brother has gone for help.*

Galen sought out the Playhouse Bounty Hunter.

"Came to us awful desperate to get you out of the Playhouse. Do you know he tried to make a bargain with us?" Dorian whistles. "Was willing to pay a pretty price for your return."

"Gal—Galen sent you?" I falter, shocked and relieved at once. The tension in my chest eases. They're here to help.

I'm so relieved at the news, I'm caught off guard when he brazenly leans across the table and flicks my jacket collar aside. I startle back, clasping a hand to my throat. "Galen sent me to retrieve a *marked*. Swore up and down you'd never give yours up." Dread floods me as Dorian clears his throat, those unsettling eyes piercing. "It would appear we've not come to retrieve a marked after all."

I narrow my eyes. It's widely rumored Dorian and his people *don't* mark, for the sake of fooling their way into the Playhouse and getting close enough to dispatch a Player. "That's a lot of talk, considering I've heard you aren't, either."

Dorian smiles slowly, neither confirming nor denying. "My eyes aren't gold, Riven."

The Diolkos slackens its pace, brakes hollering in the distance. "Sounds like our stop," he announces, that unserious, singsong voice of his making my blood run cold. "So I'm going to ask you one more time. Where is Jude Stepharros?" He smiles. "He owes me an ear, you see."

"Long gone," I return glumly, but the chances of me convincing these people of anything feel slim to none.

"Then I suppose we'll need to finish this conversation

elsewhere, when you've had more time to think on it."

Something like a rag meets my nose and lips. My grip on my knife loosens.

And everything goes black.

Intermission: Scene V

When I awaken, I see stone walls and rotting wooden beams lined with torches. Across the worn floorboards, a heavy oak door. A map on the wall. Two windows, crusted with ice, frame a furious snowstorm. It's dark outside. Still night, then.

I can't move—my hands are bound tighter than a sailor's knot on both armrests of a chair. Who's to say how they dragged me off the Diolkos and to wherever this is without raising suspicion, but it's almost impressive.

Actually, no. I coaxed a Player through a railway station and onto that train. It takes more to impress me now.

Somehow, these garbled thoughts bring a huff to my lips and the word "mediocre," before the rest of my brain wakes up.

"I'm sorry the accommodations don't suit you," says a voice with a laugh, and I lift my eyes to see a figure illuminated in the now-open door, the night dark and encroaching around him. A drift of snow rushes in, and I shiver as Dorian pushes the door closed and stalks forward.

I feel eyes on my back, hear chatter—there are people behind me. One of them whispers something that sounds like, "Don't look her in the eyes."

"I cannot stress this enough, but capturing me is truly useless," I say, realizing how dry my throat is when the words come out in a rasp.

To be fair, I *am* frightened, but after being held prisoner in the Playhouse by immortal monsters, being kidnapped by humans feels more like a time-out.

Dorian blinks at me, a passive smile drifting across his weathered face. If I look close enough, I almost think I can see wheels turning just behind that unsettling gleam in his eyes. "I don't think that's true. Have you seen this?" He hooks a finger at someone behind me, and I hear heavy steps. Then Dorian is holding a newspaper. He taps the front page. "When morning comes, this headline will be in every newspaper across Theatron."

It reads:

WHO IS ALISTAIRE HUNT?

My lips silently mouth the words along the top line. *Audiences shocked after auditionee replaces Lead Player Jude Stepharros in one of the most convincing Mimicry performances seen to date. A classic Playhouse trick, most say, though speculations about Jude's absence at the stage door have given birth to rumors about the Lead Player's health…and whereabouts.*

Still, with no face of her own yet to be seen onstage, it begs the question: Who is Alistaire Hunt?

"It would seem you have a curse, *Alistaire*," Dorian says loosely.

"Tell me something I don't know," I mutter, pulling on my bindings. They don't budge.

"A *natural*, the Playhouse would call you," he goes on. "And that creates a most unique problem for us. You're marked, you see." I wince with disgust when he presses two fingers to my collar and tucks it back, revealing the blistering, but healing, skin. "Or… you were."

I try to look over my shoulder, catching a glimpse of the cloaked audience behind me.

So *this* is the notorious resistance.

I don't know why I imagined Dorian as young. Up close, I decide he can't be younger than sixty, a hard ruggedness to his form and weathered face that suggests I am far from the most intimidating thing he has encountered.

"If you were to take the place of Jude Stepharros—" Dorian says, interrupted by my burst of laughter, which he ignores. "If you were to take his place in the cast and news were to—and it *will*—break that you are *not* from South of the Cut…well, that would make you, Riven Hesper, the very first Player from the North. In *history*. Certainly the only marked Player to set foot onstage."

"You make it sound glamorous," I feign. Cracking jokes makes it feel less serious. I know where he's going with this. There's never been a Player who hailed from North of the Cut.

And *certainly* not one who happens to be the daughter of the dead Peacemaker.

"The political upheaval alone would cripple Theatron. Throw the entire philosophy of the North into jeopardy." That unserious, singsong voice again. His eyes lock on mine. "Should you take Jude's place, your presence alone could very well open the gates wide to the North for the Playhouse."

I say nothing as his words crawl over my skin, seep into my bones.

"Is that what you want? Are you truly that selfish?" Dorian almost sounds sincere, until his voice drops to a snarl. "I guess we should expect nothing less from the Playhouse." He pauses. "Your Player-worshipping traitor of a father would be proud."

It feels like I've been slapped across the face. *Player-worshipping. Traitor.*

What is he talking about?

"Where is Galen?" I demand.

"Your brother was sent away. He should have known we do not help the likes of the Playhouse. I should have thanked him for the information, though. It made it easier to track you."

A bitter taste fills my mouth. "I am *not* their next Player."

Dorian sighs, a sad look on his face as he reaches into his breast pocket and retrieves a vial. "I'm afraid it's a chance we can't take, Riven."

The bottle looks familiar—that twisted silver cap that forms the shape of a serpent. I've seen one just like it in Jude's dressing room.

Poison of Echidna. It's lethal. Instant.

"I am going to ask you one more time." He tilts his head, smiles kindly. "Where is Jude Stepharros?"

"I don't know!" I answer truthfully.

"Are you willing to help us track him?" the woman—Eleni—counters. And I realize the real reason they've kept me alive. She saw the Craft in my eyes, knows I could possibly track him by it, probably find him if I tried.

I open my mouth, close it. *Could I?* I was willing to hand Jude over to Syrene. But that was supposed to be a *trade*.

Looking at Dorian, at his hunters, at the Eleutheraen weapons strapped to their belts...I don't think there would be any trade if they got their hands on Jude.

"No." The word shocks me more than it does them. "I won't."

Dorian twists his lips. "That's disappointing."

"Wait," I protest, bucking and pulling at my ties. "Wait, but I—I know things. About the Players, about their director—"

Dorian roughly pushes my sleeve farther up, pulls a torch from the wall. Beneath the flame, my veins shine gold.

My stomach feels like it's full of lead.

"It runs in your blood now," he concludes, resolute and emotionless.

"It can be *purged*," I insist. "My allegiance is with the *North*, not with the—"

"Yet you won't help us find him, a Player *you've* set loose on the world?" he asks. "You expect any of us to believe you're capable of telling the truth?"

I can't stand the look of his blue-gray eyes, the swift conviction behind them.

So *this* is how it ends. Not by the selfishness of a Player who trapped me but at the hands of my own kind.

Dorian pops the lid off the bottle, and the sound sends my vision tunneling. My blood burns hot—*really* hot as he grips my chin and brings the bottle to my lips.

This isn't how I'm supposed to die.

Panic shouts in my mind, and I buck, throwing my weight to the side as hard as I can.

My chair swings and then comes crashing down on my left as I pull hard on my binds. Someone yells to Dorian as my ties snap.

I roll onto the ground and make a beeline for the door.

Someone snatches my hands and forces them behind me, whipping me around so fast, the air is shoved out of my lungs. It gives me a chance to take in the rest of my surroundings—the stone walls behind me, the gleaming gold weapons strung up in display beside a narrow hallway leading out.

Dorian's entourage lines the back of the room. I don't count them—eight? Ten? I barely catch more than a flickering glimpse of their faces, hard and rugged like Dorian's, by the light of the torches.

More boots come barreling in from that narrow hall.

It takes way more of them to hold me than it should. I want to convince myself it's the adrenaline, but I know it's something else. There's Craft in my blood. I *am* stronger than I should be. Stronger than a *mortal* should be.

A lot of things are shouted, but I only care about one phrase.

"Eleutheraen gold—to hold her—"

Fear grips my spine as instinct sends me reaching for my bridge, riling my anger and tugging desperately on the Craft there—

But before I can do anything with it, I'm thrust back into my chair, and something heavy loops over my arms, pulling tight. Chains. One of the Eleutheraen links is jagged and scratches the skin of my shoulder, a violent burning sensation left in its wake.

Do something! I think furiously at myself. *Figure this out—*

But the yelling around me, the calls for Eleutheraen gold, the weight of chains cinched around my shoulders…

My world slows, my body too heavy, like it desperately wants to go to sleep and never wake up. Nausea whirls in the pit of my stomach as I pull in a breath.

Help. The word is a shout in my head, useless. I'm alone. I'm alone, and I need to get out of this—

"I don't *want* to harm you, Riven," Dorian growls, leaning down to face me when I'm at last restrained. "Were it simpler, I would gladly return you to your brother. I wish that I could."

"Then why don't you?" I challenge, but my voice is strained.

"He'll *tell* you I'm marked. That I do *not* belong to the Playhouse—" I rail against the chains but feel weaker each time I try.

To my horror, a thought crosses my mind: *What if Dorian is right?* Look at where I am. What it takes to hold me.

What if I *am* no better than a Player?

I have no idea what I am anymore. But whatever it is, it feels lonely.

"And when the world learns who you are?" Dorian says, catching his breath. I grip the armrests of the chair and grit my teeth until my jaw aches. "*Daughter* of the murdered Peacemaker! If *she* can trust the Playhouse—*join* it!—why shouldn't everyone?" He shows me the bottle again. "This is not about you. Think of your people, Riven. Your *family.* Surely you must see this is the best thing you can do for them?"

I breathe hard, exhausted. I don't want to believe him. But his words…they start to sound right, to make horrible sense.

Dorian approaches me with caution, watching my hands like they're claws. Suddenly, it's not that I'm too tired to fight him, to fight all of them.

I'm just not sure I *should.*

I stop pulling on my chains.

Dorian leans down, bracing an arm on his knee and staring deep into my eyes, like he'll find every lie I've ever told there. Slowly, my gaze drops to the poison in his hand.

The door flies open again, the wind howling through. I shiver harder.

"Sir!"

A boy, no older than fifteen with a freckled face, stands there with a worried look. "Sir, you need to see something—it's urgent." His voice is frail and panicked, eyes bouncing between my situation and something happening outside.

Dorian stills a moment, patience thinning as he says, "I'm sure it can wait—"

"It *can't*, sir."

There's a shift in the room as Dorian's people exchange

concerned looks.

"Watch her," Dorian orders to my army of babysitters and stalks out after the boy, calling for the man named Basel to follow. The one built like a granite statue lumbers out after them, enormous gilded axe in hand. In their absence, Eleni—his obvious second-in-command—and another woman who might have more muscles in her neck than I have in my entire body stand by the door, eyes on me. As if waiting for me to try and make another grand escape.

I don't.

If I expected commotion to follow, none does. Nothing. Even the howl of the wind falls eerily silent. I tune in to the careful breathing of those around me.

As fate would have it, I am sorely out of luck, because when the door creaks open, Dorian stalks back in, unbothered by whatever situation awaited him outside. He stares at me and stills, shaking his head. "Where were we?"

I brace myself for the poison as Eleni steps aside to let him through.

Do I deserve this? Part of me wonders if I might.

At least Jude said it kills quick.

There's a sly grin on Dorian's face that I don't like at all as he leans close. But when he tilts his head at me, I pause, find myself struggling to recall if it was his left ear that was missing. It *was* his left ear. Not his right. Wasn't it?

"Don't look so scared," he whispers, voice dropping so low, I think only I can hear it. "What did I teach you about your nerves? Three deep breaths."

My breathing stops altogether.

"You aren't Dorian," I say.

"Dorian? No." He smiles. Gold curls under one of his irises. "Not I."

Intermission: Scene VI

The room stills when Jude rises to his feet, face conniving as a jackal and gold spilling across his eyes.

Eleni shrieks an order to halt when one of their hunters reaches for a weapon.

Dorian—or, rather, Jude disguised as Dorian—watches in amusement as Eleni treads carefully forward, hands raised in surrender. "Where is Dorian? This doesn't have to end in blood."

Jude raises an eyebrow, looking pointedly down at me bound in my chair and then back at Eleni. "It doesn't?" He raises a hand, runs it absent-mindedly over his missing ear. *"This,"* he announces, twirling a finger at the room, "is *really* rude. I'll have an apology. Who's first? You?"

His eyes fall on the muscular woman behind Eleni, whose hand curls around her dagger. "I'd sooner cut out my tongue."

"Do it, then."

My eyes flip up to Jude as my mouth falls open to tell him to stop, but I'm not fast enough. Not before the woman's tongue falls to the floor. She starts moaning incoherently, sending Dorian's people scattering toward the walls where weapons hang or to their belts for Eleutheraen gold daggers.

"I said *hold*," Eleni shouts through her teeth, then turns back to Jude. "*Where* is Dorian?"

All at once, his disguise melds and shifts, face morphing until he's Jude again.

Blood is splattered from his sleeves to his forehead.

"Well, don't look so sad." Jude pouts, rubbing his chin. There's blood crusted under his fingernails. "You'll see his face again." A wry grin slides over his mouth. "I left it hanging just outside."

The air drains from the room. Eleni's expression clears, blank as paper. But something more vibrant than gold washes over her eyes. I want to say it's the hardness of anger or the guttural pangs of disbelief, but when she opens her mouth and utters a sentence in an old language I don't understand, it's with a darkness that sounds more like heartbreak.

Jude replies in the same tongue—old Syrenian, I would guess—then lets out a mean laugh. It's a rich and selfish sound, the sort when you laugh for yourself and don't bother to check if anyone else found it funny. The sound is beautiful when you're in on the joke and cutting as steel when you're not.

His words, whatever they were, sink into the room, into the minds of men and women with no marks to defend against his Compulsion. Weapons drop, clattering loudly to the ground.

Eleni hisses something back, and he doesn't react, a cold glint in his eyes, probably enjoying the attention as Craft pulses bright in his veins.

He raises his chin, utters another word.

A curious blankness paints the faces around me. I watch as each set of hands, unburdened by weapons, slowly pulls a torch from the wall instead.

Eleni is gripping her hands into fists so tightly, I see blood. Fighting Jude's Compulsion? *How?* She looks to the Player and whispers a word in that old tongue again. The pleading way she speaks it makes me think it's *"please."*

Jude balances a glare down at me, then back at Eleni, making a little *hmm* sound in the back of his throat. And then: "Kneel."

The room goes deathly still, the air gone. The woman glowers at Jude, just barely letting her gaze slide to her hunters clutching torches—and those horribly blank expressions.

With eyes like chips of ice, she bares her teeth, lowers herself onto a knee—

"*Not* to me," Jude snaps, that twisted smile faltering. "Come now, I'm getting bored."

I throw a reasonably horrified look in his direction, now tugging on my chains so hard, I'm surprised the chair doesn't snap. *No*, I almost shout. *Not to me. I'm not one of them. I'm not like him.*

If Eleni went any stiffer, she'd shatter. Her expression full of hate, she pivots toward me, leans down, and slowly, *slowly* bows her head. But her gaze never leaves mine—a gaze that wishes me a slow and painful death.

Why is he doing this?

Around her, the hunters hold their torches patiently, awaiting further instruction.

"Wait," I breathe.

Eleni shuts her eyes, as if to shield herself.

Jude speaks another word.

"Jude," I interrupt. *"Don't—"*

One by one, the hunters press the torches into their chests.

I can't watch, heart thundering in my ears as the room fills with screams, the reek of smoke and burning hair, and one instrument in the chorus that doesn't fit: the pattering of hurried footsteps on their way out.

When I dare to open my eyes, Eleni is making her escape through that narrow hall. I barely register Jude saying something that sounds like, "Hold still."

My throat fills with smoke as something collides with the back of my chair.

The wood splinters, and the chains release me. I catapult forward out the door after Jude, desperate to escape, my ears unable to take the screams any longer as the stench of burning flesh reaches my nose.

What I decide is worse, though, as we flee the burning house, isn't the screams themselves. But the way they start to quiet, one by one.

The silence follows us out, clinging to my clothes like smoke. Only when the cold hits my skin do I realize we've made it outside. Alive.

It's dark. The snow has stopped falling and blankets the ground. There are violent disruptions in the white, though—places where the snow is flattened and disheveled.

Dawn is on her way, judging by where the moon has drifted to make room for the horizon. Aside from this, there's nothing. Only a burning, desolate house in a quiet forest.

And blood, staining the fresh snow at our feet, a violent streak of color slashed across a white canvas. Wherever Jude dragged Dorian, I'm sure the darkened crimson trail toward the back of the house will lead me to whatever is left of him.

A thick branch, snapped from a nearby tree and discarded on the ground, drips red at one jagged end.

There's a vial buried in the snow at my feet.

It's empty.

There's no sign of the large man who followed Dorian and, to my horror, no sign of the young boy who called Dorian outside, either.

"Did y-you— The boy at the door," I stutter. "You didn't—"

"I *was* the boy."

I breathe a small sigh of relief at that, while Jude walks from the flames with little more remorse than he'd depart his dressing room. But the air is heavy with horror as I follow. My shoes find their way around the blood, my stomach turning when I notice something small on the ground, illuminated by thin rays of fading moonlight.

There, in the snow, lies Dorian's other ear.

Intermission: Scene VII

Exhaustion creaks in my bones by the time we near civilization, a village settled at the bottom of the icy hills that, in my opinion, could benefit from a nice set of stairs. The sun rises higher as we walk, morning breaking clear onto the horizon and easing the harsh winter winds. I shiver. I've never been this far north before and decide I won't be making another visit anytime soon.

Some unspoken agreement to work together lingers between us. Until Jude finds a mirror, or until I find passage back to the District, at least. I can't really follow through on my threats or carefully plotted plans to turn him over.

And if I'm being honest with myself, I don't think I could do it anymore anyway.

In the light, I notice Jude is holding his arm. The overcoat he must have traded his cloak for at some point is torn at the bicep, confirming something sharp ripped into fabric and flesh alike. He's favoring his right leg, but I can't tell what's wrong with the other one.

Dorian put up one hell of a fight, I guess.

A different question is rising into my throat, though. *Why?* I trail after him in the snow, my boots sinking into Jude's larger footprints. *Why did you come back?*

The forest is unforgivably quiet, save for the crunch of ice beneath our feet and a biting wind that seems determined to get under every layer I'm wearing.

Doesn't he feel remorse? *Something?* There's not much to read from the set of his shoulders, long legs moving through the woods with the sort of inhuman grace reserved for elk.

"That was..." My words shatter the long-standing silence. Jude doesn't flinch. But someone needs to acknowledge the last few hours out loud. I still can't banish the stench of smoke and burning flesh from my nose, the raw screams from my ears. "That was awful."

Jude stops cold in his tracks. Around us, tall, dark trunks with gnarled branches seem to listen in, the only witnesses to the grisly scene we left behind.

"Yes," he agrees. "And anything less would have painted a bright, vulnerable target on both your back and mine for the next group." He aims a meaningful glare at me over his shoulder, a crown of frost gathering in his hair. "Do you feel justified now? Is it nice to have all your suspicions confirmed, to have watched me be the monster you so desperately believe we are? Or is it possible, *Alistaire*"—he points behind us, the way we came, voice rising—"that the North is harboring its very own monsters?"

I can't help but think of that conversation with Cassia. No. *No.* The North is *good*—

I grit my teeth, unable to break my gaze from his hands, stained rust red, his rings tarnished. "You didn't have to—"

He whirls on me, hair whipping against his forehead in the wind. "You're right, I *shouldn't* have had to. That was embarrassing of you to need rescuing."

I stop short, offended. "They took my weapons. *Bound* me with chains; they were going to *poison* me—"

"Yes, sounds terrible. I can't imagine what that was like," Jude deadpans, but the sarcasm doesn't reach his eyes, which are blazing gold with Craft after whatever unspeakable power he invoked back in the cabin. "Except *I* broke free, didn't I?" A startling, angry edge cuts into his voice. "*I* was poisoned, wasn't I?"

Guilt shrouds my mind, and I recoil, but after what I witnessed a few hours ago, it chills me to think what Jude could have done *without* a dampener on his Craft.

Regaining confidence, I stomp after him. "That isn't fair."

"It *is*! It's fair to expect you to do what you're perfectly capable of. Why *didn't* you break free? You could have killed all of—" He shakes his head, takes a steadying breath. "If I didn't know any better, I'd think you were ready to let them poison you."

"Because I *wasn't capable—*"

You are not capable *of taking care of yourself.*

Galen's accusation comes back to me with startling clarity. I've been told my entire life that I can't. That I'm helpless. We quarreled over it so much at home; maybe I started to believe it at some point.

Jude looks to the sky in disbelief, a hoarse cackle escaping his throat. "You snuck into the Playhouse. *Marked.* I watched you run at Mattia with a *dagger.* Somehow, you smuggled a lethal weapon out of Marigold's mitts and lived to tell the tale. And then you used it to harass *me.*" He points a finger in my direction. "You're going to try and convince me you're defenseless? You scare the living *daylights* out of me, Alistaire! So yes, I'm angry. Because the only way that back there got as far as it did is because *you* let it."

My face flushes. "Why should you care—"

"Because *you* should care!" he roars, turning back around, closing the space between us in two strides. His hands clamp onto my shoulders, heat bleeding through the cold. "You should be *burning* with rage that someone tried to hurt you."

I should pull away, but the warmth that seeps from his grip holds me in place. His eyes search mine, flickering back and forth like he's awaiting some signal there that only he would recognize.

That anger will be the death of you, Galen's voice reminds me. I shove it away.

Jude is right. I *am* angry. I've *always* been angry.

I huff a breath. "That isn't how we handle things in the North. Death isn't always the way."

"The North!" His tone slips off its hinges, incredulous. "Of course. The *North.*" He throws his arms wide, gesturing back the way we came. "*That's* who you're defending?" He winces at the movement, from whatever's happened to his arm. "Are they as charming as whoever drove you so helpless that you walked into the Playhouse?"

"You don't know anything about the life I come from," I defend, but doubt creeps into my mind as the scratch on my shoulder burns where the Eleutheraen chain dug into it. The North did this to me.

And I'm one of them. *Aren't I?*

"I think I've gathered enough." His tone calms, irritatingly more unnerving that way. "Tell me, do they fear you more or less now that you have Craft beating in your heart? Or was it only when they assumed you did."

That strikes a nerve. I clench my teeth, cornered and desperate to change the subject. "How'd you find me?" I ask, but I already know. I can feel it still, a golden thread humming between us. A wiser woman would have severed it before leaving the Playhouse.

I'm not entirely certain why I didn't.

Jude inhales once, twice, breaths vaporizing between us. "Craft binding. We're linked." I'm about to tell him to *unlink* it when he quietly adds, "You could have at least *tried* to hold them off until I got there."

I throw my head back, exasperated. "How should I have known you were coming to help?"

For a heartbeat, neither of us moves.

"How should you have known I would—" he finally says, making a point of looking wronged. "You think I didn't know what they would've done? I'm not entirely heartless, Alistaire! In fact, I'd have been there sooner, but I was slightly detained after being *poisoned*." I shrink back as he points an accusing finger at me. "And you *didn't need me*. Say, where did that terrifying resolve of yours run off to?"

His skin has gone nearly white. For once, Jude looks sincerely furious.

Fine, then. *Good*. I'm itching for a fight.

"*You* are one to talk," I hiss between my teeth, "about *courage*."

"Am I?" he taunts. "*Do* tell!"

"You're a coward, Jude!" I shriek, and he aims a lethal glare at me. I go on anyway. "You're a selfish Player who only ever thinks of himself. One with more power than even you know what to do with and a reputation you are *terrified* to live up to. According to *you*, you'd rather go to all the trouble of using me to get out of the Great Dionysia than just facing it yourself!"

Jude's eyes flash with the dark glint of a challenge. It occurs to me in a vague way that maybe I should be more careful about picking fights with Jude, based on what I just witnessed. But at the moment, I don't care.

"And *you*," he whispers back, taking a single step forward, and I raise my head, daring him, "are determined to be *miserable*." Stubbornly, I plant my feet in place as he stalks closer. "You harp on whatever odd imaginings about yourself that that ungodly cunning force of a mind churns out, plotting and conniving but never *once* realizing—" He cuts himself off with a near-hysterical laugh. "You know what? You're right. I've done you a terrible disservice, sharing my stage with you, offering you power, strength, knowledge. I'm sure the two of us are much happier shivering out here than wandering the warm halls of the Playhouse. My fault for saving you. *Do* forgive me."

I reach for a retort, but the words hitch beneath my ribs. I *have* felt stronger, less hollow, less cold. And maybe I did like the way I felt on that stage—seen. Seen and not feared.

Something in me resents it with a fierceness.

The familiar rasp of my tone returns, and I think I've almost missed it. "That was quite the little show you put on back there to call a *rescue*."

"Well! No one else bothered," he points out and shrugs. "In fact, *someone* told them where you would be and where you were taking me. Someone fed them that information. And frankly?" He feigns a look around. "I don't see whoever that *someone* is showing up to help."

The air between us constricts. I find myself questioning if he's not mad at me so much as *for* me. But something in me resents that, too.

"Do *not* act all high-and-mighty with me," I say. "There are quick ways to kill and there are slow." I shudder at the memory of scarlet smattered across white snow. "I'll take my bets that you went for grandeur and spectacle *as usual*." I lower my tone to match his. "That's all you care about. Attention. And you always get it—from *everyone*." I realize my mistake just a beat too late.

Jude tilts his head, that mean grin returning. "You could just say you're jealous. It would save us both the time." He shrugs again, then turns to walk off, calling, "Who could blame you? The world adores me, you know."

Snow crunches under my boots, and I realize I've stalked after him.

"What, you think I *envy* you? That I want to *be* one of you?"

"No." Jude turns cleanly in the snow to meet me, making the bold assumption I won't stomp on his toes at the first available opportunity. "I dare say you prefer misery over company."

"I prefer it over your company." I flinch. I didn't mean that at all. And the hurt on his face makes it worse. But I'm committed now. "You and your Player *ego*—"

"*My* ego." He lets out a sharp laugh. "Do you know something about egos, Alistaire? Actors wield them like shields. Wear them like blindfolds. Shove them into every crack in our armor for protection. But egos *love* misery, and that's how I know you have a vicious one. Pain is protection, too. Pain will blame everything outside itself and never *once* check to see if something is broken within."

My skin goes cold. The world seems to slow as all I manage to do is stare back, mouth agape, feeling a little like I've been stripped naked in spite of my layers of leather and wool.

"Don't pretend to know my mind." I can't help myself—I reach for my ire, for that thread of *power*, and it crackles like fire in response. But I can't tell which side it comes from. I square my shoulders, tugging on that power and letting Craft burn through my veins. "You're so used to everyone ogling at how beautiful you are, you can't begin to imagine what it's like to be me—" My voice cracks like a whip. "I am *allowed* to be angry."

"Anger can be anything onstage given the right costume. It's a pretty mask, that's all. Tell me, what's behind yours? I've grown curious."

I huff a breath. "Charm is one, too—just as much." We may keep different weapons in our arsenals, but they all still cut at the end of the day. I tilt my head. "Is *that* why you came back?" He stiffens. "Because you can't stand someone wandering the world who doesn't worship the ground you walk on—"

"Is it so hard to believe that I care for you, Alistaire?" he snaps, and I freeze, all the harsh words rising up my throat dissolving. He presses a hand to his chest and adds, "Can't I be good? Just for once."

The thread between us crackles with power—and something more now. Something new.

"Or does *that* scare you, too?"

Jude's eyes glint gold in the darkness, sweeping down to take in the curve of my lips, the set of my jaw, before flickering back up to mine. And for the first time, I wonder if what I've mistaken for hatred is just a mirror.

The thought sends me a step back. Then two more.

Jude's gaze narrows on mine as my feet move away. "Fear does not make you a coward. Yielding to it does."

Coward. The word cleaves through the hard shell of my skin, nestles under it. And starts to burn. Maybe I am a coward. I do like being miserable and alone. There's safety in it, a certainty that no one can leave if there's no one to lose in the first place.

And comfort—comfort in the certainty that Jude is terrible. That *Players* are terrible. Or there was until he paraded in and started shaking up all my carefully crafted convictions.

But it may be too late. Because as he turns to leave, I say something that does truly and deeply frighten me. "Stay."

And I think he knows it, too. Because as he turns, sees both a question and its answer written across my face, he mutters something that sounds suspiciously like, "Dear heart, I think you'll ruin me."

Whatever words he has left are lost to the wind as Jude storms furiously forward—

And crashes his mouth into mine, stealing the breath from my lungs. It isn't a gentle kiss, not like the hand he slips carefully into my hair, not like the arm he coils around my waist. My mind wipes itself blank, clear as the white blanket of snow around us, the cold long forgotten beneath the burn of his touch. Whatever confusion and reservations still waver through me are lost to the roar of my own pulse as my hands find the collar of his shirt and pull him closer, kissing him back, just as foolish and reckless—

Until a shred of common sense bursts through the door of my mind.

What am I doing?

I tense, and Jude pulls away, his chest rising and falling. My own shock is mirrored in his expression as I clap a hand over my mouth. My heart races as I search for words in the air between us and come up empty-handed.

Around us, the forest holds its breath, waiting for someone—*anyone*—to break the silence.

Finally, Jude does.

"I don't care that I'm going to pay dearly for that," he says and, without explaining, walks off.

Intermission: Scene VIII

"Thank Dionysus!" Jude announces, throwing open the doors to a dark, run-down tavern with only a few patrons and even fewer lanterns.

I wonder what type of person finds themselves in such a place first thing in the morning. Though given that I'm one of them, who am I to judge?

"Your best wine, I thank you," Jude declares, sliding a few gold pieces to the bartender, then collapsing onto a peeling stool that's seen better days. His disguise is thinner than I think it should be: hair cropped short in a honey-blond color, eyes farther apart and masked in shades of blue. He's either too tired or too lazy to bother disguising his frame and height.

I take the disguise as a comfort, because I don't have a clue how to face the Jude I was arguing with an hour ago. Even though my mind has been replaying and overanalyzing it from fifteen different angles since then.

None of them make sense. None of them work with the pieces I have of who Jude is.

Worse, I'm not sure I want them to.

The man on the other side of the bar raises an eyebrow at the coin, and I don't have time to ponder where on earth Jude even *got* that money before it's plucked off the counter and replaced with a wooden cup filled with a deep-red hue.

"And one more thing," Jude adds. "You wouldn't happen to know *where* we are, would you?"

Before suspicion can etch into the bartender's face, I gesture to the wine and mutter, "It isn't his first."

"Cartonia," the man replies with a thick accent and moves away before Jude can ask for a golden chalice instead.

I drop my head in my hands, the answer digging into my pride.

We made it to Syrene, but I failed so extravagantly at delivering a Player to the council that I didn't get us halfway to the meetup point.

"Well, Alistaire," Jude says, swirling his cup. "We have quite the journey ahead of us. Four days' walk, I'd say. Three if we're lucky."

"And I wish you the very best on it," I say, ashamed by my complete and utter failure. "We'll be parting ways shortly." I know when to cut my losses.

Jude raises an eyebrow at me, and I avert my gaze to the torn scarf I used to wrap around his injured arm before we came in here. It does little to stanch the golden blood but at least hides it.

"In for a nasty surprise, those monsters..."

The words catch our attention, muttered from one man to another at a nearby table. My eyes fall on the newspaper between them. It's the same headline Dorian shoved in my face. The one proclaiming my faceless fame and Jude's mysterious disappearance.

Jude's eyes narrow at the paper, catching up.

"How can they be sure you're missing?" I whisper to him. "Just because you didn't show at the stage door last night?"

"A bit more complicated than that," he says lowly. "Sil and I were to meet with the council this morning to begin to discuss the terms of our new reentry. You can imagine they might have noticed when I didn't show."

"Heard he was sighted near the border just yesterday," the man with the beard goes on. Guess we *were* seen. "Could be anywhere by now, but *gods*. A Player on the loose..."

Another man laughs cruelly. "Hell of a show, once they catch him. They'll have to find themselves a new Lead Player after *that* trial, I tell you."

"Little point in a trial," challenges the third. "It's in the godsdamned law. They'll be in their rights to execute him. Now *there's* entertainment I might pay to see."

Jude sets his drink down on the table, hard.

"Can't get far. If he really came this way, they'll catch him before long. They've finally started confiscating the mirrors the damned Revelers brought in." The man taps the newspaper on the table. "Imagine that. Executed in his own city."

"Watch them try and replace him with this faceless bitch the papers keep going on about."

My hackles rise, and Jude slowly turns a look over his shoulder.

That anger will be the death of you.

Before I can think better of it, I place a hand over Jude's, as if to plead, *Don't. Do. Anything.*

His hand is ice-cold. We found a creek for him to wash the blood off his hands, but I can still imagine the stains there, an unsettling reminder that he isn't all vanity and stage bows. Which is something I'd really prefer not to witness in this tavern right now.

"Is that true?" I say under my breath. "That if you leave the Playhouse, they can—"

"Yes," he says. "That law is signed in Eleutheraen gold. I'm not supposed to leave—I'm not supposed to even be *able* to leave—but that's between me and my contract with Sil." He presses his fingers to his temples, like his head has started aching. "You can thank the damned *Peacemaker* for that."

My heart drops as I school my features at the mention of my father. Of course, I know all of this—ensuring the Players stay caged in the Playhouse is a legacy tied to my family name.

But for the first time, the odd nature of it hits me. "Why would Sil sign into such a thing? Trapping his own Players." It doesn't make sense.

Jude is staring at his wine like it owes him money. "That," he says, tone hardening, bitter, "is a *great* question." He raises an eyebrow at me, clearly waiting for me to do the math.

But I think I know. "Because the law was never for the benefit of mortals," I breathe. "It's for Sil's. He doesn't want any of you being able to leave. Under threat of your lives."

I reach desperately for the part of me that hates Jude. The hatred instilled since I was young. The part of me sharpened and ready to drag him before the council in exchange for leverage and my freedom.

But my anger and hatred are crushed under the weight of knowing that Jude could have run back to the Playhouse after escaping me. He could have made it back last night, before the council could file his absence. He chose to track my kidnappers and me in the opposite direction instead.

"Thank you," I say quietly, "for coming back."

He must have done it because he wants out of the Great Dionysia. Wants to use me. To exploit me to get through the casting call. He's a selfish Player and that's how—

"Loath as you are to admit it, Alistaire, you are one of us now."

I'm not sure what startles me more. That it didn't occur to me Jude could have his own moral code or the implication that I'm a castmate to be looked after.

Players kill for three reasons, I remember. *A blow to their ego, a threat to their cast, or, on rare occasion, for pure spectacle.*

"Right," I say, amused and maybe a little unnerved by the idea. "You won't leave a castmate behind."

Jude watches me. "I won't leave *you* behind."

I narrow my eyes. "Because we're linked." He must want his power back.

He shakes his head once, refusing to break his gaze. "No."

For a moment, a bright, delicate fluttering warms my chest.

I shove it down at once, horrified.

"And some might say you now owe me a debt, given that I'll be paying for it with my life," Jude says. "So, *please*, Alistaire." He looks pleadingly at me. "Come back to the Playhouse. Come back, and I will release you from our bargain."

"What?" I snap in a whisper. "*Why?* You just said yourself, going back *will* get you killed."

"Alistaire." Jude pulls his hand from mine, turning away from the bar to ensure no one sees. He brings two fingers to the collar of his shirt and tugs it down toward his shoulder, and my blood turns to ice.

That golden gash I'd noticed before has spread to his chest, peeling up to his throat.

He conceals it again and leans toward me. "I *have* to get back to the Playhouse."

Something is wrong with Jude.

At first, I think he's just run out of witty remarks and biting comebacks. Then, I think he's run out of words altogether. Sometimes I feel his gaze on my back as I walk, and I throw a look over my shoulder. Three times, I've caught him wiping his eyes, smudging the kohl beneath his lashes. Other times, he just watches me back, like he's waiting for me to say something.

Mile after mile, I never do.

"Green!" he proclaims once and pales a little when I ask what he means. "My favorite color," he explains sheepishly. "It's green."

I have no idea what's happening to Jude, but he's right. He needs to get back to the Playhouse.

A deer in the woods startles us both. We're on edge still. "Do you think there are more of them?" I ask, watching the deer leap across the nearby creek and retreat into the hills. "Those hunters?"

"Were I to wager?" Jude stumbles again and catches himself on a thin tree trunk. That's the third time in the last few minutes. "I'd guess there's a thousand of them for every one that died. There'll be hell to pay for it, dear—"

I wait for the lilting pronunciation of my alias that sounds more like *Ah-li-star*. It doesn't come. Jude is staring at me, open-mouthed, still leaning on the tree trunk and blinking in confusion. His arm has bled through the scarf I tied around it.

"I'm sorry—your name is—" He swallows, frustration pinching his brow. "I know it; your name is..."

"Alistaire," I offer.

"Alistaire!" he shouts and shakes his head. "Of course. Alistaire. Say, Alistaire," he goes on, pausing to cough into the snow. "As fun as this little adventure has been, I think it's far past time we get back."

He pushes by me. I follow, telling myself he's tired. We haven't slept in two days. That cut on his arm could be infected. Something is clearly wrong with his left leg. Or maybe he's just too self-absorbed to remember a name other than his own.

I glance back, and my excuses fall short.

A smattering of gold stains the snow.

Intermission: Scene IX

In spite of Jude's protests, I win the argument that we need to take shelter for the evening.

I slip into an apothecary on the way. Much as he refuses to admit it, whatever injury Jude suffered in his fight with Dorian is slowing us down and making his breathing labored. I study the way he's holding his arm for a moment before selecting a healer's kit with a suture needle and catgut.

We stop at an inn for the night. Jude's picked another pocket, I guess, because he has no trouble handing over someone else's coin for our stay. He Mimics a man we passed on the street, and I *know* something is wrong when he doesn't flirt with anyone at the front desk.

Luckily, our room sits at the very end of the dingy hall. Unluckily, there's a floorboard painted with shimmering Eleutheraen gold at its threshold.

Jude rolls his eyes and steps right over it, shedding his Mimicry. "Not even real," he says. "You wouldn't believe how often that's the case. Too expensive to use true Eleutheraen gold. They just like to make their patrons think they're safe."

"It isn't real?" I poke at the gold floorboard with my foot.

"Wouldn't matter if it were. Painting doorframes—it's all myth that it keeps us out." He kicks off one of his boots. "A sealed circle of pure Eleutheraen gold, which is rare, will do it. But not some random bit of gold across a floorboard. How do you think we crossed the Cut?" Discomfort leaks into his expression when he leans on the other leg to kick off his second boot. "Damned nuisance to move the Playhouse through, but any Player could traverse that pitiful moat."

"Players can cross the Cut?" Gods, *of course* they can. It was never sealed with pure Eleutheraen gold. "What about the treaty—"

"The treaty kept the *Playhouse* out. Not named Players. How could it? None of the original Players are around anymore to be named in a treaty. Sil doesn't let us leave the grounds anyway."

I stare quietly at the paint. *This* too? Question marks prod at my mind. The wall was never fully sealed. The Three Compliments Rule is complete fiction. Mimicry—fortunately—doesn't involve skinning a victim to take their shape.

How many lies did we foolishly accept as truth? How many more are there?

Jude collapses onto the bed without bothering to remove his jewelry, making himself at home, long legs dangling off the mattress. But his breaths are uneven, ragged. Wincing, he lifts himself to shrug off his coat.

My eyes widen. His sleeve is soaked through.

Jude curses as he inspects the wound. "Don't tell Cora, will you?" he says. "I made her restitch this shirt a week ago."

"Don't mess with it," I say, retrieving the supplies I bought. "And take that off."

"Such excuses." Jude frowns at his ruined sleeve. "If you want me to undress, you can just ask nicely."

I toss the healer's kit at him. "Fine. Suffer."

"All right. All right." He laughs on a wheeze, putting his hands up and wincing again at the movement. "I'll quit teasing." He goes back to working the buttons on his shirt, muttering about how Cicero will probably punish him with hideous costumes as vengeance.

I ignore the butterflies in my stomach as he tosses his shirt aside and unpack the healer's kit—making a stern point of *not* giving him the attention he's always after.

But by the heat that floods my cheeks when I glance up at the wide expanse of Jude's shoulders, the contours of muscle laced with golden veins, I think I fail extravagantly. I clear my throat and avert my eyes to the gold coin that hangs from a thin chain at his neck—a beaming Comedy mask pressed into its face. But when Jude twists to get a better look at the cut on his arm, the coin turns, revealing Tragedy's sullen mask on the other side.

Head down, I lay the gauze out on the mattress beside a long cloth bandage and a small linen pouch of coiled catgut. There's an astringent made of what might be vinegar and honey, but one glimpse at the wound makes me pretty certain none of it will do much.

The mattress sits too low, so I angle my knees on the floor and soak the cloth in the mixture before setting to work on cleaning the cut, ignoring Jude's accusations that I'm trying to torture him.

"Are you still not going to tell me what that is?" I ask of the gleaming gash I spotted on his opposite shoulder when we left the Playhouse. Since then, it's created a mapwork of golden veins down his chest and back. Whatever they are, they clearly aren't related to this cut on his arm.

And they're spreading.

The disturbing image of Gene Hunt's skin nudges at my mind.

He shakes his head once. "There's no mending that kind. Don't worry over it."

The laceration Dorian gifted him cuts deep into the muscle, closer to bone than I think either of us wants to admit. And the blade clearly didn't rake clean across his skin—in fact, it looks like it was hacked into it in a brazen attempt to relieve Jude of his arm.

"Eleutheraen gold?"

"Gilded with it, maybe," he says, making a face at his arm. "If it were pure, I'd probably be practicing my penmanship with my other hand right about now."

"How did—" I sit back, suspicious. "You didn't have any weapons." I'm not sure I mean that as a question, but he answers it like one.

"Rib cages tear open easily enough without weapons."

I almost drop the bronzed, curved suture needle I'm threading as my stomach turns. Best not ask questions I don't want answers to, I guess.

"And get that away from me," he adds sourly.

I blink. "What, a *needle*? You're afraid of needles?"

Jude makes a show of looking deeply insulted as I break into laughter, until he grumbles at me to get the stitches over with.

"Here I was, thinking Players didn't fear anything," I say, pulling the first clumsy suture through while he does his very best to appear sad and noble. I roll my eyes, wondering if he was this melodramatic before becoming immortal.

"Where'd you learn this anyway?" he asks miserably. "Or do you just specialize in victimizing poor Players like me?"

The brown sutures leave a trail of uneven, spiderlike stitches across his skin, which Jude is none too pleased about. "I was going to study healing. At school. Spent so much time looking for ways to fix whatever was happening to me, I thought I'd be good at it." I omit that I've never actually had to stitch anything up before, since I'm sure he'd dive out the nearest window. Becoming a healer sounded fine enough, but I never imagined needing to mend a Player.

I never imagined one showing up to help me, either.

I tug on the needle and thread, forming another misshapen *X*, and Jude groans—from pain or vanity, I'm not sure.

"We do, by the way," he says a moment later. "Players. We get scared, too. And maybe you're right to call me a coward for it."

I flinch, pausing with the needle raised again. That accusation ran out of my mouth a little impulsively, but I never expected him to agree with it. The astonishment must read on my face because he adds, "You don't believe me."

An angry lump forms in my throat, bitterness festering under my skin—toward him, toward the Players I grew up fearing. Toward whichever one broke my family. "I don't see what Players have to be afraid of."

His attention moves to his open hand. He closes it into a fist, lets it fall open again. "I didn't want Lead Player, never wanted the standing that comes with it. My entire life these days, it seems, comes down to reputation." He exhales.

"You didn't want to be Lead Player?" I reply, startled by his sincerity and even more curious. I put my focus back on aiming the needle through his flesh and pull it through. He's the face of the Playhouse, granted more power and prestige than his castmates. Sil seems to rely on him like a second-in-command.

He doesn't even notice the pinch of the thread now as I sew up the last of the wound, seemingly lost to his own thoughts. "I came to the Playhouse like you did. Angry and powerless. Hell-bent on vengeance at the time. The worst part is I got what I wanted."

I shudder at the idea, giving up your humanity for revenge. "Is it worth living in a cage?" *Forever,* I don't add. *Until someone kills you for your place.*

"Well, it's a very *nice* cage," he defends. "Nicer when someone isn't rattling the bars of it, too." He throws me a pointed look, and I snort. "There are worse things than being trapped."

"I don't think that's true. It seems awful."

A sharp edge of concern cuts into Jude's expression, but it vanishes too quickly to be sure if I imagined it. "It's safer," is all he says.

Damn, that suture is crooked. He's going to throw a fit about that later. But the flimsy flicker of the oil lamp on the table offers little light to see what I'm doing.

"Was it enough? To be able to let it go?" I snip the end of the thread and tie it off, then reach for a bandage. "Revenge."

"I'm still waiting to find out." Something about the way he says it sets a chill in the air.

Mattia's warning calls to my mind. *Be careful of Jude. All he knows is winning.*

"Immortality takes from you," he says. "It's a slow taking. And *power.* Gods, power takes more. Power breaks you into pieces you never knew were there. It all comes at a cost."

My hands work the bandage into a knot, a question on my tongue. "What was the cost?"

Jude watches the floor, blank. "Freedom."

My mind conjures the gates of the Playhouse, that golden cage. All the Players kept inside like expensive birds. "Was it worth it?"

His eyes flicker up. "Life is a game of playing the cards you're dealt and then justifying them so you can sleep at night." He bites down on his jaw, like he didn't mean to let those words escape.

"*Do* you sleep at night?" I tease to lighten the moment, securing the bandage.

He tilts his head, a spark sliding behind his eyes. "What, are you looking to find out? My dressing room is usually unlocked, you know. You're welcome anytime."

I roll my eyes at him, but my pulse still skitters when he raises an eyebrow at me. Out of stitches and bandages, I drop my hands, twisting them in my lap, grateful for the small distraction when the lamp seems to burn through its last traces of oil, hissing and dimming.

"Come now, Alistaire, where've you gone? Surely you have a very clever comeback. This is our dance, yes? I try to lead and you step on my feet."

I watch the curling trail of smoke from the oil lamp, opening my mouth to offer a retort—and am mortified to discover I am, in fact, out of them. So I settle for, "Are you always this insufferable?"

"Yes," he states with a sly grin and leans forward, elbows on his knees. "Are you always this hardheaded?"

My shoulders rise with a laugh. "Probably."

Jude nods. "Good. I think I'd get dreadfully bored otherwise." He goes back to examining my messy stitchwork, leaving me to sit with the thought, harmonizing with his earlier words. *You can be a great many things, dear heart. But you cannot be fewer.*

I almost wish he *would* say something unkind. Jude never flinches away from the jagged edges I can't seem to saw down, certainly doesn't bother trying to soften them himself. Half the time, he seems outright entertained by them.

But I haven't been as kind, slicing at him with my words without hesitation, like I have to put up a shield before the blow comes. Jude has plenty of sharp edges, too. And I don't think I'd change any of them, either.

"You know, I'm still miffed at you for all this." He twirls a finger broadly at our surroundings, breaking me from the thought. "My clothes are in damned ruin"—they are—"my hair is a mess"—it is—"you've turned my arm into your personal quilting project"—I snort, ignoring him and getting to my feet—"and frankly, I'm not sure why this room bothered with walls for how cold it is in here."

"Done complaining?"

"Almost." He says it all like a joke, but sincerity creeps into the punch line as he blurts, "I just wish we were home."

For a moment, it's dead quiet. The words linger like a third party to our conversation, demanding to be addressed. My throat goes dry. And when I can't take the silence any longer, I mutter, "The Playhouse is not my—"

"Please." And Jude, for once in his life, seems short on words. "Please, Alistaire."

I pause. "What is it?" It's something else that's bothering him. Something other than the cold room, beyond the dangers trailing us, beyond the ones we left behind. And whatever it is, even Jude isn't a good enough actor to hide it.

"Can we just pretend—just this once?" There's a note of weakness in his tone that catches me off guard, his teasing comments gone and forgotten. "Just pretend this ends happily."

This.

My chest tightens. He knows something I don't. "The Great Dionysia."

"I can't stop what's coming," he utters in a breath, too quick, like he didn't mean to say it. "I would." He looks up, and there's something I've never seen in Jude's eyes before, alight but dimmer than usual.

Fear.

"So can we please—" A hand in the dark reaches for mine but stills in the air like he's thought better of it. I think he tries to smile, but it looks more like a wince as his eyes dart back to the floor. "Can we just laugh and argue and pretend everything will be fine."

Pretend. I almost laugh at the idea. If there's one thing we're both good at, I suppose it's pretending. But before he can drop the hand between us, I reach for it as if a string on my wrist has been pulled. The brush of his skin is warm in contrast to the brittle draft of the room, but it seems to send a shiver up my arms anyway.

And I think I'm past pretending to myself about Jude.

My fingers wrap around his, and he watches me closely as I step into the space between his knees where he's seated on the mattress, bend slightly to study the gilded edges of his eyes, like I'll be able to retrieve every secret he's buried within them. I don't see any secrets, though.

However, the mischief has certainly returned by the time he reaches his other hand to my jaw. I'm not sure it's a question in his eyes so much as a brazen dare as his gaze flickers to my lips, but I do know a smarter woman would run for the door right about now at that look.

Unfortunately, I am not her.

"We can pretend," I agree, and press my mouth to his.

My hesitations are, apparently, not shared. As if this is all the permission he's been waiting for, the hand at my jaw slides readily into my hair, cupping the back of my neck, tugging me closer so abruptly, he almost throws me off-balance. I laugh softly against his lips, steady myself with a hand to his chest and, at the touch, almost think Jude seems to pull his next breath like he's been underwater until now, deepening the kiss.

In spite of all our time away from the Playhouse and the absurd collection of perfume bottles on his vanity, the scent of hyacinth still lingers on his skin. It wraps around me, lingers in my hair as he drops my hand to loop an arm around my hips and reel me closer to him, until I can feel the heat of his skin, the race of his pulse. Half of me is horrified at my reckless self. The other half declares this isn't enough.

I lean into his hands, allowing the invisible current that whirs around Jude to draw me in, probably the same current his countless obsessive fans feel.

The thought makes me tense.

"Get out of your head." His words are a brush against my ear as he pauses, pulls back to look at me, searching my face like he can read the thought written across it and chase it away before it can take root. "Whatever it is."

I glare back. "I'm not—" I search for words. "I'm not one of your mindless adoring worshippers," I say, insistent. Before he gets any wild ideas.

"Heart, I know," he answers with a laugh and reaches for my chin to angle his gaze back on mine. "But I'm starting to think I may be one of yours."

Whatever doubt was still lingering in the air splinters, then is crushed entirely, the space where it hovered closed by the ravenous kiss he pulls me into. Everything blurs to the heat of the hand dragging through my hair, to the soft laugh between us when his rings get tangled in it. I let the tips of my fingers play at the thin chain clasped at his neck, noticing him shiver under the touch as his hands drift down my hips, pausing at my thighs, before he uses them to pull me into his lap.

All I can hear is the beat of my heart quickening when he drags me onto the bed with him and flips me onto my back, the low laugh he lets out when I snap at him not to hurt the stitches I worked very hard on, thank you very much.

He thinks I don't catch the wince of pain on his face when he moves over me, though he just mutters something about a scratch on his leg and that it isn't anything to worry about. I don't believe him for a minute but am all too distracted by the way he busies his mouth trailing kisses down my neck instead, which magically erases whatever thoughts were circling my mind a moment ago, savoring the weight of him, the warmth.

Something about the dark makes it easier to ignore how we got here. What both of us have done. Makes me forget all about what Jude is and think only about who he is, who he is to me.

I'm still trying to figure that out—if it's a friend whose tousled hair I run my fingers through. A rival who laces my fingers with his. An enemy whose waist I wrap my legs around and cling to. Maybe someone else entirely who murmurs a question into my ear before working at the buttons there at my collar.

Whatever he is, they all seem to weave into Jude, whose heart beats a steady rhythm I feel like I've known all my life. A laugh I would recognize in a crowd. A touch that consumes me and starts to simmer, to burn, to demand more.

Until my fingers brush along his shoulder, accidentally over that strange gash that—

Jude gasps and rears back, blinking like he's confused. "I'm sorry." He blinks some more, looking around, one hand clutched to the gash at his shoulder.

A gash that has just spread farther down his chest.

I sit up, concerned. "Jude?"

"I'm not supposed to—" He winces, but the moment I try to move for him, he raises a hand between us. "Just stay—please, stay over there."

I don't know if I'm more concerned about the gash or about the fact that he's looking at me like he doesn't recognize me or where we are. I swallow, finding my throat dry. "Is something wrong—"

Muffled voices from a passing exchange in the hall startle us both into silence.

Gods. Right. There's a manhunt with Jude's name on it in Syrene. For all we know, we could be sharing a hall with more hunters. Reality seems to cut between us, all the warmth gone. My face heats as I fold my arms in, unsure what's just happened and whether or not it was my fault, if the confusion on his face is just masked regret.

"I'll take first watch," I say abruptly, on my feet and scurrying for the space by the window when the voices vanish down the hall. *Anything* to fill the silence.

Jude clears his throat. "If you insist." He wanders across the room, whatever startled trance he was in breaking.

We step back into our roles like nothing has changed.

"Let me know if anything exciting happens," he says, sauntering to the bed and trying to hide that he has, in fact, torn a stitch.

"Exciting?" I curl myself onto the windowsill, Jude's dagger (or someone's, I don't know where he got it) clutched between my fingers. "There's a bounty on your head large enough to fund a small city."

Jude scoffs as he collapses back onto the mattress. "I do think I'm worth at least a *medium-size* city."

I roll my eyes and do my best to forget whatever happened a moment ago. Through the window, stars are growing visible beyond the thin clouds over Syrene, marking the second night of our absence from the Playhouse.

The moon shines through our window like a spotlight, like it can sense a Player out of his bed and far away from home. The blue-white beam reaches across the tattered white blankets Jude is strewn over, sparkling where it meets gold at his fingertips.

The cut on his arm will heal. But that other injury—whatever it is—that spreads along his skin and leaves sharp lines of gold in its wake…I'm not so sure about that one. I'm reminded of Gene again, her skin peeling away from her flesh. "Gene Hunt wasn't a ghost, was she," I say.

It's silent. For a moment, I think he's already asleep.

Then he answers. "No. She wasn't."

"She didn't take her life onstage, either, did she?"

Another moment passes. "That's the way of the theatre," he says, quiet. "You give your life, your blood, your morals to the stage. And after that, it demands more."

Apparently, we're done with blunt honesty for the night and have reverted back to theatrically dodging questions with riddles.

Then he asks, "How did you do it?"

I raise an eyebrow. "What?"

Jude shifts, pulls a blanket over his shoulders, though it does little to conceal the light humming around his skin. "The cold. It's cold out here all the time."

I shrug. "I dealt with it. Always bothered me more than my brother growing up." My voice strains at the mention of Galen, eyes sliding to the window again, wondering if he's out here somewhere, after Dorian turned him down.

"Your brother," Jude repeats, resting his head back on the pillow. "What would he do to get you back?"

I think of Galen urging my mother out of my bedroom and shouting at her to stay downstairs when I first fell violently ill. For days, weeks maybe, the illness filled my head with delusions. I screamed at the shadows that floated over my room, thinking I was probably going to die. And I remember my brother's voice: *You're strong enough, Riv.*

Maybe Galen *did* think me capable, to some extent, trusting I would pull through when the poison took hold and turned my skin sickly gray, when ice began to crust in my veins.

I raise my hand and turn it over in the moonlight. The veins glitter now, a golden hue hanging softly over my skin. "Anything," I say, even though it's a suspicious thing of Jude to ask. "My brother would do anything."

It's quiet again.

"Alistaire?" says Jude's voice one more time from the darkness of the room.

"Yeah?"

"I'm sorry."

A laugh jumps from my throat. "What, for ruining my life and throwing me into the casting call? It's a bit late for that." My breath stills. "Or if you mean what happened a moment ago, I think that was just as much my fault."

"No, I'm not sorry for either of those things, actually," he says. "For something else."

I look at him—half asleep, bathed in moonlight, gold flickering under his skin—and realize I might not want to know what he means.

For once, I don't ask.

Intermission: Scene X

Jude doesn't take his watch later. Which is probably my fault for forgetting to wake him. So imagine my surprise when *he* wakes *me* up.

"Alistaire," Jude's voice whispers. He darts back before I can run him through with my knife on impulse. He points at the dagger, annoyed. "See, *that*. Where was *that* instinct when Dorian's damned hunters tried to—"

The door rattles, and by the way his attention shoots toward it, I think it isn't the first time.

Jude leans across me, unlatches the seal on the window, and pushes it open. I don't know who could be trying to get in, but I know that there's no such thing as an ally out here.

"How could they have found us?" I dive headfirst through the window onto the flat roof, gasping when the wind meets my neck, like ice pouring down my back.

"Well, Alistaire, the thing about being a creature that is *particularly* known for attracting attention is it makes it difficult to sneak around." He throws one long leg out the window after me as I crawl across the roof. "Simply feeling drawn to this room could be suspicious enough for some."

He maneuvers cleanly down a pipe onto the icy grass, and I attempt to follow suit. Except when I do it, I land clumsily on my hip while Jude mutters a snide remark about neglecting my combat training before hauling me to the closest desolate road, slippery with frost.

The light emitted by his skin is particularly conspicuous in the dark. Suddenly, he turns, as if a thought has just occurred to him, and yanks my hood over my head. "The rule applies to you, too, now."

I groan and try to ignore the gold glow hovering over my hands.

Fear of an escaped Player has apparently encouraged everyone to stay inside after dark. The streets are quiet as death as we go, ice crunching under our boots. Bounty posters with Jude's face paper the walls of fur shops and firewood stands. I nearly shout at him when he pauses to autograph one.

We pass more than one news rack closed for the night but full of frantic headlines. My eyes sweep over them as cold seeps into my bones.

ESCAPED PLAYER: JUDE STEPHARROS TO STAND TRIAL UNDER LAW

"They give me *no* credit," he mutters, skimming an article surmising Jude will begin slaughtering a city any day now. "I've been wandering out here two days and I've only killed—" He pauses and starts counting on his fingers, then gives up. "Never mind. Let's go."

It takes several tries to find a shop with a lock that *isn't* made with Eleutheraen gold. Soon enough, I point out a bakery and amble around the back. Jude stands watch while I pick at the iron lock with one of his earrings, then motion him inside.

Thank the gods it's warm in here. My bones might splinter if they get any colder. I sink onto the floor of the pantry, deciding the bag of flour in the corner will make a fine pillow.

Jude follows a moment later and tosses a bag of rolls at me. I greedily tear it open and scarf down four. He chews on a piece and gives up, wincing and pressing a hand to his jaw like he's in pain. Then he tosses the bread across the room and sinks against the wall beside me. His breaths are more labored than before, and he's shivering violently. Lines of gold bleed down his forearm now, that mysterious wound of his spreading farther like a disease, deteriorating everything it touches.

"What's..." I pause, unsure what I'm asking. "What's happening to you?"

He draws in an unsteady breath, stares at the ceiling. "Alistaire, tell me—tell me a story, will you?" His words come out ragged, like he's begging for water. "Please."

"I—" I freeze. "I don't know any stories." And I don't think a story is going to fix whatever is happening to him. Maybe he's searching for a distraction.

Jude lets out a breath and then struggles to pull in the next. "Right. I'll tell you one, then."

When he speaks, I'm swept into another world. His words weave into the cold air around us like a blanket, warm and sparkling. Each utterance paints a more vivid portrait in the darkness. I scoot closer, my ears eager to hear more, and he pauses.

"No, keep going," I prompt, surprised how badly I want to know how it ends.

"I thought you *hated* stories," he taunts back. And he's right, I do. Stories are bad. They're lies.

But the way Jude tells stories, I wonder how I've lived a day without them.

"I think I hate them less when you tell them," I say quietly.

He pauses, drained, then nods and goes on. When he's done, his voice is tired, like spinning the tale has taken something from him. His breaths grow more strenuous, the glow around him wavering like a dwindling lantern.

My mouth opens, and the words, "Are you dying, Jude?" fall out a little too bluntly.

He doesn't say anything for a moment. Then, finally, "Death is a matter of opinion, Alistaire. To die is to be forgotten. I imagine the world will never forget me."

"In your opinion, are you dying?"

He sighs deeply, stares at the white scar across his palm. "Yes."

I have a feeling Reality Suspension can't fix whatever is happening to him.

Turning on my side, I face him and whisper, "Does it have to do with Sil? Him and that book he always carries."

Jude winces. "Alistaire, if you care for me at all, you'll tell him this little journey back was made in utter silence. You and I, we didn't speak. Nothing of *note* happened."

A chill hovers over the words. He almost sounds frightened.

"I won't tell," I promise, wondering at what Sil might do. *Is* Sil more powerful than the Players? I'm not entirely sure *what* he is. "And I do," I add, quieter. The words cling desperately to my throat, trying their hardest not to make it past my teeth. "Care for you."

A lot, I think. Enough to follow him back to the Playhouse, if only to ensure Jude doesn't face the consequences of leaving his post when I forced him to.

Jude's brows shoot up; he's apparently shaken free from whatever trance he'd found in his palm. "Now, don't tell me that block of ice you call a heart has started to thaw," he teases, turning to face me. "I imagine it would take someone entirely irresistible to do *that*."

I shove him, but he catches my hand, laughing, his fingers wrapping around mine. In one stubborn motion, he tugs both of our hands to his chest. The sudden shift drags me across the cold stone, narrows the gap between us. Jude's eyes look more like stars this close, softer. Part of me waits for the usual unease to surface, to send prickles down my spine and swallow the warmth from my veins.

But that anger, that rattle of disgust, never surfaces. Only a rush that skitters up my veins, a feathery feeling that flickers in my chest when he tucks a loose lock of hair behind my ear. In spite of the bitter chill, Jude's skin feels like he's been standing over a fire for hours.

And I think maybe I'm done fighting. I don't want to fight the weight of Jude's arm falling over my shoulders, the warmth like summer sun that encircles me and pulls me into his chest, or the easy way he tucks his chin into my hair.

"Alistaire?"

I crane my neck up, waiting for another biting remark about that ice-cold heart of mine.

Instead, he says, "Why are you so angry? Really."

Defensiveness rises in my shoulders, but this time, I catch it and coax the sharp words back down my throat. I've been asking myself the same question. "I don't fit properly anywhere." The words take a moment to find. "And it doesn't feel fair. Like I'm this badly cut piece of a puzzle that doesn't fit with the others."

Jude considers my words, leans his head back into the wall. His chest rises and falls for several beats, the timbre of his voice lowering. "If you have to saw all your edges to fit, you're probably in the wrong puzzle." He looks down at me. "And no offense, but you have a lot of edges."

"Do you ever feel that way?" I press. "Like the person you are doesn't fit."

"I'm an *actor*, Alistaire." He laughs. "I spend *most* of my days pretending to be someone I'm not. None of us really belong anywhere." Then he smiles, and for once, it isn't a smirk or a telling grin. It's just a smile. "But life is worth finding the right puzzle."

I press the tips of my fingers to where my mark used to be, unsure I fit in any of them now anyway. I don't have any idea where I belong. "I think maybe you're right." The words escape my mouth unexpectedly, but I've thought them through. I've thought them through a *lot*. "The North—it isn't all good." And in spite of what I've been taught every day of my life, I add, "And maybe *you* aren't all bad."

He meets my gaze, and I spy something more than the typical pride and mischief behind his eyes. It almost looks like relief. "Alistaire," he begins. "There's something I need to tell—"

He pauses, chokes like he's swallowed gravel.

Then he clutches his throat, like he can't breathe, and I sit up, concerned.

"Jude?" For once, I *hope* he's just being dramatic.

"I need to—" He gasps for air between coughs, each more vicious than the last. I press a hand to his chest, where gold has begun to bleed through the white of his shirt. His heart is staggering between beats, labored and uneven.

All the color has drained from his face by the time his phantom fit ends, but it leaves his voice a thin rasp.

"It's almost over," is all he says, fading like he can't keep his eyes open anymore. The light around him dims like a candle flickering in the wind. "We're almost done."

Intermission: Scene XI

Whatever is happening at the Playhouse, it looks bad. Worse than how Jude looks, which is also very bad. He managed to sleep a couple of hours before formally announcing to me between strained breaths that "the show must go on" and insisting he was recovered enough to keep moving again.

I didn't believe him for a minute, but I agreed. We need to get him back to the Playhouse. But now that it's finally in sight, I'm second-guessing.

"Are you sure about this?" I call after Jude as we walk. Our disguises feel too thin. It took Jude most of the trip back to teach me Mimicry without the help of a mirror. Mostly because he kept losing his train of thought, jumbling his words, or breaking into more coughing fits. Each seems to leave him worse than the last.

My disguise is a shallow one, the freckled face and upturned nose of a girl we saw selling papers and shouting their hysterical headlines about Jude's escape hours ago.

"We'll have to get into the Playhouse through the tunnels. This way," Jude calls behind him.

"Tunnels?" I ask.

"Used for transporting large set pieces and props. And occasionally, yours truly."

We must be half a mile from the Playhouse still, but furious crowds are piling out around it like ants as we move over a desolate road, watching from afar. I hear shouting, and I see torchlight as the sun dips below the horizon. A Player has escaped. Broken the law. The North has been *waiting* for a reason such as this to get the upper hand.

Jude toes the ground, counting something out. Finally, he snaps his head up when he reaches eleven. "There, I think."

He points to a shed in the distance. I can't imagine why. It's run-down, with rotting wood paneling and probably a termite problem. But before I can argue, Jude takes off and throws open its doors. I follow and skid to a stop, nearly falling into what appears to be an enormous stairwell filling the entire shed, leading down. The steps aren't damp and rotting like I expect. They're encrusted in jewels. A brilliant silver railing invites us into complete darkness.

"This way, Alistaire," he calls, descending the first few steps. "And shut that door behind you, if you don't mind."

The stairs trail deep into the dark and drop us at a tunnel with nothing to light our path, save for the glow of our skin. When we reach an impasse, Jude turns right without hesitating.

"What's down here?" I ask, nervous.

"A labyrinth. Any intruders, armies, what have you, would never reach the Playhouse without a Player to guide them through it."

"It's a maze?"

A growl in the distance freezes us both in our tracks.

"A maze with surprises," he adds. "Stay close."

I trudge after him, muttering that I'm tired of "Playhouse surprises." But the constant feeling that I'm being watched, that a second set of feet is trailing my own, is enough to make me think Marigold and her freaky skull collections weren't so bad.

Jude moves through the labyrinth like it's an old playground he knows well. Three lefts, a right, straight for what feels like a mile, and then another right. I stubbornly latch on to the hand he offers, not keen on losing him a third time.

After what feels like hours, I spot the first candelabra, a beacon in the night. The dimly lit corridor ushers us into the Playhouse Archives. I follow Jude past marble shelves and to a set of steps that lead up, past the arena entryway, until eventually I spot light peeking through the seams of a closed door at the top.

We burst through it and into the brightly lit Playhouse lobby.

I fall and roll, landing on my back. Spots flare across my vision, obscuring the ornate molding and marble columns encroaching over us in blessed light after hours in the dark.

All I can think about is how nice it feels to be *warm* again.

"Okay," Jude gasps beside me, seeming to catch his breath fully for the first time in days. "Easy part's over."

He sheds his disguise but says to keep mine on.

"*You're* the one they want to execute," I argue.

"Yes, and hopefully with a trial. If the other Players see you before I can explain, I promise there'll be no trial." He ducks over to the window, where the uproar of protests and fire swells outside. "They're down there," he concludes grimly, and we head for the grand doors.

The hall, laden with massive chandeliers, twisted staircases, and rolling red carpets, feels like a walkway to the gallows. Ahead, the Playhouse entrance looms, the dance of fire and shadows just beyond the stained glass windows on either side. Indiscernible shouting slithers through.

"Why doesn't the cast just move the Playhouse away from here—leave the North?" I whisper as we walk, but my feet feel heavier with each step. Nervous. The rising chaos of whatever is happening outside is enough to make me pause, reconsider.

"They can't without me." He presses both palms to the heavy doors. "We're all sitting ducks at the moment. Alistaire?" He stops short. "You may have to do this next part on your own."

I return a reasonably confused look as Jude throws open the Playhouse doors.

First, everything goes silent.

The distinct clip of Jude's step echoes as he strolls across the terrace to the gutting hush of held breaths and eyes turning on us. The Playhouse sits at the bottom of the incline, and as we go, my eyes sweep uphill and over the masses on the other side of our gates. They watch me back, a blur of faces. Ten thousand people? Twenty? I can't see where they begin or end.

Sil is locked in some sort of heated conversation at the gate's entrance, though the overwhelming silence gives him pause enough to turn. His shoulders fall when he sees Jude.

JUDE: "Good evening, everyone! I hear I've been sorely missed."

Sil says nothing. He just runs, embracing Jude like a prodigal son returning home, and then turns to me like he's about to do the same before thinking better of it. His face changes, deep, sad lines cutting into it. "Oh, Alistaire." He shakes his head, apparently seeing right through my Mimicry. "What have you done?"

I search for the rest of the cast, but they aren't outside. Just faces—from both the North and South, I wager—so many faces staring at us.

"Sil," a hard voice orders from the gates. "Your Player has come home. Open the gates."

I turn toward the voice, and when I see who stands on the front lines, the world stills.

Eleni. The woman—Dorian's companion—who escaped Jude's hand just days ago. She's uniformed in black and silver to represent the council guard. My eyes follow the argent patterns sewn into her sleeves, trying to calculate her rank—patterns that crawl up to the open neck, revealing a glittering, golden symbol there at the base of her throat.

She's marked.

I scramble to put the pieces together. Dorian's hunters have been long condemned by the council and named traitorous to Theatron. They refuse marks for the sole purpose of *needing* to outwit a liar, should they come across one. Somehow, this woman has positioned herself into the leadership of both, poised to play whichever side suits her. Which, given that she's marked, is bold. She can't lie if caught by the council. Or, at least, she'd have to get awful clever with her words.

So *that's* how she survived Jude's Compulsion.

Jude must process all of this with the same frantic speed that I do. Eleni knows everything. About what we've done.

Worse, she knows who I am.

"Alistaire," Jude says at last, never taking his eyes off her. "Go inside."

"I'm sure we can work this out," Sil calls back easily.

"Open the gates," Eleni repeats. Her stare is focused on Jude, like she can still see Dorian's blood on his hands.

The small army behind her is nestled in the crowds, clad in the same uniforms. Their hands are weighed down with Eleutheraen chains, blades strapped at their sides. Deployed by the council, no doubt at the insistence of Syrene's ruler.

"Your Player left the Playhouse," Eleni says firmly, but there's a condescending grin in her voice. "He's to stand trial—"

SIL: "He's *returned*. What damage has been done?"

JUDE: "Alistaire, please go inside—"

TITUS: "Well, *look* who's home!"

The Playhouse doors burst open again, and the remaining Players file out. There's something in Titus's clutch, a person held like a wild animal struggling something awful under his grip. "We got you both a welcome-home present. Just *look* what we found running around inside!"

MATTIA: "It isn't enough for you people to storm our gates; now you're sending moles inside our doors?"

TITUS: "Give our love to the council and tell them this is pathetic." He grunts as the figure fights his grip, jolts in our direction.

"I'm not leaving," the man shouts. "I'm *not* leaving without—"

I see his face and forget everything else in the world.

Galen.

Intermission: Scene XII

For a fleeting moment, relief crushes my chest at the familiar sight of my brother's face. The same rushing reassurance that calmed me as a child when Galen woke me from vicious dreams full of golden eyes. He's come to rescue me from a long, waking nightmare.

Except this time, it's Galen who's surrounded by golden stares. Something in me twists, sharpens as my attention falls to the place where Titus's arms are keeping Galen's restrained.

"Let him go." My voice escapes my throat like a crackle of torchlight.

Titus raises an eyebrow. "Is that you, Al?"

JUDE: "Alistaire, *don't—*" He stalks toward me but isn't fast enough. I shed my Mimicry swiftly, my own face feeling the cool night air as the false flesh simmers away.

Galen watches me, his expression blank, bruised, *tired*. I see the word "Riv" form on his lips, like he doesn't believe what he's seeing.

RIVEN: "I said let him go." I look to Jude for help and am stunned to find no sympathy on his face. He watches Galen with the cold indifference I would expect from a Player, but not what I've come to expect from Jude.

When he looks at my brother, anger courses through his expression. Throat tight, he utters, "There are consequences, Titus. For hurting a marked of the council's."

TITUS: "Well, lucky us! He isn't."

RIVEN: "What?" The word comes out like an accusation.

Galen fights and curses as Mattia forces his collar down from his throat.

There, under the torchlight, is a dark slash through the seal of his mark. Something twists in my chest as I wonder at all the awful things he's done to bring me home.

He won't look at me, eyes hard on the ground. And I can't tell if he's ashamed of what he's done or if he's ashamed of me.

If he's *scared* of me.

"Release him." My voice drops to a biting growl ready to cut through Titus's flesh.

Titus pauses. "I'll make you a trade, *Alistaire*. Did you kill Marigold?"

The words catch me off guard, and I pause. "Yes."

Heartbreak dawns over Sil's face. "Alistaire—" he begins, but Titus shoves forward, dragging Galen.

TITUS: "And Jude. Did you kill him, too?"

I plant my feet on the marble, pressing my lips together, unsure what to say.

TITUS: "Because you might as well have."

In a single movement, Titus throws Galen down the marble steps and runs at me, going for the hilt of his blade. I have barely enough time to register the awful sound of Galen's back hitting the marble, or the shine of the blade aimed for my throat, before Jude slides between us, shoving him back hard. "Titus—*not now*."

Titus recovers, looks at Jude with eyes like hellfire. "Oh, I'll *get* to you."

A heightened awareness sets in Jude's shoulders at the invitation of a fight, one I'm not sticking around for.

TITUS: "Perhaps someone can tell me"—he addresses Sil but points at Jude—"why the *fuck* he can leave?"

I turn, my feet tearing down the steps toward my brother.

PARRISH: "I'd like to know that, too." Her voice, a mild and sweet melody most of the time, sharpens into something cunning, lethal.

"Silenus, control your Players," I hear someone call out.

My knees smash into marble at the bottom, on the landing. I reach for Galen, who's struggling to push himself up. "Are you all right?" I whisper.

"No one?" I hear Titus shout from behind us. "No one can

tell me why *we* have to stay in here and Jude can apparently leave whenever the hell he wants?" Titus heaves a breath. Then: "Open the gates. *Open them*. Now."

SIL: "Titus, stand *down*."

"Silenus, control your—"

TITUS: *"Let me out."*

I ignore the pounding of Titus's nearing steps as he races down the stairs, Mattia, Parrish, and Arius behind him. Sil is shouting something indiscernible.

"Galen," I press, ignoring the crowds watching us closely, like this is the grand finale of some sick play. "Can you walk?"

My brother coughs, the wind knocked out of him. His head is bleeding—he must have hit it when he fell.

Beyond us, the Playhouse gates scream open. Titus has apparently reached them.

"Come in. *Everyone*, come in!" Titus is screaming now, his feet apparently unable to pass the threshold. "If we can't go out there, you might as well come inside! Who the hell cares, if Jude here can break all the rules?"

For some reason, the marching of foreign boots entering Playhouse grounds makes my hackles rise. I push the noise out, turn my attention back to Galen, to the brownish bruise painted across his jaw.

"What happened?" I whisper to him.

"Riv," he begins, grasping at my shoulders. I almost think he's going to hug me, when I realize he can't. Not in front of all these people. For my sake. "You look—" He coughs a laugh. "Terrifying."

My chest eases when he makes a joke, all while looking straight into the gold of my eyes without shuddering in disgust. Then, without warning, my brother hoists himself up and grips my collar, pulling me toward him so abruptly, I let out a startled cry. Some part of me expects a blade to cut right through my rib cage.

Instead, the weight of a small item drops into my coat pocket.

"Riven," Galen says, determined, hands on my face. He dips his head in a single, subtle nod, his eyes communicating something in a language I don't understand. But still, there's a kindness in his gaze that edges on proud. A gaze that hovers over most of my memories and always promised to protect us both from Craft and Players.

And then it's gone. His eyes wipe clean, blank.

His jaw slackens. Galen's weight slumps onto me. I focus downward, where the tip of a blade protrudes from his chest. It vanishes, and Galen falls out of my grip onto the marble.

I peer upward to where Eleni stands just behind him, an Eleutheraen blade in her hands.

Intermission: Scene XIII

My mind refuses to make sense of the blade she holds. *My* blade. My father's. The one left in my bag when Jude and I fled the cabin of Dorian's hunters.

My brother's blood slickens its edge.

"A traitor to the North dies like a Player," Eleni says bluntly, like an afterthought. She turns on her heel and points at Jude, who I realize is kneeling beside me, speaking words I can't hear. "Take him," she adds.

I hear nothing else beyond the ringing in my ears and the word *"Éxodos"* leaving my lips over and over, louder each time. But there's no reality of his left to suspend.

"Alistaire, he's already gone." The words are Jude's. I ignore him and shake off the hand he places on my shoulder. Blood stains the tips of my fingers. Galen's eyes are cloudy and open, turned to the sky. Gone.

Suddenly, I'm a child again, watching the havoc unfold around me at the news of our father's cold body. Found in the very same place. Right outside the Playhouse.

"Jude Stepharros, under Theatron law, you are to stand trial for—"

I can't look away from Galen, but I hear the drag of Eleutheraen chains coming for Jude.

"Alistaire?" Jude calls, fighting as he's ripped from my side. "Look at me—*Alistaire*!"

Maybe I should be satisfied. This should feel like justice. Jude is the reason this happened. I want Jude dead. I'm sure I do.

Except Galen is gone. And not because of the Players he protected me from since I was small. But by the hands of our own people. With our father's own knife.

It's not fair. It doesn't make sense.

"Alistaire—"

I glance upward. Golden links cuff Jude's wrists. Something beneath my skin moves at the sight. Startles. Wakes up.

I have never been angrier in my life than I am right now.

Somewhere, deep inside my head, that bridge locks firmly into place, and something furious and dark courses through it.

That anger will be the death of—

"Please look at me," Jude yells, trying to get my attention when I am entirely somewhere else. "Look at me. *Riven!*"

Riven.

My world stops.

Slowly, I turn and do just as he asks. I look at Jude, a Player.

A Player who knows my real name.

"Let him go." I don't recognize the voice that comes out of me. It's not begging or even asking. The voice that comes out of me is an offer, a warning.

The four men holding Jude stagger. Their eyes whirl with confusion, like they're trying to remember how to breathe.

"It would be unwise to attempt the use of Craft on marked men," Eleni bites out, steps away. I don't bother looking up at her. It takes everything to tear my eyes away from Galen, feeling helpless. Feeling *alone.*

I am alone now. Wholly and completely.

But I am *not* helpless.

Warmth floods my veins. Crawls up my throat and slides down my tongue.

"Sil, control your—"

My mouth opens. "Eleni stands still."

It's like someone pauses the entire world. Silence strikes the mayhem surrounding us, bringing it to a hesitant stillness.

The mortals made a treaty, to keep the Players South.

Eleni stares at me, dumbfounded.

My mouth opens again, and a singsong voice comes out. "Eleni steps forward."

And when the treaty ended, a wall to keep them out.

The toe of her boot inches forward, and that's when fear ignites in her eyes, when her hand darts to the mark that *should* be protecting her from this. From me. The pitch of my voice engulfs the eruption of whispers in the crowd around us.

At the edge of my vision, Jude watches from his chains, his mouth hanging open.

"Eleni falls to her knees." My voice again, but not.

I am not helpless.

And if the wall should crumble, then marks will keep us safe.

She tries to spring forward. Toward me. She falls to her knees at the marble steps instead, her hands clasping onto the ledge of one.

And if our marks should fail us, gods have mercy on our fate.

"Eleni hits her head. Very hard." I raise my eyes and meet hers. My mouth opens one more time, voice rigid as stone and sweet as honey. "Over and over again."

Eleni obeys.

Intermission: Scene XIV

Two bodies mar the Playhouse steps.

I'm vaguely aware of the collective mania breaking out at the sight of dark blood washing over the marble, because the ringing in my ears isn't loud enough to drown out all the screaming. Eleni's body lies face down on the steps, limp, hands still clutching the ledge of the terrace. Crimson oozes into her blond hair.

A stampede pushes away from the Playhouse. Somewhere, Sil yells for the other Players to go inside.

I don't care. *"Methexis."* The word warms my throat.

The ground beneath me clears into a glassy ocean only I can see. Tendrils of brilliant Craft lock and weave deep below it. Summoned by my anger, they ascend to the surface with a violence I only draw from, as my bridge to that strange power bonds stronger. I grip hold of that darkness, that anger. Pull it inward, center it, because it hasn't just come from me. It *is* me. It's a rage so hungry, it has to devour something.

But that something will not be me.

I banish the image of my bridge and focus on the mania beyond it, but hold fast to that Craft—that *power.* It courses through me like a live flame.

A word rattles from my lips in a pitch so low, my own ears can't distinguish it. I don't even *understand* it.

Where is this coming from?

This isn't me.

Jude shouts something. I turn, and his eyes widen, frightened. Like he sees something I can't. The men holding him abandon their post, scattering and leaving Jude to struggle against his bindings.

Not to get away from the crowds, but to get away from me.

All I can think is that I want all of these intruders out—*far* away from me, from Jude, from the Players, and from the Playhouse.

The thought consumes me as an illusion builds on my lips and escapes my mouth like a curse.

In response, shadows slink from the clouds overhead and fall like dead leaves to the ground. They crawl over the marble like living creatures, chasing away the spectators.

At my command, they seep outside the Playhouse gates, where shrieks erupt like banshees as the dark illusion stretches over the crowd.

Then, one by one, every last torch in this godsforsaken crowd quiets to an ember, to smoke, and finally: to nothing. My illusion smothers the light, swallows it whole.

The air thins, cold and icy.

In the distance, the city lights of homes and buildings and shops hush and dim to nothing, like a candle blown out.

Stop this—

I can't. I can't stop it.

Darkness eclipses the moon above, a ceaseless night that falls in a blanket so thick, it muffles the screams in the distance. I see nothing except the dim golden halo of my own skin. I hear nothing except Sil calling out, presumably still for the Players to go inside.

Then the distinct clattering of Eleutheraen chains dropping to the marble.

Somewhere behind me, the Playhouse doors slam shut, and I'm alone.

Alone.

A hand grips my ankle, as if to contradict the thought, and it's warm like the sun.

I hear words I can't make out, but the voice belongs to Jude. I don't understand what he's saying. It almost sounds like another language, though it feels comforting. Familiar, in a distant way.

Even as the shouts dwindle, leaving only darkness, I stand still. Below me, Jude clings to my ankle, whispering something over and over.

I stand there—for a long time.

Until finally, I stop.

ACT III

Act III: Scene I

When daylight breaks, I'm in my dressing room.

We're back in the District, according to my window. Though I don't remember the Playhouse moving. I don't even remember leaving the terrace. I'm standing but can't shove off the feeling that I've just woken up and am not entirely certain how much time has passed.

Sil nervously eases into my room. I drop the window curtain back into place, and it's stained. A golden substance drips at my fingertips, just like Jude's had done.

Jude. He called out to me, right before it all happened.

To Riven. Not Alistaire.

Jude knows my name.

I stare out the window, trying to remember what happened. What I did and *why.*

But I'm less and less sure it was me at all.

"I thought you'd show up," I say to Sil by way of greeting. He leaves the door open behind him long enough that I can see black-and-silver uniforms beyond it—people who do *not* belong in the Playhouse.

"A moment, please—I thank you," Sil says to them before shutting the door. "I'm glad you're...awake."

RIVEN: "They're here for me." My voice doesn't sound like mine. By the way Sil stares at me, I imagine I don't look much like myself, either.

I caught a glance in the mirror earlier when I threw a sheet over it, just enough to see my pupils, blown out and bloodshot. The dull brown of my irises wholly devoured by a hungry gold that bleeds deep into the whites of my eyes and runs in dried trails down my face. The lifeless panes of my cheekbones jut out at sharp, unnatural angles, as if trying to tear through skin, which has flushed with a blush of color, less pallid. I've grown even taller somehow.

I look like one of *them*. A Player.

Sil steps closer and seems surprised when I don't skitter back like a frightened animal like I always do. Instead, I charge forward, imprints of gold trailing beneath my feet.

RIVEN: "Something is happening to me." It isn't a question, and I'm not asking for an explanation. I just needed the words to be stated out loud. I don't know who called down that horrible, ever-growing darkness. It came from my hands, but it was *not* me.

Sil nods slowly. "The stronger the motivation, the stronger the Player."

I swallow, my throat tight. "I'm angry." At whom and for what, I'm not sure. At everything. For so many reasons. "I'm so, *so* angry." And I want it—*need it*—to stop.

Somewhere below, the Playhouse doors slam shut. I look to the window, and my insides twist at the sight of Jude being led out of the Playhouse, Eleutheraen chains binding his arms to his torso. An army of fifteen uniforms escorts him down the steps. He doesn't fight them.

All I can think is, *You know my name.*

RIVEN: "They've come for both of us, then."

SIL: "I'll argue your defenses. The plague you brought—"

I turn. "Plague?"

The word weighs on my chest, the sheer impossibility of it too heavy and jarring. The Players have a long history of horrors called down on cities that angered or betrayed them. The Laughing Plague made witnesses laugh until their vocal cords tore. The Dancing Plague, a punishment that caused mortals to dance until they died of exhaustion. But *I* wouldn't have brought anything like that. I couldn't have.

I watch Sil's face, waiting for the assurance that I didn't hurt anyone.

A flash of memory crashes through my mind, like recalling

a nightmare. That woman—that woman with the blond hair, the blood...

I have hurt someone.

Just as fast, it hits me. Not a nightmare. All of it real. *Galen.* Galen is—

SIL: "The papers are calling it the Dark Days Plague." *Darkness.* That illusion I called down.

RIVEN: "How far?" I try to remember, but my memories keep slipping, blurring like I'm watching them through a stranger's eyes. I brace a hand on the wall, steadying myself. "How far did it spread?"

Sil hesitates before answering. "It didn't cross Paraskenia's border, so we can spin it as a defense. The law allowed them to arrest Jude—and do nothing else." Sil eases to the window and peeks outside while I focus on keeping the bile from rising in my throat. I stare at my hands, unsure how they could have done such an awful thing. "The trial will be speedy. The council can do many things, but nothing can disrupt the Great Dionysia."

Great Dionysia? Somehow, even the mention of the competition I've falsely enrolled in feels ridiculous in all of this.

Sil reaches into his breast pocket, plucking a small vial from within, its contents obscured by the tinted glass. It reminds me of something. I press a hand over my pocket. Galen tucked something inside it. Before—*before...*

It's still there, I conclude, feeling the outline of a vial. Though I don't pull it out in front of Sil, resolving to check later.

SIL: "Alistaire."

I blink at him, dazed, but notice the concern that shimmers across his face as he flicks the cap off the tinted bottle. "This grieves me, too. But I need you in control if you're to stand before the council."

I wrinkle my nose at the offering. "What's in it?"

"Eleutheraen gold."

I back away, as if he backhanded me. Trails of gold stain my path. It occurs to me with no small level of discomfort that this must have been how Jude felt.

SIL: "Diluted! It contains hardly a drop. I promise it won't hurt you. I only need you to come a little further back off your bridge."

RIVEN: "I thought you said Players *thrive* on their motivation." I sneer at him.

It hits me a moment too late that I've admitted it out loud: I'm turning into one of them.

SIL: "They do. But when it becomes *greater* than them, a Player is no more than a servant to their driving force."

Is that what happened? Did something else take control of me?

I draw a glance at my hands. At the gold running so bright through my veins, it shines through my skin. At this rate, the Craft living and breathing inside will eat me alive before I can do anything. I need to live long enough to finish this.

Because I don't want to go home anymore. I don't want to escape, and I don't even want justice. Behind my eyes, pieces click together, the horrible beginnings of a plan.

I want revenge.

Sil tilts my chin upward, draws the bottle to my lips. I don't fight.

Act III: Scene II

This musty cell turns out to be a fine place to stew over my plan. One I won't be able to do anything about if Jude and I are both executed today.

Not that I can think clearly with Eleutheraen cuffs chafing against my wrists. My head swims as I lean it against the cool cell wall. That small sip of Sil's tonic still burns in my throat with a vengeance that made the journey here horrendously dizzying. Enough so that I'm not actually entirely certain where I am.

If a single drop of Eleutheraen gold could neutralize the Craft in me, I shudder to think what more would do.

A thought occurs to me, and I reach into my pocket to extract the vial hidden there, trying to remember the last words Galen spoke when he passed it between us.

It's Eleutheraen gold. Pure, judging by the label—no dilution. I can't fathom how he got the money for such a thing. It feels like a message, one I'm not sure how to decrypt.

I turn my attention to the cell across from mine, seething. It's empty.

Until the door shrieks open and two men pile in, leading a third. At once, I'm on my feet.

Jude walks primly into his cell as if two heavily armed guards aren't dragging him by the elbows. The cell door slams and the guards vanish, leaving us mostly to darkness.

In a breath, I cross my cell and grip hold of the bars separating me from Jude. "How do you know my name?" I demand, my nails biting into the rust.

Without so much as wincing, Jude answers, "How could I not? The world may not recognize you under all the glitter and gold, but I saw you the night you wandered into the Playhouse. You had his face."

Suspicions confirmed, I feel my chest tighten. "Michail's." My father's.

He sneers at the name. "That's the one."

The admission slices through me. My muscles lock, waiting for the punch line. For Jude to look up, laugh, and apologize for making such a cruel joke. But no punch line comes.

Jude knows who I am. He's known since the day I walked into the Playhouse and lied to me every day since. My mind clings to disbelief, claws for something—anything—to contradict that it was all a sham. This bond between us more than my imagination.

"Gene Hunt. She ties into all of this." My eyes narrow, accusing. "She knew my name, too," I breathe. Gene recognized me. "Did she know my father?"

"We all had the misfortune of meeting him." He huffs. *"Peacemaker."*

"Did you kill him?" Jude says nothing. Nausea gathers in my throat. "My father," I repeat, certain I don't want the answer. "Did you kill him."

He raises his chin, bares his teeth. "I'd do it a hundred times over, Riven."

The shadows clear from my vision. Whatever rose-colored gauze I'd cast over Jude dissipates. He is what he is. A Player. Players always lie.

Somehow, I let myself forget. This is my fault.

Before I can swallow my anger, I push on, frantically reaching for answers and throwing out the first one that makes a little sense. "Did you love her? Gene?"

Jude looks like he might explode with laughter. "No, Riven. I'd go as far as to say the two of us didn't get along." He rolls his eyes. "She'd fall in love with anything."

Any*thing*. The degrading jab sparks a new, awful thought.

"Michail," I whisper, shocked, the pieces falling together like broken pottery. Part of me has wondered since the night I saw Gene, saw my name on her lips, like she knew who I was. "My father—*he* loved her."

Jude says nothing. But his face tells me everything.

My mind reels. A picture begins to take shape. Gene took her own life—onstage in front of thousands. The night Michail was found dead outside the Playhouse. She died, and then Michail wasn't far behind.

"You killed Gene, too, then," I conclude, visualizing her notorious onstage *suicide*.

"Whoa, now." Jude raises his hands in defense. "I didn't put anything in that cup she drank from. I just didn't help suspend her reality when she changed her mind." He throws me a look. "People often change their minds when they're dying, wouldn't you say?"

I draw a hand to where my mark used to be, defensive.

"You're right, though." Jude leans his head back to the wall. "That put me in a tough spot, Gene dying. I never competed with her in the arena, never rightfully claimed my crown as Lead Player. Her role was given to me by default. Some even thought she did it to spare me—to *pity* me." He avoids looking at me. "I have a reputation to fix, Riven. I hope you can understand."

Then it all snaps into place.

I'm not a prisoner. I'm a trophy.

"You weren't trying to get out of the Great Dionysia. You *never* planned to let me go after trapping me." My accusations coil inside me, then all come out at once. "You *wanted* to kill me in the arena. In front of everyone. Not in spite of me being a marked but *because* I'm marked. Daughter of the Peacemaker, killed in front of an audience."

"Well, there's no need to make yourself sound like a sacrificial lamb," Jude says. "Death is death; we all do it."

He never meant to let me go. I'm his key to solidifying his place as Lead Player, to going down in history for killing the first marked Player before an audience of thousands. In the name of his home, destroyed by the North.

Vengeance and triumph and glory all in one fell swoop.

"Was it you?" I blurt. "The night I entered the Playhouse, the night of the casting call. I was attacked. There was a voice—it was singing, and it..." I blink, remembering my attackers. The blood. Right before Sil walked out. "The voice stopped them."

"I think the words you're looking for are 'thank you,'" says Jude.

Gods. He saw me before I even entered the Playhouse. I was an opportunity he seized. "You're—" My voice breaks, full of fury. A knot forms in my throat. "You are so *selfish*."

"I'm an *actor*," he says, but there's hesitation there. Then he shuts his eyes tight. "I didn't mean for it to go like this."

I run through everything in my head, only in a different light this time. It all looks different now. "Destroying my mark wasn't to save me from dying. It was to keep me alive long enough to kill me in the arena," I accuse.

He winces. "It was, but Riven—"

"You didn't come back when Dorian took me because you cared. You did it because *you* want to be the one to slay me. In front of an audience. All for your precious *reputation*."

And I fell for it. I have been suspicious of Jude since the moment I laid eyes on him, and he still fooled me. My breaths come faster, my vision shaking with each admission he utters.

"Riven, please, I don't—"

"Was it a trick, saying that you'd release me? Just a false promise to get me back here?"

"I don't—"

"And if I refused, would you have just dragged me back here anyway?"

"I don't know!" he shouts, gold flaring in his eyes, the words echoing off the stone. He reels in his voice. "Riven, *listen*—"

I'm not listening. All I can think is how utterly absurd and desperate I must be to have believed Jude saw me as more than just the cursed daughter of the Peacemaker. No, Jude is too clever. He saw a weakness, a vulnerability to exploit, and he went for it.

What the hell was I thinking? That Jude had *feelings* for me? I really have lost it.

Mattia was right. All he knows is winning.

"Riven, please. Would you get out of your head and listen? I am *sorry*," Jude calls through the bars into my cell. "There are things you don't know."

"And luring me into a damned bargain, to break a curse *you* put on me—"

"Curse! Riven." Now he laughs, shaking his head. "*Look at you.* What curse?"

"My—" I freeze, eyes flickering down to my hands. The nails that fell off have grown back. The puckering veins have vanished from my wrists, replaced by shimmering gold and strong cords of muscle. But most of all: I can *feel* everything. That eerie numbness, that unforgiving ice that courses through my blood, has vanished.

It happened so gradually, I didn't even notice.

"Riven," Jude says, breaking me from my stupor. "If you trust anything of me, then let it be that I'm sorry."

My laugh bounces against the rusted ceilings above us. "*Now* you're sorry," I say, gesturing widely at our current situation.

"You may not believe me. I expect you won't, and you shouldn't. I'm full of Craft and lies. It is *all* I know. But I swear to Dionysus, Riven, I am sorry. You aren't—" Jude blows out a breath. "You aren't what I expected you to be."

I reach for my rage but come up empty. There's just hurt.

"Well," I say at him. "You are *exactly* what I expected you to be."

Act III: Scene III

The main doors beyond our cells open, and several men armed to the teeth with Eleutheraen gold file into the holding area.

"This is quite an escort for a *walk upstairs*," I state as the men draw me out of my cell by my chains like a dog on a leash.

"We aren't going upstairs," offers Jude, who I ignore. "Are we, gentlemen?"

They don't respond. They've probably been given strict instructions not to speak to us.

And even stricter instructions not to look at us, because that's when a thick folded cloth is pressed over my eyelids. I scowl as the men tie it at the back of my head, plunging me into darkness.

"Where, then?" I ask our captors, not Jude. I never want to hear Jude speak again. But of course, he answers anyway.

"By law, any witness to the crime in question holds the right to be present for the trial—"

His voice is capped by a cough and a struggle. I can't see what's happening but have a decent idea when what feels like a rag is forced across my lips and tied too tight at my neck.

Someone kicks the back of my leg, and I stumble into a walk as they guide us up some stairs.

With no vision and no way to communicate, I'm left to mull over those final words.

Any witness to the crime in question.

My entourage picks up speed, forcing my legs to move faster. I feel the sun warm my hair and hear the bustle around us. We're outside.

Our presence gains notice with each step.

Curses fly at me. I feel spit on my neck and calls for my execution. A remark flutters past my ear: "See how it feels," someone says.

I want to scream, *I'm one of you*, but gag against the rag binding my mouth.

The men prompt me into a crammed space, and a door shuts. Wheels beneath me turn and gain speed. Who's to say how much time slips away before we're carted out, then made to walk what feels like a few hundred more steps.

The anticipation in the air is akin to the beginning of a show, and the hairs rise on the back of my neck. The commotion of an audience swarms outside.

A gentle hand unties my gag, then my blindfold. Sil's are the first eyes I see. The only thing more alarming than these circumstances is the relief I feel upon seeing his face. It's guttural. Like being picked up by a parent after falling and scraping your knee as a child.

"Where are we?" I ask, throat tight.

"The First Act. This is the original arena stage in Theatron," Sil explains, moving to untie Jude's bindings. Because he removed mine first. It feels significant, and I can't place why. "Players performed here when they still walked freely."

Not that I could guess this by the windowless stone room we're enclosed in. But I remember reading about The First Act Theatre in the District well enough. I've even passed it, a hulking stone arena, long forgotten and crumbling from neglect. "They used to put Players on trial here."

"They used to *execute* Players here," Jude offers helpfully, blinking until his eyes adjust to the light. "Witnesses have a right to see the trial. Generally, if a Player has been accused, you can imagine the witnesses are many."

"How many?" I ask.

Sil ignores the question and throws our gags and blindfolds to the ground, then turns and looks pointedly at me. "Alistaire." He rests his hands on my shoulders. Disgust doesn't creep through my bones like it should. The touch almost feels comforting. Whatever Sil is to me right now, he's not my enemy.

Which almost scares me more than the trial ahead.

Whatever he's about to say is lost as a woman uniformed in black and silver appears at the door. She says nothing but motions us through, noticeably avoiding our eyes.

Sil swallows his words to me and offers instead, "Break a leg."

I feel my audience before I see them.

The tunnel we pass through spits us into an outdoor arena built of weathered stone and shaped like a bowl. The rims of the bowl are full; we're surrounded by the company of what seems like thousands. I can't bear to look at their faces, but I feel their eyes all the same.

I expect screams. Curses. *Something.* Instead, eerie silence stretches over the crowd.

The stands where my accusers sit have fallen into disuse. Thin rays of sun light the circular platform ahead as I march, keeping my eyes on Sil's back until we reach its center. It's dusty and cracked, a ring of Eleutheraen gold encircling the stage we stand upon.

Jude is guided off to my left. I spot a place near him where the line of Eleutheraen gold is broken by a hair. Unsealed.

Sil stands just behind us at the center.

Once, Players performed on this stage. Later, their blood spilled on it.

Which purpose it will be used for today is anyone's guess.

The audience rises to their feet. Many from South of the Cut have come in support of the Playhouse, judging by the number of metallic theatrical masks I spot in the rows.

Survive this, I chant to myself. *I made it this far. This isn't how I'm supposed to die.*

A line of seven men and women file out of the opposite tunnel. Theatron's council, robed in black and silver. They seat themselves accordingly at a table far upstage. The crowd sits when they do.

Finally, the magistrate enters and stops before us, with slicked-back silver hair and eyes like a fox. Those eyes lock on me and stay there until she calls, "Jude Stepharros. You stand before the council, accused of breaking your contract and violating Theatron law by crossing out of Playhouse grounds before the start of the Great Dionysia."

I innocently pretend not to notice the accusing glare he sends my way.

"Alistaire Hunt," she goes on. "You are charged with the illegal misuse of Craft by a Player and the murder of a council-appointed official—"

"She was marked. So I can't have killed her with Craft," I snap back. "And I am *not* a Player," I add before Sil can stop me.

"You are not *anyone*," the magistrate says, not taking the bait. "According to the city census and Theatron record, you do not exist."

The air grows very still. Jude shuts his eyes beside me, but I feel Sil watching keenly.

"Alistaire Hunt," she demands. "Who are you?"

For the first time in a while, the scars of my mark burn, wishing to tell the truth. I seal my lips shut, and the magistrate smiles. She knows she's onto something. "These are significant accusations against the Playhouse, Silenus," the magistrate states, turning her attention to Sil. "A Playhouse Plague. A council-appointed official dead at the hands of a Player—"

"She is not a Player. She is an auditionee," Sil argues back.

"Yet, with her Craft, she brought perhaps one of the most notable plagues Theatron has ever seen. How do you explain it?" The magistrate eyes him, daring him to answer.

"I admit, Craft has taken a particular bond to her blood. She is a natural," Sil answers, steady.

Slowly, the magistrate turns toward me. "A bond to her blood so strong, she may have influenced a woman to execute herself before *thousands* of witnesses—"

"The woman was marked," Sil says, voice hardening. "Alistaire could not have used Compulsion to influence her."

"Then how do you explain her death?"

Even as she says the words, the realization runs cold through me. Craft bonding so close to my blood, strong enough to kill a marked woman...because *I* am a marked woman, perhaps able to use Craft on a marked because I've been forced to do it on myself.

There's something I'm missing here—a piece I'm sure I'm not seeing.

Still, I tuck the possibility away under my growing pile of secrets.

The magistrate extracts a scroll from her belt, unfurls it, and reads it aloud. "Early evaluations anticipate the Playhouse's Dark Days Plague has damaged the vision in an estimated *four percent* of the affected city's population. Many more claim madness by the shadows of your hand." I shut my eyes, like that will block out the words. She must be referring to those who were close to the Playhouse, to that strange darkness that I brought. Thank the gods it didn't kill anyone.

It wasn't me. It was something else.

"Your Craft bled into the ground, darkening streets and infrastructure alike. You have damaged every last crop within the city limits, unleashing an unprecedented shortage over its population," she announces.

"An act of *defense*," Sil argues. "Alistaire's work, while admittedly excessive, came in response to an unauthorized siege on the Playhouse. She is not a Player. She does not fall under such laws."

The crowd stirs again. It's ludicrous but, technically, he's right.

The magistrate's face hardens. There's a glimmer in her eye that makes nausea churn in my stomach. "Your claims only hold steady if you can prove she *isn't* one of yours, Silenus. And to do that, you will need to prove she is *someone else*. As I've said, there is no record of you, Alistaire Hunt. No name, no family, no appearance in the census. You come from nowhere. Unless you can prove otherwise, the court has no choice but to assume illegal dealings of the Playhouse and try her as such—"

"She is *not* a Player!" shouts Jude.

"And I am not Alistaire Hunt," I say.

My voice strikes the arena like a whip. I stride forward.

RIVEN: "My name is Riven Hesper."

My chains clink as I pull my hands up, grip my collar, and yank it aside, where the raw scars of my mark shine beneath.

RIVEN: "And I am the marked daughter of the Peacemaker."

Act III: Scene IV

At first, a hush settles on the arena.

Then all hell breaks loose. Around me, spectators from North and South alike jump to their feet in protest. The council shouts for the magistrate, and the magistrate shouts for order.

I can't bring myself to look at Sil, certain what I'll find there: disappointment. Shock. Maybe betrayal. It unnerves me to admit Sil may be the closest thing I have to an ally now.

My throat tightens where my mark was, a written confession for all to see. A ruined mark is abominable in the North. And destroying it *intentionally*—unthinkable.

Moments pass in mounting chaos until the magistrate, somehow, brings order back to the court. She turns to me, her pace abrupt and her face full of disbelief as she grips at my collar and examines the scars closely. A moment or two passes before she pauses, then clutches my jaw roughly with one hand.

There's a snap of movement at my left, and I hear Sil mutter a sharp warning to Jude while the woman examines my eyes. Her hand feels like a block of ice, the touch leaving me nauseous.

Finally, she releases me, breathing hard and turning to the council for guidance. "She is marked. She was, at least."

"Riven Hesper."

I turn at the sound of my name to the robed, aging man seated at the center of the council. He raises a wrinkled hand and motions me forward.

I approach cautiously, one step at a time, taking in the council at last.

These are the revered bloodlines of Dionysus's first followers? Their faces are unremarkable, human.

Councilor Augustus Bouras, overseer of Parodos, I presume based on where he sits. He gestures for me to stop when I'm within arm's reach.

"The spitting image of Michail, then, aren't you?" His eyes track every angle of my face, like he's imagining what it would look like were I not full of Craft. "Your father was a dear friend, Riven. Theatron felt his loss greatly."

The scrutiny of Councilor Augustus's gaze is not nearly so startling as the hatred looming in the eyes of the girl a few seats removed from him, no older than sixteen. I can guess who she is by her age: Moira Atticus, successor to her father at an unexpectedly young age. Ruler of Syrene.

Just as quickly, I recall Jude's casual confession. I wonder if she suspects him of her father's murder. Regardless, she has enough reason to hate us both.

"What?" she says flatly, noticing me staring.

"I'm sorry," I say, inclining my head and turning to address the rest of them. "For what I did."

Her throat bobs, eyes hardening. "Every word from your lips is a lie." Her family swore its hatred for the Playhouse—and has ruled Syrene with that hatred for a long time. I look to Sil for instruction, but he's gone entirely still and offers no help.

"Forgive Moira's brashness," Augustus cuts in with a lighthearted laugh. "You know how the young are." He seems to be speaking more to Sil than me. "In any case, death comes for us all!"

"Not for her, it doesn't," Moira seethes, the edges of her words elegantly clipped.

"Moira," Augustus cautions.

"Is that why you did it?" she goes on. "Betrayed your people. Everything you were raised to believe in." There's something more behind her words than anger. I hear confusion, sense a sadness deep behind her lowered brow. "For this? For immortality?"

She's asking more than that. I'm her would-be *co*conspirator. Galen never named to the council who would be delivering Jude to Syrene, but she must know now it was supposed to be me.

And I failed. Badly.

"Immortality," I repeat, a smirk on my lips. "I may not live to see *next week*."

"Yes, the Great Dionysia," says another councilor next to Moira. "You and your bloodbaths, Sil."

"Why change a favored tradition?" Sil replies with a laugh.

"Your brother is a good man. He's served the council well," adds the councilor of Orkestra at Augustus's side. "He can corroborate your relation to the Hesper family?"

"He cannot," I say coldly.

"And why is that?" Augustus demands.

RIVEN: "He's dead. At the hands of your council guard." I deliver the words like a scripted line, making sure the pitch of my voice carries through the arena, even as it breaks.

Murmurs swim through the air. I tune them out. I don't hear anything. I haven't even had a moment to say the words out loud.

Galen is dead.

A droplet of gold stains the ground, and I struggle to bring my bound wrists up to wipe my eyes. Augustus studies me, and I wonder if it's sympathy I see lurking behind his cloudy gaze.

"Did you find yourself in the Playhouse and enroll in the casting call by *choice*, Riven?" he asks. It's a leading question. His eyes slide to Jude.

And there it is. I could tell the truth and end all of this right now. Jude would almost certainly be executed. By no means would I walk free, but my contract with the Playhouse would be voided.

Looking over my shoulder, I find Jude's eyes. He lowers his head, bracing himself.

Then, slowly, he nods at me. *Go on*, he seems to say. *I dare you.*

My lips move, but no words break past my teeth. A grip like a vise works its way around my throat—a feeling I know all too well. Splinters of anger claw up my neck.

I will *not* have the council execute Jude.

It's not enough. I want so, *so* much more than that now.

I want revenge.

And suddenly, I know exactly how I get out of this.

"Yes," I answer. "I entered the casting call by choice."

Shock descends over all seven faces before me at the lie as I prepare to deliver the performance of my life before thousands. And perhaps, the performance *for* my life.

"Why did you go to the Playhouse?" Augustus inquires, not believing me.

RIVEN: "For a seat at the table." I raise my chin. "A Player hurt me when I was young. *Cursed* me, you might have heard. Like many of you, I heard no music growing up, read no story, lived in fear of the Playhouse's return. And I am tired of being afraid."

I gesture at Jude with my bound hands.

RIVEN: "Their Lead Player isn't guilty of breaking his contract. *I am* for forcing him to leave the Playhouse. To show him the world outside. And look how he's returned without a soul harmed." It's a miracle Jude doesn't snort at the blatant lie.

I angle my body outward, appealing to the crowd, silently unleashing my Craft, reaching for their heartstrings and giving them a gentle tug. Testing if I *can*.

RIVEN: "My father died at the hands of the Playhouse, for his desire to seek peace between two worlds at each other's throats." My Craft flows through me, warming behind my eyes. "But my brother died at the hands of the North, the result of their fear." My voice climbs, higher and louder, as I shout to the crowd. "The Playhouse is not going anywhere. So why shouldn't the North have a seat at the table? Why *shouldn't* you have your voices heard?"

Their glassy eyes focus on me, captivated. I wonder if my speech has sought out true sympathy from them. Or if it's my own Craft looking back at me, if their tear-stained faces are wet with faux grief *I* have imposed.

Maybe their marks can't protect them from me.

I walk the platform, eyes up and chin high.

RIVEN: "I seek to become the first marked Player," I say, laying it on thick. "To represent truth and trust as a voice from North of the Cut in the Playhouse. To watch over their efforts and uses of Craft and to bridge the gap between Theatron's people that too many lives have fallen into already." *Go on. Believe me.*

My feet move downstage, to the front of the platform.

RIVEN: "Not only will I become the first marked Player." I stop and steady myself, gathering my breath. "But their Lead Player."

I can't strip the Playhouse of its power until it's *my* power to yield. As Lead Player.

RIVEN: "I challenge Jude Stepharros to the Great Dionysia."

Act III: Scene V

They cheer.

They *cheer.* They cheer until the magistrate raises her arms and demands order and Augustus stands from his seat. "The council calls for a brief recess—to discuss these most unusual circumstances," he announces.

SIL: "There is nothing to discuss." He points a finger at me. "Riven is accused of the illegal misuse of Craft. Your laws guide the actions of Players, not a marked. No such laws exist."

The magistrate straightens, jaw tight. "I'll admit, Silenus, it is an extremely rare situation—"

SIL: "With all due respect, her crimes no longer fall under the council's jurisdiction." I feel his eyes on my face. "They fall under mine."

I think for a moment he'll order Jude to kill me right then and there and brace myself for a fight.

SIL: "She is a marked who entered the Playhouse under false pretenses and illegally enrolled in the Great Dionysia!" He paces toward me, waving off the magistrate when she moves to stop him. "She stole my Player's Craft for her own use. Lied to me. Endangered my Lead Player and stole him from his home. And tell me, *Riven.*" Sil stops about two inches from my face. "Is it true? Did you kill my dear little monster Marigold?"

There's no use in denying it.

RIVEN: "I did."

"Silenus, perhaps we can—" interrupts Augustus.

SIL: "She gave up her right to your defense when she came to my Playhouse." Sil takes one breath, two. Nods to the council, then turns to appeal to the crowd. "What would you have me do with her?" he calls. "After all, she's one of *you.*"

The audience stirs in response, hesitant and indecipherable

calls popping up at the prospect of not only one of their own being executed before them but the Peacemaker's heir, their one and only voice in the Playhouse during its reentry.

It's quiet. Too quiet. Until, near the front, someone calls out, "Let her perform."

Conspiratorial whispers stir at the suggestion as Sil makes a display of guiding Jude and me to the front of the platform, grandly gesturing.

SIL: "I won't grant her freedom." He shakes his head and sighs. "She enrolled in the competition, and she will see it through. Riven's crimes are forgiven. And the Playhouse welcomes this most unusual prospect of the North's first Player." He grins, all pretense of sadness gone, but there's something in that smile that unsettles me. "Perhaps, the first step toward the mending of this broken land once and for all."

Then: the words I dread and anticipate.

SIL: "Riven Hesper will compete in the Great Dionysia. Will you have her?"

The crowd, their hearts swelled by my speech, release their approval in waves of cheers and cries that shake the stage.

Slowly, I raise my eyes and meet Jude's gaze. He doesn't look angry, or scared, or confused.

His face is full of relief.

Before I can question it, Sil calls out, "Why delay, council?" He turns back toward the mixed expressions on their faces. They hold no ground here. "We have our champion. I see no reason to delay. The Great Dionysia will begin tomorrow!"

Act III: Scene VI

News of my confession doesn't just make the local District paper the next day.

Instead, it makes the headlines of *every* paper in every town and every city across Theatron, flooding the media with rumors of caged actors in the North and teens removing their marks for a chance in the spotlight. Many report of the unmanageable, record number of patrons from both the South *and* North arriving in the District to witness the five-day Great Dionysia.

Which begins tonight. In a few hours' time.

Three days of performance.

The fourth day: an intermission for both sides to agree to a new treaty, whatever the terms may be.

On the fifth day, the finale: a battle of Craft between Jude and me that only one of us will walk out of.

As evening falls over the dining hall, heralding our last meal before the Great Dionysia, a sharp whisper catches my attention. I raise my eyes and see Mattia staring back at me from the Players' table as Arius leans in to mutter something to her.

"I will *not* share a stage with a *marked*," she hisses back at him. "Insulting."

The revelation of my mark was, predictably, not a welcome one with the Players. Except for Titus, who largely regarded the whole thing as hilarious and commended my stupidity.

But I don't find Mattia's threats any more unsettling than the tables my fellow auditionees once sat at, now empty. Like they were never here. When I inquired about where the remaining auditionees went, Sil simply shrugged and asked who I was talking about.

Sitting in the dining hall for a casual last meal feels outrageous and borderline comical as the clock ticks closer to the Great

Dionysia. *This* feels more like a performance than anything.

Outside the dining hall's floor-to-ceiling windows, an audience eagerly watches.

I numbly go back to flipping through articles. Reporters ruthlessly resurrect the story of "Michail Hesper the Peacemaker," rehashing it in an increasingly unflattering light in the South. Meanwhile, in the North, my father's story is made into the tale of a man caught between worlds. His loyalties are nearly as hotly debated as my own. Protests against my eligibility to compete began in several different territories this morning.

My mother could not be reached for comment.

I shove the paper off the table, doing my best not to care.

But something catches my eye as I toss another mindless article aside. A solagraph from my classroom from nearly ten years ago. It sits below the headline: ***RIVEN HESPER: WHAT WE KNOW SO FAR***

The image is poor and grainy, in absent shades of black and white. But I can make out the forced smile of my teacher, Professor Ariti, hands clutched in front of her. The twelve toothy grins of my classmates filed in front of the chalkboard. My younger self stands centered at the back for the sake of my height. The pinched sides of my eight-year-old mouth look more like a grimace.

It's no wonder. I remember this day. The day after I received my mark. This image couldn't have been snapped more than a few hours after I passed out in class and subsequently stumbled out of the nurse's station, groggy and irritable.

Today, I see something I hadn't noticed before in the corner of the image. First, the nurse tucked in the back, watching me with concern. She hovered for most of the day afterward. But beside her, barely noticeable in the right corner, is another face I recall from that day—a stranger, kind and unassuming, with bright hazel eyes. A healer who looked over my mark after it got infected, though I don't recall ever seeing him again afterward.

In the solagraph, it's hard to tell if he meant to be captured. His hand is raised in a polite wave goodbye, one leg already halfway through the open door. But the way his knuckles are clutched white around a healer's kit tells a different story.

My fork clatters onto my plate as I lean close, my breath stilling in my lungs.

There's a ring on his middle finger. Though grainy, I recognize the shape.

Finders Keepers. And there, across his open palm, a bandage with the edge of a long, deep cut peeking out at his wrist.

The paper shrivels at the corners as my fists clench. My heart starts to pound.

Slowly, I cast my gaze across the dining hall to Jude. He sits at the head of the table beside Mattia, easy and unbothered.

Sensing my attention, he raises his eyes to mine, alight with a challenge I've come to recognize. I follow the glimmer of his ring to his chalice, which he raises in a mocking toast.

I raise mine back in answer and drink.

Jude wanted a chance to kill me in the arena, and he will have it.

Act III: Scene VII

When I burst into my dressing room, I do the one thing I swore I wouldn't do again.

I call out to Cassia in the mirror, risk of being overheard be damned. There are a hundred pieces snapping together in my head. With each one, the picture grows grimmer.

Something isn't adding up. Jude has Mimicked and spoken to me as someone else at *least* twice before I came to the Playhouse.

He made me believe he spotted me at the casting call. That he seized the opportunity to make a show of killing the Peacemaker's daughter in the arena and reclaiming his name as Lead Player.

Now, though, I don't think that's true. Jude has been watching me for a long time.

But when I reach my mirror and press my palms to the glass, it's not my aunt's face I see.

It's Mattia's.

Sharp nails poised for my throat, she lunges through the glass and tackles me to the ground.

Her razor-like nails rake across the base of my marked throat, and I scream, pain exploding up my neck and sending dots across my vision. I throw her off me and into the small side table that collapses under her weight.

"You aren't welcome here," she growls, lifting herself from the rubble with inhuman speed. "And you are certainly no Lead Player."

Mattia runs at me again, and I throw my arms up in time to stop the jagged edge of an ornate candelabra she's grabbed from introducing itself to the side of my head. It drags a nasty cut down my forearm instead. She wants blood. But I can't suspend my reality and survive her blows without sending my life into another Player. Something tells me Mattia is not about to be a willing participant.

She *actually* means to kill me.

I go for the splintered table leg on the ground and wield it like a stake as she corners me, her sparrowlike eyes honing in on my movements.

"I remember your father, you know," she says. "Pathetic and desperate. Always watching us from afar under claims of reporting back to your council. But he envied us." She extracts a blade from her belt. "I think you envy us, too."

She lunges as my back meets the mantel, nowhere left to go. Her dagger misses my eye by the skin of my teeth.

Instead, the dagger plunges into Gene's portrait behind me, driving into the painting inches from my face. Mattia sneers as I dive beneath her armed hand, silver slicing clean through the canvas as she frees her blade.

A torrent of paper floods through the open slit of Gene's painting. The rustling of pages floating to the ground is peculiar enough to give us both pause, heaving breaths as a storm of sheets darkened with ink fills the space between us. There are hundreds, like the portrait's been swollen with them, bursting forth like feathers from a torn pillow.

Mattia watches me, and I, Mattia.

We both dive for the pages.

"Diary entries. Must be. Gene was always too sentimental..." Mattia mutters until her voice cuts into silence, mouth agape.

They aren't diary entries at all.

RIVEN:
Hello.

SIL:
You might as well come in. The show's
just about to start, you know.

The words slice into my memory, sink into my veins.

I reach for another.

TITUS:
Gods, they're annoying!

MATTIA:
You've barely spoken to a single auditionee yet, Titus.

ARIUS:
They may surprise you yet, Titus. Casting calls bring in all kinds.

My first instinct is to toss them into the fireplace and swear I saw nothing. But when I peer up, Gene's painted face knowingly stares down at me from the frame, the slit from Mattia's knife gaping from her hair to her shoulder.

For the first time, Gene doesn't look like a stranger.

I know you.

Something worse than Mattia's candelabra smashes through my mind. A dam, broken. My breaths quicken, and my head floods with songs and words, lifting a veil I didn't know was there. It feels wrong, like a treat I've stolen and hidden out of guilt.

Then, flashes. My vision burns red and gold, pain flaring through my temples until I can't think straight.

Mattia screams. It comes out like a wail, distressed and piercing.

"Stop!" I snap at her. Her calls will reach Sil. It'll summon the whole damned cast to this room.

But as I take in the mess around me, it occurs to me that may be the least of my worries.

A wisp of a shadow corners around Mattia and curls up the wall. With it, a cold breeze falls over the room. The lights begin to dim. Nyxene.

We aren't supposed to be here. Mattia isn't supposed to be doing this, saying this—

We know something we aren't supposed to know.

"We didn't see this," Mattia says shakily under her breath. Her long fingers gather pages into her arms. "Riven? We *didn't*." She tosses the stack into the flames, which flare and spit back as she levels a fierce glare at me. "Now, come help me."

What have I done? I wonder as Mattia gathers another bundle of pages into her arms.

Burning them won't undo this.

I grip as many pages as I can and stagger to my feet.

And I run.

Act III: Scene VIII

I run as fast as my legs will carry me, my fists full of yellowing pages. In the light, though, they aren't yellow at all—they shimmer like gold leaf. The texture feels familiar in my hands, soft yet untearable.

When I reach the lobby, I nearly slam into Sil.

SIL: "Riven! Where have you been? Where is Mattia? You're both late." He checks his watch. "The Great Dionysia begins in an hour."

My breaths are coming too quick.

His attention narrows on me—then to the pages clutched in my hands.

"She feels ill..." I murmur, but the words come out awkwardly.

The silence is torment. Slowly, Sil shakes his head at me. "No, she doesn't," he replies firmly, staring deep into my eyes.

He knows.

TITUS: "Gods, who is *screaming*?" He emerges from the staircase, Arius and Parrish just behind him. "Did Jude stumble across his own reflection?"

Sil's eyes bore into mine and then fall back to the pages. "Oh, Riven," he says gently, but his tone is grief-stricken. "You weren't supposed to find that."

Before he can reach for me, I bolt.

My heart hammers against my rib cage as I run, making a mad dash for the narrow corridor under the lobby staircase.

I have no idea where I'm going.

But I know something I'm not supposed to know.

There, down the hall, a set of doors I've seen before. They lead into the arena, where contenders were introduced the first night of the casting call. Mirrors. There are mirrors down there, lining the walls. I remember seeing them.

Slamming into the doors, I race down the stairs.

But with every step, I remember more.

Gold-encrusted mirrors hang over stone walls by the narrow entrance into the arena, the very same one I stood in during my first night in the Playhouse. Eavesdroppers and shadows be damned, I slam my palms into the glass.

"Cassia! Show me Cassia Hesper."

Astonishingly, an image clears: one of Cassia's old study, dusty bookshelves stacked against rickety walls. My heart tears a fraction more. After all of this, Cassia left the mirror uncovered for me.

Then: "Riven?"

"Cassia!" My voice sounds shaky and unfamiliar in my own ears.

"Riven, that isn't you. Is it?" Urgency clips her tone. Her figure steps cautiously into view. She looks much the same, save for the haggard lines beneath her eyes. I know better than to think I can say the same for myself.

Cassia eases back when she lays eyes on me, the fear plain on her face.

There's a sound like a door banging somewhere in the distance. I don't know which side of the mirror it comes from.

"I don't have time to— I..." My words jumble. Then: "Come to the Playhouse!"

In an instant, her expression shifts, distraught. "So it's true. You're one of them now."

"Cass, please," I plead, breathless as the clip of steps echoes somewhere outside the arena's entrance. I don't know how to convey any of it. "You have to stop me."

"Stop you," Cass repeats, voice low.

"You have to stop me from doing something terrible," I urge, desperate.

"If what the papers say is true, it's far too late for that."

Flinching, I steal a glance at the pages in my hands. I'm going to do worse.

"No, Riven," Cassia says, her tone indicating the conversation is over. "I will not go near the Playhouse. Not for you, and not for—"

"Fine!" I yell, my mind racing. "Then—then get a message to the council for me. Okay? Please. There's something you should know." I drag my gaze over the pages. "There's something we should all know."

A light claps on outside the hall I'm burrowed in. It summons me forward. I grip the sides of the mirror to keep my feet from moving for it.

"I risked my neck and reputation telling the council you would deliver the Lead Player to them. Instead, you have volunteered to take his *place*." Her lip curls in disgust, but there's more than that. Her eyes are full of hurt. "*What* message could you possibly have now?"

I grit my teeth. "Be honest, Cassia, please. Did my father make you—make you swear not to say—" I swallow, unsure how to even ask this. "Where did I come from?" I land on, enunciating each word, pinning Cassia with my golden stare.

Her face stills. "You are not from over the Cut, if that's what you're insinuating."

My chin shoots up. "A half-truth."

Cassia's face softens. "It's said and done, Riven. None of it matters now."

"*What* is said and done?"

"Your father, Michail…he had a cousin near the border who was killed by Revelers. Michail took you in. Insisted on it. You couldn't have been more than three." She speaks carefully, like I'm a flame to douse.

"Helene isn't my mother," I conclude. And Cassia is not my aunt.

"Michail wanted to raise you as their own. You are still *family*."

My breaths come quicker as I laugh at the ridiculousness. "Cass, I *look like him*," I shout, pointing out the obvious. Helene may not be my mother, but Michail is most certainly my father.

Cassia thinks I was an orphan taken in.

But I'm not. She was fed a lie.

She winces. "I know. Obviously, what Michail said is not… true." She seems to run out of words. I'm pretty sure the only ones left are: *Clearly, he had an affair. Clearly, your mother lied to protect him.* Michail wasn't marked. No one was back then.

Gods. What have I *done.*

"Go to the council," I say. "The Great Dionysia has to be stopped."

It was a plan. This was all a plan.

"And tell them *what* exactly?" Cassia growls, patience wearing thin.

"I don't *know*! Anything!" I say, regretting the lies I swore by in my trial. Realizing I've walked right into a trap. "Tell them—tell them they're holding me here, that I was tricked by a Player. You're marked; they can't accuse you of deception."

"They can accuse me of being outright mad," she hisses. "And I can certainly accuse *you* of deception."

"You can. And you should," I say, defeated. "Cass, after this conversation, don't believe another word I say. Ever."

Not that she needs to know this will be our last conversation anyway.

Cassia looks drained. "What is it you've done, Riven?" she whispers.

"It isn't just what I've done. It's what I'm *going* to do," I plead. "You owe me. This is your fault, too."

Cassia bares her teeth at me. "*My* fault you walked into the Playhouse?"

"It's not that I came to the Playhouse, Cassia!" I shout. "The problem is that I came *back*."

Act III: Scene IX

First, Cassia is there. Then the glass ripples, darkens, and she's gone.

The curtained entrance to the arena shivers with light, sways with the swell of music pounding beneath my feet. There's a pull in the air, like someone's thrown a hook through my chest and is tugging on it. My eyes search for the invisible string lifting my hand to move the curtain aside.

The arena is dark. Familiarity coats the scene around me.

Then, a voice.

TIG: *"Gods, I hate waiting here."* A whisper I've heard before. It comes from my left.

No. It doesn't. But it *should*—

A great *crack* startles me as lights flash on within each of the archways, illuminating us.

Except I'm alone this time. Around me, each auditionee from my first day in the Playhouse *should* stand as a glowing silhouette in the darkness. They aren't there.

I look up and watch a series of spotlights piercing the five empty spaces on the platform above, where the Players should stand. Or did.

Eerily, their spaces are empty, too.

Finally, a long, elegant shadow emerges from the sixth and largest entrance in the arena. My face hardens as Sil materializes within the arch.

SIL: "Ladies and gentlemen!"

Even from this distance, his eyes slice through me as the director marches into the arena.

SIL: "Congratulations! You should all be proud—a round of applause for this year's cast!"

Applause crashes in around me as Sil's arms stretch out to the audience.

No—applause *doesn't* come. There's no applause. No audience.

But I've lived this scene, and so I know there should be.

"Enough, Silenus." The voice that rips from my vocal cords sounds nothing like mine. It's earsplitting, drenched with the theatric pitch of the Players that should be standing over me.

Sil levels his gaze on me. "Act One, Scene Seven," he says. It takes more effort than it should to move forward; I can feel the reluctance in disobeying now. Challenging my own blocking.

"Tell me, Riven—since you're so *aware*." Sil speaks slowly, nodding at the pages still clutched in my hands. "What is it, do you think, that controls the world? Is it money, fame, love?"

My eyes drop to the loose pages. I release them, and they flutter to the floor.

"*Stories*, Riven!" he announces when I don't answer. "It is not what we're taught, who we know, what we have. What controls us—" He inclines his head, waiting for me to finish the sentence.

The answer rises in my throat, but I swallow it.

Sil sighs. "What controls us is what *entertains* us. And so I am going to tell you a story, Riven. One that will sweep the masses." He winks. "There once was a girl who grew up much the same as many. Without Craft, fearful of Players. Only, the division did more than break the world she lived in. It broke her own family. Took a parent from her grasp."

The air constricts in my lungs as the truth collapses in on me, heavy as steel.

SIL: "She's taken and branded with their righteous *marks* and made to fade into ordinariness. Just like everyone else. She is raised to hate and fear the Playhouse, just like everyone else. That is the *point*. She is *just* like *everyone else*."

"Stop," I say without meaning to, bringing a hand to my mark, feeling the scars tingle at my throat.

SIL: "Then, one day, she comes to the Playhouse and finds no evil to fuel her hate. In fact, it becomes a home. It *feels* like home. So, torn between the two, she becomes the bridge that bonds them. A bridge for the Playhouse to return to the North and be *welcomed*. Because if she can forgive the Playhouse, why shouldn't everyone?"

The carefree tone of Sil's story vanishes in his next sentence.

"Or, that's how the story was supposed to go."

The arena is still. The absence of my fellow auditionees feels overwhelming now. "Where are they?" I demand.

"They aren't in this scene, Riven."

Scene.

I kneel and grasp the fallen pages from my dressing room. They glow like the skin of a Player. Like my own skin, humming with life in my hands.

Like the Script in Sil's.

My eyes scan more of the words, dated the night of the Playhouse's return:

JUDE:
No need to be nervous. Between you and me,
this crowd is nothing but a pack of weeds
with only a handful of flowers to pluck.

RIVEN:
I'm not auditioning.

JUDE:
Oh?

This is my first conversation with Jude. Written and somehow hidden away by Gene Hunt in her own painting, fifteen years before it ever happened.

RIVEN: "Jude—he *spoke* these words to me." The gold-leaf papers bend in my hands as I clutch them harder.

SIL: "I'm sure he did!" He laughs. "In fact, I'm certain it's one of only a handful of times either of you recited your own lines. I'll admit, I'm disappointed. The improvisation was wildly unprofessional of both of you."

RIVEN: "These pages—they were in Gene's painting."

No, not pages. Script.

This is a script.

My eyes fall to the book that Sil clutches in his hands, the one that never leaves his side. The realization settles in as I note the glow of the pages. The Script that Jude is so afraid of, that he warned me to stay away from.

Sil gestures at the words in my hands, the stolen pages. "I should have known she'd go and do something like that after she tore them out. Gene *had* become a liability."

"You murdered her," I accuse. He poisoned that cup she drank from. I'm sure of it. My hands shake. "She didn't deserve that. She was a *person*, Sil!"

"Gene is *not* a person!" roars Sil, throwing his arms out. "She is a *character*, Riven."

The world stops, the silence pounding in my ears as he levels a telling glance at me.

"And so are you."

Act III: Scene X

My fourth wall shatters.

A thousand memories, faces, voices pound on the inside of my skull, seeking a way to the surface. Beneath it all, something stirs. Something stronger than me, something that has just awoken. I blink rapidly until my vision clears.

"I know," I admit at last, the shock caving into my chest.

Sil moves toward me, then halts when I raise a hand to indicate *no closer.* "I understand this is painful. But I am so *proud* of you, Riven! You've been terribly missed. What was it like, being away so long?"

There's a lump building in my chest, and it tightens painfully. "I'm not— I have a family. And I have a mother and a fa—"

"A father?" prompts Sil. "What do you know of your father, Riven?"

I straighten, my memory grappling with reality, all of a sudden distrustful of both. "His name was Michail Hesper, a hero. A Peacemaker. Wrongfully murdered—"

"No, no, no, Riven. Your father was never *wrongfully* murdered. He was *rightfully* so." Sil shakes his head. "And you are certainly *not* Michail's daughter."

He's right. I know he's right.

But something in me defiantly utters the words, "I *am*."

SIL: "You are not, Riven! Michail planted you. *Fifteen years ago*, he planted you, a Player in the costume of an innocent child, in his own family. Where you'd grow up in a city that would have no reason to suspect you of being anything more than a troubled daughter."

I blink a few times. The words sound right. But everything in me rejects them. That's not who I am. I desperately grasp on to that part of me, reach for pieces of my identity slipping out of reach. Riven Hesper. Daughter of the Peacemaker.

Hesper. Daughter.

I'm neither.

RIVEN: "Why?" The word spears out of my throat. It's the only one I can manage.

SIL: "We lost access to half of Theatron after being forced into that damned treaty the North is so fond of. *Half* our audience—for five hundred years! And the North, they used that time, learned to shield their minds. Build their walls. Marks eventually took root, spread. We were losing too much ground."

This has been a plan. A long one.

"The treaty would expire. The dust would settle, but if we were to ever win the North, take back the stage that belongs rightfully to the Playhouse, we would need to be tactical. Not by war or by bloodshed. What would that get us? An audience of corpses!" He shrugs. "There is no power to be had over the dead."

"And so you sent me," I say, betrayed. By Sil or by myself, I'm not sure.

I look at my hands, then drop them to my sides, guilt falling heavily over me. It hurts to think. Like I've been sitting at the tip of an iceberg my entire life and have just dipped underneath the surface to find what happened before my name was Riven. And everything underneath is dark and cold and terrifying.

Sil raises his chin. "Tell me who you are."

RIVEN: "My name is Riven Hesper." I answer defiantly, but as I go, my words slow and shift. Not into what I am but what I'm supposed to be. The part I play. "Daughter of the Peacemaker. I come to the Playhouse and eventually give in to my love for Craft. I kill Jude in the arena and win the Great Dionysia. I win audiences over by the masses." I pull in a breath, the realization taking its hold on me at long last. "I am a bridge that opens the gates to all of Theatron."

"Good," says Sil. "Now, tell me who you really are."

The silence lingers between us until the thing under my skin breaks it. Gold rushes through my veins and blazes bright in my eyes, casting a brilliant glow over my vision.

A second voice, one that doesn't sound like mine, speaks. And it is horrible.

"I am the first Player," I say. "Formed from the well of Mount Eleutherae. I was cast in the role of Riven Hesper fifteen years ago to take back the North."

I'm not their hero. I never was. I can't save them from the Craft that poisons their minds.

I am the poison. I am the Craft.

Act III: Scene XI

Sil claps, a proud smile on his lips.

I internally strangle the thing beneath my skin, shoving it deeper and deeper before it can resurface again. But the Player underneath is awake now, aware. It fights me back. For a blink, I struggle to remember my name, grasping at my memories like straws.

"My only Player I would trust with such a role. And you played it *well*. You nearly broke my old heart when you showed up looking like you did."

I stare back down at the page crumpled on the floor beside the others. At Jude's first words to me. "These aren't records," I say. "They're written before they happen. All of it. It was scripted."

The Script. The book that rests like a breathing entity in Sil's hands. Director and playwright. Some distant memory hovers at the edges of my mind: of reading the script for this story many years ago. Of signing on for this role.

The role of Riven Hesper. I wanted this. Or, the thing inside me did.

"That can't be." Denial throttles my mind. "My father—"

"Michail is not your father," Sil interrupts. "He was a mortal and a traitor to the North you seem to love so much."

Dorian's comment races back to me, chills my blood.

Your Player-worshipping traitor of a father.

He knew my father. Already suspected something was off.

Sil goes on. "Michail Hesper was obsessive. Selfish, bitter! He hungered for fame and notoriety and was willing to do anything for it. He came to my Playhouse—as an emissary, no less. Some vain effort from your human council to get ahead of the treaty years before its expiration."

"And you...killed him?" I say, unsure how much more of this I can take.

"I made him an *offer*, Riven. I'd turn him into a hero. *Peacemaker*, they would call him!" Sil laughs to himself. "Michail returned home with my *miraculous* agreement. A compromise. A promise to keep my Players contained in the Playhouse. By law."

His smile makes me sick to my stomach.

"Of course, after losing so many of my Players, I never planned to let *any* of you out again anyway."

Why would Sil sign into such a thing? I asked Jude.

Because it was only ever for Sil's benefit, to ensure the Players stayed contained, controlled, under threat of their lives if they tried to disobey. What worth is a director without his Players?

"But your human council seemed overjoyed, and Michail was renowned for his work as a Peacemaker. Just as I promised."

His life's work. I've always thought of him as a hero, all of it a *lie*.

"And in exchange," Sil says, "Michail would plant *you* in the North with his own family. A Player in the costume of a child. Convince your mother you were rescued from Revelers, the orphan of distant relatives."

You look so much like your father, my mother would always say. I often pondered the confusion in her voice. The dip in her brow.

As far as she knew, I was an orphan. I had no right to look like her long-dead husband. It must have hurt her every day, the insinuation of an affair living in her own home.

Even though that's not what I am.

What I am is *so* much worse.

"There, you would grow up as one of them and, one day, come home." Sil grins. "And you would bring the rest of Theatron to our doorstep with you. Willingly."

Me. A fox in the henhouse.

"But I *look* like him," I argue.

Sil scoffs. "You ought to! Your costume was designed after Michail. Notice how it's captivated your council, to see the Peacemaker's face onstage? Notice how those from the North trust you in a way they would *never* trust a Player from South of the Cut."

I'm the one to scoff now. "Trust? They were scared of me." And had every right to be.

"Small-town gossip doesn't concern me, Riven. Though I am sorry your costume wore down so badly after the marking—that must have been a frightful sight," Sil says without emotion. "Your face in the papers *does*, though."

A face all of Theatron will know. With golden eyes.

"So why kill him? Michail," I press. Surely, his death could only hurt the Playhouse's image, murdering a famous Peacemaker Sil practically *invented*.

"That was not supposed to happen." Sil frowns. "In all his obsessive visits to the Playhouse, Michail did the most foolish thing a person can do."

I brace myself. I know where this is going. Jude told me. "He fell in love with a Player. Gene."

"Yes." Sil's face falls. "Mortals are not trustworthy or reliable. They fill themselves with guilt over the smallest things." He feigns sadness. "After Michail learned the truth, he took it upon himself to break Gene's fourth wall. Provide her *proof* of what she was: a character. Temporary. Mortals decide love is not love unless it is all true! But love is man's own play, in which he often casts the wrong characters."

Sil gestures to the fallen pages at my feet, and I follow them. Pages Gene stole.

Did she go mad after realizing what she was?

I look at my hands. What *we* are. Just speaking the words makes my mind feel like it's about to snap in half.

"I—" The lurking suspicion that had hung in the back of my mind resurfaces. "I thought maybe she was my..."

"What, your mother?" Sil laughs richly. "Gene is no one's mother. You belong to no one. No one but me and my Playhouse."

Each word slices deeper, then twists like a knife. No mother. No father.

Player.

"The fourth wall is there to keep you safe, Riven. As was Gene's. One of you learns and then *all* of you are in danger. And she did just that, shared her discovery with another castmate. Jude. Broke *his* fourth wall, begging his help. It spreads like a disease every time it happens."

Jude. *Gods*, it's all of us. We're all characters.

My heart feels like it's shriveling in on itself, my lungs too tight.

"You characters are fragile, and that's all Gene was," he says. "A costume with too much control over the actor beneath. She began to break, like all characters do. Her hair fell out, her memories faded, her skin peeled right off. The Player beneath came to claim its body back, once she was made aware of her own impermanence."

His words ring true against my sightings of Gene. Her skin cracking, her eyes hollowed out and hungry. The Player underneath was trying to shed the character it played: Gene Hunt.

A role. Nothing more.

He shrugs. "The character of Gene was written with a soft heart. She was horrified of the truth of what she was. Then, discovering the end of her story, that she would die and give Jude her crown..." He shakes his head. "*That* sent her over the edge."

Her last performance is well-documented, but most people only ever focus on her death—not the breakdown she had first. Gene, racing at the audience, screaming and screaming, *"It's not real! None of this. Don't believe it. Don't believe—"*

And then falling to the ground, dying there before the audience.

Not a suicide. A murder.

"You poisoned her," I seethe.

"It did not kill the *Player*, Riven. It would take *much* more to kill the Player beneath her skin. It only killed the character she was playing, made it easier for the Player to shed Gene Hunt completely. Or, it *should* have."

Viscerally, I know this from my time here, before I was even *me*.

Our notorious deaths in the Great Dionysia are just a scripted dance: to shed one character and begin the role of another. Dead roles cannot hold on to their Players. In the Playhouse, we call the shedding of a character First Death.

When I die, I won't be able to hold on to mine. On to Riven.

Second Death is worse. Second Death is undoable. Second Death means to kill the Player underneath. It's why we're all intuitively terrified of Eleutheraen gold. It's nearly the only thing that *can* kill us, wholly and completely.

Well, that and—

Gods. Nyxene.

"I saw Gene," I argue. "She wasn't dead."

Sil's face grows grim. "Either her Player could not, or would not, shed her. It may have been selfish for me to let Gene haunt the Playhouse like she did, hoping one day the Player beneath her skin would peel off that nuisance of a costume. There are so few of you left, you know. I've had Nyxene searching for her for ages."

Well, Nyxene certainly found her, thanks to me. I ratted her out, gave away her hiding spot to the Playhouse's Stage Manager, thirsting to rip apart anything that doesn't belong.

"Gene couldn't speak." I lower my voice to a whisper. "She kept trying."

Riven. The word had come from her lips with the effort of moving a mountain. *Script.*

She was trying to warn me. To *stop* me from playing my role exactly how I was meant to, a puppet who hasn't noticed its strings.

"Of course she couldn't speak! Gene's character hasn't had any lines in ages. She has no scenes left. She isn't even a person, Riven." Suddenly, he looks sad. "Characters are easy to kill, flimsy and temporary, like you."

I wince at that.

"A poorly executed Reality Suspension is enough to kill *you*, your role. What you saw of Gene was the death of a Player."

Second Death. Permanent.

"It grieves me, but it couldn't be helped," Sil says. "Some characters are stickier than others, and there was no getting her to come out of her role. Her Player was a great loss."

The words tingle on my skin. It's just a matter of time before the Player within me tries to do the same. Peels *me* off like an old costume.

"And my father?" I wince and correct myself. "Michail?" I need to know if *some* part of it was true, whether he was my father or not. "What of him? What happened?"

Sil throws me a pitying look. "He became a liability. After Gene's unfortunate last performance, as you know, he stood and made all sorts of commotion running from my theatre. He nearly made it out, too."

"But he didn't," I say.

"Jude was faster." The director pulls in a deep breath. "Who's to say what Michail planned to do—turn himself in? Kill you? Admit to the council what he'd done? Humans and their hearts are unpredictable. It was a risk we couldn't take. In fact, his death was a damned nuisance for us to deal with. I had to correct your storyline around his absence. Very messy."

He watches me for a reaction, and I give him none. My chest is too tight. So he goes on.

"Then came marks." He nods and gestures at my neck. "We didn't know if we'd see you again after those became commonplace. A drastic measure the council justified with the Peacemaker's death. But here you are, home, just like you swore."

Something irks me, a tinge of numbness that splinters down my neck where my mark used to be, trailing through my shoulder. Slowly, I tug at my sleeve to check, and a cry builds in my chest.

Gold blisters from my clavicle to my shoulder cap, eating away at the skin like a disease. It's spreading.

It looks like Jude's wound.

"Are these lines?" I say, panicked. "What I'm saying right now?"

"No," says Sil. Anger slices into his voice for the first time. "You've gone entirely off script. Not to mention, you've made a habit of breaking the most important rule of the Playhouse."

"The fourth wall," I mutter, studying my wound.

"It isn't an old tradition or myth of the theatre. It's there to *protect* you," Sil reminds me, and he closes the last couple of steps between us.

He pulls my hand away from the blistering well of gold bleeding through my skin, like a parent examining a scraped elbow. "Look what happens when you become aware. Characters are little more than skin. They'll come right off if you aren't careful."

I jolt, tugging away.

That isn't true. I am me. I am Riven. I am *not* just skin.

Even if what's beneath my skin isn't me at all.

Act III: Scene XII

"You mean Jude has known who I am. All this time." The arena echoes my voice back at me.

"But look what his knowledge has cost him!" Sil says, swinging an arm wide to take in the entire stage. "He's hanging on by a thread. Tearing his costume. Forgetting his lines. We only needed him to last long enough to compete in the Great Dionysia and give you his crown. Then his Player will shed him, too, and begin anew."

No. The very idea of Jude being torn from himself, being tossed out in favor of a new role, makes rage boil under my skin.

He's more than that. He's more than that to me.

My mind races. Everything looks different now. How he forgot my name. Couldn't recall his own favorite color. Simple things that should be at the tip of his tongue.

His memory is only as good as my own, false and deceitful. Like a prettily painted house whose walls are filled with rot and decay.

Jude didn't run into me that first night in the Playhouse. He was *waiting*. Barely clinging to his set storyline: that of a selfish Player seeking to reclaim his crown.

"Do we all know?" I ask, my voice hoarse. But I think I know the answer.

"Thank the gods, no!" Sil huffs. "Once a fourth wall is broken, it cannot be rebuilt. Characters will start dying from that point forward until the Player sheds them completely."

A shudder racks my body. It's begun. I feel it. "Only Jude."

"Yes. You two have a most inconvenient tendency to find each other, no matter who you're playing." The director scowls. "The more aware you become, the worse it gets. Jude is deteriorating quickly now, but we managed to keep him intact for fifteen years after his fourth wall broke. I'm sure we can at *least* manage the same for you."

He shakes his head. "We *have* to, Riven. For the sake of my Playhouse, for your cast. To claim what is rightfully ours: our audience. *Your* audience. Theatron, in its entirety."

And I realize now that Sil will be satisfied with nothing less. None of us would. We Players feed off their attention; corpses can't be entertained, controlled. And the bigger our audience, the stronger we'll become.

We want them alive. We want them groveling. Willing and fooled.

Fooled by me.

So few of you left.

I survey the room where the other auditionees stood at one time. Only, now, I recognize them for what they really were: Players. Tig. Phileas. Thyone. Linos. All of them, just Players in the costumes of auditionees.

There were always more than five of us.

"There's no casting call. No competition to become a Player." I have the nerve to sound surprised. "It's all a performance."

"The Playhouse is no place for mere mortals, Riven. We entertain the hopeful actors who come through our doors and dismiss them when the first night is through." He shrugs. "The Great Dionysia is a beautiful thing. A good show! Let the mortals believe they're in control. Let them think they might reach our ranks themselves."

Each realization strikes me through the heart, though I can't pretend I didn't know, vague as the memories are.

Fate guides the feet of the willing and drags the heels of the defiant.

I shake off the words. I am more than the cards I am dealt. I have to be. *Riven* has to be.

I think I've even grown to like her.

"I am *not* just a role." Anger radiates over my every word. "And I will not be shed."

Concern bleeds into Sil's expression as he glances down at the Script and back up at me. "I will not lose another one of you." He watches my eyes, looking for the thing under my skin that knows him. It stirs when he grips my shoulders. "You are a character. And you will let my Player go after all is said and done. Do you hear me, *Riven*? This form is no more real than the characters *you* play onstage."

Something wrestles within me at the reminder. Something alive and more aware than before. I smother it. But it's there. Starving and angry and eager.

"You will *let my Player go* when it is time," he repeats, angrier now.

My heart aches, but I don't dare reach inward for it. Because it isn't mine. I'm sharing it with a monster. My thoughts, my words, my actions, all of them coming secondary to an ancient creature's desires to execute a script written long ago.

"The Great Dionysia begins tonight," says Sil, short. "A prelude to negotiations with the council in three days' time." He throws his arms out, grandiose. "I want you to change the tide! To make them believe the daughter of a man who broke the bond between worlds can be Theatron's redeeming grace. You are the bridge between the Playhouse and *them*."

He smiles proudly. "History is easier to change than you think. All you need is enough people to believe it. And you will make them believe it."

"They won't forgive so easily," I say quietly. And they shouldn't.

"No, they won't. But they will *wonder*. They will want to know *why* you chose the Playhouse over them. And your performance will break their reluctance." His hand finds my chin, lifting it to face him. "The heart is stronger than the mind, Riven. Humans abandon their stubborn truths so long as they *feel* strongly enough inclined to do so."

His eyes are still that same soft blue, friendly and calm. Not hard or malicious. The relaxed expression of someone who already knows he's won.

I shake from his grip. "No."

Sil throws his head back, exasperated. "Do you know what theatre started as? You should. You were there." He waves his hands. "*Moral* plays! Simple Comedies and Tragedies. All designed to teach an audience the difference between right and wrong. You'd be surprised how often people get the two mixed up."

Something in me considers this, hesitates. "What gives you the right to determine which is which?"

He blinks, confusion dawning on his face. "That mark *did* mess you up, didn't it?"

I don't think it did, actually. I think maybe I'm seeing the world clearly for once.

Maybe Gene did, too.

"The audience doesn't *matter*," he states. "They are on a ticking clock. One day, the clock will stop. Then I couldn't tell you anything else about them, because no one remembers. But they will remember *you*. They will come here to see *you*. They come here to escape. For meaning and for excitement. For you to explain to them what is right and what is wrong. And do you know who is more eager to escape reality than even the audience?"

I return a glare.

"*Actors*, Riven! *That* is what you are."

"And what are *you*?" I demand, unable to hold the question back any longer.

Sil stares at me with that awful smile again, far too comfortable where he stands as I boil over with fury. I expect him to claim he's a god. A monster. An evil, ancient spirit with limitless power.

His answer is none of these things, and somehow worse.

"I am just a man, Riven."

When I say nothing, Sil goes on. "Not one from *here*, I'll admit." He chuckles.

A man. A man who pulled us out of the well, drained it of its Craft, caged us, *leashed* us.

My eyes fall on the book in his hands, feeling the thrum of its power in my blood.

With *that*.

Something awakens in me at the sight of the Script—more than just the lines written for us but a power that runs deep in the Playhouse, binds us to it. To a *mortal* who stole the power of a god. Part of me longs to grab it from his hands.

The rest of me fears the consequences of touching that book. Remembers the stark emptiness that blotted out the light in Thyone's eyes when she did.

"It's a shame, don't you think, Riven? I offer humans all the entertainment they could ask for. Write them stories and songs and have my Players perform them."

"You stole them. And us."

"I improved your world," he returns, a bitterness to his tone as he laughs sharply. "And so many of them would choose to live without stories at all rather than warm their hearts with the ones I so generously provide."

Somewhere above us, the great lobby clock sings out a warning call, summoning me for my entrance. The Great Dionysia. The festival is about to begin.

The patience thins in Sil's voice when I make no move to follow my blocking back upstairs.

"What I'm offering you, Riven, is a *permanent* escape. As a Player, you never have to deal with the pangs of reality again. You can be anyone. You will bathe in the glow of a spotlight every night. You will be loved by the thousands!"

When I don't speak, Sil's smile strains. "Let's be honest. You aren't here to avenge anyone. You aren't here to destroy my Playhouse. You're here to prove to yourself you hate it. But you can't. You can't prove to yourself you're any better than an actor because you are so much worse."

"I am better. I am *not* just an actor—"

The clock chimes again, insistent.

"You aren't even an actor, Riven!" His voice claws with anger, but I know the desperation in Sil's face. Not the condescending look of a director corralling an amateur performer, but the disbelieving grievances of a puppeteer arguing with his own puppet.

"You are a *character.* One that has gone *severely* off script. You were created for the Playhouse, and you will die in the Playhouse—because you are *nothing* without it. You are not real. When the Player is done with you, she will shed you and you will be nothing again."

He takes an unsteady breath, lowering his voice to a warning whisper. "Characters that are *too aware* are of no use to me."

"Then why tell me all this? Why make me even more aware?" I yell back at him.

He tilts his head. "Have you heard of deus ex machina, Riven? It's the part of the story when the gods, higher powers, what have you, must drop in to fix things. Necessary only when something in the story has gone so horribly *wrong* that there is no other way to mend it. And you've been going constantly off script since you got home."

He walks a circle around me, and his eyes fall to my ruined mark, which gapes open with golden Craft. "Because of that. *That* will always run in your blood. But I know you, Riven. Which is why you played your role in every way that mattered. Because deep inside, this life is what you want. You are far from finished here."

I cup a hand over my mark, wishing it were still there. It was probably the strongest weapon I ever had against my own script. Against the thing inside me.

The clock chimes its final warning. I should be in costume by now, should be heading to the front doors with the rest of my cast.

"And if I fail? If the North doesn't cooperate and I can't win them over?"

His face darkens into an expression that plainly conveys, *You know the answer.*

Sil will finally give up on trying to win them. He'll wipe them out.

He'll unleash us to do it.

"They don't deserve to be slaughtered," I say under my breath.

Though, when I think of Haris, I wonder if that's more merciful than what will otherwise happen to them.

Sil's face twists, that anger just inside yanking on its leash. "Then you had better be prepared to convince every one of the council rulers sitting in their seats, *waiting* for your performance. Because if a single one doesn't open their gates the day after Dionysia—"

"Do not threaten me," I bark. "You need me. The Playhouse is nothing without an audience, and your audience is wary of you."

"Damn it all, Riven, I am simply giving you *options*. You think I want to see you hurt? You think I want to see *any* of my Players hurt? I love you. Every one of you."

My gut twists. He means what he says.

"The game is *over*," he announces. "I know every move you will make. I know every thought that will cross your mind. I know everything about you because *I* wrote it."

The ruined mark between my collarbones twinges.

"Choose to forget about all of this, best you can," Sil goes on. "Choose to go back to playing the role of Riven Hesper."

Something hot stirs under my skin. Power—to persuade, to veil, to retell, desire for eyes on me, forever—I am built of it.

"There will be no leaving the Playhouse for you," says Sil. "You will perform and win over your audience. You will finally have what you want."

"And what do I want, Sil?" I dare him.

"Oh, Riven," Sil says, pitying. "You want *everything* waiting for you at the end of this Great Dionysia. A cast that you fit into. A home that you belong in." He clasps his hands together. "An endless audience that desires *you*."

Years of disgusted looks and sidelong glances, of strangers whispering and moving to cushion more space between them and me, carousel through my mind. Then the audience singing my name, never tiring of my presence. My heart aches at the contrast.

A world where I am never alone, where I am always loved.

A world where my presence isn't too much for the space around me.

A home.

The word sings through me, plays my heartstrings in perfect harmony. My heart swells in my chest, and I feel every word I've ever spoken on my tongue, every move I've ever made in my muscles. Everything I've ever done was designed to bring me here.

Suddenly, I want it all so badly, I think I'll burn from the inside out. My heart longs for it. For home.

Would it be so bad?

"Or?" I croak at last. "If I don't perform?"

"There is no *'or,'* Riven," he says. "There never was."

Act III: Scene XIII

As I exit the arena, each blink of my eyes feels like waking from a dream, my body already moving automatically into the blocking for the next scene.

Sil's words beat against the borders of my mind. My life is only a role I play. My world is a set. All that's left is for me to perform, and to be Sil's winning piece at the end of a very long game.

And *that* wakes something inside of me, cuts through the fog.

My mind is still my own, and it's saying, *Fucking run*.

I bolt along the corridor and up the steps, gripping the door handle and flying through the opening. And smack into—

Jude.

I realize I'm staring, but I can't help it. For the first time, I recognize him, all of him. Not only the arch of his brow, the curve of his lips, the spirited gleam in his eyes.

It's something more now. Something that makes my heart drop.

JUDE: "Awful hurry you're in, Riven. Did you miss me that much?"

The line I'm supposed to say surfaces on my tongue. It reaches up my throat, the snarky comeback that leads us into our next scene, where we prepare for the show.

RIVEN: "I—"

I swallow the words, then choke out my own. "I remember you."

Jude freezes, his expression cracking at the edges. I see it in the raise of his brow.

"And I know you remember me," I say, suddenly seeing past the royal-blue theatrical garb, the metallic leaves sewn into his hair, the kohl smudged under his lashes. He's always been there.

"You have to help me stop this," I say. *"Please—"*

"Stop," he whispers, shaking his head. "Stop it, Riven. Stop—" His eyes dart past me and then back. A slit in his neck gapes farther open when he looks over his shoulder, gold seeping out. A nick in his peeling costume.

His character is breaking. Cracking right here, right now, over his skin. But I see recognition there. I hear the words wrestling in the air between us.

He grabs my shoulder, the other cradling the back of my head like he's about to kiss me.

Then something happens.

His face clears, his posture eases, the actor inside pulling Jude back into line. He drops the hand from behind my head and lets it fall to grip my arm.

And just like that, he's gone.

He turns and charges down the hall, dragging me along by my elbow.

JUDE: "I don't have any idea what you're talking about."

Cicero and Sil don't look surprised when Jude hauls me into the costume wing.

"Get her in costume," Jude says, emotionless. His death grip releases me onto a small platform surrounded by three gold-encrusted mirrors. I bolt off it for the door, thrashing and cursing when Jude pins my arms over my waist and tosses me back. But he struggles, too. I'm stronger now.

"I'm not going out there," I hiss, fighting. "I won't go through with the Great Dionysia."

"You've already missed your call time," Sil says, annoyed. "Don't make this more difficult than it has to be, Riven."

Jude clamps his hands down on my shoulders and leans too close to my ear.

JUDE: "The whole world is waiting for you out there." A cold rage is festering beneath his words. It doesn't sound like Jude. I don't think it's him at all.

I catch his eye, and there's nothing there. Just hollow gold irises. Maybe there's too little left of Jude to wrangle the monster that plays him.

The costume designer peeks his head out from behind a rack, his arms heavy with a long onyx gown. Though I know Cicero isn't a costume designer at all now.

He's a Player, just like me. Playing the role of Cicero.

"The gold hairpiece, not the silver," Sil instructs, stripping off my embroidered vest like I'm a doll to dress up.

I clutch my arms close to my waist, horrified at the state of my figure.

Jude curses under his breath.

Strips of skin have begun to peel like tree bark, gold glinting beneath. There's a long, ugly line raised across my waist, staining my cream-colored shift. I tense, slowly lifting two fingers to a particularly tattered area at my collarbone, smoothing the skin back down.

"Don't touch it," Sil orders, emerging from behind the mirror with a box that he pulls a makeup palette from, slated with skin tones that look just like mine.

He extracts a brush from its base and runs it over the wound, roughly concealing where gold bleeds, right at the scars of my mark. I grit my teeth. Like makeup will conceal the fact that my body is peeling off me. "I'm not going onstage."

"You *are*," he interrupts. "You will do *exactly* what is scripted for you or—" Sil grips a lock of my hair and pulls.

It falls right out, lands on the floor in a pathetic curl. I didn't even feel the pull.

The curse, my mind thinks automatically. No, not a curse at all. A symptom of a dying character, of going off script. The irony of coming full circle feels like a slap in the face.

"*This* will get much worse. If you have any love for your cast,

Riven"—Sil meets my eyes in the mirror with meaning—"any of them," he says again as Cicero flies in and begins sewing me into the gown, "you will go out there."

"I have no love for my cast or this theatre," I lie.

"Fine, then. If you have any love for these mortals like you claim," Sil counters. He laughs to himself, like I'm a child concerned about endangering my imaginary friends. "Then you will stay on script. You will win them all over, and you will do it peacefully."

"I won't be here to do it if I lose in the arena," I bite back. If Jude wins instead and ruins his little storyline. "Try me."

Sil throws his head back and laughs. "Then you will die, Riven. And I will have my Player beneath all of you back. And *she*, I promise you, will have no qualms about destroying whatever blocks her path, as you've already demonstrated." The smile curving his lips is cold. "I do hope we don't have to resort to it. The world is your stage. Why should we burn half of it down, after all the trouble we've gone to in order to take it back?"

My heart sinks like an anchor in my chest. Sil is right. I'm a thin skin tying a monster down from destroying half of Theatron. I can feel her beneath me. She'll obliterate everything that stands in her way.

I wonder if this is how Gene felt, why she held on for so long.

Sil plucks a gleaming crown from one of Cicero's boxes, digging it so hard into my scalp that I yelp.

There. I catch it. A sudden twitch of movement from Jude at my call, just barely a crack in that icy exterior.

"We will see you at the doors, Jude," Sil states, also catching this.

Jude blinks several times, like he's struggling to remember something. I catch his eye in the mirror, and for a moment, I think I see a glimpse of him, hesitating. "Sil, perhaps I can—"

SIL: "We will see you out there."

Fear blooms in my chest as that emptiness crosses Jude's face again, and I wonder if I've lost him for good as he returns a tense look at us both before vanishing out the door, locking onto his script again. My mouth opens, as if to call him back, but the words can't seem to escape my tongue.

He leaves me with Sil, who shoos out a confused Cicero and takes to lacing up the back of my dress himself. "No need to pit all your anger on Jude," he says.

"He's been lying to me all this—" I inhale sharply when Sil pulls the laces too tight.

He catches my eye in the mirror. "He is what he is. You may be my most resilient Player, Riven, but you had best believe Jude is my most loyal. He's been protecting you."

"Then he's done a hell of a job, given where I'm standing right now."

"Not protecting you from the Playhouse, Riven." Sil snatches one of my hands and, in a single awful movement, pinches my thumbnail, ripping it clean off. My fingernail detaches easily, like it was glued on.

I buckle, swallowing a howl of pain. I didn't feel the hair pull, but I felt *that.*

"From yourself!" Sil goes on, circling around me where I'm doubled over. He grips my chin, forcing my gaze up to meet his. "You will *not* think of the things you've learned about yourself. About the Playhouse. You will play the role of Riven Hesper, the first Player of the North, crowned triumphant in five days' time. Do you hear me?"

My fourth wall quakes in my mind. *"Methexis,"* I whisper to myself as Sil circles around to my back again and feel my Craft beckoning for me from the earth, reaching up from the ground like shadows of gold only I can see below. I reach for it, searching for comfort, for power, for *something* to make me feel less defenseless than Sil thinks I am.

But my fourth wall is broken now, and so I see what fills the abyss. What has *always* filled the abyss.

Faces. Countless faces fill the earth below me like the River Styx.

Every character I have ever played, every costume I have ever worn. All of them reaching for me. Riven is just another that will be tossed into the pit when I shed her.

"Methexis," I breathe again, and the bridge is gone just as Sil stands before me again. "Okay," I acquiesce. "Okay."

Act III: Scene XIV

When we enter the lobby, all five Players wait by the door, Jude at the front. By the confused looks on their faces, they've been waiting awhile.

TITUS: "Don't worry about it. Stage fright gets the best of us all."

He stands beside Mattia, who stares like I'm a ghost she can see through. Then, ever so slightly, she shakes her head. *Forget what we saw.*

But I see it already. A rip in the skin there at the corner of her eye, bleeding. The first tear in her costume. It'll only spread, now that she knows what she is. Mine will spread, too, like Jude's.

At Sil's command, Jude throws the doors open and steps into the night, slowing only to offer me his hand.

JUDE: "Ready, Riven? Your first Great Dionysia will be a sight to remember."

I want to refuse, insist that I won't be a part of this, that I'm done with this role. That I won't see it through to the finale and won't allow the Playhouse to reclaim the world with tricks and lies. That what we've already done to half of Theatron is unforgivable.

But my lines burn on my tongue, and Sil's threats ring in my ears.

So I answer, "I'm ready," and don't correct that this isn't either of our first Great Dionysia. We've seen all of them.

Impatient, Sil shoves me forward. I stumble, catching Jude's hand for balance as he leads us down the steps and into a path carved from the crowds. Jude's eyes flicker to the bandage wrapped around my thumb, where Sil ripped the nail from its bed moments ago. A question forms on his mouth that he doesn't ask; he just squeezes my hand a little tighter.

And traitor or ally, Player or Jude, I can't seem to let go.

The clock over the Playhouse foyer sings the song of our freedom: midnight. The beginning of the Great Dionysia, allowing the Players to walk freely for five days' time. Like dogs given extra lead on a leash. At the end of it, our roles will be completed, our contracts will reset, and the gates will seal. Sil will have his way, and even Jude and I won't have leeway to leave anymore.

We'll be trapped, just like the others. Like we've always been.

We're only being let out of our enclosure to lure everyone else in.

Our gilded cage shrieks open to raucous applause. The gates are clotted with watchful eyes, filled with awe. Gifts of flimsy jewelry, expensive fabrics, and love letters litter our path. We don't pick them up.

Whispers of *the Player from the North* taunt my ears. I tense when someone is bold enough to reach out and graze my dress.

I register nothing of the eager faces or praises. Just a distorted sea of people bordering my peripheral vision, my eyes focused on my hand in Jude's as he leads us forward.

I wanted this, didn't I? I can't help but wonder as I'm guided through with my cast. Watched. Wanted. Belonging.

Not like this, my mind counters, even as that *thing* deep under my skin shifts, filled with pride. An actor who played her role perfectly.

"Look *up*. Look at their faces, Riven." Sil speaks over my shoulder, quiet enough that the rest of my cast won't hear. "Refuse your role, and the Player you are under this pathetic exterior will paint the streets with their blood. Look up. Look at their eyes."

My will thins with each step. On all sides, we're surrounded by crowds so thick, I can't see where they end or begin, but I see their faces tracking my every move. I notice the mixture of unguarded grins and hesitant, pinched lips. Open palms that offer flowers, notes, silver.

Worst of all, though, are the marks—so many displayed, their golden seals broken, like mine. The disturbing display of loyalty stops me in my tracks. I surrendered my mark under the threat of death, and these people have recklessly surrendered theirs under the promise of hope.

I can't do this. This is wrong.

But if I refuse, this Player will shed me like a costume, and she'll do worse.

My breaths quicken, freezing and drying in my throat. Jude's arm goes taut as space stretches between us, and I don't move forward with him. Sil urges me onward from behind, but I can't move.

My hand hurts, and I realize it's because Jude is squeezing it, the edge of his Finders Keepers ring pressing into my index finger.

I stare at our hands and then up at him.

"Remember what I told you?" he whispers, and finally, I catch it. Recognition, however brief. It creeps through his exterior for just a moment, breaking past. *"Three deep breaths."*

My eyes find the coin hanging at his collarbone, winking back at me in the moonlight.

Jude was right all that time ago, I decide. We are the same.

Two sides of a shiny coin used to purchase terrible things.

Act III: Scene XV

Sincerely, I hoped never to see The First Act Theatre again after my trial. At least I'm not being led into it by chains this time, though Jude's grip could probably give those shackles a run for their money.

It's as I remember: an outdoor amphitheatre nestled at the bottom of a hill, filled with seats that climb up to the rim—though the seats are mostly full already. At its base sprawls a platform with a massive skene of white pillars lined up behind it. Stars cluster overhead, as if arranged to produce the most light directly above the stage.

Smart of Sil to move the first performance of the Great Dionysia here. Some in the North may be eager, curious, but not enough to risk setting foot in the Playhouse. He'll win them slowly first. In an open-air stage, where spectators can observe from the seats, watch from the stands, or just listen from the safety of their homes miles away.

I'm led through the crowd and around back, up a flight of stairs and into the skene at the back of the stage. I register little, if any, of it as I'm ushered through a curtained entrance and onto the stage behind Jude.

My ears pop as the audience jumps to their feet at the sight of us.

SIL: "Welcome, welcome—to the *Great Dionysia*!" His voice booms, carries over the applause.

He nods at Jude, and the Lead Player raises his eyes to the sky. A whispered word falls from his mouth.

The entire world falls dark, like a curtain closing, a set being prepared. Chants turn to excited whispers. The crowd stirs with unease, frightened by the dark illusion.

Then the world blazes gold, a burst of Craft seeping into the ground and shooting across the District. The moon shines like a spotlight, illuminating a different city than the one we stood in a moment ago, adorned in the fashion of every Great Dionysia, past and present.

My eyes track maroon flowers encircling the platform, blooming through emerald ivy. The dusty, cracked stage shines in luminous gold beneath my feet. Warmth coats Theatron's chilly air, replaced by a silky breeze that seems to hum sweetly when it passes you by.

The realization pierces me like an arrow. It's decorated as our lost home on the mountain, Eleutherae.

The audience seems to notice all at once—some with shock, others with delight—that the colors of their own clothing have brightened into vivid shades of red, gold, and purple. Most of them return a roaring wave of applause. This is more color than many of them have ever seen, much less worn.

Even I have to pause to take it in—seeing the world outside illuminated in beauty that we hoard all to ourselves.

My mind flashes briefly to the Archives, to every story ever written. Stolen away by us.

SIL: "Tonight!" His diction cuts clean through the last of their cheers as Jude and I exit the stage. "We are proud to present a *brand-new* show based on old events. As we know, those who do not learn from their histories—"

TITUS: "Have better things to do?" His heckling receives a fit of laughter as he exits.

Sil shakes his head, smiling, and turns back to the audience.

SIL: "In honor of the upcoming renegotiation of the Playhouse's home in Theatron and a *peaceful* return to the North, the cast feels a responsibility to remind the world of conflicts not so long ago, if only to avoid their recurrence. We must learn from our pasts, yes?"

The crowd stirs, uneasy. Meanwhile, we take our places offstage. As we wait, the audience stirs with anticipation, Revelers eagerly claiming the best views while those with marks take hesitant positions near the edges of the theatre until the last seat is occupied.

From backstage, I peek and catch a glance of Theatron's council being escorted into the front row. Sil's voice rings in my head: *I want you to change the tide.*

All my ideas of bringing the Playhouse to its knees shake, uneasy. Not because I'm frightened I can't beat Jude in the arena. I can. I'm designed to.

But because the thing I am beneath this skin is stronger than me, and my own nature will, I am certain, come to claim back her vessel.

You are the bridge between the Playhouse and Theatron.

I want to be. I *want* to be, I realize. And I hate that I do. I want to be here, before an audience, beloved. Home. Would it be so bad to be that bridge? Would it be so wrong—

SIL: "Let the show begin!"

The lights dim, and I shut my eyes, embracing the warmth twirling at my fingertips. Craft nips at the air.

They will want to know why *you chose the Playhouse over them.*

It's tempting. So tempting. No one would be the wiser. They'd never know I'm the true villain of their story.

For the next three days, we'll perform this new show in five acts. We won't sleep, eat, or drink. On the fourth, we'll rest—an intermission for debate as the Playhouse and the council sign a new agreement.

On the fifth day, Jude and I will fight.

The heart is stronger than the mind. Humans abandon their stubborn truths so long as they feel *strongly enough inclined to do so.*

The script for this performance is five hundred and thirteen pages, carefully crafted lines into the shape of a simple parable that waits on my tongue, stirs in my bones. One that rewrites Theatron's history, carving the new story into the eyes that watch.

Rewriting history is easy, Sil told me.

You just need enough people to believe it.

The audience settles comfortably into their seats, and the moon illuminates our stage. For the first time in a long time, North and South Theatron sit side by side.

And Sil has done a remarkable job convincing them the enemy is each other.

Waiting, I set my eyes on my glass-green shoes, the color stark against the gilded platform at my feet as I pull in three deep breaths. Jude materializes at my side, ready for our entrance.

"Jude," I whisper, feeling the call of the stage in my blood as the show roars to life. "Help me stop him." I flinch at my own words, the same ones Gene spoke to him, *begged* him.

Jude refuses to meet my eye, his gaze on the stage.

JUDE: "Break a leg, Riven."

Then the show begins, and we move for our entrance in a performance that was set, written, and cast fifteen years ago.

Act III: Scene XVI

Act I:

The first act is a story I know but haven't heard in a long, long time.

The story of a simple man. A craftsman, no less. Sil is younger in this version of events, played and Mimicked by Parrish.

I watch with dread from backstage at the depiction of Sil introducing the first Players. Us. As he drains the well dry of story, of song, of *Craft*, he assures his new Players that this is what they are meant for.

A prop book rests in his hands to represent the Script as he makes them grand promises of spotlights and splendor and endless stages. He promises this will fix the world, because he is a smart man, and he can fix the world.

They agree. It makes sense. It sounds nice.

He binds them to the book in his hands.

And the world is their stage.

Act II:

Arius's lyrical narration pulls the audience through Theatron's histories, its wars, its Players, all in captivating song and sugary words. He skillfully omits the Playhouse's part in most of it. His melodies are a corridor from a dreadful past to a bright future.

One that rests in Sil's trustworthy, capable hands.

Act III:

The third act moves into more recent years. Titus plays the role of Michail, his traitorous actions hidden from the audience. His death is framed as a tragic accident.

Still, I don't watch from backstage when his body falls from the highest level of the skene, hits the marble with a disturbing crunch. The result of a faulty railing in this version of events.

The audience wails at the depiction of the Playhouse fleeing the District in the wake of his death and the calamity that followed.

Act IV:

Nausea gathers in my throat as Mattia helps me change costumes, donning Galen's old jacket. Then I set foot onstage for the third act.

My story.

The story of a girl who grew up fearful of Players, who lost a parent to the division, who carries the same mark as the rest of the North. A girl who despises the Playhouse, just like the audience.

I'm just like everyone else.

I step onto a set drained of its color, surrounded by faded, dreary shades of gray.

Then I journey to the Playhouse, and the world comes alive, blossoms with beauty and entertainment and song that the audience yearns for, locked behind its gilded doors.

There, I discover it isn't full of evil; it's deeply misunderstood. So, torn between the two, I become the bridge that bonds them.

Act V:

All is well.

Act III: Scene XVII

I haven't slept or eaten in three days.

But when Sil calls us out to a roaring curtain call, I feel full and awake. More alive than I have in years.

JUDE: "Riven? We're up."

I startle from my daze, the show a blur of vague recollections. Sil has called our names.

Mattia sweeps into a low bow as Jude leads me onto the stage. Riotous applause shakes the platform. Screams for us to look in a thousand different directions attack my ears.

SIL: "I give you Jude Stepharros…and Riven Hesper!"

Jude bows low, then takes a sweeping step aside and gestures to me. My legs shake, anger coursing through my veins. At the Playhouse or at myself for doing exactly what Sil wanted, I'm not sure. Or maybe just at the fact that this feels *so good.*

I bow.

SIL: "Not only your stars of this most wonderful and memorable performance, but your contenders for this Dionysia's finale. You are all invited to witness Riven seek a permanent role here in the Playhouse when she challenges Jude to a final standoff in the arena."

Sil presents a book between us, pressing a quill into one of my hands while Jude signs the book without hesitation. When he's done, he looks to me hopefully.

I glance over the page. A faux contract. This is Riven Hesper's promise to the Playhouse, should she win in the arena. To stay and perform until challenged for her place.

This is just a prop. A measly piece of paper that can be torn or burned or crumbled.

My contract—my *true* contract with the Playhouse—flashes through my head. The feeling of a quill in my hand long ago, gold spilling across the page. My name, my *real* name, signed at the bottom. An eternity sworn to the Playhouse, to whatever role I am cast in.

All for this. Fame. Love. Belonging. *Power.*

I press the quill to the page and sign, a show of sealing myself inside the Playhouse until my death, should I survive the finale. The audience watches, awed by my devotion.

The leaders of Theatron observe from the front row, their expressions still and contemplative, eyes roaming over me and then Jude. Then back to me.

SIL: "Any words you'd like to share, Riven?"

I swallow, conjure the lines I know were written for me. They come out stiff as ice.

RIVEN: "It will be an honor to perform in the arena with you, Jude."

SIL: "And you, Jude?"

The *whish* of something piercing the air breaks the conversation, followed by the gasps of the audience as it soars overhead. I see a slant of gold ripping through the sky.

Then I hear myself scream.

Act III: Scene XVIII

I grasp onto Jude's shoulder as I stumble.

At first, all I can think is that my leg feels like it's been plunged into ice water.

Then I see the shaft of an arrow protruding above my knee, and pain explodes up my body, wakes something inside me. My Player. I've died many, many times, and this is perhaps closer to true death than I, *we*, have ever been.

Second Death. This arrow was made with Eleutheraen gold.

The other Players bolt on instinct, gathering around me like a shield. Jude is shouting something furiously at Sil, but I can't make out what he's saying over the ringing in my ears or the panicked audience.

A reproachful grumble that sounds like, "Hold it together," falls out of my mouth as I test my leg.

Spots cloud my vision, and I blink them away in time to see Titus pluck a spear off the floor of the stage—a prop from our show—and throw it with brutal force into the audience, met by screams so loud, my ears pop.

My eyes follow the spear as it whips through the air and buries itself in the wall of an old, broken watchtower past the crowds—embedded beside a window it missed by mere inches.

In the window is a face, one I almost don't recognize. But I know it, even at this distance.

Cassia locks eyes with me. Her hands still clutch the crossbow.

In a blink, it dawns on me. She tried her best to carry out my last request: *Stop me.*

She nods, acceptance of her failure in the resolute set of her shoulders. The Players will find her, if the crowds don't find her first. I shudder to think what they'll do. I try to mouth at her to run, to *go*. My mind is groggy, my mouth struggling to form words.

But she tried to undo it. She tried to stop me.

I think I begged her to. But the Player in me is awake, and she's angry. *Furious* that the hands of someone so ordinary almost ended the never-ending performance of a Player with a single arrow. She pushes me to my feet with a ferocity I don't possess, shoves away from Jude. She makes sure everyone in the crowd sees my hand grip the arrow and rip it from my own flesh.

A shout of agony dies in my throat, never making it to my lips as I straighten, hold the arrow in front of me, and drop it carelessly to the floor.

I'm not smiling, yet I feel the stretch of my lips pulling to either side of my face in a wide grin. I can't seem to stop it.

My perspective slips. Shifts. Isn't mine anymore. It's someone else's, and it's bleeding into my own thoughts. My desires. My morals.

I want them dead.

What? The thought feels foreign. Not mine. No. I don't. I don't—*I don't*—

But a new voice is there, and it's louder than my own mind.

I want them all dead.

Act III: Scene XIX

Jude has two noses. Four nostrils total.

That, or my vision has begun to double from this vantage point. I mutter something to the tune of, "Put me the hell down."

"Riven, if you can resist fighting me on *one thing*," Jude says, sparing a glance down at me as he slows and starts to climb. Up? Stairs? Is that where we're going? "Let it be what was just nearly your very own public assassination."

I loll my head back and catch a glimpse of the Playhouse doors as Jude carries me across the landing. Behind him, a sea of anxious faces hovers at the gates. My vision blurs again. My mind feels fuzzy, but I'm decently confident Jude plucked me from The First Act Theatre's stage and took off sometime after my legs forgot where the ground was.

My thigh feels like it was impaled with an icicle, a glacial stillness lingering at the wound.

"That wasn't supposed to happen." I focus on the glittering coin resting at Jude's neck on a thin chain, my fingers brushing his skin as I reach for it and roll the metal between my fingers. The gold is warm from being pressed to his collar.

"No. It wasn't," he agrees. "And your greedy little hands can keep that coin." He slows just a bit. There are whispers over his shoulders, onlookers with far too much interest in our conversation. He lowers his voice. "Of course I remember you, Riven. I remember everything."

He's still there. Relief pours into the part of me that cracked wide open earlier. Not quite mending the break, but it's a salve.

As he sidles through the Playhouse doors, leaving the crowds behind, I fiddle with the neckline of my dress, checking the wound where my mark was. The delicate flesh feels like it's split open, spreading. Not good.

My Player is closer to the surface, recognizing me for what I am. A costume, worn and thinning. A character to take control of before I go any more off script than I already have. That monster beneath looked out at the audience and wished them all death until I somehow managed to strangle her back into the confines of my mind.

"You pretended—earlier. With Sil." My accusation comes out a bit slurred, my mind sluggish from the Eleutheraen gold.

"I had to. You must be out of your mind to go off script in front of Sil like that. After Gene?" He shakes his head, chest rising and falling. "He won't put up with a character gaining that much control. He'll kill you. Not just you, *all* of you."

Second Death. If Sil can't control me, he'll kill me—Player and all.

"We did too much to get you here," he goes on. "I've spent years trying to keep you alive for this."

"That's funny, because I spent those years just trying to stay alive," I return, spiteful. "Some backstory would have been helpful."

"It probably would have gotten you killed." His voice drops to a whisper, like he's worried someone will hear. "Please, leave your fourth wall alone. And whatever you do, don't tell the others. Go back to thinking of me as a selfish Player who trapped you. Think of me as what I'm supposed to be, not what I am."

"You don't make it to the end of this story, you know." I let the coin drop from my fingers, staring at the exaggerated frown of the Tragedy mask engraved into the gold, resting against his heart.

"I know," he answers and throws a look over his shoulder, probably watching for Sil. A shadow skitters up the wall of the Playhouse. We're speaking off script, and Nyxene listens for such things. "But you'll see me again. As someone new."

"You won't remember."

"I won't." He moves up a scarlet staircase, the one that leads to our dressing rooms. My heartstrings wring at the matter-of-fact tone. Like it's already said and done.

"Isn't it strange?" I press. "Having all this power just to be leashed under someone else's strings?"

Jude presses his lips together. "It's the Script, Riven. The world is controlled by the strength of a pen. So are we."

Freedom for power.

We enter the common room. That rage festers deep in my soul again—the idea that a mere man could get his hands on such power. The thought is so sharp, it cuts through the fog of my mind. For a moment, I'm quiet. An idea takes shape behind my eyes. "What happens if the Script is—uh—edited?"

Jude's steps falter as he stares at me the way you might stare at a child who's just announced a horde of monsters lives under their bed. He looks so alarmed, I'm scared he'll drop me. And he does, setting me onto a scarlet chaise so suddenly, I yelp.

His eyes narrow. "We're actors. Not playwrights."

I wince at the bitter cold pain obscuring my vision from the movement before recovering and arguing, "But the Script is the reason—"

"Do *not*," he warns, "touch that book."

I push myself up. "Why not?"

"Because if it has the power to make us, then it can unmake us just the same. Gene ripped those pages out and went stark mad. We're bound by it." He spares a pleading glance down at me. "Please, Riven. For your safety. For mine. For our cast. Leave it be."

"But *think*, if there was a way to—"

I will not think on anything," Jude says, but his tone weakens, "if it means losing *you*." His hands cup my face, and his eyes lock on mine, bright with determination. "Riven, listen to me. Sil will protect his Players long before he protects the roles we play. He's right to."

I almost laugh, trying to read his gaze. "What does *that* mean?"

His hands are warm, but his tone ices over. "It means if it comes down to losing your character now, or losing *you* forever, I will skin that costume off you myself."

Act III: Scene XX

Jude's words pierce my spine; I'm unsure if he could mean such a thing. I pull back far enough to search his eyes. He tries to school his features, but there's an edge he can't hide—dark and unforgiving.

I will skin that costume off you myself.

The air in the common room seems to dissolve through the stained glass windows as I try and fail to pull in a breath. Until a shout mercifully shatters the silence.

"Out of my way, Jude," calls Arius, rushing from the hall with a tray of what looks like salves and fresh bandages. It frees us both from the agonizing stretch of quiet as Jude moves to make room and Arius kneels at my side.

ARIUS: "Don't!" He swats my hand away from inspecting the gash above my knee. "You don't want it to spread. It's already in your blood."

I roll my eyes. That ship sailed the day I was marked. But I don't argue as Arius pushes the gauzy folds of my costume from the arrow wound and checks the laceration with the gentleness of a seasoned nurse, snapping at Jude to give him space.

Jude is still staring at me like he can't believe what I've suggested. I look away, focusing on Arius instead.

Because I can't believe what he just said, either.

But when I blink, I don't see Arius at all. I recognize him for every face he's ever worn. An old friend. A gifted healer who's sewn me up a thousand times before.

ARIUS: "Definitely diluted gold. You got lucky." He flashes me an encouraging smile.

"Lucky?" I laugh hoarsely and bite back a comment about my own family not splurging enough on pure Eleutheraen gold to kill me. Though the discomfort pulsing up my leg is still enough to make me consider snatching an axe from the wall to chop it off.

Arius presses over the wound to stanch the blood. A furious string of curses rises in my throat as I grip the sides of the chaise, clamping my teeth together as the stampede that is my cast parades out of the hall.

TITUS: "Gods above! Ay, Riven, did you know you've got a little scratch on your leg there?" He jokes, but his lips have gone white, and I sense the fear rattling beneath his tone. In every life we've lived together, in every new role, Titus has numbed the worst parts with debauchery and humor.

It's like I'm seeing them all clearly for the first time, memories fighting to the surface. Faces I've known and loved, words I've said and regretted. When we Players were pulled from the well, our forms came full with humanity's deepest struggles and emotions.

The substance of all great stories.

JUDE: "Where's Sil gone?"

MATTIA: "Still out there, filling their heads with pretty words about Riven's *grand sacrifice*." I can hear the eye roll on her tongue. She's keeping her distance at the door with a solemn frown on her lips.

That fourth wall cracks a little more as I stare at her, catching a glimpse of one of my oldest friends—and greatest rivals.

I should stop thinking about this. It's making it worse. It's bringing my cast's true names to my thoughts. I could shatter everything they know of themselves, and of me, with a word.

PARRISH: "May I see?" We all startle as Parrish and her anklets jingle forward. "I've never seen an Eleutheraen injury up close before. Titus wouldn't let me."

TITUS: "Be grateful for that."

I suppress a smile at her curiosity. She's worn more costumes than any of us, never placed in any singular role for long. She gets bored so easily.

ARIUS: "It's a rude thing to ask, Parrish."

JUDE: "Never mind that. Come look, Parrish. You might as well see what we're strong enough to survive." Jude clears his throat, catches my eye. "And you *will*, Riven."

Jude. I know him better than the rest. I've loved him, his every song, every story, more than any.

"You'll survive this," he says again.

We both catch the emphasis on that last word. *This.* This is something I can heal from.

Abandoning our Script—that, I would not heal from. None of us would.

Alone, that is.

But I'm not alone anymore. I never have been.

What would it take? I wonder, looking at my cast. *What would it cost to win our freedom?*

My gaze falls on Jude, and I already know what it would take. What it will cost.

I will skin that costume off you myself.

It's going to cost me Jude.

Act III: Scene XXI

That night as I try to fall asleep, a chest full of memories cracks open, and several roles I've lived spill out. I grasp at them like straws but come up empty with a vague feeling of loss.

Under the lamplight, I roll the little bottle of Eleutheraen gold between my fingers. Galen's parting gift, proof that he was here. In a strange way, it's the only thing left to cling to that makes me feel real, human, my own. Galen must have suspected on some level what I was. Maybe he chose to love me anyway. It doesn't mix well with Sil's claims of mortals being foolish and selfish. Humans love, and they seem to do it selflessly.

A soft tone startles me from that strange place between dreams and consciousness.

It's a small voice, gentle and humming behind the mirror I draped a curtain over before going to bed. With no one to speak to, I don't need a mirror anymore. According to Mattia, Cassia was arrested hours ago. She's in a holding cell now, awaiting trial. Another person I've failed to save.

The floor is cool beneath my feet as I pull myself out of bed, attempting to keep pressure off my bad leg, though feeling has slowly started to return to it, to cut through the icelike stillness, after Arius spent several hours mending the wound.

"Dear Riven Hesper," whispers the voice as I reach the glass. A child's. "Please don't tell anyone about this. I don't think you're bad."

A very foolish child, apparently.

I've heard prayers thrum at the edges of my mirror before. This one sounds different. I pull the fabric from the glass, press my ear to it, and listen carefully.

"Please keep this a secret. I have always wanted to see the Playhouse." Then a tapping sound, like a small finger scraping at a window. "My sister says you're from here. So I was wondering if you could let me come see it? I won't tell anyone."

She's from North of the Cut, I realize with a start.

My first instinct is to frighten her. Scare her away from the Playhouse forever. Warn that she should run as far from this place as she can.

But when my hand drifts to the glass, I call a portal through instead. A small child crouches on the other side of the mirror, a thick garment cast across the glass where she's clearly pulled it to the side. She sits in a drab and dark room, bare of decoration or beauty.

She looks like I did, once.

The child jumps when I materialize on the other side, though I wager she can see little more than the glow of my eyes in the darkness. Which is for the best. I must be a frightening sight.

My tongue moves to warn her of the dangers of Craft, of the Playhouse, of all of it, but the tips of my fingers reach for the mirror instead. I close my eyes and call on the Craft thrumming in my blood. Like that day in the Archives with Jude, I cast a quiet hum from my throat.

I hear a tiny gasp, followed by a delighted laugh, and open my eyes.

On the other side of the glass, flecks of gold fall from the ceiling like new snow, showering her room in light. The mirror echoes my song, swelling and doubling the melody.

She bursts into giggles, her bare feet spinning in circles as the golden blizzard falls over her.

Something inside me smiles. *That*, I think. *Maybe that's what I'm for.*

I catch one last glimpse of the little girl, twirling beneath the stardust, before banishing the portal and covering the mirror once more.

Then I shut my eyes against the third day of the Great Dionysia and make peace with the sunrise rapidly approaching on day four. And do my best not to think about the fifth.

When I do sleep, I dream of Mount Eleutherae. At its top, a well, bleeding gold.

Act III: Scene XXII

The rest of the cast is already gone by the time I exit my dressing room, tucking locks of dark hair back with little gold pins as I head for the stairs to join them outside.

In all honesty, I'd hoped to avoid the celebrations altogether, until Titus very helpfully pointed out I can "be boring when I'm dead tomorrow." A comment that made Jude's eyes briefly flash to mine. Then he left the room rather quickly.

I hate knowing the ending.

Heading down the stairs to the lobby, I lean over the railing and catch an obscured glimpse of the festivities outside through the stained glass. Though I'm less concerned about the big party than I am about what's happening beyond it. Somewhere inside the stone behemoth sequestered in the second ring of the District, Jude and Sil are convening with the council.

A brief formality, Sil said. Before the Playhouse's newfound freedom is final. Though they left several hours ago and haven't returned.

Jude and I haven't spoken since yesterday. And the look of warning he gave me before he left—and the blatant refusal to speak off script when I tried—makes me think we aren't going to any time soon.

I press my hands to the gilded doors and step into the night.

The fourth day of the Great Dionysia reeks of debauchery, an outdoor night market hosted in the heart of the District where the Playhouse looms. Above, the sky sparkles with stars. Below, music pulses merrily in the air as I exit through the open gates.

I enter the celebrations with a limp and probably the most outrageous plan I've ever had in my life.

Even after Arius swore up and down that officials had scrubbed the District of any signs of Eleutheraen weapons, I warily watch for pointed arrows among the smiling mouths and reaching hands as I move through the festival, past tables overflowing with delicacies, cakes, and rare wines. Merchants busy around them, overwhelmed by demand, until one spots me and bursts into tears with a speech of unending gratitude that I don't deserve. It's impossible to catch all of what she says over the music, but the word "red" dots her sentences more than once, and I notice the roses woven into her black hair. Red. Color. *Beauty*—all seeping outside of the Playhouse for the duration of the festival. Probably more than most of them have ever seen.

I hurry faster down the street.

Betmasters lurk at every corner, coin changing hands over my and Jude's fates—wagers laid on who will emerge from the finale tomorrow alive.

Farther down, booths are strung with tiny lanterns that twinkle like fireflies, their vendors hawking playbills and posters, shouting their prices over the beat of drums.

"Come now, Riven," Titus bellows, emerging from a crowd of Revelers dancing wildly in the open plaza. Wine stains the corners of his lips, gold leaves falling loose from his hair and floating to the ground. "Your last night on earth calls for a dance!"

Before I can object, he grips my hand and pulls me into what I think is a dance but feels like a gallop.

"You're drunk," I observe, wincing when my injured leg meets too much pressure after Titus attempts to dip me.

"You're correct." He throws his head back and laughs. "See? At least I can admit when I'm something no one likes very much." He spins me, brushing too close to Revelers that form a circle around us, their ears itching to catch a word of conversation among Players.

TITUS: "I know the feeling, though, you know." He sticks a foot out for emphasis, the one an arrow sliced right through. "Never stops hurting."

RIVEN: "Comforting."

Then we're dancing again.

"Titus, I need to"—I lower my voice—"talk to you about something. An idea."

Titus grins wickedly. "Oh? Trying to make Jude jealous? Sure, I'm in."

I frown. "Not that."

"So long as your *idea* doesn't involve me going inside. I'm fucking tired of that place and plan to enjoy my freedom while I've got it." He raises an eyebrow. "And don't think I've forgiven either of you for leaving us all behind to go on your little adventure outside. Damned unfair, that was."

Titus blinks a few times at his own words, shaking his head in confusion. He doesn't realize he's slipped, gone off script.

Recovering, he locks his arm around my waist, hoisting me into the air and whirling us twice before setting me down.

TITUS: "I'm impressed, Riven. You're either about to unite a nation or start a war. Between you and me, one of those sounds *much* more interesting." He playfully waggles his eyebrows at me. "I haven't gone to battle in a long time."

I flinch at the reminder and turn to peer up at the second ring of the District beyond the square. Nearby, Sil and Jude sit among the council. I wonder what's happening now.

RIVEN: "Let's hope it never comes to that—" My words are interrupted by a riotous auction commencing down the street over props used during our three-day performance.

TITUS: "Yeah, well. I imagine it's inevitable when they find out what our boy Jude is trying to argue in there."

I hesitate, tripping over my own feet.

RIVEN: "What?"

TITUS: "After your little incident last night, Jude's trying to claim Eleutheraen gold shouldn't be allowed within a city's reach of the Playhouse. A danger to us, you know."

RIVEN: "But—" I stumble over my words. "But they're arguing for the Playhouse to have full freedom to travel all of Theatron." Titus nods. I clear my throat and lower my voice. "That…that would ban the use of Eleutheraen gold *entirely*."

TITUS: "Use. Ownership. Trade. You name it. They're claiming the last fifteen years have been filled with propaganda and that Michail—well, your father—fell to his death on accident." Just as it was framed in the play. "Clearly, you're here with us, so you're not too broken up about it."

An incredulous laugh bursts from my throat. "But most of the North is marked with Eleutheraen gold—"

TITUS: "They're proposing a grace period for everyone to have their marks unsealed. All Sil sees is a lot of potential Playhouse goers. Besides! I hear you've already started a trend in some cities."

I shake my head. "The council will never agree to that."

"Won't they?" Titus grins. "They might have some stubborn heads on the council with marks of their own. But rumor on the street is..." He leans in, brushes his lips to my ear in a whisper. "One of our Players can use Craft on the marked." Titus gives me a conspiratorial grin. "It might have been dark outside when it happened, Riven. But I watched you kill that woman. There was a mark on her neck."

He means Eleni. I lower my eyes, looking away.

"Gods, you must have hated her! Making her do it herself like that. Nasty way to go." He spins me around. "You're right, though—the council will never agree. They need all seven committed, and... well, that was quite the show you put on in Paraskenia."

I wreaked havoc with that plague of darkness. Made it *very* clear Players cannot be trusted.

TITUS: "Don't look so grim! War is fun. Gods, what's she doing up there— Parrish!" He jerks his chin at the ivy-covered wall of brick, where Parrish has scaled halfway up, dress hiked to her knees. "Get *down*."

She pauses to pout over her shoulder. "There's a piece of ivy there at the top that I want for my collection."

TITUS: "You don't have an ivy collection."

PARRISH: "I didn't say it wasn't the first piece."

He shakes his head, gives up, falls back in step with me.

TITUS: "So! What is it you wanted to tell me? I'm all yours, Riven."

I brace my mind, trying to assure myself this *is* the right thing to do. That this is not a terrible idea. He spins me again, but this time, when he pulls me back to him, I lean in and whisper at his ear. His rich laughter vanishes.

I don't say much. Just a word. A name.

But it's one he hasn't heard in a long, long time.

Titus's hand freezes on my lower back. He looks into my eyes, smile fading, recognition breaking across his gaze.

ARIUS: "Riven! Have you finally run him out of words?" Our castmate breaks from the crowds, a blissfully ignorant grin on his mouth as he claps Titus on the shoulder. "You're more impressive than I thought."

But Titus is still frozen, staring at me, struck silent.

It spreads like a disease every time it happens, Sil said.

Good, I decide. *Let it.*

Across the street, Mattia's eyes bounce between Titus and me, calculating. She shakes her head at me, solemn.

Before Titus can speak, I pull away and disappear into the crowd, stealing inspiration from the first face I notice and Mimicking it over my own. Then I slip into the night, unrecognizable, elbowing through Revelers until I break away from the party and make for the stone steps leading up to the second ring of the District.

If the North refuses to cooperate, Sil will give up and wipe them out. I know that as well as I know my own lines. But the plague I caused wasn't scripted. It wasn't supposed to happen, and now it's thrown a wrench in Sil's grand storyline, made the council resistant.

And they *have* to concede, because if they don't…

I walk until I reach the enormous columns bordering the Archeion of Dionysus. Stepping over the chamber threshold, I drop my Mimicry mask and follow Jude's voice echoing through the stone halls. Eventually, it leads me to a set of carved doors.

"Syrene will be safe," Jude is saying. "I swear it to you, upon my blood and my stage—"

Moira's voice laughs coldly. "Jude Stepharros, I have never heard a more worthless promise."

"Then allow one from me." My voice strikes the room as I throw open the doors, but my heart wrings with the words, the betrayal I'm unleashing on my home, even if it's the only way to save it.

And definitely the only way to prove my loyalty to Sil.

He needs to believe I'm on his side. That I've given up.

Still, my stomach twists.

RIVEN: "Your mines of Eleutheraen gold have run dry. Your forces are weak and your resources almost nonexistent. You may fight with what you have, but you won't win." With a single breath, I've broken my promise to Galen to not speak of the shortage.

Even Sil didn't know about that.

I'm sorry, Galen. I've let him down in so many ways.

But this time—*this time*—I'm going to make it right.

The room freezes, all seven sets of council members' eyes on me, reflecting horror. Moira looks on me with hate as I lay cards that aren't mine on their negotiation table.

Jude stares at me, astonished, and it's an effort to meet his gaze. Like he'll be able to read the decision behind my eyes.

But Sil—he smiles, the most horrible smile I have ever seen. "My, Riven. How we've missed you this evening."

Act III: Scene XXIII

Later that night, I follow my scripted blocking up to the Playhouse terrace, much as I resent obeying it. For right now, I have a role to play. By the slow, stumbled chatter, I assume I'm late for my entrance. They've run out of lines.

TITUS: "Riven!" His voice booms as I emerge, but I catch the tension in his smile. "Ladies and gentlemen, we are looking at either a new star Player or a corpse with a very nice jawline."

Mattia kicks him.

MATTIA: "Do you think you could make it more than a few sentences without being such a shameless flirt?"

TITUS: "With wine like this and a face like yours?"

ARIUS: "Join us, Riven. There's drink to go around."

TITUS: "So, drink! Like there's no tomorrow." He winks but holds my gaze a beat too long, our earlier conversation written behind his eyes. There's a small place below his ear where gold peeks through, the tiniest crack in his costume.

Moving to the couches, I seat myself in the space beside Parrish—realizing it isn't incidentally empty but unwittingly reserved. More of it, scripted.

I catch Mattia's attention, where she's plucking figs from a bowl. Her gaze bounces away from mine. There's a new rupture of gold at her hairline, spreading like a web. The Player in me sees it and feels disgusted, noting the urge to shed a deteriorating costume, empathizing.

But *I* am the costume, and I'm still here, so I shove those thoughts away.

RIVEN: "Any word on the council?"

Arius grimaces. Titus laughs.

MATTIA: "From what I hear, I don't think Jude will be joining us tonight."

JUDE: "Actually, he will."

We all turn to where Jude stares blankly at us from the top of the steps.

I wonder if anyone else notices the messy way his gold irises have begun to bleed into the whites of his eyes. His handsome features, sharp before, are almost inhuman now.

"Any news?" Parrish chirps.

JUDE: "It would seem your speech moved them, Riven." Moved them. A kind way to phrase *plucked every line of defense from their fingertips.* "They've surrendered. Signed onto Sil's new terms, to go into effect beginning tomorrow, after the Great Dionysia winner's been crowned." He finds a seat across from me but avoids my eyes. "The Playhouse has won."

Silence shivers over the words.

Then my cast breaks into cheers, wine is poured, and chalices are clinked together.

I've done it, exactly what I was designed to do, taken the world for a stage. Handed it to Sil on a platter.

I hate to admit part of me feels good—*complete.* Playing my role as it was intended.

JUDE: "Confiscations of Eleutheraen weapons and the dismantling of resistance groups will begin immediately after. I expect none of it will go down cleanly."

TITUS: "Well, enough of this doom and gloom! One of you will be dead tomorrow, and that's exciting."

The mere mention of the arena sets a chill in the air. As the quiet chorus of banter carefully sculpted around me plays out like a piece of sheet music, I clutch the Eleutheraen gold vial in my pocket, wondering what Galen would do, would say, if he could see me now.

ARIUS: "Well, Riven?"

I snap to attention, unsure what the question was, until I realize I *know* what's been said, because I remember reading this scene. Red wine splashes over the sides of a crystal chalice Arius sets on the table. "Any predictions?" he clarifies. "About tomorrow?"

Parrish nudges me jokingly. "Suppose you'll join us forever? We've got the whole world to perform on these days."

I look widely at my cast. Jude's knuckles are white around his cup. I raise my own.

RIVEN: "Ignorance is bliss."

Our final night slips away with the shift of stars and the clearing of crowds below, though some hopeful onlookers sleep outside the Playhouse gates, craning their necks up toward the terrace.

The Players make their exits in pieces. First, Mattia, who always retires early. Then Parrish, who stretches, yawns, and mutters something about checking on her "experiment." Then, stubbornly, Titus, who awakens from his drunken stupor at this proclamation.

Finally, Arius rubs his eyes, then floats down the stairs after the rest.

Alone, Jude and I say nothing to each other.

This scene is over. We're supposed to go to bed, too. Being the obedient Player Jude always is, he numbly gathers his coat from over a chair without a word.

Fine. With my shoulders tight, I turn stiffly and stalk toward the stairs, making my peace with the thought that the next—and last—time we'll see each other will be in the arena.

"Riven," he blurts as I pad down the first three steps.

It's the first unscripted word he's deigned to utter since that conversation yesterday.

I throw a look over my shoulder, brow gathered. We're out of lines for this scene. And Jude has made his alliances clear. "He speaks," I say dryly. The lights in the stairwell leading to the common room flicker, dimming. We're off script, but somehow, it feels more natural than the words that were written for us.

"This is the safest time to talk—when we return to our rooms at night, before the lights shut off." His voice is tight. "The same way it's okay to smile and wave and break character during curtain call. The curtain is starting to shut."

I pinch the corners of my mouth into a cold half smile. "Then I had best get backstage before it does."

I scamper down a few more steps before he calls, exasperated, *"Riven."*

But my next entrance, to my dressing room and then to my bed, is calling. I'm sure he can feel his own blocking, too.

"Please," he adds stiffly, like the word takes a lot of work. "I know you're mad, and you're right to be. But can we please— Just please talk to me."

I try to tell myself it's silly to be angry with Jude, that I can't feel any more betrayed by him than by myself. That we both accepted our roles, no matter how long ago it was.

But only one of us seems intent on seeing it through to the end.

And I am not just mad about that. I'm furious.

I breathe, look at him. "What, Jude?"

He watches me, suspicious as I climb back up the steps. "You helped the Playhouse evade a war tonight. I know you too well to think you did it out of the goodness of your heart."

I sense the real question beneath his words, though. *Can we go back to safely playing our roles now?*

The torchlight flickers, then starts to dim. As it does, I catch a glimpse of him, an actual glimpse, of every face Jude has worn, every voice he has spoken to me with.

"I want to know why," he says.

You may be my most resilient Player, Sil told me, *but you had best believe Jude is my most loyal.*

I hate that, in a sense, Sil has won. I don't know if I'm looking at an ally or an enemy. Maybe some unholy combination of the two. But until I find out which, I do have a new part to play, and it will be a tricky one.

My mouth opens. It takes effort to form the words. Words that aren't a line, that my tongue was never supposed to form. "Because I choose this," I say. "I choose every life we will live after this. I choose our stage and this Playhouse. My home."

The place where my mark once was twists with phantom pain at the lie.

But Jude doesn't seem to notice me wince. Instead, he closes the space between us in two strides, throws his arms around me, and he weeps.

Act III: Scene XXIV

Hugging Jude feels like coming home and shutting the door after you. It feels like the peace and stillness that follows. In spite of how mad I am at him, my resolve softens, my anger briefly melting away into the warmth of his chest.

But my ribs feel like they're about to crack, so I wheeze out, "Jude, would you please put me down—"

"Do you know what it is to miss a person for fifteen years?" He tucks his face into my hair. "I'll put you down when I'm ready."

The lights flicker again, so I guess Jude's metaphorical curtain is already closing. Noticing this, he tenses, sets me on solid ground, hands finding my face. "Gods, it all went wrong." His eyes are bright, restless. "I wasn't sure you'd make it home."

I exhale a laugh, but it comes out bitter as I press my palm to my throat. "Yeah, well. I almost didn't."

The corners of his smile fall. "That wasn't supposed to happen. I tried to—well, to stop it."

He did, just with a different face. Almost dragged me back to the Playhouse and foiled Sil's carefully laid plans. And in the end, left me with a warning.

Come with me or you will suffer.

"And then afterward," he says, quiet, "I still listened for you, just in case."

A blurry memory clicks into place. Nights I couldn't sleep after the marking, exhausted from pain but alive with a rush of anger. I blamed it all on my so-called *curse.*

But deep in the quiet, during the longest nights, I heard singing. A soft, rich humming from the drawer of my nightstand, where my mother's hand mirror hid. One night, I even opened the drawer, pressed my fingers to the glass. As years passed, I grew certain I must have dreamed the whole thing.

"I heard you," I say, realizing. "It—" *Made me feel like I wasn't alone.* "It helped."

"You were so far away from home, with no idea who you were. And I thought maybe hearing—" Jude stops, shakes his head. "I don't know what I thought. You were getting weaker and weaker. Then, one night, everything just went silent."

Galen was furious when he discovered the mirror. Tossed it right out the window.

Jude runs his fingers through his hair, staring off somewhere. "And *Michail*—gods, he wasn't supposed to die. I messed it all up, Riven."

"You stopped him from—" I shiver, not finishing the sentence.

Jude swallows, nodding. "That last performance with Gene. She'd already broken my fourth wall, and she made a big show of telling Sil she'd burn the Playhouse down before shedding her role—as if she could just leave and go live a simple human life. I think it's all in the world that she was ever after. She just wanted out."

Something winds tighter in my chest at the thought. That we *can't* go live normal lives. I'm proof enough of that.

And I want out.

The corners of my eyes burn, and it takes me a moment to understand why. I can barely recall who Gene was to me, but something stirs in my heart—the same deep and irreversible sense of loss that caved into my chest when my brother was taken from me.

I realize I've stepped away, put space between us, and Jude notices, too. Is looking through me the same way he did that day in the snow, like he's desperately trying to pluck the magic combination of words out of the air between us to convince me he isn't some unfeeling monster.

Slowly, I nod at him. *Go on.*

Jude's throat bobs. "When she collapsed, I looked up from the stage and saw Michail rise from his seat. Then he took off for the doors." Jude shakes his head, as if to shake off the memory. "The curtain fell, and I've never run so fast in my life. I cornered him before he reached the lobby. I don't know what he meant to do, but he had a knife in his hands—that *same* knife you brought in here. For a moment, it was like there was no script. No lines."

His eyes wander to a far corner of the terrace. "He ran, tried to escape. At some point, we ended up here. And I..." He scrubs a hand over his face, not finishing the sentence. "It was all too late. I'd broken character, badly. That's when *this* started getting worse—" He moves into the last of the torchlight by the ledge, tugs one sleeve up far enough to reveal where nicks of gold mar his skin. "It spread slowly at first, but the damage was done."

He drops his hands to his sides and looks pointedly down toward the landing, where Michail's body was discovered.

"The audience was filing out when they found him. It messed everything up. And after Sil made such a big show of the *Peacemaker*." His voice wavers. "Fear spread. The North declared marking children not long after that. Sil let me out to check on you—make sure you survived, but I..." Attempted to drag me back to the Playhouse instead. I picture the Player I saw, her voice sweet and conniving, luring me away. "Well, I might have not *exactly* followed the instructions." He tries to laugh, but it comes out hollow as I look to his scarred hand and refrain from reaching for it. I draw my shoulders in instead, the guilt weighing them down. I could have hurt him much worse that day.

"Hell, *I'd* have gone instead, but Sil, he—" Jude grimaces, and I wonder if I'm imagining the shame coating his expression. "Sil didn't think any of the rest of us would survive that long out there."

Judging by how quickly Jude fell apart during our little adventure through Syrene, Sil was probably right about that.

It's quiet for a moment. A familiar, nice quiet.

"Were they good to you?" Jude clears his throat. "Your—your family." He sounds nervous about the answer, unsure what sort of hands I'd been left in.

"I don't..." It hurts to think. It all looks different through this lens. I sigh. "You first."

"My family never existed, now that I think about it." He shakes his head. "I'm not actually from Thymele. I have all the memories as if I were, though, because *Jude* is from Thymele. I can't always tell the difference between what's real and what's not."

That's often the case in the Playhouse.

I collect my memories—real, *true* memories.

"I was raised by a mother." In my mind's carousel of recollections, her eyes darted away from me more and more as I grew, her lips white with worry. "But I think maybe she was scared of me, knew something was wrong." Part of me knows not to blame her, not to be bitter. After all, I grew up looking like Michail. At *best*, I seemed like the evidence of an affair. At worst, the suggestion of an affair with a Player.

I'm neither of those things. And worse.

But none of it dulls the sting of her stiff, one-word answers to me growing up. The way her shoulders tensed when I passed. The flinch in her expression when I spoke. The way she'd only ever peer above my head and never into my eyes.

"She chose not to be a mother to me either way."

The words settle between us.

I think harder and decide, "That man planted a Player. *In his own home.* All for fame and recognition and the obsessive love of another woman—Gene, a *character* just like me, who never really existed—"

"You exist," Jude says firmly. "*I* exist. Just...differently from everyone else." He looks thoughtful for a moment. "Is what he did so unthinkable? Betraying the world for love."

I watch him back. "No," I say. "I don't think it's unthinkable at all."

That's exactly the problem.

I clear my throat. "But I grew up. Normal, I thought, until they took me to be marked."

A shadow passes over his eyes. "I thought the marking would kill you. But Sil swore the safest thing we could do was let it play out and trust that you were strong enough to make your way home to us. I still snuck out once more after to check on you, and he nearly had my head for that." Jude watches the moon, full and bright above us. "And then I waited, wondering if it was enough. If you were alive or dead."

This isn't how I'm supposed to die. That thought sliced through me the night I was attacked at the casting call. Because that wasn't the end of my story.

Now that I think about it, I know exactly how and when my role ends. I read it ages ago.

A shudder skitters up my spine.

Another torch blows out.

"I watched from the window the night of the casting call, waiting for you to come home. And you did, just like you promised," he says. At the memory, I imagine myself standing outside the Playhouse, entranced by that voice that seemed to clasp around my heart like a fishhook and pull my feet forward. I think I could have listened to it forever. I think I *have* listened to it forever.

"But you didn't look anything like you were supposed to." He stares down at the gates like he sees something I can't, his voice breaking. "You were skin and bones. Your face was gray. And gods, the way you *looked* at me, like you were terrified and disgusted at once when all I wanted to do was pick you up and never put you back down."

And I subsequently made it my personal mission to be a thorn in his side. *Gods*, he didn't deserve half of what I put him through.

"I thought—" I gather the words, but they sound *ridiculous* now. "I thought Craft had poisoned me. Everyone did," I say, watching another torch start to dim. "Food never made me full. Blankets never made me warm. And gods, I *hated* it when anyone touched me..." I trail off, cringing. "Everyone's hands were always sharp and cold and—"

"Food doesn't sustain us; performing does," he interrupts, clearing his throat. "Craft is the only thing that can warm your blood, and you were all but cut off from your bridge by that mark. And touch—" He shudders, too. "You're a Player, the antithesis to reality. Humans, though—they're full with it. They can't escape their reality. It's why they flock to us for distraction. Their touch *should* repel you."

I look at him. "I was never cursed."

"You were *starving*," he says with a humorless laugh. "And subsequently poisoned by that mark, which just sped up the progression and probably damaged the bond between your role and—" He doesn't say it. Between my role and the monster that plays it.

Sil's *most resilient Player*. I frown at the thought.

"And then you paraded into the Playhouse, deathly unwell from so many years away, and all you wanted to do was *leave* again. You didn't know half your lines. Then, for you to insist on keeping that mark!" He throws his head back, looking exhausted, and I remember all his desperate attempts—not to train me for a competition but to bring me back to myself.

While I fought him every step of the way.

"And when you finally *did* let me burn it off, you just hated me more." He raises an eyebrow at me. "I thought we were making progress until you showed up to my dressing room with that arrow aimed at me. Which you were *not* supposed to do, by the way."

I grin back. There's something oddly comforting about it, a small relief. That even if so much of it was supposed to be scripted, we weren't. Jude leans back onto the ledge, the dimming torchlight casting his hair in summery shades of auburn, crosses his arms, and finally seems to relax a little.

"Why didn't you just tell me by that point?" I ask, leaning onto the ledge beside him until our sleeves brush.

He laughs weakly. "I almost *did*. About a hundred times, I wanted to tell you. But a fourth wall can't be unbroken. Once we know, we know." He adjusts his rings, like he's looking for a distraction from the thought. "You taking me out of the Playhouse was never supposed to happen. It pushed me so far off script, my memory started slipping out of place. My costume. Everything."

Dread slices through my chest as I realize what I did. He hadn't even been able to recall my name. "I'm sorry," I say, not sure that I am. My favorite parts of Jude have never been planned moments in a crafted storyline. They've been whispered words in the dark, stolen looks backstage between scenes, sly attempts to outsmart each other in the margins of a script we were given no choice in.

I'm tired of the two of us being bound to one man's grand narrative. I imagine the entire world is.

But I notice a new nick splitting between my thumb and index finger, a rip in my costume and a consequence of this conversation—I'm not sure we have much choice.

Jude's eyes follow mine to the damage, softening. "It's horrible knowing, Riven. It's lonely, not to mention dangerous." He reaches for my hand where it rests on the ledge, examining delicate skin where my costume has begun to fray like he's afraid of making it worse. "I didn't want *this* to happen to you, too." With a sort of carefulness entirely at odds with the character he *should* be playing right now, he presses my palm to his chest, and I can't help but note the familiar rhythm of his heart, a pulse that sounds more like music when I think about it. He pushes up my sleeve, the warmth of his fingers lingering where the flesh has already begun to peel away. His face falls. "And it is anyway."

Fear gathers in a lump in my throat, but I swallow it down. He's right. It has. Even if the worst of the damage can be hidden behind a high neckline, the deterioration has started to spread in small, thin scrapes. I doubt Sil will always be able to fix this with makeup.

At some point, Riven—everything I am—will fade to make way for someone new.

Some old part of me wants to stomp and scream that it isn't fair. But I think I've done enough screaming into the void about unfairness to last me into the next lifetime. Maybe sometimes things are just unfair.

That doesn't mean I'm done fighting.

I draw back, and words cut loose from my mouth that I'm definitely not supposed to say, but I mean all the same. "I don't want you to go," I utter, and mean it, all my anger crumbling.

Jude plucks a piece of ivy from the column beside us, absently rubs it between his index finger and thumb. "I'm not going anywhere. You'll see me again, with a new face. A new name. A new role. And I'm sure you'll drive me to my wits' end then, too."

A new piece of ivy grows in place of the broken ivy almost immediately, like the old leaf was never there.

"I won't know it's you," I counter, and I hate the way my heart lurches when I speak. His fourth wall will be rebuilt. And after Riven, mine will be, too. Still in this cycle, still in this cage. "And *you* won't know."

He holds the ivy over the ledge, and we watch it float down together. "I'd know you with any face and by any name, Riven." His golden eyes meet mine, and his words wrap around me like a familiar blanket. "Any voice, no matter how cutting. Through any gaze, no matter how loathing. I would know your touch through a closed curtain and the sound of your step when the last spotlight has gone out. I have known you at the beginning of each performance, and I will bow with you at the brink of every finale."

Finale. That word seems to wedge itself between us, a rift driving us further apart.

I pull in a breath, an easier one, lighter, and lift my gaze from where it's stalled on the flecks of gold peeling off my hands—from flesh that's ephemeral—to watch the light in Jude's eyes, which isn't. He and I may be sewn with the same eternal thread, but it still comes unraveled at the end of each show. We're running out of time.

A thought hovers at the edges of my mind—that slash of lipstick written across Jude's mirror. I thought a fan must have written it. *If not in this one, then in the next.*

Not a fan's handwriting, and not his. Mine. I grin. "If not in this one—"

"Then in the next. I *do* love it when you leave me notes," he confirms with a smile. "And I say that calls for a toast!" Jude wanders across the terrace to the table, full with our abandoned chalices. He plucks two and fills them with what's left of the wine, returning with less than half a cup between us and shoving the greater of the two into my hands. "To the godsdamned finale?" he asks, raising his cup, a glimmer in his eye.

That word again. *Finale.* It rings melancholy in the air as I meet his gaze and raise my chalice. "To the godsdamned finale."

Act III: Scene XXV

All my worst ideas start with this feeling. A subtle spark that tingles at the back of my head.

Jude frowns. "That's your scheming face."

Okay, maybe not all that subtle.

Another torch blows out and startles us both. We should be in our dressing rooms by now. But I'm not ready to go inside yet.

That thought—that horribly risky but *very interesting* idea—sparkles in my mind's eye, but the words aren't quite there yet. And with it, a deep sense of knowing—knowing I will win our freedom if it kills us.

Looking at Jude, I wonder if it might.

Down below, the nearest city in the South stirs, still bustling with excitement. On the opposite side, in the distance, the North stands silent and watchful, like a garden without sunlight. Somewhere below in the District, the council sits around a table, bickering over the Playhouse's newfound reentry without ever realizing they've each stood witness to a very elaborate show.

Above it all, I can't help but notice how the moon shines down on both sides of Theatron in equal measure.

Without warning, I abandon my cup and hoist myself onto the railing, balancing on the soles of my feet as I cling to the ivy wrapped around the nearest column. Jude drops his chalice and rushes in my direction, calling out, "A *moment's* peace, Riven. I am *begging*. Now, what are you— Ow!" My foot loses its purchase and kicks him square in the chest.

"Sorry," I apologize over my shoulder, already lifting myself up the ivy and onto the ornate dome that caps the terrace.

If all the Craft in the world rests in our veins, the world ought to have a taste of it, too. It was theirs once.

When I peek over the ledge, I catch a glimpse of the crow

statue atop the dome frozen in flight, its marble wings stretched to the sky. "Up here!" I pull my body onto the very top of the Playhouse, Jude already close behind.

"And what are we doing up here?" he calls after me, climbing onto the ledge. The wind grabs at his hair, throwing it sideways across his face, which in turn looks annoyed.

"We're taking bets." I spin and go for the coin around his neck. Jude doesn't move as I snap it from its chain.

"On what?" he asks, raising an eyebrow.

"On the arena."

His shoulders fall. "We *know* how that ends."

"What if we didn't?" I ask. In my head, my spark of an idea takes firmer shape. And that shape is a mountain, with a well at the top. "What if it didn't end the way it's supposed to?"

His expression strains. "Riven."

I hold the coin up between us, the moonlight winking off the stamped frowning mask, then turn it over to reveal its joyful counterpart. "Call it. Comedy or Tragedy?"

Jude rolls his eyes. "How optimistic are we feeling? In a Comedy, everyone lives happily ever after. In a Tragedy, scarcely anyone lives at all."

"Is that your answer?"

"No," he replies and saunters forward. His hands find my jaw, slide back into my hair. The gleam in his eyes could give the stars overhead a run for their money. "My answer is that the finale has already happened. We just haven't performed it yet." The coin suddenly feels cold in my hand, the words heavy in the air. It must show in my expression, because he adds, "I've never pretended to be a hero, Riven. I have no interest in it."

"What, you'd sooner call yourself a villain?" I mean it as a joke, but my throat tightens and the words come out stiff.

"All that stands between a hero and villainy is proper motivation," he says. "Love provokes the hero as violently as it does the villain, and it's merely who tells the story that determines which is which."

His words sink into the silence between us. I can't help but wonder which one of those *we* are but decide the question is better left unanswered and, slipping out of his reach, toss the coin. It flips once, twice, maybe three times between us before plummeting back down, where I catch it on the topside of my palm, pressing my other hand over the answer.

"Well?" he prompts. "What's this prophetic coin say?"

I peek, then peer up at him. "It doesn't matter." Then I spin and fling the coin as far as I can. It soars and soars until it stops—freezes—there in the sky. My hand stretches out to it, feet inching closer to the ledge until Jude jumps forward to grip the back of my dress and hold me steady.

With the flick of my wrist and a whispered command to my Craft, the gold illuminates. Just a small burst of light at first, a fractured coin. But while Jude mutters something about not being able to trust me with any of his jewelry, the pieces unfurl in a sparkle of light that first doubles, then triples. Then bursts—the illusion echoing across the night sky like a sea of golden stars.

Below, the city seems to sparkle under the light chasing away its shadows.

A gentle tug on the back of my dress. "I guess I didn't care for that particular necklace anyway," he says. "Let's not forget our neighbors."

I follow Jude, this time, to the South's side while he pulls a ring from his index finger. There's not a sound to be heard save for the music of our feet racing around the dome, recreating my illusion until the entire sky lights up with gold like a brilliant sunset.

Far below, doors fly open, windows sliding down for heads to peek out in curiosity. We grin at the delight that squeals in the South and laugh mischievously at the initial panic that eventually softens into relieved confusion in the North.

Wind in my hair, I snap my fingers and watch my tiny stars fall like golden frost, a mirror to my illusion from one night before. For the first time in a very long time, the world outside glows brighter than the Playhouse.

Jude and I settle ourselves on the ledge, our legs hanging over the drop like children on a log. We might have stayed there forever, had someone not written the words for us to come down. Nyxene will begin searching for us soon, wondering why two actors are out of bed.

And so, eventually, we gather ourselves and stand, ready to go. To sleep, to wake, to take our places for the finale. And my idea for how it might end.

I try to parcel the words, to stop him long enough to hear me out, but, "I'll miss you, Jude," falls from my mouth instead before he can climb back down the ivy. Even though we both know that that isn't even his real name.

He slows on his way to the ledge, shoulders shaking with laughter. "Good." He turns, flipping his palm to the sky to show me that ugly white scar slashed across it. "Then you'll know how it feels."

I linger, like the clock down in the lobby will quit ticking if I only stay still enough. But part of me suspects Jude is looking forward to shedding this costume, to rebuilding that fourth wall and living in ignorant bliss again. I'd be tempted to, at least.

When I don't move—because I don't want this part to be over—Jude relents. Saunters up to meet me, smirking like a fox. "I'm never far off, Riven. I've never *been* far off. What is death but a brief intermission? A moment backstage." He brushes a knuckle to the delicate skin behind my ear, glides it down my jaw, and tilts my chin up to meet his gaze, which seems brighter than the moon that haloes his silhouette. "A quiet place to try on a new costume and then find you. And even when I'm not there onstage with you, I'm an eye in the audience."

He's worn a lot of costumes through time, and even if I can't remember much, I wonder if this is my favorite—the smile, at the very least, I decide. Always sly and clever, like it's hiding the last verse of a forgotten song. Hair that glints like torchlight at the ends, eyes as bewitching as they are gentle—and, at the moment, disarmed. As if drawn there by some invisible thread, I move to brush my thumb over that single freckle below the left one, shoving away the bitter sense of dread that prods at my heartstrings.

That idea starts to gleam in my mind, shinier by the moment.

"I am applauding your every move, listening for each and every line. And at the end, I'll be at the stage door to meet you," he says, and his hands are so warm and familiar, I can't help but lean into them, wrapped in the scent of hyacinth and not caring that his rings will get twisted in my hair. "Whether in the next life or the one after, I'll wait there in the wings until it's time again."

I'm not ready to let Jude go. But as he slides his scarred palm to the back of my neck, looks on me with eyes that I think I've spent most of this life and several others dreaming about, I don't think I ever will be, either.

His lips brush against mine—not for the first time, but possibly for the last. I find myself memorizing every movement, every touch, holding on to the moment like it'll slip through my fingers, the same way Jude is holding on to me.

The kiss is nothing like that day in the snow. It's soft, lingering. My arms slip around his neck, drawn into his current, and I lean into the hand he winds around my waist, the fingers he spears into my hair as it shifts, deepens, turns into the sort of kiss reserved for the last act of a performance.

Kissing Jude feels like the strike of a match on a bitterly cold night. It feels like waking from a nightmare only to catch the glimmer of a sunrise.

It feels like that last piece of a long-scattered puzzle finally clicking into place.

Until the clinking of what sounds like a fallen chalice freezes us both.

Jude whips his head toward the ledge, eyes searching, and I'm suddenly very aware of the subtle clatter of movement down below. *Sil?*

Then the accompanied whispering of shadows.

Not Sil. Nyxene.

"Don't move," whispers Jude, who's gone as tense as the crow statue behind him. I hold my breath, but in the quiet, my mind drifts to Gene and the message she gave her life delivering. *Riven. Script.*

Moments pass in rigid stillness, and eventually, Nyxene departs—probably to search other crevices of the Playhouse for her missing actors. Taking the hint, we retreat back down the ivy in shared silence, in time to witness the only remaining torch snuff out, leaving trails of smoke in its wake. Jude's shoulders drop. "I'd say that's our cue, Riven."

He turns for the stairwell, but before he reaches it, I blurt out, *"Wait."*

And at last, my very, very dangerous idea spills out of me.

"Do you ever think about the well?" The words are heavy. I'm *definitely* not supposed to be saying them. "If we came from it, doesn't that mean we were...free at some point?"

Jude goes still but doesn't turn. His voice drops to a low, quiet warning. "The well is deadly to us." He moves to leave again.

"Is it?" I press, and he pauses again, his shoulders going tight. He knows me. He knows where I'm going with this. "Why? If we *came* from it. Maybe it only—only wants back what was taken. *Us.* Our Craft."

The gods never poisoned the well after we rose out of it. Maybe—maybe Sil *polarized* it by emptying it of our Craft and our power, until it became what it is now: Eleutheraen gold. When he caged us, bound us to *his* Script.

Slowly, Jude shifts to look at me. His expression might as well be made of stone, but I go on anyway.

"Wouldn't that mean there was a time when Craft belonged to the world?" I ask. "A time before it was all stolen and hoarded here. A time before we were greedy—"

He huffs. "Has it ever occurred to you that maybe I *like* being greedy?" His eyes dart away, like he didn't mean to say that.

"But *think*, won't you?" I swallow and hurry a step toward him. "If there was a time before this, there could be a time after it. Couldn't there? Before the Playhouse." The Script flashes through my mind. My voice strains, thin. "Before Sil and that *book*—"

"That book gives us power," he says, his voice going taut. "If we aren't subject to it, we're subject to *them*." He jerks his chin at the ledge, to the cities beyond. "You think *we're* liars, tricksters. But humans—humans do terrifying things with power. *For* power." He turns to look at me, and his eyes gleam, steadfast. "Before, we knelt to the world, not the other way around."

Loath as I am to admit it, his words ruffle my prideful feathers. He's right; I do like this power. I like being in control.

But I also think he's wrong—wrong about the people. Wrong about staying trapped here.

In my head, through a cloud of foreign memories, I almost glimpse it: Eleutherae, a mountain that peaks over the hills, bleeding gold in a place lost to men. A well at its top. My heart aches for it, misses it.

"If there was a way to fix this, would you?" I let my eyes drift from him, out to the world beyond. To the dull and joyless life marked and Reveler alike are accustomed to. To the life *I* was accustomed to. "Fix what we've done."

He scratches the back of his neck, hesitating. "I'd say the two of us are a little late for redemption, love."

"We're not." I shake my head, wishing I could brush the guilt from my shoulders. "*You're* not. There's time to undo this."

"No, there's not." He heads for the stairs, and my heart drops. "Good night, Riven."

"Wait, *Jude*—I know there's a way we can stop—"

"Enough," he snaps, gripping the railing. His eyes flare. "A castmate is *dead* because of me. Can I undo that?"

My mouth shuts, opens again. "What happened to Gene wasn't your—"

"I should have *stopped* her, Riven." His words speed up, like he's been holding on to them a long time and now they've all come tumbling out. "She said all this same nonsense, too. And if I'd gotten her to give up the delusion of escaping this place—if I'd gotten her to comply with the damned Script—*none* of it would have happened. She'd be here. With a different face, fine, but—" He shakes his head.

I want to interrupt, to reach for him, but I can't move. I'm not even sure if he's talking to me or to himself. We get so little say in our own words, and I wonder if he's been needing to say these for a long time.

"Sil killed her for refusing to play her role. He poisoned that cup and warned if I didn't help him, if I couldn't prove where my loyalties lie—" *Jude is my most loyal*, Sil's voice taunts in my head. "He'd have no choice but to write my role off, too. You think she didn't try to suspend her reality? I let her die, Riven. And then she went on to suffer that horrible halfway existence. Because of *me*."

My gaze lands on the ground, stays there. I don't have words that can fix this.

"*That* is why I never told you the truth of what we are, why the others can't know. There are consequences for defying the set storyline, and I won't lose another castmate over it."

He stops for breath, all his tender words from moments ago slashed away by the sharp edges of guilt in his tone. "There's no forgiveness for that. No '*undoing*' it." His eyes shift, harder now. "I will not lose you, too. So whatever you're scheming in that devious mind of yours, drop it now."

"No," I argue and charge after him. "What Sil did wasn't your fault. At least *listen* to me—"

Every angle of his face ices over, and the shift is so seamless, I don't dare move any closer. "If there was a way out, I'd have found it," he says. "I won't gamble our lives searching for loopholes. What happened to Gene will happen to you the moment he suspects—" Jude cuts himself off like it's bad luck to say the words out loud. "It was me who led us through those gilded doors at the beginning of all of this, Riven. I will be the last to walk out of them. And I will play whatever role I have to if it means holding on to you. Let the gods judge me a villain for it. I will see you in the arena, you will win, and that is the end of this story."

I rush forward. "Jude, *wait*—"

"I surrendered everything to make this world our stage." He steps out of reach and vanishes into the darkness of the stairwell. "And heart, I'd sooner burn it down before giving it back."

Presumably, Jude goes to sleep in his dressing room.

I do not.

In the darkest, quietest moments of night, I slip out into the cold, watching for Nyxene over my shoulder. But frankly, I'm more afraid of Jude catching me.

I make one visit, two. Then a third, and a fourth, and a ninth.

By my last, Nyxene and her shadows have spotted me and are furiously snatching at my heels, aware that I'm out of bed and severely off script.

But not aware that I've spoken to every single one of my other castmates under cover of darkness.

As dawn begins to break, I've set the stage for the finale.

Act III: Scene XXVI

M*y name is Alistaire Hunt.*

As the morbid excitement of the audience rampages through the vents and carries into my dressing room, all I can think of is that first lie. That first mistake. It's enough to drown out Parrish's humming as she buzzes around my head like a bee, weaving threads of gold into my hair. At the moment, she looks so meek, it's hard to picture her ever winning her own blood battle to claim her place in our cast.

PARRISH: "It's all right; it isn't the first time someone's wondered." I must have been staring. She taps at my jaw to get me to turn and starts painting my lips. "They always underestimate the small ones. I was put in the arena with Marcus at the time. He was new enough to be the perfect degree of prideful—the sort that made him laugh at my efforts."

RIVEN: "What did you do?"

PARRISH: "Most Players with a knack for Compulsion imbue new emotions in their audience, but my talents lie in the exaggeration of what's already there. Marcus was overconfident, and I amplified that to a sort of blissful unawareness. Pretty easy after that. Oh, don't look so shocked! Jude wouldn't do that. Not his style."

I shift uncomfortably at the reminder. I'll be locked in with Jude until one of us is dead.

And based on last night, he seems perfectly fine with that being him.

PARRISH: "But that said..." She bites her lip, goes back to braiding. "Watch your surroundings. Don't trust them, I mean. In the arena. And Jude, he always goes for throats—"

SIL: "Drama queen, always has been." Parrish and I look over our shoulders to find Sil at the door, a flat, square box in his hands. "Turns everything into a bloody performance whether he's supposed to or not."

The unwelcome memory of Dorian's ear in the snow flashes across my vision, while Parrish moves to excuse herself rather quickly.

She catches my eye before she goes, though, gives me a subtle nod. Then presses her hands to the door; I catch the smallest rip in her elbow, the gold exposed beneath as she vanishes.

SIL: "But *you*, Riven." He rests the box on my vanity as the door clicks shut. "You are patient. Clever. Leave him to his ego and theatrics, and Jude will destroy himself."

With a *click*, the box snaps open, revealing a tangle of golden leaves fashioned into a thin, glittering wreath. Sil removes it with care.

"Remember," he says, positioning the wreath over the crown of braids atop my head. "Everything you see in the arena isn't happening." The sharpened edges dig into my scalp, but I don't let him see me flinch. "Stick to your bridge. Do *not* let Jude have control over the illusion."

My pulse races as Sil brushes the intricate plait Parrish styled over my shoulder, and I think my hair must have grown a foot in the time I've been here. The face in the mirror looks so unlike the one I came in here with.

Strangely, I think I miss the old one.

SIL: "Don't make the mistake of thinking he'll take the first shot he gets. He isn't there just to kill you." His hands settle on my shoulders, locking eyes with me in the mirror. "He's there to make a show of it. Break a leg, Riven," he tells me. Just as he's told me before every Great Dionysia before.

Sil moves for the door, and my mouth opens. "You've gone to great lengths, Sil—keeping all of us together. Safe. Here."

He stills at the unscripted line, hand at the doorknob. "Such is the burden of a director." His words are clipped at the edges.

"It's curious—how you ended up with the Script the way you did."

I can see from here the muscle ticking in Sil's jaw. "Some Playhouse mysteries may never be solved," he says, showing his teeth an awful lot.

For a moment, Sil doesn't look like my director. He looks like what he is: a selfish man with the hands of a thief and alchemist. Wielding the stolen power of a god, to use and to exploit for his own purposes.

I wonder if Sil was as powerless as me once. Desperate, hungry, angry. Maybe a day existed before greed overtook his bones and throttled his every desire. But if there was, it doesn't matter now.

Nothing is enough for a selfish and simple man. Nothing short of ruling the world.

"Your audience is counting on you," Sil says, tone short. "See that you don't keep them waiting."

The door snaps shut behind him with a little more force than necessary.

I retrieve the weapons Parrish laid out for me: two daggers, which I secure beneath the flexible layers of my dress, slit high on either side of my hips for easy movement. A long, polished bow. A quiver full of arrows. I pull the thirteenth one out, examining its point. Then, drawing a breath, slip the small golden vial that Galen gave me from beneath my neckline, where it hangs on a chain.

My eyes burn, but my hands are sure as they unscrew the vial and dip the point of the arrow into Eleutheraen gold, assuring myself I won't have to use it. That it will never come down to this.

Jude's words from last night counter the thought. *I will play whatever role I have to if it means holding on to you. Let the gods judge me a villain for it.*

But I will not play a role anymore.

I will not be Sil's pawn, tool, or weapon.

I will not be the villain of his story.

And as gold dries on the arrowhead, which I stow carefully back into my quiver, I can only hope Jude won't be the villain in mine. The vial vanishes beneath the neckline of my dress.

I'm about to head for the arena when a gentle hum snags my attention.

The voice beckons me back to the mirror, a soft melody emanating from the other side. I've known it since it sang to me through the mirror years ago, comforting me when I was frightened.

He hums the very same tune now, though in a lower, richer tone.

Slowly, I place my palm to the mirror. The glass ripples at my touch.

Then it warms, and I imagine a second palm meeting the other side of the glass. I can almost see the white scar slashed across it. From the depths of my memory, I recall the words to the tune he hums. A forgotten rhyme from an old play.

Until next time,
Until then,
So long until
We're back again.

Act III: Scene XXVII

"R*iv-en, Riv-en!*"

The chant swells from the opening of the stairwell, louder with each step as I descend into the darkness. It stirs something in me, a sense of dread, clashing with the thrill of a performance. By the time I reach the landing and step into the tunnel at the bottom of the Playhouse, the audience feels like a riotous storm that shakes the walls and matches the pounding of my own heart.

The Playhouse draws its strength from its audience. A theatre grows weak without them, Jude told me once. And I can feel it now in the thrum of magic rising from the ground. My eyes track the gilded edges of the tunnel around me as they gleam brighter. The gold spreading. Warming.

Every move forward feels like scratching an itch. Everything my role was created for boiling down to now. My steps echo in time with the crowd chanting the name of someone who doesn't exist—someone entering a trap full of sparkling chandeliers and red velvet seats.

Light darts through the breaks in the curtain up ahead, calling me forward.

SIL: "Ladies and gentlemen." His voice bellows, overpowering the cheers. "It is my honor to welcome you tonight to this, the finale of our Great Dionysia!"

Their screams for blood vibrate in the ground and satisfy the hunger of the Player within me inching closer to the surface every hour. My hands find the slit in the curtain, parting it.

SIL: "Please welcome: *Riven Hesper*!"

The spotlights flood my vision as I step through the curtain, and the arena roars to life. My ears pop at the crash of applause, my head spinning with the blur of faces dotting the circular space, which is fashioned in the same golds and reds of the auditorium above it. In the podium seats closest to the ring, I find my cast, their expressions twisted with forced indifference. Mattia gives me a subtle nod. Titus winks at me.

At the center between them: Sil.

In the second row just behind him, the council watches, faces taut.

A grin stretches toward my ears as I drop into a dramatic bow.

But when I lift my face, take in the crowds, I realize this isn't the arena I remember.

It's grown. *Growing.* Twice the size I thought it was.

The Playhouse expands to suit however many wander through its doors. Or, in this case, through its mirrors—hundreds of them, lining the entryways beyond the stands, open portals for mortals everywhere to wander in.

As stragglers file into the rows and spectators shriek their approval of my entrance, the Playhouse seems to tremble. To quake. To soak up the devotion and attention of those who have wandered right into the belly of the theatre.

Its walls groan, widening around me, making space for more and more patrons. Overhead, the ceiling rises farther away. As its walls stretch, they crack.

Gold Craft rushes in to fill the spaces between.

SIL: "Joining tonight's finale..." He pauses with flair, and unease builds in my chest, my pulse roaring in my ears. "Lead Player *Jude Stepharros*!" Before Sil can bite down on the last syllable of his name, the crowd is on their feet, thunderous cheers relentless as the curtain across the opposite entrance sweeps open.

Jude moves into the arena with otherworldly grace, his stature nearly reaching the apex of the opposite arch as he straightens. Golden veins travel like vines from his hands to his neck, glowing beneath the white of his shirt, open at the collarbone. Glittering symbols are painted across his chest to disguise the damage of his costume peeling away.

Sewn into his dark hair is a matching wreath, not unlike my own, except the edges stick out, dull and rusted. Sil widely publicized that Jude would be wearing Gene's wreath to *honor her memory*. She notoriously finished off her own opponent by slashing their neck with the gilded edges of her crown.

A grim understanding sinks in. I'm certain Sil's intentions with it reach far beyond any publicity stunt. Forcing Jude into wearing a reminder of what happens when we don't obey our storylines, a crown heavy with guilt.

In one of his hands, a spear.

Jude doesn't seem to notice the audience, his eyes pinning me to the place where I stand, burning with the same determination that's hammering in my chest. The rest of the world blurs to noise and color.

He bows. A single, elegant movement—too calm for what's coming.

I shove down the fear rising up my throat. A confession hovers on my tongue. To Jude, for what I'm going to do. To the audience, for what I am. To myself, for what I'm not.

The air between us hums.

In my mind's eye, a coin is tossed. Flips in the air.

Jude looks up. The lights catch the gold in his eyes, the faint shimmer of Craft. The noise of the crowd falls away.

The coin flips again, Comedy's and Tragedy's faces glinting with each turn.

Across the arena, Jude's lips form the shape of three words.

Three deep breaths.

My lungs comply before I can think. The dread in my chest feels so heavy, I'd rather play any other part than this right now.

SIL: "Let us begin."

The coin flips once more. And falls.

Jude does not break his gaze from where I stand.

Until now. As his arms rise to the skies, he throws his head back. A word seems to form on his lips as his eyes burn like torches.

All at once, a cover of night shakes the ceiling.

Then, like a blanket, the illusion of darkness collapses over the arena.

And I feel myself falling.

Act III: Scene XXVIII

A fountain gurgles pleasantly beside where my head lies, my body stretched out on the cool marble floor. I seem to be in some sort of grand hall or atrium.

Where am I? How have I gotten here? My mind is too foggy to recall.

My stomach twists like a braided rope. There's something I'm supposed to remember right now. Somewhere I'm supposed to be.

"Riven?" calls a voice, echoing down one of several long hallways surrounding the fountain.

I inhale a sharp breath. I *know* these walls.

"Riven," says the voice again. Female. Older. Deceptively sweet and patient. Fear slides into my veins, cold and nauseating. I know that voice, too. The woman who etched my mark as a child.

Clambering to my feet, I make a dive for the farthest corridor from the voice, ducking into the first unlocked room I find. The room is bare, save for a long table littered with tools used for Eleutheraen marking.

"There you are."

My blood freezes at the sight of the woman standing by the table. Graying hair, stout shape. She isn't threatening. But the scars at the base of my throat burn like hellfire when she tilts her head at me.

The woman smiles, her teeth slightly crooked. She dips a sharp instrument into a pod of Eleutheraen gold.

I stagger back for the door.

"Come now, Riven," she says. "Don't be frightened. This is how we do things here." She spits that last part, unable to hide some edge of disgust.

That's what wakes me up.

"Jude," I whisper, more to myself than to him.

Not real. Illusion.

Jude had access to my memories during that first Reality Suspension. And he's resurrected one of my most frightening recollections to parade it before an audience. Not that I have any idea where the audience *is*. The illusion is too thick, too all-consuming.

Mattia warned me to remember that the Great Dionysia is as mental as it is physical, a battle of deception. The goal is to destroy your opponent's sense of reality so thoroughly, they don't know to fight back, don't even know *who* to fight back.

It's hard to combat an opponent when you can't tell what's real and what's not.

My gaze flies over the stone walls around us to the windows, hunting for the eyes of spectators beyond. I don't see them, but I feel them. A shiver races along my spine as I realize what I'm dealing with. We draw our strength from our audience, and Jude's is growing. A lot.

It all looks so *real*.

The woman clicks her tongue. "Sharp, aren't you? But then…" Her bored eyes dip to the gold pod in her hands. "You let them do this to you."

I startle at his bold words, and the woman laughs, but it's Jude's voice that comes from her mouth this time. "They can see us, dear heart. But I'll take care that they only hear what we want them to."

He's playing tricks with the sound.

"Sorry for all…*this*, by the way." He gestures broadly to our surroundings.

Right. He's painted this awful scene intentionally *for* the audience, a memory so many of them know well from their own lives.

"But they're expecting a show, and we might as well give them one." He nods encouragingly. "Fight back, Riven."

"No." The word rushes past my lips. "I…I can't."

His brows fall, like he's misheard. "You can." Apprehension curls around his voice. "It's okay. I'm ready."

"I won't." My voice strains. I reach for the courage to speak words I couldn't last night. "I won't fight you. I'm done with this script, Jude. And with every other."

His costume falters, dissolving from his true face all at once, like every other thought has cleared from his mind, and I know I've struck a chord.

He's heard those words before, from Gene.

Jude's expression twists with disbelief, and his attention darts to the windows, as if Sil is right there at the glass, watching us, still pulling the strings. In the breath of a second, his demeanor goes rigid with resolve. "Then I suppose I will have to convince you."

"Funny," I say. Something in his tone makes me want to reach for the arrows resting at my hip, but I force my hands to stay at my sides. "Because I came to do the same thing."

His eyes flash up to our surroundings again as he grits his teeth, maybe nervous that his masking of our voices has slipped, that Sil will hear me. A muscle feathers in his jaw as he turns his gaze back to mine, taking in my words. My intent.

I want freedom.

And Jude—Jude has always chosen power. His cast. Me.

His eyes stir like storm clouds, and I can feel he's on the precipice. His promise last night rings in my head. *I will play whatever role I have to if it means holding on to you.*

His face goes cold, and my stomach sinks. He's made his choice.

He will play the villain in tonight's performance, just as Sil wanted.

Act III: Scene XXIX

"So be it," he says, his hands balling into fists.

At the dark shift in his voice, I take a defensive step back.

JUDE: "There are three things I will have you know before the end of this, Riven." An edge cuts into his words as he recites the line. "One, that *this* is not your home."

He throws his hands out, gesturing widely to the windows, where the illusion of the District awaits outside. Instantly, they shatter, glass scattering everywhere. A piece bites into my palm when I duck to cover my face.

JUDE: "No matter where you go, no matter who you become, and no matter what you do, you will *always* come home." He bites down on each word. "Home here, where we belong, home to the Playhouse."

At that line, an anger in me wakens. Being trapped here in the Playhouse. Being planted in the real world like a festering wound. Being used like a chess piece.

Do not *let Jude have control over the illusion*, Sil's voice prompts in my head.

I move fast, doing exactly what I did on this day ten years ago when I was marked: I start to shove the worktable over, only now, with the strength of the Player I know I am. My arms thrust it at Jude with a force that pins his back to the wall.

The crash of the impact shudders through the stone walls as I grip the handle of the door and summon a command under my breath. The foundations of his illusion splinter, rumble. A groan peels my attention back to Jude, who pushes the workbench off, jaw tightening, the proud glint of a challenge accepted in his eyes.

The walls shake as I slip outside and slam the door shut on him. His mirage collapses, the houses and streets he conjured crumbling to ash.

"Methexis," I utter, and my Craft rushes in response.

I need to buy time before Sil realizes something has gone wrong. Make it seem like I'm fighting back until I can get Jude to reason with me.

I kneel and speak to the ground. *You are not dust*, I tell the rubble as it swirls uneasily, like something living is beneath it. *You are limestone. You are war-torn. You are an ancient city.*

Two can play at his memory game. I saw his recollections, too.

The dust rises, solidifying into tall, cracked columns topped by heavy marble domes. I sing to the stone until it smooths into a winding path between dry grasses. The tips of my fingers prod at the sky, summoning a white moon and a foreboding wind. The scent of fear stifles the air, sharp and bitter.

I draw from my bridge until the illusion molds into the shape of a different city: the lost ruins of Thymele. The same city I saw in Jude's memory—a false memory made up for his role.

But whether the memory is real or not, Jude remembers every bit like it happened.

I creep along the empty streets of my illusion until I find him.

He faces away from me, statue-like at a crossroads, his attention roaming warily. Shoving my heels into the ground, I back behind the thick trunk of a tree and watch from afar.

Then his shoulders shrink inward like a child's, eyes shifty and uncertain as he blinks up at the sky, like he can't remember what he's doing or why he's here.

I reach out, nip and pull at his mind with Compulsion until nothing exists except this moment, this memory. "You are young." I weave deception into my tone as the wind carries my whispers to his ears. "You are scared."

The earth rumbles again as the wind thickens, black with smoke. I raise my mouth to the sky and command it to turn red as blood.

Finally, with a flick of my wrist, I resurrect the illusion of stakes rising from the earth, the burned golden remains of our fellow Players scorched upon them. Flames race through the streets, tearing toward Jude. He cries out, staggering back.

He may not have lived this memory, but the Player in him knows the scene well. We all do.

Jude collapses to his knees, staring at the burning Players on the hill, no longer the terrifying creature from a moment ago. He looks small, vulnerable. I catch a glimpse of the hopeful thing he is at heart, before fear and pride hardened him.

I conjure a mask for myself: that boy I saw in Jude's memory, morphing inward, younger, innocent. Dipping my thumb into the ground, I swipe ash over my cheek and notice the rough calluses of my costumed hands.

Then I run into the burning city. As someone familiar, a friend. Someone he'll trust. *"Jude!"*

He blinks in my direction, eyes wide and frightened. Recognition blooms in his expression.

I motion for him to follow me, running for the shelter of the city's temple built to honor the first Players. Under my breath, I conjure the distant chorus of slaughter, a gust of shattering limestone. Jude's feet pound after mine, all the way to the columns of the temple.

I don't need Jude to let his guard down. I only need him fooled long enough to lure him toward one of the heavier columns.

Embers fall over the city like rain as we dart through the temple's courtyard, the night sky deepening into a darker, angry red. I lean down, brushing my fingers to the stone. *"Tremble,"* I tell them and straighten before Jude notices.

The ground obeys, shifting beneath us. Jude swears and runs between two of the columns as the marble splits at our feet. He whirls, running his hands through his hair, eyes wide and blinking, like he knows something is off about his surroundings but can't place what it is.

I watch the pillars, straining my Craft toward them. *"You are weak,"* I whisper to them.

Jude pauses a few feet from the columns, shoulders rigid. His gaze narrows at the faded tile at his feet, then up at the columns.

"You cannot stand," I tell the pillars as Jude approaches them for cover with caution. He kneels to the ground, plucking a stick from the tile defensively.

I close my eyes and focus. *"You will fall,"* I command them.

But when I open my eyes, Jude isn't by the pillars. He stands only a few feet from me as the column tips behind him. With a thunderous crash, the falling support beam shakes the foundations of the earth. Overhead, the dome ceiling lurches inward, begins to crumble.

Then I register the object in Jude's hands. Not a stick. A pointed silver spear, the one he held when he stepped into the arena.

No sooner have I grasped the turning tables before Jude pivots and throws the spear. The head slices across the air.

A sharp pain explodes through my side.

JUDE: "Impressive. You had me a moment." His tone drawls, putting on a show for the crowd as I lay gasping, the spearhead buried in my side. My torso feels wet, warm. His steps approach. "You should have chosen someone else to Mimic." Jude's brow draws together in annoyance at my mask, which dissolves from my skin. I'm unable to hold the illusion any longer. "Lukas never made it out of the city. Wasn't fast enough. I told you I escaped alone." He tilts his head. "Why are you drawing this out, Riven? I've given you several opportunities now. Finish it."

I gasp for breath, but it falls right out of my lungs. Pain scorches from my side and pulses through my body. This isn't enough to kill me—Jude knows that. He just wants me angry enough to fight back. And he's right. That anger is warming behind my eyes, starting to burn in my throat.

He knows if I won't follow the Script, the monster beneath my skin will.

"I won't fight you," I rasp. "I am *done*."

Jude whips his gaze up like he's heard something strange, searching the false world around us. Then he winces, clutching a hand to his temples. As he does, something twists in my mind, and I feel it, too. *The Script.* Our performance has gone awry, and the near-irresistible urge to submit to the words written for us is calling us back.

Something like panic flashes across his face. Then, quick and merciless as a whip, Jude grips the end of the spear before I can pull it from my side, and twists.

"*Fight me*, Riven!" he roars as the city crumbles, my illusion slipping and breaking as the urge to suspend my reality, to let this body die for a moment, overwhelms my thoughts. Darkness bruises my vision. Above us, cracks in the temple dome spread like tree branches, ready to fall in a hailstorm of rock and debris. Marble splits beneath my back.

My mind begs for rest, to release the illusion and embrace the shadows hovering over my vision, eager to take me. I am so tired of fighting.

Surely, Sil knows by now. Knows something has gone wrong.

JUDE: "The *second* thing I will have you know before the end of this." The skin across his left eyebrow is splitting, gold bleeding viciously down the side of his face. His costume tearing more as I push us further and further off script. "There is no true good, and no evil. Only those powerful enough to decide which is which."

My eyes narrow at the chain around his neck—bare now. The coin gone.

Two sides of a shiny coin used to purchase terrible things.

I will not be used anymore.

In the distance, I hear screams. The roar of the audience. Someone calling my name.

Jude gives the spear a final twist, shouting at me to *fight back*, but blood roars in my ears over his words.

Then: exactly what Jude wants. Something visceral and unforgiving boils in my blood, rises to the surface. The Player beneath my skin, summoned by the dangerous realization that I'm refusing my role, a marionette yanking on its own strings.

White-hot Craft bursts behind my eyes.

My gaze turns on Jude, and fury frames it. *I'm going to kill you.*

No. I sever the thought, strangle the overwhelming intention to fight, to kill, to rip the spear from my flesh and slash it across Jude's throat.

Shadows eclipse my vision, my blood burning through my veins. With a cry, I throw my hand onto the marble and voice to the stone a final command.

Before Jude can react, the dome falls and the ground splits open, swallowing us both.

Act III: Scene XXX

My fingernails scrape at the splintering floorboards, cold and rotting. Then the smell hits me: snow and oak.

Pain cleaves through my side as I push myself up to take in my surroundings, one hand clumsily stanching the blood and discovering shreds of my dress drying into the rapidly healing spear wound.

I'm alone in a cabin. And I've been here before. *Dorian.* I recognize the chair I was tied to in the corner.

Fear bobs in my throat when I notice the bottle, there at the very center, its serpentine silver top. Poison of Echidna.

"Go on," a voice growls. It sounds like Dorian's. "Since you loathe your life so."

I picture the bottle I'd seen, wrapped in layers of satin in Jude's dressing room. He must have brought it into the arena. Not to force to my mouth, but just to see if *I'd* do it.

Because I almost had, that day Dorian waved the vial in my face. I'd considered it.

Now I grip the poison and hurl it at the wall.

A sparkle of glass sprinkles over the floor like rain as I stagger to my feet and run for the door, grabbing the handle and yanking it open. I hurry outside, the shock of snow pressing into my sandaled toes nearly making me stumble. But I keep running, weaving among twisted branches and jumping over fallen logs.

Night is thick in the air, and everywhere I look, there's nothing—nothing but the stretch of tall, dark trees and twisted branches along the side of a steep precipice of ice and stone. I slow to catch my breath and walk over to the edge of the cliff, peer down at the rushing black river far below.

I steel myself, but hair rises on the back of my neck and a cold shiver rolls down my spine. I'm being watched. "Where are you?" I call out. The ache of sleet soaks my heels. "Show yourself."

A long shadow emerges from behind a tree.

My hand presses at my side to stem the flow of blood. A prop metal spear wound isn't enough to incapacitate me, but my legs have begun to wobble as the figure moves in my direction, slow and deliberate. I dread the light, waiting for it to shine over Jude's face. But when he steps into the dim moonglow, it's not Jude.

It's worse.

My lungs cinch, recognition cutting into me.

Galen steps forward into the snow, blinking with confusion. Moonlight shadows half his face. Normal. Relaxed. Kind. His head drifts lazily to one side. "You should really be getting home, Riv. What are you doing out here?"

The calm timbre of his voice unglues my anger, my resolve collapsing like my illusions a moment ago. It's enough to make me wonder if, after a long, terrible nightmare, I've woken up. All I want in the world is for him to be real.

"Galen," I breathe, though I know it isn't possible. Even if every detail down to the small scar above his cheek is intact and—

My eyes lower to the crimson stain that blooms from his chest. Small at first, until it spreads. A startled sound pushes from my throat, followed by the sort of unfettered rage that sends my feet rushing forward.

Galen catches hold of me, his hands firmly gripping my elbows. *"This,"* he whispers harshly, inches from my face. But that crackle of hostility doesn't fit his voice. He never sounds angry. "*This* is what humans do. To you. To me. To everything good and everything we love."

The words tug at my heartstrings. Galen wasn't killed by my kind. He was killed by an ordinary human.

"They don't know right from wrong. They have to be *taught*," he presses.

The scent of blood stings my nose. I shut my eyes, begging my ears for silence, when all I hear is my brother's voice.

"This is what they take when given the *chance*, Riven."

There are a million things I would tell Galen if I could. But none of them surface. And this is not Galen. Bitterness festers in my chest, grows. The air around me hums, alive and thunderous.

I want the illusion to go away, to *stop*. But I can't focus. It's too convincing. Part of me isn't sure it *isn't* my brother, that he hasn't somehow emerged from the dead to rescue me—

"Don't let all this death be for nothing," he says.

My eyes snap open, meet his gaze.

Gold slices across his eye like a live ember—and it's enough. Jude.

I'm in the arena with Jude.

This isn't real. He's trying to provoke me with every vile thing the world has done to me until I break.

I grip him closer to me. "Trust me," I say. "I won't."

Then I take a sharp step back, off the cliff, casting us both into the icy waters gnashing below.

Act III: Scene XXXI

The ground is dry, but I am soaked, shivering from the cold—though I'm faintly aware of the feeling of warmth gushing from the gash in my side. It's so dark, I can't see. My whole body aches, my memory burning with confusion. The finale wasn't supposed to go on this long.

I'm far off script, and I just want it to be over.

I want to be home.

That word shudders through me, warms the ice in my veins. Bleeds out from my fingertips as I lie here, staring at a blank, dark sky.

Home.

One by one, lights—*stars*—flower across it, illuminating a brilliant white moon. *Home.*

The hard ground beneath my back softens. Silky moss blooms from the dirt, emerald green and spreading like paint on a canvas from where I lie. *Home.*

My back begs for rest as I roll onto my side and push shakily to my feet. Under my sandals, a path of white glitters like seafoam, pouring over the hill and then up to the top of a mountain. *Home.*

An eruption in the earth tingles beneath my step as I climb uphill. Cracks break across the mountain, trenches that fill with gold and trickle from the top like intricate lines on a map.

A hum swells in the ground, music I can feel more than hear pulsing in the air.

Onward, alone, I go, brushing the tips of my fingers along the bark of a tree. It responds with blooms of sapphire and violet on its heavy branches. I breathe out, and the wind answers, a light breeze that nips at my ankles, tugs at my hair.

If a crowd watches me from somewhere afar, I don't hear them. All is silent, save for the chime of the stars. Golden streams and pebbles that glimmer like pearls pave my path. Everything that once filled this place before it was drained, destroyed.

My home. Eleutherae.

I'm alone, and it occurs to me for the first time that maybe alone isn't a bad thing.

My feet move through Eleutherae like my heart beats in the earth, until I reach the top of the mountain, where every golden stream meets in one pool.

The well we came from. It stretches in a large oval, maybe twenty feet across, gaping like an open wound upon the hill, luminous as my own skin. Golden, alive, and ancient, soaking up starlight in a hazy swirl of brilliance that's almost too bright to look at.

In its reflection, I don't see my own face. I see a hundred, and then a thousand, all of them morphing and shifting. I know each of them, their stories still awake and breathing in my blood.

On the other side of the golden pool stands Jude, unmoving.

Or, what's left of him. Our tumble down the cliffs pulled skin from his frame, leaving new gashes of gold in his flesh. The cut on his eyebrow slices all the way down to his lips now.

His eyes flicker from the well to the mountain sprawling below us, to every glittering star watching from above like an eager audience.

We aren't *really* here. We're still in the arena.

But this is where we're supposed to be, and Jude knows that, too.

He approaches the well with his shoulders tight, expression distrusting. Then swiftly kneels before it, peering deeply into his own golden reflection. When he finally tears his gaze away, looks to me, cracks form in his eyes, that same ruin that dwells in my own.

Rising slowly, he begins to make his way around the well.

"Jude," I say, careful. "Please. Come home. With me."

"This place doesn't exist anymore, *Riven*." The words rip from his throat so viciously, I startle. "Eleutherae is gone."

"But the well isn't," I plead as he comes to a sharp stop a few paces from me. "We were stolen. Trapped *here* in the Playhouse. And we've been in this cycle for a long time."

"The Playhouse is our home," he snaps. "It's all we have left."

"It's not." My heart pounds, unruly, but my resolve doesn't waver. "We're more than weapons, and you're more than your fear of not being one." I breathe and reach for words. For the ones I mean more than all the others. "Don't make me leave this place without you."

That does it. Jude's face clears, fully and completely. Void of expression.

A merciless silence stretches between us for one breath, two.

He knows I won't play Sil's role any longer.

By now, he knows I have no intention of winning the Great Dionysia, either.

Then his face shifts, stretches like a jackal. Without warning, he bolts, runs at me, hand poised for my throat.

But I'm faster. I draw my bow and the Eleutheraen arrow from my hip, halting Jude where he stands.

He freezes, an arm's reach between us, every muscle going still as stone as he watches the point of my arrow poised at his heart. At its golden tip.

The shift of power between us is instant. The hand he'd trained on my throat drops uselessly to his side, defeat welling in his face, pure and resolute, with the quiet hint of a smile. But I'm not fooled. I know Jude has begun to count his breaths in case he needs to hold the last one.

Until he nods, daring me. *Go on*, he seems to say. *End it.*

Though I can't see them, I feel the stares of the audience around us, locked in dead silence. Gritting my teeth, I push everything else out.

"The third thing," I demand, my voice hoarse. Jude shuts his eyes, resigned, and I press on. "The third thing you would have me know before the end of this. Tell me what it is."

Jude's eyes flutter open, bright with determination. "That

I have loved you." He raises his head, voice steady, certain. "Unreasonably. Entirely. Unfairly and, gods know, selfishly. In every life that I have lived."

My fingers hesitate on the bowstring. Just once, I nod. "Then forgive me for what I have to do in this one."

In a breath, I twist, leveling my arrow at the moon glowing overhead, and release it.

Act III: Scene XXXII

For a moment, the world is silent.

Then the sound of an Eleutheraen gold arrowhead ripping into the very heart of the Playhouse crashes through the stillness. My arrow found its mark, piercing the marble dome directly overhead and what lies above it: the stage.

The Playhouse quakes violently as what seems like millions of cracks crisscross the dome, reaching farther and farther.

In a breath, our illusions dissipate like dust in the wind. Eleutherae slips away, replaced by the horrified cries of an audience watching, bewilderment filling the arena as the lights flicker.

Drawing a second arrow, I aim at Jude, who watches me, open-mouthed, as chaos erupts. Before he can make a move, I level it at his chest and breathe one word.

"Run."

His jaw shuts to clenched teeth. Defeated, he turns and runs from the arena like a bolt of lightning, disappearing beneath the arch.

The audience rises to their feet in confusion, panic closing over the arena as I catch sight of Sil shouting orders at the rest of my cast to file out.

Shutting out the voices, the shuffling feet, I home in on my inner world, my bridge.

"Methexis." Power reaches up from the ground, warmth beckoning. I draw from it, from the depths of my motivation, until Craft pulses through my bones so strongly, I think they might melt.

I lure that power to the surface of my tongue and look at the audience.

"Leave," I command, Compulsion dripping from the words. "The mirror closest to you. Now."

There's no hesitation. All at once, the audience floods toward the exits, unable to resist the command. Rapidly, the arena begins to empty.

In the center of the chaos, I embrace every bitter reality I've fought for as long as I can remember: of what's unfair, of what's imperfect, of what's temporary. Of what I can't have, of what I can't control. My body is breaking under the weight of my own anger, and I can't hold on to it any longer.

I inhale—*three deep breaths.* And finally, *finally* release it.

I forgive every moment of it.

Something shatters deep in my head, and I feel the Player in me shriek, her grip on me slipping as the bond between us fractures.

When I look up, I find Sil, his eyes ablaze and burning holes into the place where I stand. But as the marble splits open at my feet, fissures racing up the walls like a cracked teacup, he turns with furious resignation and runs for the exit.

And so do I.

Act III: Scene XXXIII

My legs grow heavier with each step, the Player beneath my skin alive, awake, *furious*, grasping for control but no longer able to puppet me so easily.

When I emerge into the hall outside the arena, Compelled spectators seem to be making frantic exits through every mirror portal in sight.

And if every mirror is open, that means at least *one* thing so far has gone according to plan.

Sil will have fled to the Greenroom, where he expects to find the other Players.

But I flee to the lobby instead, where the Players will have actually gone.

Hopefully.

I spy Arius's long golden hair first, and relief washes over my very bones as Parrish pokes her head out from behind him while Mattia and Titus wander in from the opposite side.

"For the record," Titus calls at me as I tear into the lobby. He cracks his knuckles. "Opening all the mirrors at once is a fucking nightmare."

I fly into his arms with a hug before doing a brief head count. Not just of Titus, Arius, Mattia, and Parrish—but of Cicero and Cora from the costume wing. And of the ten nameless crew members dressed in black and masked with deliberately plain faces, five of whom played the roles of my fellow auditionees only weeks ago and have been resting in the temporary, unnamed roles of stage crew ever since.

All of whom I paid a visit to last night after my attempt to get Jude on board failed miserably.

At my confession, I watched as the memories of their lives, of who they were, who they are, and who they will be next crashed over their eyes, as the shared ache for home shimmered in their faces.

Each made an agreement with me, and for a moment, the victory of that was enough.

But Jude's absence might as well be a presence in and of itself.

"All here?" I take notice of the clump of hair missing from the side of Titus's scalp. Gold swells beneath it. He took the fourth wall break first, and maybe the hardest.

Parrish's palms are lined with ripples of gold. There's a chip in Arius's nose.

"All who matter…and then some." Titus nods at Parrish and the obscure jar of trinkets, rehearsal room keys, and what might be a live grasshopper resting in her hands. She shakes the jar at Titus and murmurs that she can take whatever props of hers she wants, then turns to me.

"Where is Jude?" Parrish asks, shifting anxiously from one foot to the other. "I thought he'd come."

My eyes burn. I thought he'd be with me, too. I felt certain he would change his mind. With a small shake of my head, I say, "Let's get out of here."

I cast a fleeting glance at the clockface hanging grimly over us, its hands taunting me and indicating ten minutes until midnight, which marks the end of the Great Dionysia. My heart outpaces its ticking as the window on our freedom narrows. Our contracts will seal the gates once more at the stroke of twelve, keep our feet from crossing the threshold until the next one. Sil's leash on us, ready to tighten.

Hurrying toward the grand entryway, I throw open the Playhouse doors. They crash loudly into the night as I descend the steps. A waiting crowd outside screams their surprise, gathered at the gates and anticipating the celebration of a victor—not the chaos of thousands flooding back through the mirrors in desperate escape as cracks climb the sides of the Playhouse. No one understands what the last few hours have meant for the

Playhouse, for Theatron.

Only that something has gone deeply wrong.

Taking my place at the front, I turn to watch my cast file down the steps. Arius throws me a smile. I nod back, remembering our hushed conversation from the night before. *I followed you out of the well*, Arius said. *I will follow you back in.* He took to the idea fastest, eager to mend all we've broken. I can't help but think his short fables of wisdom and consequence will return to find eager ears. He tells them so well.

Parrish, whose tales I expect children have missed dearly, hops down the steps, filing off to my left. *You know*, she said last night, stroking a stuffed animal as if it were alive, *I've grown sick of this place. A little cage-like, don't you think?*

Titus grins at me, though gold has torn through the left side of his smile. His stories make me laugh the most. *Well, Riven*, he said. *It's been a pleasure performing with you. Now, let's get the hell out of here.*

Mattia gives me a resolute nod on her way down. I have no doubt the world will once again fall in love with the sagas I've heard her craft—epic and sweeping adventures that keep even me on the edge of my seat after all this time.

I expected her to fight me, to be the hardest to bring back to the reality of what we are. But ever since her run-in with our scripts hidden in Gene's portrait, her skin has thinned, her costume becoming heavy and worn after hundreds of years wearing it.

She only looked at me and said, *He won't go, you know. Jude.*

We move to the landing under the watchful eyes of a baffled audience screaming for our attention, the moon high and bright as I raise my face to the sky. Gold sinks over my vision as my cast readies to move the Playhouse one last time.

The ground rumbles violently as the theatre sinks into the ground, black mist billowing over us and obscuring the world beyond the gates. The air strains taut as the wails of the audience fade. Above, the sky darkens until we're fully immersed, left with nothing but the golden light streaming from the Playhouse windows.

At the sound of the doors opening, I turn and freeze at the figure tearing from the doors like a hellhound. Jude.

For a moment, a weight releases from my chest. He's changed his mind. He's here. We can all—

"Riven, *stop*," Jude shouts, his voice like a crack of thunder as he races down the steps.

At that word, at the fury that sharpens it, my hope gutters and slips away. Something between fear and dread takes its place as he closes in, the angles of his face morphing monstrously.

But the theatre is already rising up again, the ground rumbling and snapping as the Playhouse reaches its final resting place. Around us, the shapes of hills and burned trenches materialize, the sky a dusty gray.

All that remains of the real Eleutherae. Home.

The moment Jude recognizes our surroundings, fire ignites behind his eyes, so overrun with Craft that I can barely see the whites of them.

As the Playhouse settles, he turns on me, his face full of dread. Not just as he takes in Eleutherae but as he notices the rest of our cast. His eyes dart from them back to me. "What have you done?"

I lower my hands, step forward, and, in spite of all my resolve, of *knowing* he meant it last night when he refused my idea, I reach for him. "You can come with us. Please."

"It isn't that simple," he pleads between uneven breaths. "You don't know what will happen if we leave."

"Maybe." I look beyond him, at the Playhouse doors at his back. "But we know what will happen if we stay."

"Riven," he tries again, his tone softer now, playing a familiar melody on my heartstrings, like the right words will mend everything. I wish they would. "I am not your enemy. Surely you remember that."

I press my lips together, unsure either of us knows what we are to each other in this moment.

"What I remember," I say, "is growing up in a world without music. Without story, without color. Without anything that I am made of. And it isn't fair—to me or to anyone." My breath catches. "Maybe if I'd never left the Playhouse. Maybe if I never learned what we took—"

"You won't fix the world this way." He moves forward, and I move back. The child I saw in the mirror flickers through my mind. "We *can't.* And even if we could, this world wouldn't deserve it."

I wish the anger would come back, but none is there in his face, just a winking ember of hope. Something in me wavers, grabs hold of his words and starts to examine each one—because I think he's right. I can't fix the world. I don't know how. I don't even know how to fix all the damage we've already caused.

"I don't need to save the world," I whisper, and as his expression breaks, I force the next words from my throat. "But I won't be used to destroy it, either."

That ember of hope goes out, and something dark ignites in his eyes instead, alive with unholy rage as his hands shift with light, maybe to try and order our cast inside, maybe to move the Playhouse away from here—I'm not sure, and I brace for a fight.

But as the mist clears, Jude goes still, his eyes moving beyond me to our home. Eleutherae.

It's not the paradise I conjured in the arena. It's burned and vile. The flowers are flat and withered, choked by dry weeds. The sky drifts overhead in ugly shades of dark gray, mist too thick to see the stars. No matter how many years pass, Eleutherae can't heal. Not when all of its Craft has been drained, stolen.

His jaw tightens as he turns to take in the Playhouse behind him, the hairline fractures webbing up its sides.

And I see it as he lowers his brow, tilts his head—that inkling of doubt. He drops his shoulders, looks to his cast. "All of you?" he calls out, his voice hoarse.

Silence answers.

I'm not sure what exactly does it. If it's the twisted words throttling the air between us. The crumbling theatre, empty of our cast members' laughter. Or maybe it's the audience of one still inside, controlling our worlds with the tip of a pen.

There are worse things than being trapped, Jude told me once. *It's safer.*

"Nothing bought with fear is worth having," I say quietly.

Jude steps back like I've slapped him, disbelief drawing his expression taut, as if he's replaying everything that led to this moment and can't puzzle out where he went wrong.

Until his eyes fall on me, then drift to the closed gates beyond, and finally, finally it dawns on him. He lowers his chin, like he's about to nod, to speak something, *anything*—

His expression breaks, pinching with pain. Jude lurches, grasps at his chest like he can't breathe. At the same time, my spine goes stiff as steel.

He doesn't have to say what's wrong. I feel it, too. A pull in my blood to go back into the Playhouse, a visceral warning that we've all run our storylines rogue.

Sil. Sil and the Script.

"He's coming," is all Jude gasps out, and before I can respond, he races past me, storming for the gates.

The world seems to groan beneath our feet as he throws them open to Eleutherae, where there's no audience to greet us. "Go," he says, turning to us. No one moves. "All of you!" he roars. *"Go."*

The stillness breaks at the command. I draw a breath of relief as my cast startles and turns for the exit without arguing, filing quickly through the gates, where they'll begin their short trek to the well on top of the mountain.

Mattia throws a questioning look over her shoulder at me as she departs, and I nod. *Go. Right behind you.*

I turn to Jude, expecting him to follow, but he's already tearing back toward the steps. His stride falters, then stops short when he reaches me, meets my eyes like he's looking at them for the last time. "I will not apologize for loving you, dear heart," he says. "But I hope you'll forgive me for having done it so dreadfully."

The words are as cutting as they are a salve, but there's something unspoken just beneath them that makes my heart plummet. "Jude, why are you saying—"

"For the same reason we've *never* made it out." He holds my gaze, decision made. "I've tried. I've read this story a hundred times."

"We've—" I uselessly grasp for my memories, but they're blurred at the edges. "We've tried to leave before?"

"He'll call us back so long as he holds the Script. One of us was always going to have to stay behind." Jude breathes, looks longingly at our cast as they begin their walk to the well, and those eyes that were full of fury a moment ago soften, cloud with fear like he's sitting front row at a play of his own nightmares, like he knew he was always cast to be left behind. "You were right to call me a coward all that time ago, Riven. But, gods, I love trying to prove you wrong."

It was me who led us through those gilded doors at the beginning of all of this, he told me. *I will be the last to walk out of them.*

"I'll hold him off as long as I can." His voice is steady as he drops his hands, but the shallow breaths rising in his chest betray him, the color draining from his face as he looks to the waiting doors of the Playhouse, beckoning him, and two words ring like a bell through my head.

Not yet.

But before the thought reaches my lips, he runs back up the stairs, stopping only to look over his shoulder, something unreadable in his expression. "Be free, Riven."

Then he's gone, vanishing inside the Playhouse.

And all of a sudden, it's silent.

I stare at those gleaming doors, which hang open like the jaws of a beast, and I almost think my shadow has followed his back in.

I won't leave you *behind*, Jude once told me.

"Damn it all, Jude," I mutter under my breath, stubbornly changing course as those two words crawl along my spine. *Not yet.* My legs ache as I run up the steps of the Playhouse and fly through the entrance just as a loud, brassy song vibrates through the ground.

The chime of the grand Playhouse clock declares midnight.

Behind me, the gates seal.

Act III: Scene XXXIV

I don't dare call for Jude as I hurry through the Playhouse antechamber. The last thing I need is for Nyxene to hear me shouting. We're both so far off script, there's no telling what the Stage Manager will do if she finds us.

But Jude won't be able to hold Sil off by himself—not so long as Sil holds that Script.

A shudder racks my body as I pass by that gilded arch of ghastly faces I noticed the first night I stepped into the Playhouse. They don't look like they did that night.

They're melting, their bright smiles drooping into tragic expressions. Everywhere I look, rust flowers across the walls, mold eating away at the gilded edges.

The Playhouse groans beneath my feet like a sinking ship, welcoming its captains who have returned to sink with it. Each step forward sends tiny fractures skittering across the open, empty floor. There's one relief. Thank the gods, the audience has fled.

My pulse races as I hurry through the melting arch.

Parting the torn curtain, I enter the lobby, discovering a rotting display of golden chandeliers and split railings leading up cracked stairs.

And Jude, striding halfway across the room, comes to a sharp halt at the sound of my step. His shoulders shake with laughter, and I think he curses before turning to cast a glare my way. "Of course," he says. "Why would you stay put? My fault for expecting you to do something you have absolutely never done." He's trying to sound lighthearted, but the strain in his tone gives him away.

"Every finale." I repeat his own words from last night back to him as I run across the lobby. "You said *every* finale."

The ground rumbles again as the nearest column ruptures violently up the center and into the ceiling. The Playhouse is not a building. It's an illusion, one crumbling quickly with all of its Players off script and abandoning their roles.

Something between mutual understanding and a grim sense of acceptance settles in the air between us. "We'd best not be late for the last one, then," Jude says, offering his hand.

Overhead, one of the chandeliers droops lower, hanging precariously crooked.

This theatre is about to collapse on both of us.

Jude sighs. "I'm going to assume you have one of your charming little plans cooked up."

"It's definitely one of my worst, yes," I agree as dust flutters down like snow.

"Riven," he says, eyes following the damage. It's falling apart about as fast as we are. "Whatever happens..." He searches for words.

"I know," I say, nodding and catching my breath, picturing what I wrote across his mirror. "In the next, then."

I take his hand as we run over shattered marble, past portraits whose shapes and colors have begun to sickeningly bleed into each other, their frames sagging toward the ground.

"I'll admit, love," he says, "I have never been so grateful to see your scheming face."

Act III: Scene XXXV

Places look different when you know you're seeing them for the last time.

I'd never noticed the greenish tint of Player Rhea's eyes, but I note them as we pass her fading portrait. She lost her battle in the arena after a seventy-five-year run.

Though I realize now I'd recognize Arius in any role.

The peeling red paint on the wall has a nasty slit in its side, and I almost brush my fingers over it as we pass. Parrish told me it was from Titus drunkenly challenging Jude to a duel that lasted all of twenty seconds and ended in Mattia threatening to suspend both their realities.

As we cross the corridor that leads backstage, I look up the staircase that ascends to the catwalk and, for some reason, imagine Gene smiling down from it. Never a stranger hunting me in the Playhouse, but an old friend trying to stop my fate from becoming hers. Maybe she'd be proud.

Our heels echo as we close in on the stage, and I clutch Jude's hand a little tighter the farther we go, counting our steps. One for every song sung. Another for every tale told. A third for every dance performed. A step for every page flipped.

A bow taken for all that we are. Story. Craft. Every tale has our magic sewn into its bindings, bits of stars and laughter and whispered secrets only Players know. It's far past time they were set free. For someone else to tell them.

I wish the walk would last longer but figure *longer* will never be enough to satiate nostalgia. Even if it's just a fancy cage full of false memories. We've walked these halls in hundreds of different shoes together; it has to be enough.

My plan is structured in the same fashion that all of my plans are: feeble, reckless, and prone to fall apart at any moment.

"Do you believe what they say about Fate?" I ask Jude, my breath catching in my throat the closer we get to the stage. I can't help but glance down at the Finders Keepers ring peeking between our fingers, searching for comfort in it. "That Fate bows to no man."

"Yes," Jude replies and looks down at me. "I think she'd be terrified of you, though."

Departing the wings, we step onto the stage. One way or another, for the last time.

Act III: Scene XXXVI

Marigold's razor-sharp teeth flash through my memories as I tiptoe past the curtain and into the empty auditorium. *The stage*, she said.

"I think our contracts are here—Marigold seemed to think so, at least," I tell Jude, nervous to raise my voice above a whisper. Nyxene may be lurking elsewhere at the moment, but I hardly think it'll take Sil long to track us down. It unnerves me that I *don't* feel my strings being pulled right now.

I need to destroy our contracts before that changes. Every groan of the Playhouse sends me further on edge.

The stage is cracked like a sheet of ice, shattered in places. Somewhere far below, my arrow is lodged into it from my battle in the arena. I pick my way across, avoiding sharp cuts of marble. Something twists in my heart at the sight of the red velvet seats we've performed for again and again and again—torn and discolored now.

"We're relying on *Marigold*?" Jude complains, stopping to kick the dust of the ruined set pieces from his shoes. "Lovely. Do you know she tried to bite me once?" He trips on some debris and swears under his breath.

"Do you have a better plan?" I hiss over my shoulder.

He huffs. "I wouldn't dare. Trying to change your mind is like trying to move the sun." Then adds in a murmur, "Ill-advised and probably impossible anyway."

"Quiet," I say, navigating the platform.

"What did you do with her body anyhow?" Jude asks, ignoring my instructions as usual. "Parrish said they couldn't find it."

I'm about to throw him a confused look when I see it. Up ahead. It's easier to notice in the stage's utter ruin—a square of marble that peeks out just a little too much in the rubble. Picking my way over the destruction, I kneel at the center of the platform, flattening my hands over the square and feeling my Craft sink into the stage. A sigh of relief releases in my chest as the square pops open—

Just as quickly, my heart freezes, the world tilting. Behind me, Jude lets out another curse.

It's empty. Nothing inside. This is a simple trapdoor.

Our contracts. They were here, weren't they? "I thought—Marigold, she tried to tell me our contracts were kept *here*...here in the stage—" I run out of words, look up at Jude, whose wide eyes reflect my own. It was a bad plan. It was a weak and foolish and miserable long shot, and we knew it. "I'm sorry—"

The door at the back of the auditorium closes with a thud, and my eyes flash up.

SIL: "I'm not sure there are many words left between us, Riven." He delivers the line too cheerfully, and my whole body goes tense as his steady pace carries him down the aisle, like a single ticket holder strolling in a few minutes late for the final act. "Is that how it is? I give you the world and you burn it down."

I jerk my head up, my neck stiff from ignoring my blocking. My pulse starts to race. "Maybe the world isn't yours to give."

He laughs quietly to himself. "Your contract isn't hidden in the stage, Riven. You think I'd trust my Marigold with such knowledge?"

I press my lips together, defiant, picturing that chain shackling her to the Playhouse. No. No, probably not. But resentment burns in my veins, wanting, *needing* a way out to be here. To be in reach.

"I understand you've convinced your cast to go to the well." He sighs deeply, like our escape is a mere inconvenience to his day.

"'*Convinced*' is a strong word for a group of Players desperate to return home," I bite back. My gaze falls to the empty trapdoor, willing our contracts to magically appear. "The one we were stolen from."

SIL: "You came willingly."

My eyes flash up. "And now we are leaving willingly."

SIL: "Not all of you." He nods toward stage right. "I nearly worried she wouldn't follow you back in."

The words make my spine lock. But the silence behind me is worse.

Slowly, I turn. And my heart drops into my stomach.

Because the creature staring back at me is not Jude. But it's just as familiar. An empty, cruel grin works across his face.

JUDE: "Yes, I know. Follows me around like a lost puppy." He shakes his head at me, pitying. "I told you, Riven. Did you think leaving would be that easy?"

Act III: Scene XXXVII

The realization doesn't slam into me with blunt force. It doesn't punch me across the gut or crack through my mind like a peal of thunder.

It's a dreadful, silent knowing that curls deep in my bones and begins to burn.

I rise to my feet and stare at Jude, taking one step back, two. His eyes are hollow, but there's an amused cruelty glinting behind them. It dawns on me all at once.

Jude is gone. He's *been* gone. His character was meant to die in the arena.

And, looking at him now, I realize he did. He has no scenes left, no more blocking. Just the monster beneath and a cutting gleam in his eye.

The air rushes from my lungs, freezes me in place.

"Give him back," I say under my breath, a patient warning as my hands curl into fists and I glare at the monster. Rage coils hot under my skin. *"Give him back now—"*

Jude cocks his head like a bird, and a blank shadow falls over his gaze, a smile like cut glass carving across his mouth. "Lonely way to die, Riven. Even for you."

My blood roars in my ears at the cold statement, words Jude would never say. My pulse thuds so loud, I don't hear Sil climb the steps of the stage, don't notice him at all until I turn to bolt for the other wing, where the director blocks the exit. My breaths come quicker, my eyes landing on the book in his hands.

A laugh nearly rips through my throat at the sheer irony, recalling my own steps that led me to the Playhouse not so long ago, eager for freedom, for *power.*

I look at my hands, stripped of most of their skin. Not free. *Powerless.*

"You don't need to search for your contract," Sil says. "I took the liberty of breaking its seal myself. Your freedoms are done and so are you, Riven." His stare never leaves me. "I offer you every story in the world, and you choose the one where you die on my stage."

Something bucks in me at the thought. *No.*

This is not how I'm supposed to die.

Before I can consider the consequences, I jolt forward, reaching for the Script in Sil's hands, like I'll be able to stop him from ending my life, from reeling my cast back to this cage. Like I'll be able to search its pages and find Jude between its lines, discover some way to call him back.

But my legs go numb, and Sil laughs pityingly when my knees hit the marble with a *crack*, just barely out of reach. Though even from here, the power purring over the Script's pages feels hot enough to rip through my skin. It probably would have shredded my flesh if I had managed to grab it.

"There's no need for all this drama, Riven," Sil says as I stare up at him with a hatred that burns at my core. "You're eager to know how your story ends! That's perfectly understandable. I'll show you what it says."

I don't want to know. And yet—I can't help but look as he leans down, tilts the Script in his palms so I can see the words. Before me, the pages almost seem to pulse, to *breathe* with power that has leashed us for ages.

And I begin to read.

Frost threads up my spine, wraps its chill around my heart as I go—drinking in words that throttle control over my castmates' lives.

Words meant to end mine entirely.

Each one cuts into my skin, sinks into my bones. But especially the last two:

Nyxene enters.

The doors at the back of the auditorium fly open.

Instinct shouts at me to move, but a primal sort of terror slams into my chest, freezes me in place as a thick torrent of shadows bursts through the doors, moving toward me like a storm cloud.

Then the darkness gathers shape, unfolding into a monstrous, massive heap of twisted, overly long limbs that taper into obsidian claws.

The walls of the auditorium creak, like the weight of Nyxene crawling through the entrance will rip them down. Then I hear it: a low, animalistic clacking, drowned out by a cursed chorus of tangling whispers, hissing and unrecognizable, uttered in vile tones that fill my ears.

A scream catches in my throat, and I choke it back. My eyes widen, following those branch-like limbs as they stretch longer, skittering and clattering up the dome all the way to the catwalk, then slinking down the scarlet curtain—and tearing it clean through the center like expensive paper.

And within the darkness, a dozen quicksilver eyes.

Nyxene.

All at once, the marble feels like someone's spilled ice over it. I buckle, inhaling, but the air thins in my lungs, too cold to breathe. My own name slips my mind.

The horrid whispering and clacking from the back of the auditorium creeps forward, accompanied by sharp, jutting movements as Nyxene closes in on the front row, each piercing *click* prickling across my skin like pins. I flinch away, my breaths coming so quick that my vision starts to spin.

"It's as I told you, Riven." I clench my teeth and open my eyes as Sil shakes his head down at me, that smile never faltering. "Characters who are too aware are of no use to me. I did try to avoid this."

Gripping my fists so hard that my nails bite into my palms, I steel myself and dare a glance back at the velvet seats.

Nyxene's shadows skulk through the orchestra pit now, those jagged claws reaching for me, a beast cornering its prey.

Panic clutches at my heart as I tear my gaze from the sight, searching the words Sil holds before my face as Gene flashes through my mind. The day the shadows tore her apart. Not just her role but *all* of her. The memories seize me as I stare at the Script, at the end of my story.

Second Death.

Fate bows to no man.

If this is mine, Fate will not take me without a fight.

I gasp for breath, but the air feels like icicles stabbing my lungs as I draw on my strength—praying I have *some* left.

But as Nyxene crawls onto the stage, I can't seem to get to my feet. I grasp for my Craft, steeling myself to fight, ready to do it alone. Still, part of me looks to Jude for help, knowing deep down it's in vain.

There's no comfort to be found in his eyes, just a glittering edge of amusement that has bile rising at the back of my throat. I should have run when I had the chance. I should have gone with the others.

There's a way out. There has to be—

JUDE: "Don't worry over it, love. Death can't be all that bad." He shrugs, gaze empty. "And anyway, you seemed so scared to live."

For a second, the words knock the air from my chest, each burrowing deep inside and twisting until something snaps.

"Jude," Sil says. "Go back to your dressing room and wait for your castmates. Avoid all this unpleasantness—"

But before he can finish his sentence, those taloned shadows at last prowl onto the platform, the whispers echoing my name in my ears as Nyxene encroaches on that delicate radiance that shimmers around my skin like a live flame.

"What, and miss out?" Jude meanders past me, laughing. The cutting sound of it echoes and punches swiftly through my heart like a drum. Nyxene's grotesque clicking looms closer while Jude saunters on, bored. "You know me."

There's a slight stiffness to his gait, to the set of his shoulders. He wanders behind Sil like he's searching for a better view of what's about to happen to me as Nyxene's menacing limbs stretch across the marble.

But when he looks down at me, his steps come to a sharp halt, and there's an all-too-familiar mischievous gleam in his eye. "I cannot resist a spectacle."

At the familiar words, my gaze narrows on his, searching.

Jude winks.

Oh gods. It's him. It's *him*.

Well. I suppose I shouldn't be shocked he couldn't resist one last performance.

But just as fast as the wave of relief unclenches the terror from my chest, something even worse takes its place.

I barely have time to register it—the intent behind this charade, the calculation playing across his eyes a mere second before he moves.

Jude can't hurt Sil.

But Nyxene can hurt Jude.

And as Nyxene circles me, ready to strike, Jude lunges for our director's throat.

"Well then, Sil!" Jude announces.

He grits his teeth through a bitter laugh.

It's as Nyxene's shadows go dead still—and change direction at Sil's startled roar of rage—that the Script tumbles from Sil's hands and Jude growls, "To the godsdamned finale."

Act III: Scene XXXVIII

It feels like years ago now. Years since the first night I stepped into the Playhouse and Jude gave me its most important rule. *Nyxene protects Sil above all else.*

And for the first time, in every memory as anyone I have ever been, Sil looks terrified.

"Over here, love!" Jude shouts at Nyxene, gripping hold of Sil and dragging him backward. "Come this way. I'll be dealt with first, yes?"

Do not—ever—*lay a hand on Sil*, Jude warned me. We can't. Our contracts won't allow us to kill him.

Jude can't kill Sil. He can't snap the neck that he hooks his arm around, can't break the arm he uses to haul him toward the wings as the director thrashes and furiously bellows at Jude to release him.

But my heart plummets as I realize what Jude is doing. What he means to do.

Nyxene follows obediently, lured away.

He's buying me time.

"No!" I push to my feet, bolting after Jude, but I can't hear my own voice over the high-pitched growling of Nyxene's shadows, the demonic clattering like a violent storm tearing through the Playhouse.

Roaring in Jude's direction.

She will rip the marrow from your very bones.

As I tear across the stage, golden Craft blooms to the surface, so hot it scorches the soles of my feet, flooding the auditorium.

But the power isn't mine. It's Jude's. He's siphoning it, pulling every bit of Craft left in the grand illusion of the Playhouse. Gold oozes through the cracks of the stage like an open wound, rushing over the ground and toward its keeper in a brilliant tidal wave.

Immortality takes from you. His words ring loud in my head, snatch the breath from my lungs. *And power. Gods, power takes more.*

If Nyxene doesn't kill him, pulling this much Craft into his body to try to shield himself from her will.

A twisted limb of shadow lurches into my path, and the marble between Jude and me shatters on impact. I scream, covering my eyes and searching for a way around the debris as Jude calls out, *"Riven!"*

I jerk my chin up, and my heart stumbles at the sight of strips of his skin peeling, *melting*. Craft burns through his blood and what's left of his costume as he restrains Sil's outraged attempts to break free.

Power breaks you into pieces you never knew were there, Jude told me once. *It all comes at a cost.*

And as Nyxene surges after him in sharp, twitching movements, her hissing whispers swelling into shrieks.

Through the light, Jude's eyes burn like hellfire. *"Script!"*

The word slams into me, pushing me into action.

I whirl to where Sil dropped the Script to the ground, like all the answers will be written out on the floor around it. What does he mean? I can't touch it. Gene did. She ripped pages out, and it did nothing.

Riven. Script. At those words, the world tilts. The fleeting image of Gene's last moments—her very same last words—blazes across my mind. *No. No. No—*

Still, I grasp for the Script—but my vision scorches white, and I snatch my hand back. Damn it. *Damn it.*

My heart thunders in my chest. Jude bought me time. He bought me time, and I can't waste it. But this is one of those instances where I sincerely wish Jude *didn't* have unhinged confidence in my capabilities. Because I don't know what to do. I don't know how to save either of us.

What feels like a blizzard hails over the stage, freezing my hands as Nyxene screeches past.

I jerk my head up, like I'll be able to decode what the hell he means through looks alone, only to see shadows hacking through the golden veil of Craft Jude is desperately wedging between himself and Nyxene, every muscle in his body straining with the effort. Still, he won't release Sil, dragging him farther.

A flash of terror scorches through me as a jagged claw emerges from the dark like an onyx blade.

And rips into Jude's shoulder.

His scream slices through the air, unholy and otherworldly, shaking the foundations of the stage. Overhead, Craft bleeds down the walls, like the whole Playhouse cries with him.

At the call, I bolt across the stage without thinking, running at Jude and abandoning the Script—and whatever he meant—behind me.

But Nyxene is faster. One of those branch-like limbs lashes out, and a night-black talon slices at my neck. I choke, warmth flooding down my collarbones as I grab at my throat, gasping as Craft pours out from the wound—

When my hand brushes something. A chain hanging there at my neck.

A vial.

Script.

My world freezes.

I turn and face the Script, grabbing the Eleutheraen gold at my neck. A little prop Sil didn't know I had. The chain clatters to the stage as I tear it from my throat, and I feel the earth rumbling beneath me as I run.

Ripping those pages out won't change what's been written. But maybe—

Jude lets out another wretched cry, and the sound nearly drains what willpower I have left to keep my legs from locking as I bolt in the opposite direction across the platform and land before the Script lying open on the ground.

It thrums with power, brimming with every character we have ever played. With every story we have ever performed.

Maybe Galen was right. Maybe the world is unfair, and maybe fate cannot be escaped.

But maybe—just maybe, it can be rewritten. It has to be.

Jude shouts something, but it barely sounds like him. I can't even make out what the words are—they break, cut into a scream that rakes nails down my heart, a guttural snarl heralding the end of a losing battle.

I look up, and Sil's eyes blaze back from the darkness as Jude pulls the two of them deeper into the wings. My director's enraged gaze locks on the Script, which is out of his reach.

I am finally out of Sil's reach.

I clutch the vial like a sword between us and look to Jude one last time, finding him in between seconds of dying golden light as Nyxene shreds into the last of his Craft. But the sight it illuminates cleaves whatever is left of me in half.

Thin scraps of skin stretch over Jude's face like he's wearing a brilliant mask, one of his eyes coated in a filmy layer of gold so thick, I wonder if he can see through it. The left side of his body is torn in devastating, gruesome layers, where Nyxene shredded through flesh.

My hands shake as I twist the cap off the vial. This Script was the possession of a god. I don't know that there's any way to destroy such a thing, a power strong enough to raise a Playhouse and trap us into it.

But if it has the power to cage us, I have to believe maybe it can free us, too.

It will. Fate herself will have to deal with my wrath if it doesn't.

As Jude drags Sil backstage, luring Nyxene away, I raise the vial, conveying the question with a single warning look.

His eyes lock on mine, and his words peek through my memory as he nods once, and as the light around him dims.

To die is to be forgotten.

Flickers.

I imagine the world will never forget me.

Goes out.

The last thing I see is the Finders Keepers ring on his finger, glinting in the darkness as I say, "Find me."

And tip the vial over the Script.

CURTAIN CALL

If reports from the ship sailing the Maskira Sea near Eleutherae that day are to be believed, it all happened at once: A flash of light flooded every opening of the Playhouse—which most claimed had risen from the ground only moments before to begin with.

The sailors had no choice but to believe their eyes: The Playhouse had returned to Eleutherae.

Then the shattering of windows, the crash of marble. An eruption of golden flames shot toward the sky and all the way up the hill, the heat so suffocating, the first mate would tell stories of how it tingled on his skin for days, how all the fish floated right to the surface, dead.

And just as fast, the Playhouse was gone, turned to ash.

But this was only the second most surprising thing that day.

Figures stood around the mountaintop in that same moment, then descended right into it, vanishing in the well, their bodies a surge of light brighter than the moon.

"Look," someone called, face angled at the sky where the flames of the Playhouse whipped through the clouds, melting them like ice.

All at once, a flood of light cascaded over Eleutherae's destroyed ground in a rage of golden fire that razed through the weeds and ash and left patches of brilliant color in its wake.

Then golden stars broke overhead, illuminating the mountain in all its ancient, lost beauty.

Of course, no one would believe the sailors. They might not have believed their own eyes, either, were it not for the lone survivor stranded at the edge of Eleutherae, hailing for passage on their ship.

An audience member, the man told them, who had not escaped

before the Playhouse moved.

Though, when they asked the man what had happened, he refused to say much. “Just a brief intermission, I think,” he explained and, to their surprise, smiled. “Even the most tireless of actors needs a short reprieve to prepare for the final act.”

The man vanished the moment they docked back in Theatron.

After the Playhouse disappeared from the District, speculation stirred that the Players would return for vengeance. That the disastrous finale had broken the thin threads of peace, and the Playhouse would come back to curse the North as punishment for its one and only tribute ruining the festival.

Instead, something peculiar befell Theatron the very next morning.

Children woke with songs on their lips. Storybooks opened to long-forgotten tales, their blank pages thrumming with golden life.

Warm air broke overhead, flooding the sky with yellowy light and fracturing the chill that had haunted Theatron for as long as anyone could recall.

Rather humorously, confusion plagued Theatron as the dulled hues of lips and hair and eyes and clothes deepened into vivid shades of color, like bright paint spilled over a gray canvas.

Absurd claims vowed the statues of Players across the land had developed the strange habit of blinking their golden eyes when no one was looking.

Most surprisingly, those with marks watched with great alarm as the golden symbols upon their necks vanished, nullified and no longer of any use.

Meanwhile, the cloudy, golden-glazed eyes of Revelers mysteriously cleared, their obsession with the Playhouse gradually replaced by memories and stories of their own lives.

Years later, talk of the Players would settle, then dwindle, and finally, fade into the sparkling things of myth and legend. Mere humans would even build stages of their own and fashion masks to wear upon them. They’d perform Comedies free of Compulsion and Tragedies free of true death.

One day, it would be argued whether or not these things ever had a place in theatre to begin with.

However, stages everywhere would find themselves plagued by preposterous reports of hauntings—rumors of cast members no one recognized gracing the stage during a show or of rips in costumes no one had worn. Often, of props that would curiously go missing, never to be returned. Frightened stagehands would swear of steps heard in dressing rooms long thought empty and mischievous laughter fluttering in the wings when no one was around (often accompanied by bickering).

One thing, however, did not change.

Children looking in mirrors everywhere would claim to see shifts in the glass, revealing the image of a great white mountain, and to hear voices speaking on just the other side. Voices that would sing to them, whisper stories into their pages, and tell them the stage's greatest secret: the theatre is not a place one merely visits.

In fact, some of us never left.

[APPLAUSE]

[APPLAUSE]

[APPLAUSE]

ENCORE

The curtain flies back open, and the audience roars its applause. It's almost enough to drown out the murmured words next to me.

"My hair did *not* look like that." A snort comes from the seat to my right. "What is that, a wig?"

"They spelled my name wrong on the program." The second complaint comes from my other side with dismay. If anyone heard him murmuring frustrations over the incorrect treatment of injuries onstage during the third act, no one said anything.

"Would the two of you be quiet?" I utter, clapping my hands louder and hoping no one can hear my companions. They always forget how their voices carry. "Subtlety is an art, too, you know."

Not that we're all that skilled at subtlety. They both chose their old names and faces for the occasion. Most of us did.

"I could have done without the dance breaks," groans Mattia from the row right in front of me. We strolled in late and couldn't get seats together. "I don't call that subtle." She looks over her shoulder. "Embarrassing, actually, I'd argue."

Applause buzzes over the theatre as the ensemble dips into clumsy, uncoordinated bows.

"He'd have scolded us to high heaven for that," chirps a voice behind me, and I turn in time to see Parrish's greedy fingers pocketing what appears to be one of the prop daggers from the show.

I offer her a scathing glance. "When did you slip out?" And get backstage somehow.

Again.

She shrugs. "I got bored during the third-act reveal. Did he really talk that much? I don't remember."

"Who remembers? It was ages ago," I say, to avoid admitting that yes, of course I do.

I remember everything.

We all might have avoided the reminder, were it not for the highly publicized premiere of a brand-new play, one entitled *My Home the Playhouse*—an anonymously penned script that supposedly washed up in the mail of a producer. A "brilliant new show based on the beloved myth of the Playhouse and its Players," according to the marquee outside.

"The script sang with a sort of enchantment," the director writes in the opening note of the playbill. I narrow my eyes and turn the page to the next line, where he jokingly adds, "Some magic perhaps akin to what we imagine the Players themselves might have had."

Admittedly, none of our egos could resist when word of the premiere circulated. Though I'm shocked none of us got kicked out after a certain *someone* threw a tantrum over nothing but balcony seats being available.

"Fucking nosebleeds, I tell you," Titus says at my right. "They need a bigger theatre. How many do you think this place seats? Two thousand?" He drinks deeply from the flimsy plastic mug of wine he picked up during intermission—he keeps complaining about the cheap plastic and cheaper alcohol, but he went back for seconds and thirds anyway. "Tiny crowd, I say."

I let my eyes sweep the theatre. The house is packed—I squint, searching for an empty seat—but I suppose he's right. It doesn't hold a fraction of the Playhouse's capacity.

The group of lanky crew members clothed in black who manually controlled Nyxene—a unique invention of wires and lights I can't seem to work out the magical mechanics of—shyly make their way across stage next.

In spite of myself, I shudder.

The actress in the role of the Prop Master bows next, receiving shockingly enthusiastic applause. The actor in the role of Galen Hesper follows. I'm sure he did a fine job. I excused myself to the restroom during most of his scenes.

The Players, one by one, bow next, and something about the sight makes my chest tighten.

The music changes, churning with long, dark chords that I personally think feel like overkill, but who am I to say.

Then he enters—a man, *just a regular man*, I remind myself. A man with white hair and a pristine suit. They forgot the rectangular glasses. The audience roars its approval of a villain well played as he takes his bow and joins the rest of the cast.

The music shifts again, swells into the familiar overture from the beginning. A hush falls over the crowd as anticipation thickens the air.

At last, the stars of the show emerge from behind the curtain, and the audience springs to their feet as they stride downstage.

The leading man bows first, his face obscured by far too much gold paint. They really went overboard with that. Beneath it, though, the actor doesn't look much like *him* at all. None of them ever do. I've seen hundreds of his favorite roles portrayed over the years, stories we must have performed thousands of times onstage together. But I've never seen his face since that day.

I've searched, though, wandering the halls of theatres, sifting through old stories, peering into the shadows behind spotlights, wondering if I'll catch a glimpse. Sometimes I think I do—I hear a familiar laugh flitting between the notes of a favorite song, or a shared joke nestled in the lines of a forgotten play. I notice the slightest scent of hyacinth in an abandoned dressing room.

Which I'd still argue is a better use of my time than starting wild rumors that saying the name of a cursed tragedy onstage hails ill fortune. And then hurling aforementioned ill fortune at the performance if someone does.

Unlike a certain castmate to my right.

The leading actor smiles brightly and takes a dramatic step back, one arm out to—

I don't know if she looks like me. I can't remember my face all that well; I'm not even confident I put it back on right for tonight. I had so little time to get used to it, to memorize its lines, its details.

Some part of me misses it still. Maybe some part of me even misses the set pieces painted to look like marble, already rising back into the fly loft. Misses the comforts of my old bed, the fireplace in my dressing room—alight with artificial bulbs for fire safety in this rendition. It's a miracle none of us burned down the Playhouse by accident before we did it on purpose.

The actress bows and gestures generously back to her costar, who offers a nod of gratitude.

As a unit, the cast waves to the orchestra who accompanied the performance with heavy drumbeats during the bloody finale. Next, they gesture to the crew who executed marvelous feats of sugar glass for the shattering mirrors in the Greenroom and set changes so smooth, I'm shocked humans do them without magic.

All too soon, it's over, and we're filing out of our little red seats, spilling into an overly crowded lobby. Though it takes a half hour of convincing Parrish to go return the dagger she thieved back to the prop room so we can leave, and the lobby is all but empty by the time she acquiesces—and subsequently returns with several stolen anklets instead.

"The show made me miss mine," she pouts on the way out.

"Coming?" Arius asks as I linger at the will-call window.

"Right behind you," I answer, but I hesitate as the last of our group vanishes through the exit, vehemently arguing over portrayals of themselves and who was better-looking.

Alone, I take in the lobby—a modern space built more for practicality than opulent beauty. Its plain block staircases don't look anything like the spiral steps I used to climb to my dressing room. The wired iridescent lights on the ceiling don't carry the same warmth of the Playhouse's glowing lanterns and golden candelabras. There are no painted portraits of us lining its corridors—those have been replaced by printed posters lined in plastic, advertisements of this show and others thought fictional.

I'm almost certain every theatre is haunted. And I'm almost certain its ghosts are us.

And still, in spite of its lack of elaborate chandeliers and looming clocks and golden gates, I can still feel it. The warm breath of story humming in the air. The small children seated in the back rows, thinking they've just caught a glimpse of true magic for the first time. The sleepy dreams of tired actors retiring in their dressing rooms, giggling over onstage mishaps and whispering of who came to see their show. The celebration of a story well told.

They've done a fine job with it, I decide. I'm sure they will for a long, long time.

"Did you enjoy the show?"

I turn at the voice, adjusting my silk gloves. I thought I was alone. Behind me, obscured under the shadowy awning, a man holds the door of the theatre open.

"I did." I smile and pass through the open door. Down one side of the building, a small crowd flocks around what must be the stage door.

The man lets the door fall shut behind us, and when he does, I glimpse the slightest glimmer of gold on his finger, the surface of an engraved ring gleaming softly in the moonlight. "Did you?" I ask politely.

"Not really," he replies, and as we step into the night, I notice how the streetlights overhead shimmer across his hair—a dark shade of copper.

But it's the freckle below his left eye that gives me pause.

"Between you and me"—he grins, and the whole world seems to fall still. I almost think the stars lean forward to catch his next words. "I've never cared for Tragedies."

Acknowledgments

Firstly, thank you to my Heavenly Father, who was writing my story while I was writing this one. It all makes sense now.

No part of *A Stage Set for Villains* survived from the first draft to the last. I like to joke the hardcover is blood red because of how many times I ripped this book apart. Getting it right took a village, and I have a long list of people to thank for that!

A BIG round of applause for my agent, Ellen Goff. Thank you for loving this book and believing in it from the get-go in all its (very dark and brutal) glory, for your constant encouragement, and for always having my back. You are a legend.

Thank you so much to the team at Mayhem Books for making this dream come true. To my editor, Liz Pelletier, for taking a risk on this book, which was an absolutely massive undertaking to edit—thank you for your unwavering confidence in this story, your fierce (and hilarious) protection of Jude, and for reminding me "we have all the time in the world" during our race against the clock and whirlwind editing marathon to the printer finish line. And of course, for your attention to script tags (did we get it right in the end??). I pinky swear to set the ENTIRE next book on a train! Choo choo, Liz. ☺

My sincere thanks to Stacy Abrams, who copyedits at the speed of light, to Hannah Lindsey, a magical book-fixing wizard, and to Jen Bouvier, who loved this book first. Thank you also to Rae Swain, Mary Lindsey, Madison Pelletier, and the entire editing team who worked to make the book shine, as well as the production team—Justine Bylo, Curtis Svehlak, Brittany Marczak, Molly Majumder, and Heather Howland—who helped make the inside pages look stunning. To the many who provided notes during the buddy read, I can't thank you enough for your feedback. Thank you to Victoria Chew, Melanie Smith, Erin Lowrey, Cai Cramer, Hannah Li-Paz, Meredith Johnson, and Lindsey Staub on the marketing and publicity team for the tireless work. To the art team—Elizabeth Turner Stokes, thank you for this DREAM of a cover. I will never get over how you managed to visually capture this book so perfectly. And thanks to Bree Archer and Liz Wayant, who helped make sure the book jacket design looked perfect, as well as Amy Acosta and Kdeja Correa for their excellent eyes to detail. And last but not least, thank you to Katie Clapsadl and Heather Riccio. Thank you to all the wonderful partners at PRH UK and Bonnier Germany for bringing this book to readers worldwide.

Okay, family next. Thank you Starberry, my best buddy and sister, for reading this book MULTIPLE times, picking me up off the floor when the doubt dragged me down, and for shoving food in my general direction when I needed it. Thank you to my big sister Helen, the first person to read this book—I am FOREVER indebted to you for your brilliant idea to turn the fifth chapter into the Overture. And to my sister Sheila, for lending your incredible artistic talent in designing the Playhouse symbol. Love you, Shmeebs. Thank you to my (very big and wonderful) family—to my mom and dad for their love and support, my Omi who's been cheering me on since day one, and my sisters Linzy and Cassidy who always encourage me. And thank you, Grandma—I wrote so much of the first draft in your apartment. I miss our little chats.

Publishing is a roller coaster, one made much more fun with good friends at your side. Here are some of mine who are owed about a million thanks.

Thank you, J. Elle—for so, so many things, but especially for your steadfast guidance, advice, and for believing in me and this book before I ever gave you reason to. You're a treasure, and I am fortunate to call you friend. A big thank-you to Sabaa Tahir, for your unmatched wisdom and many long phone calls—you inspire me constantly. Many thanks to superstar Lydia Gregovic for generously taking the time to read the book of a total stranger and offering invaluable feedback. Thank you also to Ayana Gray, Ali Hazelwood, and Ronni Davis—I adore you all dearly. Thank you Lydia Rader and Elli Esher—we've come a long way since fourth grade Authors' Club, huh? And a shoutout to Alex Aster, who barely knew me but said, "You know, you seem like a writer," and then took the time to read the query I was too scared to send to literary agents—and kindly heartened me to do so.

A huge thank you my oldest #bookstagram buddies Elizabeth Sagan and James Trevino for your tremendous support and beta reads when this book was at its most vulnerable. Thank you for providing feedback that helped this book not fall apart and offering kind words that helped ME not fall apart. ("Came for Riven being funny, stayed for the man-made horrors beyond comprehension" still makes me laugh.)

Shoutout to the Grump Army. We will take over this world someday.

Thank you to my Penguin family, but especially to Felicity Vallence and Alex Garber—for your endless support and patience.

Lastly, as tempted as I am to gatekeep some of the most captivating music I've ever heard, it wouldn't be fair. I first felt the pulse of this book while listening to a song by The Amazing Devil and am forever grateful to have stumbled upon their work.